ALSO BY ROXIE NOIR

The Loveless Brothers

Enemies With Benefits

Best Fake Fiancé

Break the Rules

The Hookup Equation

One Last Time

Wildwood Society

The One Month Boyfriend

The Two Week Roommate

Dirtshine Series

Never Enough

Always You

Ever After

Standalone Romances

Ride

Reign

Torch

Safekeeping

Convict

The Savage Wild

USA TODAY BESTSELLING AUTHOR

ROXIE NOIR

CHAPTER ONE
IMOGEN

I lean over the conveyor belt, peering into the inky blackness of the x-ray machine. My heart rate is over a hundred, easy, my palms sweating. I can't stop moving my toes inside the boots that I've already put back on and laced up again, and I'm pretty sure I'm sweating right through the anti-perspirant that swears it's 'prescription strength' on the packaging.

I hate airports. Hate them.

Everyone says they hate airports, but for me, they're a perfect vortex of all the things that turn from me a quiet-but-regular person into a seething ball of anxieties and insecurities.

Lugging a million pounds of luggage around while inevitably tripping over my own feet, because I'm wearing ten layers and an enormous scarf that my mom made me take, as if I didn't prepare adequately for a summer in the arctic circle and a *scarf* is going to help? Check.

Standing in lines, the horrible feeling that I'm going to be late and miss something important hanging over my head, no matter how early I get there? Check.

No matter what, having to scramble to figure out which pocket my ID and boarding pass are in, because no matter how organized and calm I am ninety-five percent of the time, airports bring out the anxious, scatterbrained wreck in me? Check.

And worst of all, worse than everything else combined, the throbbing mass of people, all impatiently standing in line, wishing they were somewhere else, talking and laughing, glaring at me while I get my shoes off and pile things on a conveyor belt and try to find my gate and hold up lines while they radiate annoyance at my very existence?

Tons of people, just *looking* at me, watching me, waiting for me to get on with it?

Yeah, I hate airports.

I bend over the conveyor belt yet again, staring down the chute, trying to ignore the people chattering behind me even as I tell myself that everyone has their own problems, there's no way on earth they're talking about the weird, sweaty girl who seems like she's losing her mind in the security check line.

What if they are? my stupid brain whispers.

You're bending over in fleece-lined leggings, it's totally possible that they can see your underpants and they're laughing because today you wore the—

I straighten up, take a deep breath, and force myself to halt that line of thinking. Instead I focus on the bright blue carry-on luggage that's just now coming out of the x-ray machine and onto the rollers.

One of the guys behind me steps forward, heaves it down, makes brief eye contact, and walks away.

He was behind me in the security line. I'm almost certain of it, though maybe he went on the other side of the metal detector when the lines split and we both went to separate tables—

"Whose is this?" a short, stout TSA agent shouts, holding up my black plastic carry-on in her latex-gloved hands.

Oh God. Oh God, they found something and now they're going to think I'm a terrorist. What did I even have in there?

"Me," I say, holding up one hand like I'm volunteering an answer in class.

"Step over here, please," she says, nodding me toward a stainless-steel table at the end of the line.

I grab my laptop bag and enormous winter coat and follow her, nerves jangling, feeling like there's a spotlight shining directly on me and *everyone* in this security line is tracking me with their eyes.

Even though I know they're not. Even though my rational brain knows that humans think almost entirely about themselves and rarely care what anyone else is doing, I can *feel* their attention on my back, I swear.

The woman thumps the bag down on the table, unzipping it and thumping it open. I feel a surge of relief when I realize that I remembered not to put all my underpants and bras on top this time, for exactly this reason.

"Where are you heading?" she asks like a disinterested robot.

It's a security question, my brain spits at me. *Answer it right or you're going to a small locked room for a couple of hours.*

"Northern Canada on a research expedition," I say, my voice coming out in a squeak. I push my glasses up with one finger against the side of the heavy black frames, a nervous habit.

She glances at me.

Don't look like a terrorist, I think.

"A research expedition," she says without a question mark.

I clear my throat.

"I'm connecting through Vancouver to Yellowknife, and then there's a chartered plane from that airport that'll be taking the whole team to this town called Inuvik, and then we spend the night there and take trucks the rest of the way to Tekkeit research station which is on the Arctic coast, you know, way up there, hahaha."

It's not a real laugh, it's a nervous laugh. The security agent pretty much ignores it.

On top of my clothes is a huge tangle of cords, wires, plugs, chargers, and other electronic ephemera that I gathered this morning at my parents' house and shoved last-minute into my carry-on. She grabs it with one gloved hand and deposits it onto the steel table, looking annoyed.

As she does, one loop of my laptop's power cable catches the corner of the folder underneath it, and as she pulls the cords and wires out of the suitcase, the folder slides off the top.

It falls to the floor, contents scattering everywhere.

"Oh!" I exclaim. "Watch out, that's all—"

I stop, mid-sentence, when I see what the folder *actually* contained, and I suddenly have a horrible, brief vision of grabbing it from my desk and jamming it into my suitcase.

It's all 8.5 x 11, glossy, full-color pictures of musk oxen.

Mating.

The preferred term is *in full rut*, meaning the camera caught these animals mid-penetration. Some of the males are bellowing, mouths open, and in one or two the photographer unfortunately managed to get a small glimpse of musk ox penis in there, just for fun, I guess.

Or to make this moment as spectacularly awful as possible.

The security officer doesn't move for a long moment, just looks down at the pictures on the floor, eyebrows raised.

My entire body is suddenly so hot that I feel like I've

been struck by lightning. I'm completely frozen in place, my muscles refusing to listen to me, tears welling in my eyes because now everyone *is* looking at me, horrified by my pictures, thinking that I'm some kind of weird pervert who carries these pictures onto planes so she can sneak into the bathroom and, I don't know, get off in there thinking about two animals that look like shaggy ottomans having sex—

"I'm a biologist," I finally manage to squeak out. "I'm going to the research station because I got a grant to study the effects of climate change on musk oxen mating patterns, because they're considered particularly vulnerable to global warming and we need to study them and their populations to predict how the arctic region is going to be changing in the next fifty years or so, because you know the northwest passage is already open since all that sea ice has melted—"

I stop to breathe, but she's already bent down to pick up the photos. I realize that my mouth is moving twenty times faster than my brain right now, so I just stop, gripping the edge of the steel table, trying to focus on the cool, hard, metallic sensation beneath my fingers.

"Sorry about that, sweetheart," she says, standing as someone else hands her a small stack as well.

"It's okay," I whisper as she stuffs all the inappropriate pictures of musk oxen back into the folder, and everyone who turned to see what was happening goes back to whatever they were doing.

The security agent grabs one of my external hard drives, carefully separating it from the tangle of wires, sets it aside with a quick glance at my face.

"I see weirder every day," she tells me, grabbing the other hard drive and doing the same thing. "I promise you I've seen *plenty* of things way worse than something you'd see at the zoo."

I just nod. My face is on fire, and I still wish I could disappear, but I can feel the panic slowly fading away, the edge coming off.

At the very least, I don't think I'm in danger of having a panic attack right here, right now, in the middle of this airport, so I just smile, thank her, take deep breaths and keep focusing on the way the steel table feels under my hands.

I move my fingers to a cooler part, concentrate on that. The woman finishes untangling all my electronics, pokes gingerly through the rest of my bag. Finally, she seems satisfied, and pushes the whole mess back at me.

"There you go, sugar," she says, and I wonder where she's from originally. "Have fun doing your research."

See? You made it through security alive, and no one is even looking at you.

Mostly.

"Thanks," I say, my heartbeat finally close to normal as I stuff my cords back into my bag.

———

THE SOLARIS INTERNATIONAL AIRPORT isn't exactly huge. It's not even exactly mid-sized, because it has seven gates and maybe twenty flights coming in and out per day, which goes up to thirty or thirty-five during ski season.

It's only technically an international airport because one of the six cities you can fly to from my tiny northern Idaho hometown is Vancouver, British Columbia. If we weren't so close to the Canadian border it would just be the Solaris Regional Airport.

As soon as I approach my gate, I know that something's going wrong. Every other gate at this tiny airport has a few people in it, families taking their ski gear home after one last trip or business men heading to Seattle or Vancouver, but gate three is packed, the line winding all the way out into the hallway.

The flight's delayed. Forty-five minutes, the screen over the counter says, so I ignore the knot in my stomach and the voice in my head that whispers *you're going to miss your connection in Vancouver* and sit in the gate opposite mine, which has considerably fewer people.

And I wait. It's an airport, my flight's delayed, and I'm so wound up and anxious that I can't concentrate on anything, so I just play stupid games on my phone and glance over at my gate every thirty seconds.

After half an hour, it changes.

NEW SCHEDULED DEPARTURE TIME:
10:05 a.m.

My chest clenches, because now I'm *definitely* going to miss my connection to Yellowknife, and I don't know how many flights there are daily from Vancouver to Yellowknife, but it can't possibly be very many, because Yellowknife isn't very big.

As I watch it, the screen disappears for a moment, then comes back:

NEW SCHEDULED DEPARTURE TIME:
10:35 a.m.

I'm going to have to go talk to someone. A person. At the desk, and I'm going to have to wait in line and explain myself and hopefully not bring up mating musk oxen while the people behind me get annoyed at my very existence while I try my best to insist that yes, I really *do* need to be where I'm going, thanks.

There's a reason I like musk oxen better than people. I like being out in the wilderness alone, no one else for miles and miles, and the animals don't care if I watch them having sex and take notes.

I don't think they even notice, to be honest.

I go to the desk. I wait in line, behind a blonde ski bunny type who gets on her giant bejeweled cell phone and complains to everyone she can reach about how *ridiculous* this is and how *completely absurd* these delays are, she can see the radar on the weather app on her phone and the storm isn't even to Vancouver yet, it's way outside the city and there's no way that it'll interfere with the flight…

Finally, it's my turn, and the woman behind the desk is one of those impossibly perky, friendly, vivacious types. She's clearly already dealt with a ton of unpleasant people today, including Bedazzled Cell Phone in front of me, and she's still got a genuinely pleased, happy smile on her face.

"Hi!" she says. "Where ya going?"

I don't understand extroverts.

"Well, ultimately, I'm going to a scientific research station a few hundred miles from Inuvik, Canada, but right now I'm just trying to get to Vancouver so I can catch my transfer flight to Yellowknife, but I think I might already be too late?"

You're over-explaining, I tell myself.

She blinks at me a few times, the smile still on her face, eyelashes brittle with mascara.

"Can I see your boarding pass?"

I hand it over. She scans it.

"This has you ending in Yellowknife," she tells me, an adorable frown wrinkling her brow. "Are you sure—"

"That's right, the flight after that is chartered so it's not on the same boarding pass, so I guess I just need to get to Yellowknife and then the rest is my problem, right? Haha."

She taps at the keyboard for a few moments, the cute frown still on her face.

"Yellowknife," she says reflectively. "Gosh, that's way out there. Not a lot of flights, huh?"

"I don't have to route through Vancouver," I offer, the panic starting to rise in my chest because that did *not* sound good. "I can go through, I don't know, Calgary or something too, that's fine."

"I'm looking at those," she says, leaning her chin on one hand, the other still tapping away.

Her eyes flick over the screen. I wait, more anxious with every passing second, because I just want this to work without all my plans falling down around my ears.

"I think I could route you through Minneapolis to Edmonton and to Yellowknife the day after tomorrow?" she finally says, still blinking at the screen. "This is kind of a doozy, but better late than never, right?"

No! my brain screams. *The chartered flight for Inuvik with your colleagues and your equipment leaves tomorrow morning, if you get there after that then you'll be left behind and you'll either have to figure out how to get there yourself or you'll be shit out of luck and stuck in Yellowknife and then you'll owe the Bright Foundation all that money...*

I pull myself together. Have I ever mentioned how much I hate airports and flying and everything about this?

A lot. I hate it a lot.

"Is there any possible way I could be in Yellowknife by tomorrow morning?" I ask, trying to keep my voice from shaking. "The research plane leaves then, and there aren't other planes, and I really need to be on that one, otherwise I'm afraid I'll be stuck there..."

I trail off as a door to the outside, behind the desk, opens and all the flight attendants currently re-booking flights for irritated customers turn their heads and look, like they're expecting someone. The girl I'm talking to, in particular, clearly isn't paying attention to me anymore, a little smile playing around her lips as she watches.

And watches.

Now I'm watching too, wondering what's so great that's coming through that door. Hopefully it's a flight from here to Yellowknife, but I've got a sneaking suspicion it's not.

Nope.

It's a guy in a bomber jacket, hands shoved in the pockets as he pushes the door open with his back, shouting something to someone on the other side, letting the cold air into the airport like he doesn't give a crap about anyone.

I roll my eyes. People can be such dicks sometimes.

But just as I open my mouth to say *hi, can you get back to doing your job*, something about the guy catches my eye. I don't know if it's his messy brown hair or the way his shoulders hold the door open or his laugh or the way he seems so *casual* right now about being the center of attention.

Maybe it's just the way he stands there, one foot on the ground, perching the bottom of the other against the door.

For the millionth time that day, my stomach starts to tighten and swirl, a familiar sensation if ever there was one.

Because this all reminds me of someone I used to know. Someone I haven't seen in at least ten years.

Someone I'd rather not see again if I can help it.

The guy laughs. He shoves the door a little wider, tosses his head. Shouts something and then lets the door fall shut behind him, absorbing everyone's gaze like he was born to do it and it's no big deal at all.

I push my glasses up my face, wide-eyed, so nervous I'm nauseous.

I know who it is, and I wish I didn't. I wish I were hallucinating. I wish I were having a nightmare.

Just keep walking, I pray. *Don't notice me, don't look over here, just leave and go get a beer and burger and be a dick to your waitress or whatever it is douchebags do at an airport at eight-thirty in the morning…*

I hold my breath, head down, peeking up through my hair.

He starts to walk away, and I let myself feel a tiny glimmer of hope that this near run-in will stay near.

Then, my flight attendant waves both hands in the air.

"Hey!" she shouts. "Wilder!"

He turns toward us, and I want to die.

CHAPTER TWO
WILDER

"**W**ilder!" Amy calls.

Shit. I was hoping she hadn't seen me, even though I knew she probably did. If I'd known she was gonna be at that desk I'd have gone into the airport through another door so I could avoid her.

The whole *point* of hooking up with a flight attendant is that they're hot and never in town. I could have sworn that she told me she was gonna be in Vancouver or something this week, so I thought I was safe.

Guess I should have listened better. Or at all.

I turn, and I'm greeted by four over-white smiles, every flight attendant currently behind the WestJet desk staring at me. Amy waves, looking like a little kid.

"C'mere!" she calls.

I don't really want to, but I head over. I've got shit to do, flight logs to turn in, maintenance to oversee, not to mention I'm supposed to be scouting a location for another hotel with my dad this afternoon, and if I'm not prepared for that I won't hear the end of it.

I wave back, and she laughs, a bubbly laugh that's perfectly suited to her.

"The flight to Vancouver got canceled and I'm trying to find this poor thing a way to get to Yellowknife as soon as I can," she says. "I've never even *heard* of Yellowknife before, but it's way up there!"

She gestures at the *poor thing* across the desk from her, and I give the girl a half-second glance. Brown hair up in a messy bun, boots, leggings, ten layers of giant coats and sweaters and a whole mess of luggage next to her.

But just as I look away, she moves, and it catches my eye. Shoves her glasses up with one finger, held perfectly straight as she touches the thick black frame and not the lenses.

"Yellowknife, huh," I say, walking closer to Amy but not letting my eyes leave the girl in front of the desk.

You know how sometimes you see something, or you hear something and for exactly one second it's like you're back somewhere else, in the past, and you don't even know how or why but there you are?

Amy says something but I'm not next to her. I'm not at the airport any more.

I'm at Solaris High School, watching a girl in a long skirt and combat boots sprint as fast as she can away from me, for the woods.

"There are *really* no flights to this place," Amy's saying. "You sure it's real, hon?"

Finally, the *poor thing* in front of the desk looks up, and she's exactly who I didn't want her to be.

Someone I haven't seen in ten years. Not since she bolted away from me that night.

Not since I watched her go, still furious and guilty and vindictive. Still aching for her, wishing all at once that she was staying, that I'd never met her in the first place, that I'd hurt her even worse than I did, that I could take everything back.

"Imogen Gustavo, no shit," I say, forcing my voice casual.

Imogen doesn't say anything. Big fucking surprise, but her face turns bright red and she looks away, toward a wall, like I'm not even there or something.

Like she can't even be bothered to look at me. Like I'm not good enough.

It all comes roaring back. My hands in my pockets tighten into fists, even as I remind myself that this is going to be a thirty second conversation and then I'm free of this girl for the rest of my life.

"Wilder," she says, her face like stone. "Hi."

"Do you guys know each other?" Amy asks brightly, still clicking away on the computer, completely oblivious.

"Sure," I say, suddenly feeling cruel, like I'm seventeen all over again and Imogen's standing there in her eyeliner and combat boots, looking away from me. "We went to high school together."

Imogen's face flares. She pushes her glasses up again, the same gesture that I know so *fucking* well because I watched it every day for ages.

"Yep," she says, and looks away again.

"Haven't seen you in years," I say, coming up next to Amy behind the counter, standing too close to her. "How's it going? Still know the difference between elves and fairies?"

She shoves her glasses up yet again, and finally, she looks at me. Imogen laughs hollowly, like she's just being polite, which she probably is.

"Doesn't everyone know the difference?" she says, her voice pitched a little too high. "*Lord of the Rings* is one of the highest grossing franchises of all time."

"Oh, I *loved* those movies!" Amy says, still tapping away brightly at the computer, oblivious to what's going on in front of her. "Don't tell Wilder here but if Legolas asked me out I totally wouldn't say no."

She glances up at Imogen and raises one eyebrow, like it's some kind of girls-only secret that a movie star is attractive.

I sling one arm around her, my other fist still clenched in my pocket because this is purely for Imogen's benefit. It took all of ten seconds for her to make me feel sixteen again, like I need to prove myself. Even though I was hoping not to see Amy again for a while, here I am practically claiming her in public.

Just so Imogen knows I can bang cute flight attendants if I want.

"Hey there," Amy giggles. "I'm at work, you know."

I give her my most charming smile, hoping it's not a scowl.

"I don't see your boss."

"Come *on*," she says, battling her eyelashes, murmuring at me like there's no one else around. "Don't get me in trouble. At least not here."

Imogen's just watching us, her face still beet red, totally impassive. Even though I haven't seen her in ten years I still know that means she's *pissed* underneath, that I'm finally getting some reaction out of her.

"How bout I get you in trouble later?" I ask Amy, letting my voice drop to the rough growl she liked so much a few nights ago.

"Wilder!" she whispers, but she's clearly thrilled. Up until now I've barely even acknowledged her in public, and now I'm acting ready to hump her over this desk.

I might do it, too. If Imogen were here to watch.

If I could see the look on her face when I did.

Amy taps a few more keys, then sighs, prettily frustrated.

"Hon, I just don't think there's any possible way I can get you up there by tomorrow morning," she says. "There's only a handful of flights per day, and you sure can't go direct from here. I can get you to Calgary or Edmonton, maybe, and then you can try your luck again?"

Why is Imogen Gustavo going to Yellowknife?

Yellowknife is way the hell up there, somewhere I've only flown private clients a handful of times, mostly our millionaire investors who had to leave their resort chain board meetings and get straight to their mining company board meetings.

Imogen sighs, tapping her nails on the counter in front of her, like she's thinking. I take my arm from around Amy, watching Imogen tapping incessantly.

"Sure, that's fine," she says at last. "I mean, better than nothing, right?"

She adjusts a laptop bag over her shoulder and gives Amy a fake smile, not looking at me even once. Like I'm just a guy-shaped prop or something.

"I'm really sorry, hon," Amy says. "If you *really* need to get there, you could charter a flight if you had the money, but it would probably be expensive, and not a whole lot of pilots are willing to make that flight, especially this time of year. Weather comes up pretty fast over the Canadian Rockies and anything much smaller than a jet can get messed up pretty bad."

Imogen's fingers twist together, still nervously tapping on the desk in front of her, eyes dropping to look at a speck of dust or something that no one else can see or cares about. The polish is chipped from her blue nails, the skin ragged around the edges of them, like she's been chewing at herself again.

Guess that hasn't changed, either. God knows I still remember sitting in study hall, age seventeen, watching her across the room as she flipped through a thick textbook, shoving up her glasses and biting her nails.

Wishing that I were thinking about literally any other girl in school.

"How much *is* a charter from here to Yellowknife?" she asks.

"Probably at least a couple thousand dollars, hon," Amy starts. "But like I said, it's gonna be hard—"

"Ten thousand at least," I correct her without thinking.

The few times I've made that flight I've done it free, for bigwigs who sunk millions into my family's resort business, but that's the bottom end of the going rate.

Amy looks at me, head tilted prettily.

"You do that flight?"

I snort, shoving my hands back into my pockets.

"I don't make a habit of it," I say. "But I've done it a couple of times, yeah. Gets pretty hairy over the mountains sometimes."

"You should give her an old friends discount," Amy suggests brightly.

I almost correct her right there, almost laugh in her face that *old friends* isn't really what Imogen and I are.

"I can't do it," I tell her, point-blank.

Amy laughs, shrugging her shoulders at Imogen.

"He takes rich people heli-skiing," she says. "You know, when you fly some guy in your helicopter to the top of a mountain and then they—"

"I know what heli-skiing is," Imogen says, her voice flat, cutting Amy off.

Amy frowns slightly.

"Sorry," Imogen says, forcing a smile at the other girl. "I mean, I'm from a ski town, you know? I didn't know you were lugging rich guys around now, Wilder. Makes sense, though. Perfect job for you."

She smiles a too-bright smile. It's fake, and I'm sure she's got some cutting reason why flying a helicopter loaded up with rich skiers is the *perfect* job for me because that's Imogen and she hasn't changed in ten years: quiet until the claws come out.

"It's actually *really* dangerous!" Amy cuts in, petting my forearm with one hand. "The last guy who did heli-skiing here crashed into the side of a mountain. It was awful, but there was a really big demand for it and Wilder here was just out of the Navy, so he stepped up."

She beams at me, but I feel fucking useless. Imogen's standing here and Amy's trying to make me sound like a war hero for ferrying rich assholes to the top of a mountain.

"You *sure* you can't do it?" Amy asks, blinking up at me. "She's got a flight out of there tomorrow morning, to… where was it again?"

She has no idea. Amy thinks that she's being nice, getting me to take some non-threatening nerd on a plane ride. Imogen, with her glasses and her brown hair and her fidgeting, doesn't threaten her at all because Amy is pretty and confident and bubbly in that popular-girl way.

It's not Amy's fault that she doesn't know. How could she?

"Inuvik, and then a research station," Imogen says.

She presses her lips together. She adjusts her glasses. She drums her fingers.

"I'll give you fifteen thousand when we get there if you take me," she says softly.

CHAPTER THREE
IMOGEN

Oh, my God, what am I doing?

I don't have fifteen thousand dollars. I don't have *two* thousand dollars, or at least, I don't have two thousand dollars I could spend on a plane flight. Every last bit of this research trip was paid for with a grant from the Bright Foundation, with every penny accounted and re-accounted for.

"Your parents finally win the lottery? I used to see them always buying tickets," Wilder says, his bright blue eyes flashing, his voice mocking.

Anger crawls through my chest, tightens my hands as my mind goes blank, just like it always does during confrontations.

"No," I say, forcing my voice not to shake. "I got a research grant from a foundation with a lot of money."

"I had a feeling they still hadn't quite made it," Wilder says. "How's your old man, by the way? Every time I see him out there teaching a new batch of kids how to ski I'm afraid he's gonna break a leg."

"He's fine," I say, my voice brittle. "Listen, the Foundation will pay you once we get to Yellowknife, I just have to get there and explain the situation."

It's not true. There's absolutely no way that the Foundation is going to approve fifteen thousand dollars for a private flight and I know it.

But Wilder doesn't. For all his pompous mockery, for all his flirting with flight attendants twice as pretty and half as smart as me, for all his making fun of my parents and acting like God's gift to earth, I'm betting he hasn't got a clue how the scientific granting process works or where the money comes from.

"Why do you need to be there so bad?" he asks, leaning his elbows on the table.

"Because the arctic research season is short, and I don't want to miss my plane."

"You can't charter a flight the last leg?"

"It wouldn't be cheaper."

Also, I don't actually have fifteen thousand dollars.

"You sure?"

I swallow hard, my spine ramrod-straight. My heart is beating so hard I'm probably developing a medical condition, I'm sweating, and I *know* my face is bright red.

But this is my chance to kill two birds with one stone: get to where I need to be on time and screw Wilder Flint out of fifteen thousand dollars.

It's the least he deserves.

Wilder just looks at me, his blue eyes hard and indecipherable as they've ever been. The flight attendant behind the counter, the one he practically started humping in front of me, is still smiling emptily at the two of us, like she's done a grand job of solving some problem.

"Yeah, I'm sure," I say quietly. "How about it?"

I can practically see the gears in his head working, trying to think through the reasons that I, of all the people on this entire planet, might want to be in a small plane with him for hours on end.

"Help her out!" the flight attendant bubbles, but neither of us pays her any attention at all. "Come on Wilder, you're such a good pilot, it's your chance to do something nice for someone in need!"

She rubs his shoulder, looking up at him, and finally he glances back at her, both his hands staying in his bomber jacket pockets.

"All right," he finally says. "Hope you like small planes, because that's what fifteen grand gets you. Private hangar, thirty minutes. Have all your shit with you already."

He turns on his heels and walks back through the door he came through in the first place, flinging it open and striding through, a couple of heads turning, and my stomach plummets instantly.

What on earth am I doing?

I can't do this. I can't, this is stupid and dumb.

He's probably going to piss me off until I grab the rudder or whatever and plow the plane into a mountain, just to make it stop.

"Great!" the flight attendant says, clapping her hands together.

Really. She really does that, claps with happiness, because I guess not everyone knows that Wilder Flint is actually a misspelling of Satan Himself.

My fingers curl against the desk top and I have to fight the angry urge to ask her if she's fucking him, if she thinks he cares about her at *all*, if he's shown his true colors and humiliated her just yet.

It's coming, I want to tell her. *Just run, you poor sweet dumb thing.*

But I don't. It would be an act of mercy, really, but instead I leave her to her own devices with Wilder.

"I guess I've got a flight," I say, trying to smile at her.

"So… where's the private hangar, and how do I get my stuff?"

———

THIRTY-ONE MINUTES later I'm on one of those mini-trucks that are always scooting across the airport tarmac, loads of gear in the back, next to a very gruff guy who doesn't seem to know more than two words.

I don't mind. It's not like I can handle small talk either, particularly when I've spent the day tying myself into anxious knots at the airport, which culminated with getting a plane ride from the one person I really and truly *hate*.

It's not dislike. It's not distaste, it's not mild annoyance. Believe me, I feel those ways about other people regularly, and this isn't this.

I really, truly, deeply think that Wilder's a bad person. He's the kid of the richest guy in Solaris — and while Solaris may be small, it's the wintertime skiing playground of billionaires, so that's saying something — and he's the kind of snotty rich kid who punches down.

Punches hard. Punches fast, leaves you reeling.

The tiny little strange truck pulls up to a giant hangar, and the guy driving looks over at me expectantly. I clear my throat, my face flushing slightly because I'm about to talk to a stranger and when you've already got social anxiety problems like I do and then have the day I've had, you blush at every single provocation.

"This is it?" I ask, since for all I know he could be taking a snack break.

"Right," he says, his eyebrows going up.

I remember to smile as I dismount the strange, tiny truck.

"Thanks!" I say. "Let me just get my stuff, it might take

a minute, there's a whole bunch of it because I'm going away for a while and so—"

He doesn't care, stop explaining yourself.

I shut up. I don't think he was listening to begin with.

Someone else brings a cart for my stuff over, another gruff guy with stubble and an age of forty-to-sixty, and we load it up. Gruffster Number One drives away, and I push my cart into the hangar, feeling like a bug in a terrarium.

A little bug, not something cool like a hissing cockroach or a unicorn beetle or a tarantula. Not that tarantulas are bugs, they're arachnids, obviously, which every six-year-old knows—

"You the girl going to Yellowknife?" a woman in a bright yellow vest asks, jolting me yet again out of my own thoughts.

"I think so?" I respond.

She gives me a look, glancing up from her clipboard.

"You going to Yellowknife?"

"Yes," I say.

She snaps her gum.

"You a girl?"

"Um, yes," I say.

"Over there," she points. "Baby Flint is waiting for you. Best get out before the weather gets here."

I look over at where she's pointing to: a plane that seems *way* too small for the flight I'm about to take. I don't even like flying in those little jets with two seats on one side of the aisle and one seat on the other, I don't know if I can get into this thing and dear God especially not with Wilder and weather on the way—

"I thought the weather was over Vancouver?" I finally say.

"Technically, darlin', we're surrounded by weather day in and day out if you'd like to get philosophical about it," she says. "But the *bad* weather is currently sidling over from Vancouver to here, so if you want to get out I'd suggest sooner rather than later."

"Right," I say, giving my head a quick shake. "Thanks."

That's another problem of mine: run-on sentences in my head turn into one-word answers, even when the conversation I'm part of isn't a one-word-answer conversation. I get a lot of stares as people wait for me to finish what I'm saying, only to awkwardly realize that there isn't more as I'm frantically trying to think of something else to say.

Like just then, for example.

I grab my cart. I throw my weight behind it, shoving toward the tiny plane I don't want to get on with the pilot I can't stand, who's still the worst person I think I've ever met despite being considerably more world-weary now than I was in high school.

As I shove my way over, sweating again with nerves and exertion, I finally spot him. Doing something on the underside of the plane, messing with it, wearing overalls stripped to the waist and a black t-shirt underneath.

If it was anyone else I might stop and stare, because objectively speaking, Wilder Flint is a very attractive man. I don't know what he's doing but he's reaching up, tightening something on the plane, but it's making all the muscles in both his arms flex and release, over and over again, the coveralls just barely hanging from his hips.

I don't think about what he looks like underneath them. I don't think about the fact that, unlike plenty of our high school classmates, he *clearly* hasn't let himself go.

I don't think about the fact that once upon a time, I knew his body like a map.

Fall off, I think at the coveralls, despite myself.

If there's someone who deserves a public pantsing, it's him.

Except Wilder wouldn't care. People like Wilder don't get humiliated or embarrassed. When something happens, everyone laughs, he says some stupid, witty one-liner, and everyone forgets about it in thirty seconds.

They don't cry about it for weeks. They don't let it keep them from their few friends, or let it control their lives, or let it—

Shut up, brain.

"Wilder," I say, just so I can't stand there and think any more.

"Imogen," he shouts, his voice echoing off the metal body of the plane. "Nice of you to come by."

I know I shouldn't take it literally. I know.

I do it anyway.

"You're flying me to Yellowknife," I say back, my voice nearly swallowed by the space inside the hangar.

He looks back at me, arms still raised over his head. There's barely-hidden anger in his blue eyes, his entire body radiating dislike.

"Yeah, I remember the conversation we had fifteen minutes ago," he says, not turning the rest of his body. "Contrary to popular belief, I do have the full working brain of an adult human."

He turns back to the plane, my mouth going dry. What do I say to that? What would anyone say to that, is there even a response a person could make? It's his fault to begin with, he was the one who acted like it was interesting that I was here and then I couldn't think of anything else to say.

I clear my throat, trying to un-scratch it.

"I've got all my stuff with me," I say. "Should I start loading it in? Some of it's kind of fragile, camera equipment and stuff, so I should probably do it myself."

Wilder jumps down from the step ladder he's standing on, whips a rag off his shoulder, turns to face me. The lines of his face are tight, his jaw clenched as he uses it to wipe his hands off, though the rag is so dirty that it's probably just getting him even greasier.

"Yeah, you wouldn't want my dumb ass handling anything sensitive," he says slowly, flicking his eyes at me. "God knows what I'd break. Just tell me if there's something I can run at real fast."

I meant *if someone breaks my stuff it should be me*, not *I think you're clumsy and going to break everything*, but I don't say that.

I just wonder what his problem is. He hurt me, not the other way around.

"I'll load it. Just get me there, okay?" I say sharply and turn away from Wilder so I don't have to look at him anymore.

I hate this. I hate this the most of anything I've hated all day, and today's been a doozy in terms of hating things.

I hate the way he transports me back to Solaris High School, age seventeen. I hate that he makes me literal and awkward in exactly the same way, makes me feel like I'm puppeteering my body from somewhere outside it.

I hate the way he obviously still thinks that *he's* the one who was wronged, that *he's* the one who should have some kind of vendetta about our past, as fucked up as it is.

I hate that I watch his stupid hands and his stupid forearms and think about winter nights in his dad's Mustang. I hate that I look at his stupid face and despite knowing better now, it still sets off a thrill in the pit of my stomach.

But more than anything?

I hate that I know I'd do it all again.

CHAPTER FOUR
WILDER

Imogen grabs the cart full of her stuff, shoves it toward the back of the plane where the cargo door is. I'd bet she has no idea how to open it, but I'd also bet that there's no way in hell she's ever going to ask me how to do it, either.

She probably thinks I don't know, that it's too complicated for me. Honestly, it's a wonder that she's having me fly her anywhere. I'm stunned she doesn't think handling a plane is way above my pay grade.

I don't know why I agreed to this. Fifteen thousand dollars is nice, but a huge chunk of that will be going to fuel and airport costs, and it's not like I need the rest to pay my rent or something. My parents are the Flints, and they own almost every resort in Solaris, the place where billionaires come to ski — I'm doing just fine, thanks.

I slam the door over the fuel valve shut, lock it, wipe my hands again. Imogen's having trouble with the cargo hold door, but I turn my back on her and walk to the front of the plane, looking out the massive hangar doors.

Dark gray on the horizon. General feeling of doom and gloom all around; being a pilot you learn to watch the skies, listen to weather, know which way the wind is blowing. All that.

What's coming in from the west in a couple of hours is nasty for sure, but if Imogen ever opens that *fucking* hatch we'll be out of here long before it hits, and then in a couple hours I'll be to Yellowknife and rid of her again, hopefully destined to see each other once every few years at a restaurant when she comes and visits her parents.

I look back. One of the mechanics is helping her open the cargo door, smiling at the pretty girl with glasses, probably flirting with her or some shit, showing her how he can lift her heavy, delicate camera equipment.

I turn back to the storm looming to the west. I hope he drops it. I hope that everything she's taking to the frozen north on her research trip gets smashed and she's got no reason to go any more, and I hope that she cancels this trip at the very last second and walks back out of my life.

You could cancel it, I think.

She'd be pissed. Devastated. Think of her face when she got so close to getting what she wanted, only to be stuck in Solaris a little longer all because of you.

Yeah, none of that is true. I don't want to never see her again.

I just wish I wanted that.

———

"Hurry it up back there!" I shout.

Imogen's worriedly looking into the tiny plane's cargo hold, then back at her phone. Probably going down a checklist or some shit, shoving at her glasses every couple of seconds, her other hand clenching and unclenching.

She's nervous. Just a pile of nerves, a wreck. Good, because I feel like I'm crawling in my skin thinking of being alone in a tiny cockpit with her for five and a half hours.

Imogen doesn't answer me. She doesn't even look back. Surprise, surprise, so I jerk open the cockpit door and toss my Navy-issued duffel bag into one of the back seats we won't be using. I'm not planning on staying in Yellowknife more than overnight — hell, if I can, I'd rather come back here right away — but I'm not dumb enough to make this flight unprepared.

The plane's already got food and water rations stocked. Not a lot, but we stay prepared for bad shit to happen. Flying where we do, it would be stupid not to.

Imogen finally puts her phone into her pocket, reaches up, tries to heave the door shut on tiptoe. It swings but doesn't catch, and she stumbles backward, her heavy boots squealing against the concrete floor.

I lean out of the cockpit, watching. I could go help but why not let someone else come to the rescue? Maybe the mechanic who was already flirting with her. He can fucking do it.

She tries again, obviously summoning all her strength, winding up hard to get the stupid cargo door shut. It's not even that big, it's just an awkward angle and Imogen's on the short side to begin with.

It doesn't work. The door almost shuts but then opens into her again, and this time I'm already out of the cockpit and to the other door, reaching one arm up and slamming it closed before she can pathetically stumble backward again.

"Come on," I tell her, turning back around and heading for the cockpit, calling over my shoulder. "If you want to get there without crashing, we gotta go *now*."

I don't look back, just hop into the cockpit, close the

door, start checking gauges. It's not really true that we're racing the storm or in any danger from it at all — it's gonna make takeoff and the first hour afterward a little exciting, but that's it. If there was any *real* danger I wouldn't be flying this plane over a thousand miles of bumfuck nowhere.

Her face appears in the other cockpit door, down below, and she shoves her glasses up her nose with *that* gesture. She's wide-eyed and wild, her hair coming free of her bun, her cheeks slightly flushed, her lips just barely parted.

Imogen's pretty. That's never been the question, not even when she was the weird girl in high school who wore purple lipstick and tons of black eyeliner, her hair over her face constantly. Pretty is pretty, doesn't matter what you do to it.

"Is it really that close?" she asks me, breathless. I think it's the first time all day that she's volunteered a sentence to me.

"The storm?" I ask, casually.

Imogen just nods.

I point at the dark gray on the horizon and she looks over, anxiety written all over her wide brown eyes and the taut lines of her face.

"You tell me."

She pulls out her phone.

"Because I was looking at the weather app, and the radar feature says it isn't that close, it's still way closer to Vancouver which is the problem and the whole reason I'm here in the first place, but if it's that bad then we can't risk it, right? I mean, I can't do any research at all if I'm dead on the side of a mountain..."

I wait for her to finish her sentence, but she just looks at me. Apparently, she's done, and I shrug, lean back in the seat.

"Whatever you decide, don't take too long or the decision's made for you," I say, not looking at her. "I can get you there if you're willing to trust me."

I know she doesn't trust me. Of course she doesn't. She's got every reason not to and we both know it, but right now I'm *daring* her.

Imogen looks at the horizon with the storm. Studies it. I can practically see equations flying around her head, numbers and symbols and shit, and then she looks back at me.

And she studies *me* like she studied the storm. She studies me like she did when we were in high school, in that way that made me feel like nothing more than an equation she'd solve before moving on, interesting only as long as I was a problem she couldn't figure out.

I feel that way again, right now, like she's simplifying me from *me* into a system of numbers and letters, assigning me importance, noting me down and crossing me out so I look through the plane's windshield and away from her searching eyes, somehow unknowable behind those thick-framed glasses.

I hate this. I lean back in the pilot's chair and crack the knuckles on one hand, determined to look nonchalant about it. Like Imogen isn't getting to me right now.

"Okay," she finally says, shifting her backpack on her shoulder, grabbing the handle on the inside of the plane door and hoisting herself up.

"Okay? That's all?" I ask, still slouching in my seat. "I'm about to fly you hours and hours to bumfuck Canada, risking my own life with the weather like this, and what you've got is *okay*?"

She's half in the doorway, standing on the step outside, her shoulders hunched over since it's shorter than she is.

"What? Okay, I'll pay you fifteen thousand dollars," she says, pushing at her glasses. "How's that?"

"Transactional."

"Good. It's a transaction."

I guess she's got me there.

Imogen sits on the edge of the copilot seat, reaches out, slams the door shut, takes off her backpack, tosses it into one of the seats behind us. I think she's about to buckle into the copilot seat, like any normal human in her situation would, but instead she shoves her way between my seat and hers and sits behind the copilot's seat, buckling up and then staring out the window.

That's how this is gonna go, then. Not that I thought it was gonna go any other way, but there's a small, stupid part of me deep down that thought maybe she'd sit next to me for the four hours we've got in this tiny little plane together.

That small, stupid part thought that maybe we'd have a conversation about what's happened since high school.

But there's also a part of me that knows that, after what I did to her, I don't deserve any conversation. It took me the better part of ten years to finally admit it. I still don't want to, because right now my gut reaction to Imogen is to look in the plane's mirror at her face and get fucking *angry* at her, think she deserved everything I did to her.

It's stupid. It's childish. But it's what I've got.

I've mellowed out, though, even if she hasn't. The military will do that to you, remind you there are more important things than getting what you want. Hell, age will do that too.

"Ready?" I ask, feeling like a fucking chauffeur.

Her spine is ramrod-straight. She's looking out the window, her pulse beating hard in her neck, hands twisting in her lap.

"Yeah," she says.

Yeah.

It's all she's gonna say and I know it, so I start flipping switches.

CHAPTER FIVE
IMOGEN

He finally stops looking at me and starts flying the damn plane. It's what I'm here for, after all, and when his eyes stop darting back to me at last I can finally relax a little, lean my head back against the seat and think about everything else that's tearing me into tiny little nervous wreck pieces right now.

For example, I don't even like flying on small commercial jets, and this plane is *tiny*. I feel like I should be pedaling something to make the engine run properly, and I'm supposed to be heading over the Canadian Rockies in this thing?

Or I could worry about the fact that I don't have the fifteen thousand dollars I told Wilder I'd pay him, that he somehow didn't demand up front. But then again, that kind of makes sense — for being the worst person I've ever met, for someone who chewed me up and spit me out before I was even eighteen, he's always been oddly trusting.

When we get to Yellowknife, he's gonna be pissed. But all we had was a handshake agreement. He can't sue me, right?

Besides, before he knows it I'll finally be off at the research station, just me, a couple other scientists and herd after herd of musk oxen to observe, and both of those species — scientists and musk oxen — tend not to be too loquacious.

Or, at least, scientists tend to skip the small talk, which is a blessing to someone like me who can never think of a single thing to say about the weather, even in the arctic.

What on earth am I supposed to say, anyway? *Yes, it's cold?* That seems pointless.

Hey, the sun is shining, but it's cold anyway? Why would you say that to someone who clearly already knows both of those things?

Scientists, on the other hand, are unlikely to discuss the weather but could tell me for hours about their paleoclimatology research breakthroughs, like what core ice samples and fossilized tree rings tell us about volcanic eruptions in pre-history.

That I'm interested in. *That* seems like information worth knowing and imparting.

"Buckle up!" Wilder shouts behind himself, over the roar of the engine.

I'm already buckled — have I mentioned that this tiny plane is making me so nervous that my hands are shaking? — but I double-check my harness, tugging it tight over my winter coat and the seventeen layers I've got underneath.

We taxi out of the hangar slowly, onto the runway. We're pretty far from the commercial jets, but the Solaris airport is pretty tiny so we're not *that* far.

Up front, Wilder's flipping switches, checking dials, talking into a headset and guiding the plane's steering apparatus all at once, doing everything with a natural, casual dexterity that… well, it suits him.

There's something soothing about it, watching him do

all this plane-flying-stuff like it's second nature. And there's something different, too, because back when I knew him even though he was the star of our high school football team — of *course* he was — he was still a teenaged guy, and *graceful* isn't a term I'd use on him.

It is now, though. There's an odd careless grace in the way he's doing all this, his hands thicker and rougher than I remember them, a few small scars on the backs.

We turn. We taxi. I frantically, rhythmically, obsessively run through mental lists of everything I need, everything I have, everything I could possibly want. Just going somewhere on a weekend trip makes me anxious, and I'm headed off to four months in the Arctic where the only flights in or out will be for emergencies.

Everything about this feels strange, dreamlike. I can't believe that I'm actually going to the Arctic for four months, where there will be hardly any other people. Even though I made about a thousand lists, I'm still certain that I forgot *something*, and the thought gives me a queasy feeling in the pit of my stomach. It's not like the middle of nowhere has a drug store I can just run to.

Plus, I'm in a tiny plane — four seats and cargo — with Wilder Fucking Flint. That alone is more nightmare than dream, though at least he hasn't said anything too horrible or nasty to me yet.

He will. I'm sure he will when he finds out I don't have fifteen thousand dollars, not that the son of Solaris's very own resort mogul needs a measly fifteen grand. I'm sure he drives a car that costs five times that much. He's probably spent fifteen grand on skis or something and not even noticed.

"Roger that," he says up front, speaking into a headset. "I've got visual confirmation that the secondary runway is clear for takeoff..."

I look out the window, pushing my glasses up my nose even though they're already all the way up.

What if he's taking me because he thought of another way to humiliate me?

The thought creeps into my head, unbidden. There's a mirror on the dashboard and I can see his ocean-blue eyes scanning the ground in front of us, not paying me any attention at all.

That's ridiculous, I tell myself. *No one takes someone else on a plane flight just to do that. Right?*

Wilder says something else into his headset, and then suddenly, he's looking right at me in that mirror, his gaze oddly intense.

It was always oddly intense. Ten years ago, he used to look at me all the time, his gaze *oddly intense* just like this.

"Ready, Squeaks?" he asks, his voice low.

My heart drops into my stomach at the nickname, and I'm barely even aware of what he's saying.

Squeaks. I haven't heard that in years, and suddenly everything is rushing back, spinning wildly out of place, and I feel like I'm stuck in a waking dream that I can't leave.

"No," I say, my voice trembling and high-pitched.

He pushes a button, moves a lever.

"You know there's only one answer to that question at this point, don't you?" he says, his mouth forming itself into a cruel half-smile.

There's a handle on the inside of the plane, next to me, and I grab it and pull, push, twist, but it's just a handle. There's no door.

"Let me out," I say, my voice closer to normal. "I changed my mind. I don't care about the fucking musk oxen any more, I can't do this."

The plane starts moving, rolling forward.

"Do what?" he asks, his voice controlled and casual.

"Be in this plane with you," I say, my knuckles whitening on the handle as we go faster and faster. "Stop. Come on."

The plane doesn't stop. It's going faster and faster, and even though for a split second I think about somehow getting to the front seat, opening the door and barrel rolling onto the runway, I know it's a stupid thought and there's no way I'd survive it.

"I thought you had important research," he says, his eyes back on the runway as it slides by, disappearing underneath the plane. "Aren't you going up there to save the world or some shit, Squeaks?"

"Don't call me that," I say through gritted teeth.

"You used to like it."

"I don't anymore."

One single flash of memory: the hot tub in one of the Flint Resorts. It was outdoors, drizzling, the cold air a contrast to the steaming water as Wilder Flint hovered over me, fingers sliding up my thigh, lips against my ear.

Come on, Squeaks.

"It was a good nickname," he says, and the plane lifts from the ground.

There's a single moment where I feel weightless, between the takeoff in the tiny plane and the fact that I feel like I'm dreaming, hallucinating, experiencing some night terror or something where Wilder's back in my life and calling me Squeaks and we're alone together while he torments me.

The plane rises, and I turn my head to the window, closing my eyes as we fight gravity. I hate this part of flying in a real plane, and this tiny thing makes me feel like we're dangling on a string, likely to be dropped at any moment.

"You know the most dangerous part of flying, don't you?" Wilder asks.

"Yes."

"Takeoff and landing," he goes on, like I didn't say anything.

I breathe deep, eyes still closed, feeling every single bump and lift and drop as the plane rises and rises.

"I know," I say, because of course I know that. Everyone knows that.

"But especially takeoff," he goes on, casually. "It's so easy to climb too slow, ram into something, climb too fast and stall out…"

"Fly the damn plane and stop talking to me," I snap.

I swear to God the plane wobbles in response, and my stomach clenches.

"Whoops," he says. "Better stay buckled, there might be some turbulence."

"Don't do that," I say through gritted teeth, sheer terror winning out over shyness for once.

"I didn't make the crosswind," he says, voice still cool as can be. "Flying's dangerous, you know. If humans were meant to fly we'd have wings."

He looks back at me in that mirror, eyes the color of an alpine lake and just as cold. I don't think alpine lakes are generally wicked, though. Bodies of water don't tend to have moral attributes.

"It's dangerous because you're making it wobble in the air and you're likely to get us both killed just to prove some stupid point," I say, my mouth running faster than my brain.

"That's the most you've said all day, Squeaks," he says, eyes ahead again, darting between the windshield and the vast array of instruments on the plane's dashboard. "I'd say it's the most noise I've ever heard you make, only…"

I don't take the bait. Even if I haven't seen Wilder "World's Biggest Fucking Asshole" Flint in ten years, I'm not stupid and I know what he's doing.

"Just fly and quit fucking around before you tear a wing off or something," I say, my heart a drum line in my chest, thudding and thumping and stuttering.

"It takes a little more than a bad crosswind to tear the wings off an airplane," Wilder says.

The plane wobbles again, and I grip the handle even harder. He's not looking at me, but I can see his eyes flash in that stupid mirror, the barest hint of a smirk across his face, and I know he did it on purpose.

"Hell, I've done barrel rolls in this baby before," he says. "Maybe once we get out of radar range I'll get you up here and teach you how to get out of a nosedive if you ever need to."

I *know* he's just messing with me, but the thought of being in a plane as it dives, intentional or not, makes my chest tighten until I feel like I can't breathe.

"What do you mean, out of radar range?" I ask, just to distract myself from the thought of plummeting like a rock toward the earth.

"I mean the dead air between one control tower and another," he says.

I frown, because I don't like that either. I know I'm going way, way, *way* up there in Canada, but I figured that at least until Yellowknife we'd be in constant communication with... well, someone.

"There are towns between here and Yellowknife," I point out.

"Not that many."

"But there are."

His eyes flick back to me.

"You nervous about being all alone with me on this tiny

little plane?" he asks, his voice sharp and mocking. "You used to like being alone with me, Squeaks."

My hands go cold, and my face goes hot. I turn my head away, looking out the window of the airplane. It's streaked with water droplets as he heads through a cloud, everything bouncing more than I'd like.

Wilder's even making the weather cry, I think. It's a stupid thought. The weather obviously has no emotions and would be unlikely to care about the actions of one human even if it did have them.

"No," I lie.

I force my voice to be still, calm, and I keep staring out the window for a long moment as I figure out what I'm going to say next.

The moment stretches out, gets longer. It's not like talking has ever been my strong point and neither has Wilder.

Don't let him get to you. He's always known what buttons to push, how to get you to react. Mom always said he had a blood instinct, like a mountain lion or something else ruthless.

Mom says a lot of things. She believes in astrology and spirit animals. She refuses to do anything important when Mercury goes into retrograde, so when I was in school I always had to explain to teachers why her student-teacher conferences couldn't be the same week as everyone else's.

But she's right sometimes. Like about Wilder.

Suddenly, I realize that I haven't said anything in a couple of minutes. I've just been staring out the window, thinking, practicing for when I finally *do* say something.

"You know—"

I scrunch my toes in my boots for bravery, then cut Wilder off.

"I'd appreciate it if you could simply make the plane flight I'm paying you to make and stop harassing me," I say, trying to keep my voice steady. "I really just want to get to Yellowknife so that I can go about my research, and if that means I have to be in this plane with you for hours on end, so be it, but I'd prefer that we not discuss anything in the meantime."

Wilder looks at me in that mirror. Just *looks*, his eyes flicking back and forth between me, the instrument panels, and the windshield which is light gray and still streaked with rain.

"Do you think people can change?" he asks, his voice low and quiet.

I'm not even sure I heard him right over the roar of the engine, but he watches me until I answer.

"Not really," I say, meeting his gaze.

"Yeah, me either," he says, and looks dead ahead. "I'll tell you when we're approaching our first fuel stop."

Just like that, our conversation is over.

CHAPTER SIX
IMOGEN

"That's where you're wrong," Miss Gardenia said, addressing the gathered board members of her father's company. *"Mr. Robbins didn't die of a heart attack after all, I'm afraid."*

The plane hits a bump in the air, tilts, straightens out, and then we descend suddenly and abruptly, my heart in my throat, but the turbulence is over in seconds.

I press my lips together, glare at Wilder's reflection in the mirror but he's not looking at me. He's looking at the controls, which I guess I told him to do a couple of hours ago, so I should probably be glad that he's actually doing it.

The ladies of the board all put their hands to their bosoms, gasping. The gentlemen looked astonished as Miss Gardenia, amateur sleuth, glanced from face to face.

All but one looked astonished, that is.

The plane dips again, tilting the other way, and I look up from the murder mystery I'm trying to read on my tablet and glare at the mirror.

"Quit it," I say, but Wilder doesn't look up at me, just keeps frowning at the controls.

Suddenly the plane shudders, and I have the unpleasant

sensation that I'm trapped inside a living being that's trembling, shivering, like something is really *wrong* and I have to shut my eyes, take a deep breath.

Airplanes are mechanical, I remind myself. *It can't just decide to fly another direction, it doesn't have a brain, it just does what Wilder tells it to do.*

Small comfort, except I'm fairly certain Wilder doesn't hate me enough to take himself down with me. Close, but not quite. Not this literally.

The plane dips again and this time I can feel it go nose-first, both wings fluttering side-to-side in the air, and white-hot jabs through my brain like an icepick to my cerebellum.

It's fine, I tell myself over and over again. *This is just turbulence, it happens in every plane, you can just feel it better in this one…*

I look out the window, but the scenery hasn't changed. We've been flying through gray fluff for the past hour or so, and while that itself isn't dangerous it makes it impossible to tell which way is up or what altitude we're at.

Both my hands are shaking, so I grab the seat underneath me and squeeze as hard as I can, until my knuckles go white-blue and I start to feel a little better.

Wilder still hasn't looked at me. He's still frowning, scowling, both hands on the steering apparatus of the plane as he glowers at the instrument panel.

The plane evens out, stops shuddering like a frightened animal. Slowly, my heart goes back to normal, thumping away in my chest, and I loosen my grip on the seat. I don't know the first thing about flying a plane, but all the dials and knobs and levers and gauges look more or less normal — nothing is bright red and flashing, at least, so that's got to be a good sign.

Please be a good sign.

Finally, Wilder looks up, into the mirror, meeting my eyes.

"Sorry," he says.

I'm still too tense and keyed up and terrified to say anything but, "It's okay."

"Just a little weather," he says, as if he has to force the words from his mouth. "Hazards of a small plane. We're getting around it."

His eyes dart back to the instrument panel just as my ears pop again, that familiar little lurch in my stomach, and I realize that even though we've been descending for a while we're *still* descending.

"Are we landing?" I ask, my voice coming out high-pitched and tight because we're not supposed to be making our fuel stop for another two hours, and then Yellowknife is another four or five. Right now, we shouldn't be doing anything but flying along straight and steady while I read my murder mystery in the back.

"No," Wilder mutters, flipping a switch and pausing his hand over it.

Nothing happens. Maybe nothing is supposed to happen, but I'm not sure. Then he taps a gauge a couple of times, each tap harder than the last until finally he bangs the side of his fist against the thing, making me jump against my seatbelt.

Something's going wrong. I don't need to know the first thing about flying to know that the pilot isn't supposed to punch the instrument panel, and the sudden knowledge has my heart in my throat along with my stomach and most of my organs, threatening to spill out everywhere.

"What?" I ask, even though I'm dizzy with panic.

"It's noth—"

The plane drops out of the clouds all at once, like a

curtain's been lifted in front of us, and the mountains come into sharp relief.

I thought we were twenty thousand feet up. We're not.

We're way, way lower and losing altitude fast.

I'm frozen. I don't do or say anything, just goggle out the plane's windshield at the craggy mountains below us so much closer than they should be.

This is another asshole joke of Wilder's, a voice whispers in the very back of my brain.

He's trying to get you to cry, freak out, do something else embarrassing so he can go back to Solaris and tell all his douchebag bros about it, because you know that people never change, and you were stupid to take this deal in the first place.

That's not it. I don't know how I know but I do, because there's a cold fear in Wilder's eyes that matches the fear in the pit of my stomach that tells me this isn't a joke, this is real as hell and bad.

"What's going on?" I scream-shout, way too loud, over the roar.

"Are you—"

The engine cuts off before Wilder can finish his sentence.

"—Get buckled!" he shouts, as if I ever unbuckled myself on this tiny, psychopath-piloted plane, but I tighten my harness anyway, hands shaking, until it's so snug I can barely breathe.

"The engine went down, and I don't know why," Wilder shouts. "Hold on and fucking pray or something."

As if he has to tell me. I'm hyperventilating, eyes squeezed shut, hands clamped on my seat and head down. In the sudden quiet I can hear myself sobbing, my ears still popping like mad, my whole body shaking, and I can't tell if it's me or the plane doing it.

I'm sorry, I think over and over again, the only thought I can muster as faces flash through my head: my parents, my little brother, my long-dead grandfather, my best friend from graduate school, my mentor who set up this arctic gig for me in the first place.

I'm sorry, I'm sorry, and I don't know what I'm sorry for but it's all I can think as we careen toward the snowy ground, the wings creaking and the wind roaring against us louder and louder and then Wilder is shouting and I'm screaming and sobbing that I'm sorry—

CHAPTER SEVEN
WILDER

I'm swimming. Snorkeling, the water around me this perfect, clear blue as I skim over the top of a coral reef, colorful fish darting back and forth below me.

There's an octopus. A lionfish, a shark, a school of colorful blue-and-yellow fish and an eel and I'm just entranced by the beautiful, colorful bounty that nature has to offer.

I dive. I need to see it, need to be closer so I dive and it's only as I do that I realize I didn't go down, the water came up. Somehow the water rose above my head and the coral reef and the fish are all forgotten as I look up through the scratched plastic of my goggles and realize that I'm here, but the water is still rising, higher and higher over my head and I think *wasn't I supposed to float?*

I kick up, hard as I can. I might be wearing fins and I might not, I can't tell, and I sure can't look down because down is bad, up is good, up is where I'm going. I kick again and again, hard as I can.

My lungs scream. My legs scream. I've forgotten how to swim and now my hands are just claws, like I can grab the water above me and wrestle myself up, feet no longer moving in any kind of rhythm except for the most desperate one, fluttering and dancing and I'm almost there, to the ever-rising surface as the air leaves my lungs in a rush, bubbling upward and it's only a couple of feet, if it would just stop moving I could get there—

I wake myself up gasping, choking, chest tight in my harness. Sweat is dripping into my mouth as I open my eyes, look around frantically, tear the harness off and rub my face between my gloved hands.

I gulp air like a madman. I twist and struggle against my seat, the very last thing you're supposed to do at a time like this because for all I know my neck and back and skull could all be cracked wide open and I'd have no idea, but it's impossible for me to do what I *should* right now and all that's available is what I *have* to do.

I finally find the latches on my harness, release them, get myself out of the straps and half-fall into the empty passenger side seat. Everything hurts, all at once, and even though I register that, the adrenaline galloping through my veins makes that fact just another one in the whirlwind racing through my head:

This hurts what happened where are we the plane crashed I crashed the plane there's snow over the windshield is anything broken are we hanging over a cliff like we're in a movie what about mountain lions are there mountain lions will the plane explode can the plane explode is Imogen okay

fuck

Imogen

fuck

I haul myself up, feet on the passenger door because the plane's at a fifteen-degree angle, port side over star-board side, and I finally see Imogen.

She's slumped against her own harness, head hanging

down, her wavy brown hair half out of her bun and rioting around her face, her arms dangling at odd angles even though her feet and legs are perfectly prim and straight, in front of her, bent at a ninety-degree angle like she's patiently sitting at a chamber music concert.

"Imogen," I say, my breath puffing out in front of me.

It got cold fast.

She doesn't respond.

"Imogen!" I shout, but nothing happens. It feels like the small space and the cold suck my voice away into nothingness, a strand of hair floating around Imogen's head as she hangs there, limp, and all I can think is *oh my God I killed her, I fucking killed her.*

I climb over the angled seats. I kneel next to her, my own limbs not totally trustworthy, the tilt of the plane threatening to topple me onto her, but I manage myself, brace my feet, take off a glove and put my hand on her neck.

Still warm. Blazing, even, her skin hot under my frozen fingers and it only takes me a second to find the desperate thump of her jugular, strong and reassuring as anything.

I exhale in relief, knee braced against her seat, the wisps of her hair tickling my wrist as I leave my hand there for a long moment, reveling in the reassurance that I haven't killed anyone. Not today, at least, and not Imogen, not yet.

I slump into the other seat next to her. There are a thousand things that I should be doing, a thousand checks I should be making. I should be uselessly radioing for help and transmitting coordinates and checking our supplies and scouting out our location, but right now, just for now, I sit in the other seat and look at Imogen, unconscious, her head back now and her lips parted, glasses off.

I'm shaking. I put my glove back on, still shaking because I just crashed a plane in the middle of the Canadian nowhere and there's no training for this, no guidebook, no clear path to survival at all.

———

I DON'T KNOW how long I sit in that seat. I don't think it's very long, but I have no gauge, no way to tell besides the sunlight outside the snow-covered windows of the plane, but given that we've had full cloud cover all day, that's nearly meaningless.

My head feels like a rock tumbler of thoughts, all crashing around, colliding into each other with gems like *you need to find food* next to *Dad is going to be so pissed about the plane* to *it's like that snow fort you were always trying to build.*

Finally, I get up. I don't think anything's broken, now that the glut of adrenaline has passed and I can feel pain properly. I've broken plenty of things — I grew up skiing, played football, then joined the military, I know broken bones — and nothing feels broken now.

The pilot's side door is impossible to open, either bent or too covered in snow, but I manage to push out the cargo door on the rear port side to a small avalanche of white powder and I get out of the plane at last, heaving a deep sigh because while I'm not claustrophobic it's easy to get that way when you think you might be trapped in a Cessna 172.

And I look around.

There's nothing.

That's not true. We're in the middle of craggy mountains, steel-colored granite peeking through the snowy mountain tops, the green-black of fir trees down below, the sky above another gray swirl that makes it hard to tell where the sky ends and the snow-covered earth begins.

The plane is down, the nose buried in a couple feet of

snow, the port side wing sticking up and the starboard side wing buried under a mound where it plowed under. From the angle of the plane it's probably bent or broken anyway from the crash landing, not that it matters because the plane is never leaving this spot again.

It's freezing. It's windy. It's impossible to tell the time of day, because the altitude and the cloud cover means that day looks the same from morning until night which means I have no idea how much light is left. For the first time, I realize that the plane's not yellow because it's a fun, flashy color, it's yellow because if it were white it would blend in perfectly with the snow and no one would ever find it.

But when I said that there was nothing, I meant there's no civilization. Besides the airplane behind me there's no sign that humans have ever existed, that we ever crawled our way out of the mud and onto land. It could be 2500 BC for all I know. We could have flown back in time.

Imogen and I are alone, together, in the deep wilderness of the Canadian Rockies, battered and bruised, one of us still unconscious.

Despite everything, my stomach flips over at the thought. Yesterday I really thought I'd never see her again, and I was fine with it. Happy about it. I still thought about her a hundred times more than I should have, for a girl I hadn't seen in ten years, and every single time I did there was the same mix of anger and guilt, revulsion and lust.

I could leave while she's unconscious, I think. *No one would ever know. Even if they found her body somehow, no one would know that I left her here while she was alive.*

Just grab your emergency supplies and start walking downhill.

I don't. I can do bad, heartless things, but not that bad and not that heartless.

I heave the cargo door open again, shove my way past the luggage that tumbled everywhere when the plane went down. It's probably full of broken shit, glass tumblers and fancy microscopes and other science equipment, I don't fucking know what.

I shut the door, unsteadily move forward. Imogen hasn't moved, but there's a piece of hair floating in front of her face that moves with every breath, so I know she's still alive, head leaning back against the seat.

Slowly, I pick her glasses up from the floor where they flew, miraculously unbroken. I fold them, put them in her lap. She doesn't move, and for the first time in years and years, I study her face, no thick frames and lenses between us.

I remember the first time I saw her like this, without them. We were in the alley behind the movie theater where she worked in high school, September, warm enough that we weren't wearing coats. She'd just gotten off work at midnight, still smelling of buttered popcorn and cleaning product, looking at me suspiciously, like she was surprised I'd shown up.

Imogen had asked me if it was a joke. I told her it wasn't. Not then.

The strand of hair floats up and down, in front of her face, in time with her breath.

CHAPTER EIGHT
IMOGEN

There's a light.

We're about to crash and then suddenly there's a light, with no time in between the two things, just one scene turning into another like a switch has been flipped.

I stare at it, uncomprehending. We're not moving any more, at least, or at least I think we're not moving. Maybe we're moving and I can't tell, or maybe I'd dead and heaven is this blurry flickering blue-orange light and toes I can't feel.

Fingers I can't feel, either, but I can feel my head and the rest of my body and it all hurts like hell, half stiff and half sore and all bad.

I move my fingers. I realize that my hands are in gloves that I don't remember putting on, and I flex them, knock them clumsily into something. My glasses, neatly folded from the feel of it, and without thinking I put them on and bring everything into sharp relief at last.

I'm still in the plane. Still in the seat, slumped half against it and half against the window, the orange-blue light only a reflection in the windshield and mirror.

All my joints move. If I'm dead at least it's not that bad. It hurts but it's not that bad and I shove my mittened hands over my hair, wonder if in the moments before the plane crashed I put on mittens and just don't remember it. I don't even know if I had mittens, I'm not usually the mittens type but it's true that they're more efficient than gloves at storing heat, just less dexterous.

"You awake?" Wilder's voice asks behind me.

I guess he survived too. I shouldn't wish otherwise. It's not nice and I'm a nice person, not someone who wishes death on other people, but the prospect of spending even more time alone with the one person I'm fairly sure is my own personal hell is daunting.

I flail at the release on my harness until it comes undone, pull it away from myself, joints protesting though I don't think anything is broken. I turn in the seat and finally look at him, sitting on a suitcase on the floor of the plane, two feet behind me.

The whole plane cabin is at a slight tilt, making me lean to one side. Wilder's got a tiny camp stove flaring in front of him, propped up so it's level. That's the light I saw reflected a moment ago.

My lips are chapped, my mouth dry.

"We're gonna die of carbon monoxide poisoning," I tell him.

There's a tiny pot sitting on the tiny stove, obviously all part of some emergency kit he's got. Wilder doesn't respond to me, just rips open a package and peers inside.

I'm still slightly woozy, dizzy, having a hard time keeping my balance even seated in this little plane.

"Do you really want to survive a plane crash," I say, and swallow, squeezing my eyes shut. "Only to die of a totally preventable—"

"I propped the back door open," he says without looking at me.

I glance back. He's right, the door to the cargo area is propped up with a rock, but even that makes my brain go all spinny so I close my eyes again.

"That's not enough air circulation," I point out, eyes still closed. "If you're going to use that thing in here we need real ventilation."

"This is plenty of ventilation," he says. "Unless you wanted to die of hypothermia instead."

"It's making me dizzy."

"Carbon monoxide doesn't do that."

Shit, he's right. I've still got my eyes shut, and I'm still fighting the tilt in this airplane cabin, trying to maintain control or something like it.

"It's probably the concussion," he says, still not looking at me. "Those'll do that."

I take a deep breath, leaning sideways against the headrest of the seat, letting my eyes drift closed. There are so many questions that I need answered, like where we are or how we got here, but I'm just so *tired* that I let myself rest like this and fade away.

It's carbon monoxide poisoning, my brain whispers right before I'm asleep again. *I always knew Wilder Fucking Flint was going to be the death of me, one way or another.*

THE NEXT TIME I wake up it's light. Not *really* light, but I can tell that it's not night time any more, the snow-covered gray light of dawn seeping through the tiny plane's windows.

I'm not in the seat any more. I'm on the floor of the

plane, lying on top of an emergency tarp or something, coats piled on top of me.

And I have to pee. Jesus Christ, do I have to pee.

I shove myself up with one arm, every joint protesting, not to mention my bladder. It makes my eyes water, but I grit my teeth, force myself up to sitting.

Everything is sore. Everything, every single part of my body feels like I've been hit by a truck, not to mention the plane is at an angle so everything feels strange and off-kilter and also, I feel like I might puke.

And I don't know where we are. I don't know if rescue's coming, I don't even know where Wilder is right now but those are all problems that can wait until after I pee.

I get on my hands and knees. Every part of my body hurts and my glasses are off again, so the inside of the airplane is more lights and shapes than anything else.

I inhale, exhale, will myself not to pee my pants and glance to one side. Right in front of me, on the floor, is a shape I'd recognize anywhere, in any context, no matter what.

My glasses, neatly folded. I grab them and shove them on, finally able to see, and with one last deep breath, I push myself to a squat.

My right ankle screams in pain, and I fall over. My elbow smashes into the floor hard enough to bring tears to my eyes.

"Shit," I gasp out, not even able to move for a moment. My ankle's hurt badly, maybe broken, and I'm afraid I just peed myself, maybe broke my elbow at the same time.

I'm going to die here.

This is the end, this is it, I'm going to die in a crashed plane in a puddle of my own pee and it's because I trusted Wilder again like some kind of idiot.

This has to be a nightmare. It has to be. There's no other possibility.

"Wake up," I say out loud.

I don't, but after a moment, the pain in my elbow and ankle starts to fade. I get my hand on the floor, shove myself to sitting again. This time I manage to stand on just one leg, my good leg, and I hold myself up against the two back seats of the Cessna, head bowed against the freezing cold roof.

Painfully, I hop forward, using the top and sides of the plane to balance myself, and when I'm almost to the cargo door it swings open, a puffy black form standing right outside it, looking at me like I'm gum that got stuck to the bottom of his shoe.

"Where are you going?" Wilder says.

I breathe hard, swaying against the side of the plane.

"I need to pee," I tell him.

He heaves the door wider until it sticks open in some snow, then steps through it. Holds out one gloved hand.

I just look at it.

"It's a hand," he says, a hard edge in his voice.

"I know it's a hand."

"What happened to your ankle?"

I wobble, then steady myself against the metal side of the plane, still staring into Wilder's eyes. They always made me feel like I was drowning, but now they make me feel like I'm being dragged underwater, held down until I can't breathe.

"You crashed the plane," I say, my voice sharp. "The fuck do you think happened?"

His jaw tightens, but he keeps holding his hand out.

"Is it broken?"

"I'm not a doctor."

"All those fancy degrees and you don't know if you broke a bone?"

My bladder is *screaming*.

"Just let me go pee," I say, keeping my voice flat because I don't want him to know that after all these years, he still gets to me like this.

"I'm trying to help."

"I don't need help, I need you to move so I can get off of this plane that you crashed and go pee."

His eyes flash, but he moves, ducking his head and coming into the cabin, bracing himself against the ceiling as well. I pretend he's not there as best as I can, focusing all my attention on the door I'm heading toward, the bright white of the outdoors beyond it.

I hop. It sucks, because my good leg also hurts and because the interior of the plane isn't really high enough for this, but I'm sure as hell not crawling to the door in front of Wilder so I grit my teeth and bear it.

I've made slow, painful progress almost to the door when my knee buckles underneath me.

I scrabble at the doorframe but I'm not fast enough and my mittens are too slippery to grab the cold metal, and I'm about to go over when Wilder grabs me around my waist, catching me.

Don't pee yourself.

I don't pee myself. Wilder pushes me back onto my one good foot and I grab onto the doorframe for dear life, hopping forward once more and hauling myself out of the plane.

I don't say anything. I don't even look at him, because once we get rescued from wherever we are I'm not giving him any ammunition. I'm not letting Wilder go back to Solaris, with his rich friends and rich clients who hire him to helicopter them to the top of a mountain, and tell them about how when he miraculously survived a plane crash the girl he was with peed herself.

Wilder's humiliated me enough for one lifetime.

The moment I'm out the plane's back door, the wind whips through my hair, my ears and nose instantly frozen, my eyes watering. Somehow I didn't think about how cold it would be out here.

My head still feels sloshy, dizzy, like it's stuffed with cotton. I think Wilder's right that I got a concussion, because it feels like I can barely string two thoughts together. Just the mental task of *get through the snow* and *go pee* is taking enormous effort, much more than it should. It should hardly take any.

The snow's two feet deep. Hopping is hard, but I half-lean on the plane and half-scoot my foot through the snow until I'm closer to the tail, a spot slightly sheltered from the wind, and then I brace myself for the hard part, both physically and mentally.

Peeing outside in the cold is the *worst*. Every time I go on a research expedition I swear up and down that I'm going to buy one of those pee funnels that they sell to women so we get our business done without exposing our entire butts to the elements, and then every time I feel too ridiculous to actually make the purchase.

But right now, squatting on one leg, wind howling around me and air temperatures probably somewhere around zero degrees Fahrenheit, I'd give anything for one of those stupid things instead of freezing my vagina off out here.

Cold aside, it feels good, though. When I'm done I yank my pants back up as fast as humanly possible and lean against the tail of the airplane, finally able to think about something besides my bladder.

My brain still feels like it's operating at half-speed, but

at least that distraction is gone, and I can think about some-thing besides whether I'm going to pee myself.

I inhale. I close my eyes. I exhale, willing myself to stop feeling like my head is stuffed with fluff, and I open my eyes.

And blink.

Shit.

I don't know what I was expecting, but we're in the middle of *nowhere.*

CHAPTER NINE
WILDER

I sit on one of Imogen's cargo boxes, waiting for her to come back. And waiting.

And waiting.

Maybe she left, I tell myself. *Could have decided to just walk away rather than be stuck here with you.*

Hell, Wilder, she wouldn't even make eye contact just now. You kept her from cracking her head open again and you didn't even get acknowledged.

I flex my hands into fists, look down at them.

Then I stand, head to the plane door, and peek out.

Imogen's just standing there. She's wearing her huge coat, pants, mittens, and boots, but no hat or scarf and it can't be more than ten degrees out here, her body tilted to one side as she leans back against the side of the plane, staring off into the distance like she's lost.

Which, technically, she is.

We're in the middle of nowhere, somewhere high up in the Canadian Rockies between Idaho and Yellowknife, much closer to Idaho than Yellowknife since we're clearly still in the mountains, but that only leaves what, a few thousand square miles of wilderness?

It's my fault. I was flying the plane.

"Squeaks," I call out, leaning from the door.

She looks over at me, eyes contemptuous behind her thick glasses.

"Don't call me that."

"Come back in here."

She looks forward again, at the view. I can't blame her, because even on this mostly-cloudy day with the wind whipping up tiny snow devils all around us, it's beautiful.

I managed to land on a gentle alpine slope, above the tree line, craggy rocks sticking out all around us. In two directions are rocky cliffs dropping off near-vertically; in the other direction is a rock outcropping that looks like it leads to another outcropping that leads to the top.

The only way down from here is a granite boulder scramble. I can't even see most of it, but it looks sharp, cold, and maybe impossible. Not the ideal landing place but I didn't have a lot of options at the time.

We're at the top of a valley, rugged rocky peaks sticking up to the left and right, the tops of a few buried in the clouds. A couple hundred feet down the fir trees begin, green-black in the filtered light, stark against the pure white snow. I can't really see deeply into the valley from this angle, but it's safe to assume there's water down there. That's generally how these things work.

"You'll freeze," I call to Imogen.

She presses her lips together, blinks slowly.

"Is that so bad?"

"Supposed to be the worst way to die."

"I thought that was burning to death."

"You aiming to find out?"

"Hard to make a comparison, isn't it?"

For no reason at all, I see a flash of the past: Imogen, moon-drenched, in the passenger seat of my car. Staring ahead just like this, impossible to read what she was thinking.

Only then I'd drive out to the middle of nowhere and kiss her in the middle of a field. I'd sneak us into a room in one of my family's empty hotels and take her glasses off. Show her everything she was missing by studying too much.

I swallow the memories, a shiver working its way through my body as the wind slices through the space between my glove and my coat. I did some bad things when I was a teenaged asshole but sneaking around with Imogen is one of my favorites to remember.

Even given how badly it ended.

Sighing, I tromp out into the snow. Imogen looks over at me, shoves her glasses up with the mittens I put on her while she was asleep. The clumsy movement gets snowflakes on the lenses.

"Come on," I say, reaching out one hand.

She looks at me, wobbles on one foot.

"I don't bite," I tell her, swallowing *not unless you ask me to*. "What the fuck else can I possibly do to you besides crash this plane, break your ankle, and give you a concussion, Sque—"

Her eyes flash, and I grind my teeth shut against the nickname I know she hates.

"Imogen," I finish.

She looks at me for a long, long time, like she's trying to figure out something about me.

Then, all at once, she gives in. Imogen lowers her eyes and the steel goes out of her spine as she takes my hand in hers, so cold she's shaking. I swallow hard, grit my teeth together, and put her arm around my neck.

Neither of us says anything as I help her back into the

plane, most of her weight on me. It's only thirty seconds, maybe forty-five at the most but it feels like forever.

It feels like I've gone back in time, back to things I shouldn't be doing and a girl I shouldn't be seeing, the girl who ended up bringing out the worst in me. No, that's not true, because everything started with her bringing out the worst in me, too.

Maybe *the worst* is most of what I am.

I help her into the plane, and her arm leaves my neck. She holds onto the ceiling and doors as she hops in, heavily sits sideways on one of the Cessna's rear seats. I heave the door shut behind us, and it's suddenly quiet and still.

I open the plastic box with the emergency supplies and grab two bottles of water, hand one to Imogen. No sense in getting dehydrated. It's an unpleasant way to die, not that any of them are fun.

"Where are we?" she asks at last.

I slump against the wall of the plane, slowly slide down it until I'm on the mess of the parachute that I pulled out last night. It was the first thing I found to lay Imogen on after she passed out again, sitting upright, and I was worried she'd hurt herself even worse.

It's useless as a parachute now, but that was true as soon as I crashed this plane into a mountain.

"I don't know," I tell her.

She stares at me, like this information is taking a long time to process.

"Didn't we have a flight path?"

"We did," I confirm, a heavy, sinking feeling in my chest. "But I think we left it a while back."

"A while?" she whispers.

I lean my head against the cold steel of the airplane's side, trying to gather my thoughts. I've fucked this girl over worse than ever before, and without even meaning to. Sure, last time she moved out of town, but now she might die and it's my fault.

"Something happened, and I don't know what," I admit, eyes still closed. "But about three hours after we took off from Solaris, my instruments stopped working. I think there was a short in the panel or something, on these tiny planes sometimes water can get into the dashboard and make everything go haywire, I don't know."

"It's not even waterproof?" she says, her voice incredulous.

"They're supposed to be," I say, feeling helpless. "They get checked out by the mechanics before every flight we go on and nothing like this has ever happened before…"

I take a long glug of water and wish she'd stop looking at me because I hate the way she looks at me. I hated it even back then, when she looked at me like one of her pinned bugs under a microscope, like something disgusting she'd put on a slide.

"I don't know," I say. "There was some kind of catastrophic failure. I should have caught it sooner, turned back, radioed, maybe then we'd have still been within range of someone who could have heard us. But instead everything went **FUBAR** and we dropped out of the clouds before I knew what was happening, only a couple thousand feet up, and…"

It's not the whole truth. I don't even know the whole truth myself, but I do know that instrument panels in well-maintained aircraft don't *just stop working*. My father's owned this plane for years, and nothing in the Flint Resort fleet has ever *just stopped working*.

Yeah, the last guy who flew the skiing helicopter crashed it into the side of the mountain. That was a huge disaster and it took my parents years to recover from it, though I was still in the Navy then, so it didn't affect me too much.

But the thing that they mostly kept out of the news was that the pilot of that helicopter was drinking. They found an empty flask in the wreckage, and none of the skiers, who all got dropped off before the crash, had any alcohol in their systems.

I've got a bad feeling that something is amiss. Not that this plane is sabotaged — I'm a rich kid, not an international spy — but something went amiss before this flight, something I don't know anything about but got caught in the middle of.

"How long have you really been flying?" Imogen finally says.

Her voice has gone a little fuzzy, even though she's drinking the water, her eyes getting heavy again, and despite myself I'm worried. She was out for a long time, and that means her concussion wasn't minor.

"Long enough," I tell her.

"That's not a number."

"You always did need those."

"What's that supposed to mean?"

I take a long drink of water, because hell, I don't know what it means. I only know that Imogen makes me feel small, stupid, and insignificant, and despite that, she's *still* been haunting my dreams for ten years.

"It means that there are things in life that can't be quantified, Squeaks. Sometimes measurements are useless, they're not the be-all, end-all," I say.

She pushes her glasses up, mittens still on her hands.

"You're trying to tell me that the number of years you've been a pilot is somehow *unquantifiable*," she says, sarcasm dripping from every word. "Because unless you and I have very different definitions of the word *year* and perhaps even the very concept of time, I'm pretty sure there's a number that answers the question, 'Wilder, how long have you been a pilot?'"

This is the worst part, when she's *right* and she's a haughty bitch about it.

"Since I was nineteen," I finally answer her.

"Eight years?" she says coolly, looking out the window at the snow piled up outside. "That wasn't so hard, was it?"

I close my eyes and don't bother answering her.

CHAPTER TEN
IMOGEN

I hate this.

By *this* I don't mean having a probably-broken ankle or being stranded in a tiny airplane way up in the Canadian Rockies. I don't even mean being stuck with someone I sincerely hoped I'd never see again in my life.

I mean this fucking concussion.

I feel like an idiot, like my brain is running at one-third speed and can't even do the simple calculations I'm asking of it. Like it's a computer that keeps returning some sort of error I've never seen before, and I have no idea how to fix it.

I lean my head against the seat back of the chair I'm sitting in. I take my glasses off, fold them in my lap, because all of a sudden, I'm so *tired* again, even though it's freezing cold and I should be panicking.

That's the other thing. I should be, at the very least, *really really worried* about our predicament but I'm not. Those emotions feel like another area of my brain that I just can't access right now. It feels like the only thing I *can* get to is the nearly overwhelming desire to take a nap.

It's the concussion, I tell myself yet again. *You're not stupid, you've got a brain injury and the best way to heal that is by sleeping, all those myths aren't true...*

———

I WAKE up on the floor again, deeply nestled in the parachute. I'm not warm but I'm also not freezing, which is probably the best I can ask for.

I sit up, careful of my ankle, and recognize the familiar blur of my glasses, folded a foot in front of me so I grab them and put them on.

I think Wilder put them there. I think he put me here, lying on the parachute, and he folded my glasses and put them neatly in front of me because he knows I can't see anything without them.

There's always the vague possibility that I woke up mid-nap, hobbled over here, and did that all myself but I don't have a history of somnambulism so that's unlikely.

"You should eat something," Wilder says from off to my left.

He's chewing something himself, sitting on a large cargo box filled with clothes, some binoculars, a few books, and toiletries. In front of him, on another of my boxes, he's got a map spread out and he's leaned over, staring at it.

"I'm not hungry," I say, because it's true. If anything, I'm slightly nauseous, and even though I know that's a side effect of the concussion and I haven't eaten in nearly twenty-four hours, probably, I still don't want food.

He turns and looks at me, blue eyes flat.

"I don't care," he says simply. "If we need to leave suddenly I'm not dragging you down that boulder scramble with a gimpy ankle *and* half-starved."

He tosses me something, and I jerk my head out of the

way, half-trying to catch it and failing completely. It falls to the floor behind me and I reach over to pick it up, because hand-eye coordination has never been my strongest suit.

Hell, my dad has been a ski instructor for probably forty years now and I can barely get down the beginner slope. At least I finally mastered the bunny slopes around age fifteen.

"Eat that," he says. "And then I'm looking at your ankle."

It's some kind of meal-replacement bar, one of those really serious ones that crazy people have in their bunkers that looks, feels, and tastes pretty much like a brick. I don't even argue with Wilder for once, just gnaw off a corner and start chewing, because deep down, I do know that he's right.

I eat. He keeps pouring over the map, legs wide, his elbows on his knees as I try not to look at him.

It's not like I can see his body right now, under fifty layers and three parkas, even though I've got a pretty good idea of what it looks like. It's not like the full force of those eyes is on *me*, not like we're in the backseat of his dad's car out in the national forest while my shirt comes off.

But there's something about Wilder, even just sitting there staring at a map, that's alluring. He was always so cocksure about himself, always so smooth and calm and in control in a way that no other teenager ever was, and it turns out that years of flying in the military only made it worse.

And he knows it, and I think he knows I know it.

Only so many things to do while you're trapped here, waiting around to be rescued, I think.

Out of nowhere, panic sparks inside me. My stomach clenches and my head snaps up, and even though the anxiety doesn't feel good it feels familiar, like maybe I'm getting back to myself at last.

"What do you mean, in case we have to go somewhere?" I ask, suddenly suspicious.

He turns his head, looks at me.

"I mean in case we have to leave the plane behind," Wilder tells me.

I shake my head.

"That's the very first thing you always learn in wilderness survival," I say. "Stay where you are so rescuers can find you, otherwise they'll have far too large an area to search and you'll never get found, ever."

"You took wilderness survival?" he asks, voice disbelieving. "What else did you learn, Squeaks? Want to make us a fire by scraping two rocks together near some tree bark?"

"It's required for anyone doing arctic research," I say, as if everyone knows that. "Of course I took the wilderness survival seminar, I wasn't about to—"

He leans back on his hands, grinning, and my stomach tightens even more.

"Your *seminar* cover what to do when you're probably a hundred miles off course, your radio's not working, and you've already been missing for most of a day?"

I swallow.

"It hasn't been that long," I point out, trying to stay calm even as panic blossoms in my chest, its ugly tentacles reaching through my ribcage. "We were only due in Yellowknife late yesterday afternoon, and I'm sure they've allowed for some extra time due to weather, so it's unreasonable to expect anyone just yet."

"We didn't make our fuel stops," Wilder says quietly.

The tentacles grab hold.

"We were due in Fort Samson just about a day ago at this point," he says. "We've been out of radio contact for a hair over twenty-five hours, and that's more than enough time to sound the alarm. By now they'll have confirmed with Coalstoke that we didn't make our second fuel stop and haven't been in contact there either, so the options are clearly either that we ran away to some lovely Pacific island together or we've gone down."

He pauses. It's a long, long pause.

"You hear any rescue planes, Squeaks?" he asks, his voice low but sharp.

"We've got the black box transmitter," I point out.

Wilder just cocks his head, the corner of his mouth hitching up the barest little bit.

"The what?"

The tentacles that grabbed hold of my ribcage start pulling, the panic deepening as I look around the tiny plane, reality setting in at last.

I don't actually know what I'm talking about. I don't even know if that's what the black box *is*, I just know that planes have some sort of homing beacon. I'm not a pilot, I don't know anything else about it.

You should, I think. *I can't believe you just got onto this plane with Wilder of all people and didn't at least google what they are, how they worked, just so you could be one percent prepared for something like this...*

"You know," I say, hoping my voice isn't shaking even though I feel like I can barely breathe. "The, um, homing beacon transmitter that sends out a signal via satellite wavelength and pinpoints our GPS location to the rescue crews looking for us."

That was total garbage nonsense and I know it, just big right-sounding words tumbling out of my mouth one after another. *Satellite wavelength?* The hell is that?

"Of course," Wilder says, letting the words drip from

his lips. "The homing beacon transmitter. Well, I gotta say I haven't heard those rescue planes either, Squeaks."

I think my concussion is healing, or at least it's healed to a certain point because the sudden knowledge that he's right about this brings the full gravity of the situation crashing down onto me in a way that hadn't happened yet.

We crashed a plane. In the wilderness. Just the two of us.

And Wilder doesn't think anyone's going to come rescue us.

"Oh my God," I say, and my vision starts to swim in front of me, blurring and narrowing. "Oh my God," I whisper.

I can't breathe enough. There's not enough air, because we're at altitude and in some tiny plane that's probably sealed tight and we've been breathing so much oxygen and also my ankle is broken, and I'm not smart any more, I'm dumb now because I hit my head so hard when we finally landed—

"Imogen," Wilder says.

My vision starts narrowing. I drop the ration brick I'm holding and tug the neck of my parka apart, the zipper grinding. Somewhere deep down I know that I'm only having a panic attack, but that knowledge never helps when you're having one.

"Hey," he says, his voice suddenly tinged with concern.

"I can't breathe," I whisper, even though I'm breathing faster than a frightened rabbit, the air whooshing uselessly in and out of my lungs.

I watch him heave the door open through a gray mist, and the fresh air feels good on my face even though it's freezing. I shut my eyes, lean back against the plane's metal skin, and I try to remember how I deal with these but all I can think is *we're going to die here we're going to die here.*

"Imogen," Wilder's voice says, and he's right in front of me.

He's got my hands in his, and he's squeezing them. He's warm.

going to die here going to die here

"Open your eyes and look at me," he says.

I don't. He squeezes my hands harder.

"Look at me!" he shouts, and my eyelids fly open.

Wilder is right there, his face a foot from mine, his hard eyes sky-blue and locked onto mine.

"You're gonna breathe with me, okay?" he says. "Ready? In."

He sucks a breath in, long and slow. I watch him, but I can't stop panting, Wilder's words barely registering over the roar in my brain.

"*Imogen*," he says, and for some reason my name gets through the static and suddenly, I'm listening to him.

"You're not breathing with me," he says, stating the fucking obvious.

My vision keeps narrowing, the black closing in, and now all I can see is him: blue eyes, tan face, cold-bitten red lips, a face I've literally seen in nightmares and anxiety dreams. When I wake up the sheets are always soaked through with my sweat.

I shake my head. I can't. I can't do this right now, still gasping shallowly for air like I'm drowning.

"Yes, you can," he says. "All you need is one second. Get control of yourself for one second. Breathe with me."

I want to scream *I can't, you don't understand, I can't because we're going to die here* but then Wilder squeezes my hands again and it's exactly enough.

I get one second.

My breath hitches, my lungs jerking, but then I get past that spot and breathe deep, along with Wilder, both of us together like we're one creature. Like he's my lifeline.

Instantly, the black fades. The sparkles zagging across my vision fade. I'm still shaking like a leaf as Wilder breathes out, still leading me, and then we breathe again.

And again.

Wilder stays there, just breathing with me. I don't know how long he does but I eventually stop shaking. The pain in my chest leaves, and even though it still feels like something ugly is wrapped around my ribcage, trying to get my heart to stop beating, I don't think I'm going to pass out any more.

When he lets go, he doesn't say anything. He just hands me the rest of the nutrition brick I dropped along with the half-full water bottle, and I take them from him.

I gnaw the block, I drink the water. Wilder gets up, closes the door until it's just barely cracked, sits on the floor opposite the plane from me with his ankles crossed.

"You gonna be okay?" he asks finally, his voice rumbling through the total, snowy silence.

I chew the last of the nutrition brick and nod, swallow the rest of the water behind it. I'm still rattled, still feel awful and nauseous and pretty sure we're going to die, but at least I can breathe, and I didn't pass out.

"Thanks for not attempting CPR," I tell him, because I guess we're being nice to each other right now. Not biting his head off is probably the least I can do. "Someone did that to me once because they thought I was having a heart attack. Nearly broke a rib."

"That's not what you're supposed to do for a heart attack, either," Wilder points out.

I crumple the wrapper in my mittened hand, wondering if the plane's got a trash can. Though I guess the plane *is* the trash can, since it's not like it's ever leaving this mountain again.

We're probably not ever leaving this mountain again, either—

"My dad has panic attacks," he suddenly volunteers.

I just stare at him in surprise.

"I'm not supposed to tell anyone, ever," he says, shrugging. "Obviously."

"Marcus Flint has panic attacks," I say, mostly to myself.

Wilder's dad is a consummate businessman, through and through, and it's pretty clear that his success is due entirely to him being complete, utter, and total fucking asshole. Everyone in Solaris respects him, sure, but no one *likes* him, because he'll do just about anything if he thinks it might make him money.

When I was a kid, he bought all the land around the only public park in Solaris, and then somehow managed to convince a judge to use eminent domain to buy that land for a pittance, too. In exchange he promised to build another playground, and he did — at one of his resorts. I've never even seen it.

An elderly woman got food poisoning and nearly died after eating in one of his restaurants. He sued her for defamation.

"He doesn't have them so much anymore," Wilder says, leaning back against the plane's metal skin. "Not surprising, given that he's practically on horse tranquilizers now."

"I've been there," I volunteer. "Those things will calm you down, that's for sure."

He's probably talking about the big guns — Xanax, Klonopin, that stuff. I've taken them before, but I don't like to make a habit of it. At least for me, they flatten out every emotion, not just anxiety.

Sure, when I'm on them I don't have panic attacks, but

I can't enjoy cupcakes either. I've been striving for a good seven years now to find the happy medium between the two things.

"No shit," Wilder says. "But before all that, it was up to my mom, my brother and me to figure out how to talk him down from one. Life got a lot more pleasant when we could. He had one in front of an investor once, and of course it was our fault for not..."

He's looking out the window over my shoulder and the sentence trails off, but in that moment, I'm suddenly seeing *him* again. Wilder Flint, the boy who once stole flowers from my neighbor's yard to give to me.

The boy who kissed me behind the movie theater. The boy who gave me my first hickey, which I stole some of my mom's oil paints to hide. It didn't work very well, for the record.

The boy who did all those things while he had a girl-friend. Melissa. The pretty, popular cheerleader. Of course.

Wilder was the richest kid in town, the star football player, the jock with the nice car and cool friends and no curfew.

He couldn't be seen around with *the nerd*.

"He deserved them," I say, my voice flat again. "Though what he really deserved was a heart attack."

Wilder's eyes flash, and his face goes back to being hard, closed off.

"Fuck you too," he says, and stands.

CHAPTER ELEVEN
WILDER

I t's a long, cold night. Somehow, even though we're the only two people for probably five hundred miles, Imogen manages not to speak to me.

Even though I make her emergency rations for dinner. Even though I give her another water bottle, help her outside so she can pee because she refuses to pee into a container inside the plane.

Total, stony silence. It would be remarkable if it didn't feel so completely awful.

We sleep on opposite sides of the plane, not that far away from each other. She's wrapped in the parachute and a ton of coats; I've got the emergency blankets and the rest of the coats.

I think she actually sleeps. I barely do.

Because if we want any chance at survival, we need to leave this plane. It's obvious by now that no one is coming. I'm not even sure if this plane had a flight transmitter — that's the *black box thing* Imogen was talking about — and if it does, it's obviously not working.

I've got some suspicions about that, but I've been trying

not to think about them. Right now, it's not that important *why* the plane went down, it's important that we figure out what the fuck we're going to do next.

If we stay here we'll die. I'm almost certain of that. We'll eat all our food, drink all our water, but that means that by the time we decide to head to a lower elevation and try our luck at finding civilization or a road or a fishing outpost or *something*, we'll be fucked.

Unlike Imogen's seminar, I've actually done some of this stuff. I've spent time alone in the cold forest, making shelters and building fires and trapping fish for food.

I'm not a Navy SEAL or something — I just flew their planes, I always knew I wasn't a lifer — but I think I'll be okay for a few days.

But I don't even know if Imogen can get down the rocks to the tree line. She won't let me look at her ankle, so I don't know if it's sprained or broken. I don't know if her *only* option is to stay here.

And if it is, I don't know what I'll do.

I could leave tonight, I think. *Then I wouldn't have to face that decision. No one would ever know.*

I stare at the tilted ceiling of the plane, watching my breath hover in the cold air.

It would be easy. Just go.

I roll over and try to fall asleep again. It doesn't work.

———

"You never did tell me where we are," Imogen says the next morning. She's chewing on another of the disgusting granola bars as I heat some of the MREs that we kept in the plane's emergency kit. They're only a year past their expiration date.

"I don't know where we are," I tell her.

"You had that map out."

"Do people look at maps when they know where they are?"

Imogen chews, swallows, glugs down some water.

We're running low on that, I think but don't say anything.

"I'm asking because I thought there was an outside chance you managed to figure it out," she says, her voice cool. "God knows you were looking at that thing for long enough."

"Sure, Imogen," I tell her, settling back on some cargo. "I've known exactly where we are this whole time, and I've secretly been talking to rescuers via radio just to torment you, because I'd also rather be here, in this miserably fucking cold airplane, than back in Solaris sitting on a couch and watching movies."

She colors, her cheeks going a splotchy pink.

"It wouldn't be the first time you tormented me for no reason," she points out.

"So my plan was, what, to wait until you showed up at the airport needing a ride? Then deliberately crash into this mountain *miraculously* without killing either of us, and then make you wait it out?"

She gets pinker, and I swallow hard. I'm tired and I'm hungry and I'm cold and Imogen has always been able to do this to me, take any emotion at all and turn it up to eleven.

"No," I say. "Maybe I'm behind your research grant to begin with. I dangled that in front of you just to get you here. I've been planning this for years," I snarl, sarcasm dripping from my voice. "You're *that* important to me, Imogen. It's all true, I've been planning one more way to make you miserable all this time."

She shoves at her glasses, face bright red, but she doesn't show any expression. If I didn't know better I'd think her eyes were glassy, but I'm sure it's just the sunlight.

"I don't know why you'd go to all that trouble," she says, her quiet voice tightly controlled. "All you'd have to do to make my life miserable is show up somewhere. It's not hard."

"I wish I'd left without you," I say.

Her jaw clenches, and she swallows.

"Nothing's stopping you," she points out, voice flat and cold as ever. "You can go freeze to death and once I get rescued maybe I'll try to convince them that they should come look for you as well, though I wouldn't hold my breath."

"You're that certain," I say. "You really think that if we just stay here, someone will magically come and rescue us."

"It's not *magic*," she says, her voice dripping with disdain. "That's the entire point of having radio contact, having the emergency beacon, all that stuff. That's why the plane is *bright yellow*, Wilder, because everything I've ever read or been told has been to stay where you are if you get lost or stranded and *let rescuers find you*."

Her voice is rising slightly in pitch as she keeps talking, edging on hysteria.

"We don't have either of those things," I say quietly, even though I know I should drop it for now. "We don't have radio communications and we don't have a transmitter. All we've got is a bright yellow plane in the middle of thousands of square miles of cloudy snow storm."

"Just because you don't know how something works doesn't mean it doesn't exist," she says, disdain dripping from every syllable. "All planes have them."

I clench my jaw, the disgusting taste of the MREs I've eaten for the last day rising in my throat, because I want to shout at her, ridicule her, tell her that we're going to die here and it's going to be her own fault that I'm the last person she sees.

If we had a transmitter, someone would be here by now. The storm has cleared. It's been over a day since we were supposed to make contact again. No one is coming.

I don't say anything to Imogen, I just stand from the cargo box where I'm sitting and shove it out of the way, then shove aside the one behind it and the one behind that.

"Those are fragile," Imogen says. "Be careful."

I ignore her. It doesn't matter if they're fragile, because her microscopes and shit are never getting used for their intended purpose. They'll be up here forever, probably with our skeletons next to them.

I reach the metal back panel of the airplane, in the tail section, run my fingers over where the rivets are holding it all together. This plane is probably twenty years old, and between that and our hard landing, some of the metal panels have separated a little.

I walk back through the airplane, past Imogen's nervous face, and fish the toolbox out from under a seat, then walk back.

I grab the hammer. I heft it in my hand, unsure that what I'm about to do is a good idea.

Do you want to find out, either? I think.

Easier to leave and never know, probably.

I ignore the thoughts and swing the hammer, claw side first, right into the place where two metal plates meet. There's an ugly noise and in my peripheral vision I can see Imogen flinch, still sitting on the floor with her bad leg extended in front of her, half-wrapped in the parachute.

I pull with all my might, letting my anger at her fuel my strength, the knots bunching in my arms as I try to tear this goddamn plane apart, swinging the hammer and pulling and grunting over and over again, sweat pouring down my back as the metal shrieks apart, exposing the insides of the plane, wires and electronics and more metal.

God, it feels good. After being helpless for this long it feels good to *do* something, to have some small accomplishment even if the accomplishment is tearing a single piece off of a plane.

Finally, it's nearly off, bent in half, and I swing the business end of the hammer at it with a clang, bending the panel back further, cold air leaking in from the hole I've opened in the plane's interior skin.

I'm sweating, panting for breath. Tearing steel off a plane is hard work, and I toss the hammer onto the ground with a heavy *thump*, then stick my gloved hand inside a nest of wires and pull.

And pull. And pull until all of it's out, on top of Imogen's suitcases and cargo boxes, just wires and wires of different colors, different patterns. None of it looks particularly high-tech or fancy, just wires and wires.

"Any emergency beacons in here?" I ask. "You see anything, Imogen? Let me know as soon as you do, being the expert and all."

I can't turn and look at her. I think I know the look on her face, a combination of horror and anger, the same splotchy red-and-white as before.

"It has to be in there," she says, her voice barely shaking. "I thought it was illegal not to have one, I checked that on the way—"

"Tell me more about what's fucking *legal*," I say, reaching my full arm back into the space and coming up with nothing. "Please, tell me how it should be here and isn't because it's against the law not to have one of these things that you're going on about. Because it's not back here, Imogen, and it's not in the front either and this plane isn't very big."

I finally turn and look at her, the pink splotches draining from her cheeks, her brown eyes wide behind her glasses. Despite everything she's sitting bolt upright on the floor, leg stuck out stubbornly in front of her, the look on her face like she's barely holding back tears but hates me anyway.

"You checked the front?" she asks, her voice quiet.

I thought she'd shout. Maybe I was hoping for it, that we could really have it out right now, scream at each other for a while. But instead she sounds deflated, broken, and I feel like she slipped a shard of glass through my stomach.

"While you were asleep," I admit.

I'm suddenly deflated, and I sit heavily on one of the plastic cargo tubs, drop my head into my hands because I was so busy proving Imogen wrong that I didn't realize that I'm also fucked.

There's no transmitter. No beacon. She's right that there should be. It should have been either in a spot below the instrument panel up front or behind that panel in the back, but it's neither and there's really nowhere else for the thing to go.

I don't have an explanation. I don't have a reason it's not there.

I don't have a reason for anything. I can't even tell Imogen why everything on this plane suddenly failed and it crashed, because *I don't know.*

"Oh," she says, her voice changing completely in that one word, and I instantly feel terrible again.

For this, for her, for everything I did ten years ago and everything I've done since and anything else I'll do in my life. Even if Imogen is a difficult asshole sometimes who treats me like I'm an idiot, she doesn't deserve to die here. With me, of all people.

"I'm sorry," I say. "I was still hoping someone would show up."

"I don't think they will," she says, her voice quiet and distant, suddenly kind.

"I don't think so either," I say softly. "I think either we leave and take our chances, or we die here in this tiny plane."

"You're not supposed to leave," she says, mostly to herself, tilting her head back against the metal skin of the plane. "You're never supposed to leave, that's the thing everyone always says, you're supposed to stay put..."

Her voice trails off into silence, and I don't respond because I don't know what to say.

CHAPTER TWELVE
IMOGEN

"You should go," I tell Wilder.

I don't mean it. Not in the least, because as much as I hate him being the only person around for thousands of miles, the thought of being here, of freezing or starving slowly to death in this plane, is infinitely worse.

But it seems like the kind of thing I'm supposed to say right now, even if I don't mean it. Like I'm noble and brave or something instead of a terrified girl with a busted ankle who can put on a brave face for about thirty seconds before admitting how afraid she is of dying alone in the wilderness.

"Alone?" he echoes, looking up at me.

He's slouched forward, his elbows on his knees, and he looks up at me like he's seeing me for the first time. I push my glasses up, feeling like I need to do something and grateful for the extra layer between me and the world.

"Why?" he finally says, sounding genuinely puzzled.

I just point at my ankle, stuck straight out in front of me.

"We can splint it," he says, his head still cocked as he frowns as my foot. "Between that and your boots it'll probably hurt and we'll be slow, but we can get you down."

"There's a boulder scramble between here and anything else."

"I didn't say it would be fun, I said it would be doable."

"Wilder," I tell him, my voice close to a whisper. "It's broken, I can't go down a boulder scramble."

He looks at me for a long time, rubbing his hands together in his gloves, the knot in my stomach pulsing and tightening and loosening. I'd forgotten his stupid ability to bring out every single emotion in me, all at once: anger and disdain and nostalgia and this weird, almost tangible *longing* that sometimes comes out of nowhere and blindsides me like a Mack truck on the interstate.

And then he smiles. Wilder fucking *smiles*, takes off his gloves, stands up and steps over to me.

"It's not broken," he says, crouching.

"I can't walk on it."

"No, you can walk on it a little," he says, reaching his bare hands out toward it.

Instinctively, I jerk my leg away, gasping in pain as it scoots awkwardly across the floor.

"If it were broken it would hurt a whole lot more," he says, his voice suddenly gentle and patient.

God, it's like Wilder is two different people sometimes: this guy, the nice one, who's strangely competent and in charge, who seems to know what he's doing, and the raging asshole with pure venom in his eyes every time he looks at me.

"Can I see your ankle?" he asks, his voice quiet.

Instinctively I want to shout *no, get away from me I don't ever want you touching me again* but instead of letting my animal brain control what I do, I take a deep breath. I swallow.

And I nod, moving my leg back toward him.

Wilder settles onto his knees without saying anything. He pushes the bottom of my fleece-lined leggings up to my mid-calf, his warm hand rougher than I remember against my skin.

Don't remember, I order myself, leaning my head back against the plane, my hands clenching in mittens.

He holds the toe of my boot steady in one hand and unlaces it with the other. I've got thick wool socks on underneath heavy-duty over-the-ankle hiking boots, and he undoes the double knots in my laces, tugs them through the eyelets, loosens the tongue of my boot so gently I can barely feel it even though my ankle is swollen and prickling.

I didn't know he could be this gentle, I think.

Yes, you did, I remind myself as he takes the boot off, cold air slowly filtering through the thick sock.

"Sorry about the smell," I say, because I haven't taken my shoes off since we crash-landed.

"I've smelled way, way worse," he assures me, a slight grin on his face. "Trust me on that."

He pulls my sock down over most of my foot until it's just over my toes, his fingers lightly traversing the pebbled indentations that it left on my foot.

My ankle is swollen and light purple, ugly shades of green and blue around the periphery of the main bruise. Even though it's midday, the sun is filtered through the layer of clouds and the layer of snow covering half the plane's windows, and I wonder if the colors on my ankle are right.

There must be some sort of light tricks at play here, I think, willing myself to stop concentrating on Wilder's hands touching my ankle this gently. *Like a prism effect or something where it's going through the frozen particulate matter up in the clouds.*

He takes my foot in one hand and the bottom of my calf in the other, his hands strong and firm and amazingly *warm*, and he rotates my foot slightly.

I make a face, and he looks over at me.

"That hurt?" he asks.

I just nod, wishing he'd stop, but he keeps doing it, his eyes searching my face.

"But not too bad?"

"Not too bad," I agree. "It's way worse when I put weight on it."

His hands move, sliding around, fingers digging into the swollen flesh around the joint. I'm holding my breath, thinking about how my foot must smell awful and how I haven't shaved my legs in the past week, since I was going to the Arctic after all to look at musk oxen and not expecting someone to touch me. Even just to see if I have a broken ankle or not.

"How much does that hurt?" he asks, still prodding.

"Some," I say. "I'm not kicking you in the face or anything."

"And thanks for that," he murmurs, teasing me. "Wiggle your toes?"

I wiggle.

"Can you rotate your ankle?" he asks, finally letting me go.

I rotate the ankle, dutifully, while he kneels next to it and watches.

"It's not broken," he finally says, rolling my sock back over my foot, pulling it up over my ankle. "Just sprained."

"I still can't get down that boulder scramble," I say, remembering how much it hurt just to get outside to pee. There's no way I can just hop from rock to rock with my ankle like this, and Wilder sure can't carry me, not that he would, which means that there's no way I can get out of this plane.

I take a deep breath, forcing myself to stave off the panic. It's always worse at times like this, when I'm under stress and haven't been eating or sleeping well, and good God are all of those things true right now.

"We'll wrap it up," he says. "There's no ankle splint in the emergency kit but with some good bandaging and if we lace your boot up real tight, I think we can manage getting you down the scramble."

We.

I don't trust Wilder Flint. I don't even like him, except for in moments like this when I catch myself thinking he's okay, though in my defense right now he's actually being okay.

But it's not like I've got a choice. Well, I mean, I do obviously, but my choices are pretty much that either a) I trust Wilder Flint just enough to go with him, or b) I stay here, in this plane, and die of either hypothermia or starvation or dehydration or a lovely combination of all three.

"I'm not light," I warn him, heart clenching.

He lifts my leg gingerly, sliding my boot over my toes and foot. I could put my own shoes back on but for some reason I let him do it, because sitting here with him, letting him be *nice* to me feels…

Well, it feels nice.

Of course he's being nice, there's no one else around, I think.

"Last year I had to wrestle a former NFL linebacker down a double-black-diamond ski slope," he says, adjusting my boot around my ankle. "I think I can handle you."

"Were you on skis?"

"Not at that point," he says, a smile in his voice. "We don't — well, we *didn't* — screen for skiing ability before we would take someone heli-skiing, and let's just say this guy didn't have very much. You know how much force it takes to break a ski?"

"Oh, my *God*," I murmur, because the answer to that is *a lot of force*.

"He did that, and as you can probably imagine, it fucked his knee up pretty good."

Wilder tightens the laces around my foot, glances up at me.

"Too tight?"

I shake my head, and he starts looping the laces through the hooks over the ankle of my boots.

"Anyway, I figure if I can get three hundred pounds of screaming man-meat down a ski slope far enough for the rescue toboggan, I can probably get you down a couple hundred feet of boulder scramble," Wilder says, double-knotting my laces.

"Now you screen for skiing ability?" I ask, trying not to smile and failing.

"Exactly," he says. "Anyone who wants to heli-ski has to take a day of private instruction first. We got a couple of complaints, but most people appreciate that we're not just letting incompetent maniacs down a difficult mountain with them."

His hand is still on my leg, one finger on the stubble-laden strip between the bottom of my leggings and the top of my socks, and we just look at each other for a long, long moment.

There are a thousand things that I want to say, a thousand things I want to ask Wilder, starting with *why are you being nice to me now?* and ending with *why did you ever pretend to be nice to me in the first place?*

But I don't ask either. I'm not sure I want to know the answers, if I'm really being honest with myself. And right now, I'm having an odd glimmer of a world where we've never met before, where we're two strangers who have to get down a mountain together.

"Besides that guy, who's the worst skier you ever had to take up?" I ask, and Wilder laughs.

CHAPTER THIRTEEN
WILDER

We leave at dawn the next day, or what passes as dawn here. The clouds keep getting lighter until they don't any more, and it's then that I have to assume the sun has risen and we can leave.

"Wilder," Imogen says softly, still sitting on the floor as I shove the door to the tiny airplane open, a bit of snow swirling in.

"Hit me," I say.

She raises an eyebrow, and I grin at her.

"What?" I ask.

I'm feeling jaunty, almost giddy because despite everything I *like* this. I've always liked the adrenaline rush of danger, of knowing I might not make it back.

It's why I've been skiing and snowboarding the hardest runs in Solaris since I was a kid. It's why I joined the football team, why I joined the Navy and wanted to fly planes, it's why I volunteered to fly a helicopter to the top of a mountain when I got out.

It's probably why I ever messed around with Imogen in the first place, besides the fact that she drew me in like nothing I've ever felt before. She was different, strange, uncharted territory that I didn't understand.

Also, I had a girlfriend. Melissa Hedder. The red-haired, ponytailed head cheerleader. The girl I was *supposed* to date, the girl I could show off to my friends and family and who I could be Prom King with.

Image is everything. My father taught me that, again and again. The man is a fucking maniac for his *image*, and it's worked for him.

Sneaking around with Imogen behind Melissa's back was a high I'd never felt before, a pure rush that I couldn't get enough of, the one-two punch of being with Imogen and doing something I shouldn't have.

Until it all went down in flames, anyway.

"Are you sure we're doing the right thing?" she asks, and it jars me from my memories of high school.

"You mean leaving?"

She just nods, and I swallow, because I'm not. I have no idea whether anyone's out there and looking for us or not. I have no idea if they'll find us if they are.

"No," I tell her, because Imogen's smart, probably smarter than me, and I'd be an idiot if I tried to pull the wool over her eyes.

"But you think this gives us the best odds."

"I haven't run it through a spreadsheet or anything," I tell her.

There's a slight smile playing around her lips.

"I could do that, if you want," she offers, her eyes laughing. "My laptop's probably still got juice in it. I'm sure there's a point of diminishing returns when you consider staying at a crash site where no one's rescued us yet versus setting off into the wilderness on our own with nothing but our wits."

"And a hatchet."

"You've got a hatchet?"

I just point to the left side of the huge pack I'm wearing, a hatchet strapped on. It's probably not the best way to carry a hatchet, but it's not like I've got a good one at the moment.

"Oh, well, if you've got a hatchet," Imogen deadpans. "By all means, let's go."

Inside me there's a flicker of *something*, some spark lighting in the dark and trying to catch. I don't know what it is, whether it's familiarity or friendship or the sudden recognition that this feels like things did between us, once upon a time.

I walk over, hold out one thickly gloved hand to Imogen. Her eyes alight on it and even now, there's a moment of hesitation before she grabs my hand with hers and I heave her to her feet.

We don't talk as I help her into her own heavy pack and adjust it, her slight frame surprisingly sturdy as I yank on straps.

That's another strange thing about our situation: the plane was well-stocked for an emergency situation like this. All Flint Holdings, Inc. planes are outfitted with the worst-case scenario in mind, since they're small planes that are regularly flown over rough terrain. That this one still had its emergency gear means that it's been regularly maintained, checked, its stuff updated.

There's no reason for the instrument failure, no reason that we crash-landed way out here. I'd suspect sabotage but that just seems ludicrous, because sabotaging planes happens in spy movies, not real life.

Imogen walks for the door. She's slow, but I wrapped her ankle up pretty well this morning, and she's barely limping at all. I just hope I'm right that it's only sprained, not broken, because that seemed like what she needed to hear.

I'm *pretty* sure it's just sprained, but I've only got a little bit of emergency medical training. I'm not a doctor or even a medic, but as she steps out of the plane, her foot sinking into snow that comes halfway up her calf, I don't think Imogen's in that much pain.

She stands there, looking over the scene in front of us. I come out of the plane behind her, shut the door, turn the handle to seal it just for good measure.

Imogen watches me do it, looks at me with eyebrows raised. I shrug.

"May as well," I say, but she's looking at the horizon again and I'm looking at the way that the mountains reflect in her dark eyes.

"It's pretty out here," she says quietly.

"It is," I agree, because she's right.

It's beautiful. It's one of the most beautiful places I've ever been, with white mountains poking their jagged gray tops above the tree line, the sun bursting over the ragged ridges. Everything about them is sharp, hard, unforgiving.

It looks dangerous, desolate, cold, like ten thousand avalanches waiting to happen, but this landscape still has a draw on me I can't explain or escape.

Imogen's looking forward, toward the boulder scramble, face set, gloved hands holding onto her backpack straps by her hips.

"Okay then," she says, partly to me but mostly to the wilderness all around us. "Let's do this."

———

It's a quarter mile, maybe less, to the big rocky patch, but neither of us talks on that walk. Imogen keeps looking back over her shoulder at the plane slowly getting smaller behind us, like she's afraid she's left the stove on or something, but she doesn't say anything.

I landed the plane on a long, snowy flat spot sort of near the rocky ridge of a mountain, maybe a thousand feet above tree level. At the time I didn't exactly have a choice, but now I wish I'd stayed calmer, guided the plane down lower, maybe landed on a frozen lake or something because getting down is going to be rough.

On two sides are steep drops that aren't quite sheer cliffs, but they're close enough that I'm not risking them, even now. The third side of our plateau rises in a long, slippery gravel field up to the sharp peak of a mountain, all hard rock and ice, the ridge line so steep it's bare of snow.

That leaves us with one choice, a slick boulder scramble down to a steep snowy field, the huge rocks pitted with ice and snow. I have no idea if they're stable or if we're about to set off a landslide. Once we're down it I have no idea if we'll just be stuck on another ledge that's even harder to get down from.

But I know it's pretty much our only chance, and it's better than the chances of rescue, which have dwindled to nearly zero.

When we get to it, we stand above the long gray patch, staring down. Up here most of the rock is granite, hard and unforgiving, and here the boulders are patched with the white of snow and the lighter gray of ice, the occasional brown of dirt where the wind has blown the snow and ice away.

"What if we're not where you think we are?" Imogen asks suddenly, breathing hard beside me.

There's a hint of accusation in her voice, but I turn to look at her, meet her beneath her hat and behind her glasses, and strangely there's nothing. No malice, no flash of enmity, just an honest question.

"What's it change?" I ask, taking a long glug from my water bottle. I don't have a lot left, but once we're down in the valley there's going to be something running through there.

She expels air from her lungs, looks around at the scenery, hands on her hips while she catches her breath, because walking through eight inches of snow at serious elevation is tiring work.

"Maybe we should go the other way," she says, looking back over her shoulder at the plane and the ridge line above it, the yellow bright against the snow. "Over the mountain, and then there might be another valley with more people on the other side…"

I consider her offered plan quietly for a long moment, looking at the sharp, bare mountain.

"Do you really think you can get over that?" I ask.

She pushes her glasses up her face, appraises it.

"It could be better than getting down this," she says quietly.

She looks away and I study Imogen's face for a long, leisurely second, letting her look away while I look at her.

Imogen's pretty. You know those movies where there's a nerdy girl who puts on a dress and makeup at one point and suddenly she's totally hot? That's kinda how Imogen is, or would be, except it's blazingly obvious that she's pretty with her glasses on and with no makeup, face pale and cheeks red and a hat jammed down almost to her eyebrows.

I always knew it. Fucking everyone in high school always knew it. We used to talk in the locker room about which girls were secret freaks, and her name always came up, every single time, back when *freak* just meant *girl who'd fuck*.

Only I stayed quiet about her back then because the other guys could speculate, but I *knew*.

Imogen heaves a breath out, the white puffing in front of her face and then disappearing almost instantly in the dry, cold air.

She's also scared. That's obvious too, and whether or not she realizes it she's looking for ways to put off committing to one course of action and cut herself off from the others. I saw it all the time flying in the Navy, guys panicking at the last second that they were doing the wrong thing.

I see it all the time in the helicopter, rich men who brag to their friends about how great the powder is at the inaccessible top to some mountain only to ask me to fly around for a fucking hour, trying to find something they're not terrified to ski down.

At least Imogen's justified and not here by her own fault.

"You really think you can get over that?" I ask.

Her jaw tightens, the muscles flexing below her skin.

"I could."

"Now? With your ankle and your pack and no clue what's on the other side?"

"My ankle's not that bad."

She's lying. It's swollen and purple, and it's slowing her down a *lot*. I can tell the only reason she's not limping is because I'm here and she's not about to show weakness in front of me.

"No?"

"I could do it," she says defensively. "If there's something better over there, a ranger station or a radio tower or something."

I shove my gloved hands into the pockets of my outermost parka, annoyed that we have to do this *now*, when we're so close to making real progress.

"Well, is there?" I ask, a bite coming into my voice. "If you've got secret knowledge, or if Stanford installed x-ray vision on you, the time to tell me is *now*."

Imogen rolls her eyes.

"Actually, the time to tell me was two days ago when we first crash-landed, but I'd forgive that if you were a top-secret government experiment," I go on, the words still pouring out. "I'm sure they've got secret biotech that they install in their best and brightest—"

"All right, I fucking get it, Jesus," Imogen snaps, glaring at me. "The devil you know and shit. Fuck, just go down the fucking boulders already."

"I guess Stanford didn't teach you to be ladylike," I say, just to taunt her.

"I guess the Navy didn't teach you not to be a mean asshole," she says.

I step onto the very first boulder, make sure I've got my balance, walk out onto the rock and survey the land below me, Imogen's words rattling around in my head.

"Nope," I finally answer.

"Or how to fly planes properly," she says, just to get a final dig in as she steps up onto the same rock as me, wobbling slightly for balance, not looking at me.

Anger flares deep inside me and I want to grab her shoulders, shake her, shout *it's not my fault we crashed something went wrong* but instead I clench my teeth, look at the splendor of nature, study the rocks below us. And I remind myself that right now, in our precarious position, isn't the time to get into a useless, meaningless fight with Imogen.

"There," I tell her, pointing at another rock.

Her eyes narrow. She pushes up her glasses.

"What about—"

"You have to look at the whole path, not just the first step," I cut her off, not in the mood for her know-it-all-bullshit just now. "From there we go there, and there, and there, and we keep our options open and are less likely to need to backtrack."

She presses her lips together. The color goes out of them, but she doesn't say anything.

"I'll go first," I offer, and hop off our rock.

CHAPTER FOURTEEN
IMOGEN

When Wilder jumps, my heart goes straight into my mouth. I mean, it's been there for most of the past few days anyway, concussion notwithstanding, but I feel the sudden urge to grab his arm, yank him back and say *oh my God don't that's dangerous.*

"Come on!" he says, standing two feet away on the next boulder.

The cold wind curls around my body, trying to find the places where my insulation is lacking. The sun's outrageously bright, blinding light bouncing off hundreds and thousands of acres of snow, making me squint at Wilder and the rocks and the sky above and the earth below.

I shift my weight. My ankle complains, but I try to ignore it.

It's two feet. Not even that. It's nothing.

I grab the straps on my backpack, take a deep breath.

"Imogen, you'll be fine," Wilder says, stepping forward and holding out a hand.

Yeah, you pussy, you'll be fine. Stop overthinking it, stop imagining that your ankle could give out at the worst possible second and you'd stumble into that, probably break a leg when the weight of your—

"Do you need help?" he asks, his voice suddenly gentle, the mockery gone.

That does it.

I take a deep breath and *leap* over the small crevice, landing on my good ankle several feet away from the crack and ignoring Wilder's outstretched hand. It could have been twice the size it was and I'd *still* have made it, for God's sake.

"See? I knew you'd be fine," Wilder says, his voice irritatingly smug.

I don't look at him. I don't want him to see the tears in my eyes for no reason. I don't want him to know how much that unnerved me, because even though I know there are perfectly good reasons — I've got a concussion, my ankle hurts, food is scarce, it's cold and we're probably going to die — for me to be a wimp about this, that doesn't mean I want him to know.

"Great. Thanks," I say, my voice flat as I look around, blinking. "Where next? That one?"

"Yup," he answers, and we take off slowly across the boulder field.

IT'S LONG. It's hard, and it's unpleasant, and I lightly wrench my ankle at least once, but we're getting closer. Every few rocks I look up, back at where we came from, and watching it get farther and farther away makes me feel slightly panicked but mostly good, like what we're doing is really working to get us somewhere.

We're almost at the bottom when I realize something's wrong. So far, I've been tiredly just following Wilder, watching where he goes and doing the same, sometimes handing my pack up or down to him if I can't manage with the thing on, but now he's just standing on a broad, flat rock, pacing back and forth.

Like a lion in a cage, if the lion were wearing a thick parka, and it sparks a bolt of panic in me because we *can't* go back now, we have to get off this rocky part of the mountain somehow and it's already late afternoon.

We'll freeze to death if we stay on the rocks, I think. *It'll be windy and cold, we need to get to somewhere that we can find at least some shelter, not to mention a little water, and God knows we can't keep moving in the dark because we'll just slip on some ice and then we'll definitely die—*

"There's a snag," Wilder's voice says, low and calm despite the thumping in my chest. "C'mere."

I swallow and walk over to him, standing in the shadow of the rocks above us. He's looking across a gap to another boulder, that one at an odd angle, the sides jagged.

"We gotta jump this," he explains, and I look down.

It's big. Wide. Too wide, probably four feet and it's straight down, the bottom dark and forbidding and probably filled with spikes and wolves and spiders and mud.

There's no way I can climb down it and back up the other side, but no way I can jump it, either. The rock on the opposite side of the gulch is angled up and slippery-looking, like even if I got a foothold there I'd slide right back off of it and into the gulch.

"We can't jump that," I say, hoping my voice sounds reasonable and not shaky.

"Sure we can," Wilder says, adjusting his pack slightly. "If these were just two lines on the ground, you wouldn't think twice about it."

"But they're not," I say, cinching my own pack tighter in my nervousness. "This is one giant rock and that's another giant rock, and there's a seventy-foot drop between them—"

"It's forty if it's a foot."

"—there's a huge drop between them and *that* rock looks hard to land on, and my ankle is all fucked up, so I really think that we should head back and find another route down—"

Wilder jumps. Motherfucker makes it look easy, just *leaping* across this mile-wide gap and landing on the other side, leaning forward and grabbing an outcropping to steady himself before he turns around to look at me, grinning.

"See? It's fine," he says.

It's not fine. Nothing about this is fine, nothing about this is good or normal or even kind of okay because I'm on a bare granite rock in the middle of nowhere with a busted ankle, a concussion, and this person who I absolutely positively completely *hate* more than anyone else.

Vaguely, in the back of my mind, I know I'm being kind of unreasonable. It's a big jump, yeah, but I'm not unraveling right now because of that. I'm unraveling because I'm hungry and cold and tired and my stupid ankle hurts and because I childishly want to be at home, in front of a fireplace, or even in an Arctic research station sipping tea and discussing the mating habits of musk oxen.

Anywhere but here. With *him*.

"I can't," I say. "I'm going back, I'm gonna find another way down, that's just too far and if I fall and get hurt I'll be really screwed…"

"There's not another way," he says. "C'mon, throw me your pack."

"Of course there's another way," I say, my chin jutting out a little. "Maybe three hundred feet back, when we climbed that one rock with the big quartz vein in it there was another way we could have gone—"

"Cliff," he says.

"No, it wasn't, there was another rock down there and then we'd have had to—"

"We'd have had to scramble up an incline full of loose rock which only got steeper at the bottom," he says. "You really think sliding to your death is better than jumping over a little crevice?"

"That's not little when you've got a sprained ankle."

"Throw me your pack."

I grip the straps, heart racing, because despite *everything* deep down in my heart of hearts I don't want to trust him.

"Imogen," he says, holding out one hand.

I stare at it.

"If there were a better way down, I swear we'd be taking it," he says, an impatient edge finally in his voice. "I promise I'm more interested in getting off this boulder field and to shelter before nightfall than torturing—"

"Okay, okay," I say, yanking the buckle at my chest apart and shrugging it from my shoulders. "Okay. Fine."

I heave it down, grab it in both hands, and fling it across underhand. Wilder catches it easily, slings it to the ground behind him in one motion, making it look as easy as the jump.

Everything was always easy for him, I think bitterly, out of nowhere. *Sports, people, me.*

Especially me.

"You coming too?" he asks, tugging at his gloves.

I stand at the edge, looking down. The light is just starting to fade and I swear it's darker now than it was two minutes ago, though it could just be my imagination.

Don't think, just jump.

Just jump.

I stand there, frozen, my body refusing to do what I keep telling it to.

Use your good foot to push off of, there's a nice little ledge-thing right there, maybe if you got a few feet of running start…

I back up, wondering if that's the best way to make it across the ravine, with a running start.

But if I try that, maybe I'll hit my bad ankle wrong and then I'll trip or fall down and then I'll be really screwed…

I come back to the edge, look down into the darkness.

"It's not that far, I promise," Wilder says, standing on the other side, feet braced, one hand out. "Come on, I'll catch you."

I shift my weight, calculating. If I jump off my good ankle then I stand a better chance of making it across in the first place, but then I'd land on my bad one and I might *really* break it this time and then I'd be screwed for the rest of this stupid journey, but if I jump off my bad ankle then I might just go into the pit of despair and then I'd never—

"Imogen," Wilder says, but I barely hear him over the noise in my own head.

—make it out, and that's definitely worse but at least it wouldn't prolong my suffering, right? Better to just die instantly and be eaten by wolves than to limp through the wilderness for another day or two, making Wilder drag me—

"C'mon, Squeaks," Wilder says, and my head snaps up.

He's grinning. The fucking asshole is *grinning* at me, like he knows I won't make it and he's ten seconds away from not having to haul me for miles and miles through the snow. He's grinning like he gets to call me whatever the fuck he wants because he thinks it's funny, like even out here he's above me somehow, like he can ruin my life however he wants—

I leap.

I don't think about which foot I'm jumping off of and I don't think about the wolves and spikes below, I just think about how there's no way I'm letting Wilder be the only one to survive this and before I know it I'm on the other side, his strong arm around my back holding me steady as my ankle tries to buckle underneath me.

I grab onto a waist-high outcropping, catch my breath.

"Told you," he says.

"Fuck you," I say, standing on my good ankle, my sprained one held off the ground.

He just laughs. *Laughs.*

"Even here?" I ask.

Now that I'm on this side, nerves shot, I'm near tears, forcing myself to hold them back because I'll do almost anything not to cry in front of him.

"You can't go without reminding me of that dumb fucking nickname *even now* when we're stuck out in the middle of God knows where?"

He puts a hand on my shoulder and I shove it off, furious.

"I moved a thousand miles to escape you," I say between clenched teeth. "The least you can do right now is pretend we're strangers."

"You got across, didn't you?" he asks softly, hoisting a pack onto his back.

"That's not the point," I growl, testing out my ankle, facing away from him. "The point is that I want you to go *one single day* without bringing that shit up, because you probably don't know this, but I arranged my entire life around getting away from you and now I'm gonna have to start that over."

I hear the snap of a buckle closing behind me, and I squeeze my eyes shut, trying to force myself not to cry.

You're tired and hungry and et cetera, et cetera, I tell myself.

Plus, it's probably below zero here in the shade, if you cry the tears might just freeze to your face and think about how miserable that would be.

"You gonna start getting away again right now?" Wilder asks, something sharp in his voice.

I bite my lip, test my weight on my ankle, don't turn around to look at him.

"Or were you gonna wait until I caught you when you jumped? Maybe you were gonna wait until we got down off this mountain, *then* you were gonna pretend like we're strangers who've never met?"

"You're the reason we're here," I say quietly, staring off into the distance.

There's a slight scraping noise, and I turn to see that he's picked up my pack as well, slung it over one shoulder. His eyes are blazing, the wind beating a few strands of hair around his face, underneath his hat.

"I'm the reason we're *alive*," he says. "Anytime you want to say thanks for that, just let me know. Otherwise we gotta get moving before sunset."

Wilder turns and starts walking. We're still stepping from boulder to boulder but from here, the steps get smaller and smaller until the rocks give way to a wide, flat snowy patch, the snow halfway up our calves.

I jam my hands into my pockets, feeling furious and guilty all at once. I'm not wrong and I know it, but then again, neither is Wilder, who's up ahead of me carrying eighty pounds of our gear while I follow along behind him carrying nothing.

Don't think, I tell myself, despite the fact that trying not to think has literally never worked for me. *Just get through this, get to the tree line, find some shelter from the wind and eat your disgusting MRE and make it through the night.*

I follow behind Wilder, stepping in his footsteps when I

can, and we don't say anything to each other for a long, long time but I keep thinking. I think about mistakes I made ten years ago, I think about mistakes I made today.

I think about arctic foxes and musk oxen, telephoto lenses and permafrost. I think about dropping the folder of pictures in front of security at the Solaris airport and how that seems like nothing now.

And I think about what I told Wilder to get him to take me on this plane flight: that I'd get him fifteen thousand dollars in compensation.

That fifteen thousand feels a lot worse right now.

CHAPTER FIFTEEN
WILDER

Carrying both packs at least warms me up, and it's not long before I'm starting to sweat, little rivulets running down the back of my neck and into the t-shirt I'm wearing underneath the other fifteen layers I've got on.

I know Imogen hates being called Squeaks. Of course I know.

But it worked, didn't it? She's trudging along behind me, through the snow, instead of stuck back there on that boulder thinking herself into tears, and that's what matters.

We're gonna get to the tree line before it's dark, and we'll find some sort of shelter and have some minor protection from the elements, all of which is way better than being stuck on the side of a mountain, out in the open.

"Wait," she calls out, and I stop in my tracks, take a deep breath, look up at the sky. The sun is low, just about to go behind the mountain, and that means it'll be getting cold before long, but I turn to look at her.

She's standing there, hands on her hips, panting for breath. Glaring at me from behind her glasses.

"Is my water in my pack?" she asks.

I sling it to the ground, find a water bottle, toss it to her. We're running low, and I'm a little worried, but not too much. There's water down below us, and at worst we can melt snow.

"Thanks," she says, and guzzles it between gulps of air. I drink some of my own water in the meantime, looking down at the tree line. It's another half hour away, maybe, but it'll be darker once we get there and we still have to find shelter.

"I'm not used to the altitude," Imogen says, still short of breath. "I lost my lungs for it when I moved to Seattle. I can take my pack, though."

She moves toward me, stepping in the footsteps I've left behind myself, holding out one hand.

"I've got it," I tell her, shouldering it again.

Imogen looks at me like she's about to argue with me, but then changes her mind.

"Thanks," she says simply, pushing at her glasses. "Sorry to be a burden."

I smile. I can't help it, because it's such a ridiculous phrase, so dramatic for something this simple.

"A burden?" I tease. "Who are you, my great-grandma from the old country?"

Imogen makes a face, but then it softens, and she wrinkles her nose at me.

"You've got my pack, so you're *literally* carrying my burden," she points out.

"Only because you're an out-of-shape gimp who'd slow us both down if I didn't," I say. "Don't tell me you've got asthma, too, because I'll just leave you right here in the snow."

"That's one classic nerd affliction I escaped," she says, trudging ahead of me, her heavy boots crunching into the snow. "I got the astigmatism, terminal clumsiness, and hand-eye coordination of a newborn panda, but no asthma, at least."

I fight the urge to say *good to hear, Squeaks*, just to see how she'd react.

"I'm surprised you never got contacts," I tell her. "I figured that in ten years…"

You'd have realized how hot you are and ditched the glasses.

"I thought about it," she says, the two of us trudging downward. "I even tried them for a while, but…"

"But?"

Imogen sighs, her breathing starting to pick up again. Hiking through snow is hard, and doing it at around twelve thousand feet is beyond taxing.

"But poking my finger into my eye gave me the heebie-jeebies so I couldn't do it," she admits.

I start laughing, because of everything I know about this girl, that's somehow surprising.

"What, you're surprised that I got weirded out by something?"

"I once watched you slice into a dead frog's eyeball and hardly move a muscle when it squirted all the way to the ceiling of the bio lab," I say. "I'm surprised that eyeballs weird you out."

"Not *eyeballs*," she says, starting to pant. "Poking my own personal finger into my own personal eyeball is what got me."

"I bet that frog eye is still up there," I say.

"Depends on how often they clean the ceilings at Solaris High."

"I don't think it's too often."

Imogen is quiet for a few steps, her breath whistling in and out of her lungs.

"Think the fetal pig blood is still on the doorframe

where Alicia Petroski screamed and smacked it out of your hand that one time?"

Even though my lungs are burning, half with cold and half with altitude, I laugh.

We were in eleventh grade biology, and I'd engineered getting paired with Imogen as my lab partner. I told my friends that it was because *obviously* she'd be the smart one who did all the work, and I'd just tag along for the easy A.

That day, we were dissecting pig fetuses, and for once I was to class early. I was a dumb teenager, so I decided to see if I could scare Imogen, shake loose her stony cool exterior for once.

So I hid behind the door with a pig fetus, and when she came in, I shook it in her face and shouted, the dead pig eyes level with hers.

Imogen jumped, but she barely blinked, more annoyed than anything. But Alicia was right behind her, and Alicia's why I got two weeks of detention.

She screamed, smacked the pig out of my hand, stared at her own hand, screamed again, started crying hysterically, and then ran down the hall waving her hand over her head, like it was tainted or something. Alicia was always kind of dramatic, but it was a whole fucking scene that ended with *three* teachers trying to get her out of the girls' bathroom before calling her mom to come get her and take her home.

Imogen, on the other hand, was irritated that I'd been manhandling the pig, which might make dissection more challenging.

"*That* they probably cleaned," I say. "And I thought you said it wasn't blood, it was the dye they put to highlight the veins or whatever."

"There was probably some blood," Imogen admits.

"Now you tell me."

"Would it have stopped you?"

"Not a chance," I admit.

"Poor Alicia," Imogen muses, a hint of amusement in her voice. "Terrorized by a dead pig when she came in that day only expecting to slice one from stem to stern."

I watch her back for a moment, the unsteady way she's walking through the snow, lifting her feet high and plunging them back in, and I lick my lips, watch my breath expel in a puff.

In two steps I'm caught up to her and I turn, looking at her face, her brown eyes glinting with some dark amusement behind her glasses. The sun's gone behind a mountain now, and the shadows are turning everything blue, making her look even paler than she is, her lips even redder.

"You thought it was funny," I say.

Imogen doesn't answer right away, just lurches right and then left, watching the tree line get closer.

"I would never," she finally says, but the way her lips twitch give her away.

"You *would*," I say, plowing into my ten-year-old memory of high school, a memory that's both not about Imogen and about nothing else. "Come on, the way she ran down the hallway waving her hand in the air?"

Imogen bites the inside of her lip, looks at the ground in front of her.

"I might not have minded watching her get taken down a notch," she finally admits. "You know she got an A in English that year because she agreed to let Dan Ramirez grab one of her boobs if he wrote all her essays for her?"

I just laugh.

"Only one boob?" I ask, thinking of the things Imogen and I got up to a couple of months later, things that went way beyond single-breast touching.

"Through her clothes. Two-minute limit," Imogen says, exhaling hard in a cloud of steam. "Because she was the kind of girl who'd trade sexual favors for homework and also the kind of girl who'd be a stingy bitch about it."

"So if she'd let him grab both boobs, it'd be a different story."

Imogen exhales, and I can't tell whether she's laughing or not.

"Dan and I were in Mathletes together," she says. "After he got her the first A on a paper I told him he should use that as leverage and negotiate, but he never did."

There's a twinge, a turn, a twist deep inside me as Dan's face floats to mind: dorky glasses, bad haircut, scraps of a mustache that didn't do him any favors.

"You two were friends?" I ask, my voice five percent sharper than I want it to be, but Imogen just laughs, her eyes sliding over to me.

"We were," she confirms. "We talked about boob grabbing *all* the time, though. Just boobs, boobs, boobs. Mathletes was a really wild time."

I'm silent for a moment, not at all sure what to make of this new information.

"I'm kidding," she finally says. "Dan dragged me into an empty classroom at a competition once and then swore me to absolute and utter secrecy before stammering his way through the situation with Alicia's boobs."

"You mean boob, singular."

She just laughs.

"You ever trade grabs for grades?" I ask. Not because I think there's a chance in hell that she did, but because we're talking instead of fighting for once and I think I like this.

"*Please*," she says, crunching through the snow. "I got all my own A's. Even in gym, all you had to do was put on those stupid shorts and look bored while you pretended to try kicking a ball."

"Hey, I was good at gym," I say.

"And you got a B in biology, didn't you?"

I go quiet, because there's a slight edge to Imogen's voice. Things like that are coming back to me: the way she sounds when she wants to talk about something and doesn't, the way she sounds when she's in a group and forcing herself to be brave, the way she sounds when we're alone and she's like this, normal and sharp-witted and relaxed, not nervous or anxious.

"True," I say. "B plus, actually."

"You're welcome," she says.

There's a moment where my gut reaction is to be angry, furious that she's like this again, high and mighty and acting like she's Queen of Smart Things.

But then I look over at Imogen, cheeks and lips mottled and red, breath puffing in front of her face, and I realize she's smiling. Teasing me. The anger drains just as fast as it came, and I'm left walking down a mountain and remembering junior year.

We had study sessions together, and that's where everything started. Well, not exactly. It started when I went up to Imogen in class one day and asked if she'd be my lab partner.

She blinked at me. Pushed her glasses up. Looked around, like she was trying to see if there was *anyone* else she could possibly pair with, then back at me.

Sure, she said, her voice clipped and shrugged.

Then we were lab partners. She wasn't even a very good one first, always annoyed with me, bad at explaining things, never even bothering to make eye contact when she ordered me around while doing everything in lab so I wouldn't fuck it up.

But after I got detention for sending Alicia into hysterics, Imogen warmed up to me a little, and then a little more, and then one day I asked if she'd help me study and she surprised me by saying yes.

Her parents were the relaxed hippie types, mine just wanted me to have better grades than I did, and my girlfriend Melissa couldn't have cared less that I was hanging out with the school dork, so we could study alone together, whenever and wherever we wanted.

And believe it or not, I *did* actually learn some biology, though I also learned a lot of things that were way more interesting.

For example, she tasted like raspberry chapstick and had a tiny mole an inch above her left nipple. She's ticklish behind the knees. She likes being on top.

Then, the shit hit the fan.

Imogen and I go quiet, the only sounds the crunch of our boots trudging through the snow and the gasp of air in our lungs. My shoulders start to ache from carrying the weight of both packs, but I don't say anything.

She's wounded. She's not used to this, and I am.

And I can't deny the deep-down truth much longer, the truth that I don't hate Imogen. Not really. I couldn't see that ten years ago, and I'm not exactly Mister Insight now, but I'm finally starting to realize that.

Whatever this is, it's more complicated.

CHAPTER SIXTEEN
IMOGEN

We reach the tree line before full dark, trudging through the spindly, twisted trees at the very edge of it and quickly plunging down into the tall, full-grown pines. The needles are springy underfoot, the snow considerably lighter here, the wind a shadow of what it was out in the open.

I'm relieved in a way I don't entirely understand, like the trees around us give me comfort. The forest at least feels familiar, and without speaking, we both find a divot in the ground, next to some rocks and protected by a small stand of cedars. It's covered with pine needles, and we both kick away pinecones without speaking, then sit, the depression just fitting the two of us.

"I don't know if I can ever stand again," I admit after a long time spent staring ahead of us, into the dark. "I think my bones have melted into slush."

Wilder doesn't say anything, just smiles, grabs the MREs out of our packs. I watch as he pours water into the heater, sticks the MREs in, puts the whole thing back into the box. It's another cool survival thing I've read about but never actually seen in person, and it surprises me how easily Wilder does it all. He doesn't even have to read the instructions.

"Do you eat these a lot?" I finally ask.

"Not if I can help it," he says.

"You're good at making them," I say, and Wilder just laughs in the near-dark. It was a dumb thing to say, but my brain feels melted along with my bones, so I just laugh too, eat the food when it's ready, don't say much of anything else.

And quietly, to myself, I wonder if I'm falling for it again. Even though out here, there's no one else to impress, no one who'll laugh if I'm humiliated, I'm still suspicious of Wilder's niceness.

Of course I am. I'm human. I learn from my mistakes.

Once upon a time, ten years ago, when I was younger and dumber and just plain *inexperienced*, I let Wilder Flint get to me. I still wish I hadn't, but after lots of therapy, introspection, and most importantly, after not seeing him for a decade, I've forgiven myself for that oversight.

People are rarely insightful at seventeen. Sure, I knew it was wrong to do what we did while he had a girlfriend. I was stupid to believe him when he said that she was his *official* girlfriend because his dad wanted him to be Prom King — possibly the dumbest thing I've ever heard, in retrospect — but I've forgiven myself for all that.

I made bad choices. I moved on.

But *damn* if it's not kind of working again. Even in the snowy alpine tundra, smack dab in the middle of nowhere, with survival anything but guaranteed, Wilder's charming. It's a slightly different charm — he's rougher, his eyes are different, he handles himself in a grown, masculine way that he didn't before — but it's still charm and I'm still falling for it.

No. Not falling for it. I'm just being *slightly nicer* for now, while it's the two of us, and if by some miracle we make it out alive I don't even have to talk to him again.

We finish dinner without saying much, crunch up the leftover packaging into tight balls and shove them back into our packs. I drink the last of my water, and Wilder drinks almost the last of his. We haven't come across a stream or anything yet, but it's obvious that we're heading toward one sooner or later, so I try not to worry.

Not that it works. Running out of water sends up one of those signal flags in the back of my mind that just waves, constantly, catches my attention again any time I try to look away.

Wilder catches me staring at my empty water bottle, nods downhill.

"There's water down below," he says. "And I've got some left if you need, plus we can melt snow."

I should say *thank you*, but I don't.

"That's incredibly energy-inefficient," I say, looking around us. "It takes far more heat to convert frozen water to liquid than you gain from having the water you've melted in your body. Not that there are calories in water, but it's necessary for—"

Wilder's just looking at me, and I stop talking. I swallow, licking my dry lips, and even though it's too dark for him to see I can feel my face warm up because I'm still anxious about the water and explaining to a grown man that it doesn't have any calories.

"You know what I mean," I finish lamely.

"Do you mean that expending energy not to get dehydrated in the wilderness is probably worth some extra energy?" he asks, his voice slow and teasing.

I wish he'd stop looking at me. I wish I'd stop feeling awkward and seventeen when he did.

"Right, that's what I meant," I say.

"Thought so."

There's nothing left to do but pull the few extra layers we've got — mainly the parachute and two tarps, but better than nothing — out of our bags, huddle together under them, and then stare up at the sky, trying to fall asleep.

It takes minutes for Wilder's breathing to even out, getting slower and deeper. It's soothing and hypnotic, and I'm jealous as hell because despite my best attempts, I'm freezing cold and my mind is racing.

I'm out of water, I'm with Wilder, we're in the middle of nowhere, I'm out of water, what if the rescuers are looking for us right now, will they find our footsteps? Will they follow them? Will they lose us on the boulder scramble, not be able to figure out which way we went?

Why's Wilder being nice to me? Was that flight attendant his girlfriend?

I'm out of water. What if he's wrong and there isn't water somewhere nearby?

But *is* she his girlfriend? Does Wilder *have* a girlfriend?

Why do I keep wondering that?

Ten Years Earlier

We're in a conference room at the Granite Springs Resort and Spa, and I'm sitting cross-legged in the middle of an enormous mahogany table, the fully illustrated steps of mitosis spread around me.

It's mid-November in Solaris, the low season. There's not enough snow yet for ski season to be in full swing, and though within a month all the resorts will be filled with people coming for winter holidays, they're not here yet so we had our choice of rooms to use for studying.

Wilder set it up, obviously. If I set up our study locations, we'd be at my parents' kitchen table with my mom making us tea every ten minutes and my dad shouting the answers to *Jeopardy* in the next room.

"All right," Wilder says, leaning over the edge of the beautiful table, hair flopping in front of his blue-green eyes as he studies the handouts I made. "Mitosis is the process of cell division."

"Right," I say.

So far, so good. We've got a test tomorrow, and I think I'll do okay — though I could spend another hour studying, why not — but Wilder called my house and *begged* me to come help him study.

He's hard to say no to. Even though he's just my lab partner, even though he only wants my help passing bio, there's something magnetic about him. Something that makes me smile at the dumb stuff he does in lab and that makes me trek across town in the half-dark to a huge resort where the front desk staff gives me the side-eye when I walk in.

Something that makes me think thoughts about Wilder that I shouldn't think because I know better. Even if he weren't going with Melissa Hedder, it's not like I'd be next on his list.

"Phase one," he announces, jabbing a finger at a sheet of paper. "Prophase. Phase two, metaphase."

"Yes and yes," I say as he grabs the sheets and lines them up. There's way, way more to it than this, but it's a good start.

"Three is anaphase, and four is telephase," he says,

lining those up too. "And after that comes cytokinesis, and then there are two cells where there used to be one and both cells can just chill for a while."

He looks at me, a half-smirk-half-smile on his face, and despite myself I smile back, pushing my hair back, tugging my black long-sleeve shirt down in the back just in case I'm showing skin.

"They don't really *chill*," I say, and Wilder just laughs.

"Okay," he says, and climbs onto the table to sit next to me. "Now you want to know what happens during each of these, right?"

"I mean, I know what happens," I point out, pushing my glasses up my nose with my left hand. "You're the one who wanted to study, so yeah, I guess you should tell me more about them."

Why's he sitting next to me? He never does this.

And why am I babbling on like the world's most literal dork?

He reaches across to touch the prophase sheet, and his forearms brushes against my knee.

My heart nearly leaps out of my chest, and I hold my breath.

"Step one," he says. "This is when the… what's it called, shit. The metanucleic spindle? Starts to capture chromosomes and the nucleolus disappears."

His forearm brushes my knee again, tan against the alabaster-pale skin peeking through the holes I've torn in both knees of my jeans.

Say something, I tell myself. Correct him, it's the mitotic spindle, Jesus Christ, Imogen you're just sitting here like some sort of idiot because the boy you've got a crush on touched you by accident, get a grip on yourself—

"You cool?" Wilder asks, and now he's looking at me.

His hand pulls back, settles on my shoulder, and I force

myself to smile at him, even though I think I might be sweating a little.

"Totally cool," I say, in the least-cool possible way. "It's actually the mitotic spindle."

"You sure?"

"Yes."

"I mean that you're okay, not about the spindle," he says.

My spine feels like poured concrete, like if I move it might crumble into pieces, but I nod anyway.

"Imogen," he murmurs. "What are you so nervous about?"

I shake my head, but I can't shake his eyes, boring into mine like two lasers, blasting through my corneas and looking directly into my brain.

"What do you mean?"

"You just seem jumpy."

I swallow, my mind going blank with nerves.

He can't do this. He won't, you're really getting the wrong idea about this, there's no way Wilder Flint likes you this way—

"Your face is really close to mine," I blurt out.

Then I turn bright red. Then I hold my breath, because I can't believe I just said that out loud and oh my god *what is wrong with me.*

He leans back on one hand, a smile forming around his mouth, though his face doesn't get much further away from mine.

"Huh," he says, the smile moving to his eyes. "Weird. You mind?"

I open my mouth, then close it. Then open it.

"No?" I say, my voice barely more than a squeak.

HE'S PUTTING THE MOVES ON YOU. FOR REAL, THIS IS HAPPENING, WHAT THE HELL IS GOING ON. HE HAS A GIRLFRIEND AND EVERYTHING—

Wilder kisses me, his mouth warm and soft.

I don't move. For a long moment I'm perfectly still in shock, just sitting on this table cross-legged while his face is pressing against mine, nauseatingly unsure what you're supposed to do when the hottest guy in the entire school kisses you out of nowhere while you thought you were studying for biology class.

His mouth moves against mine, his head tilting.

Suddenly instinct or *something* kicks in. My eyes slam shut, and I kiss him back, tilting my head, and then he's got my head in his hand and his fingers are in my hair and I'm leaning forward, into the kiss, my teeth awkwardly against his lip and his mouth opens and his tongue is there.

I'm thinking *that's his tongue oh shit oh shit*, but I touch it with my own, exploring him and being explored and then they tangle together and my hand goes around his neck without me even meaning to do it.

The kiss feels like it lasts forever, and when we finally pull apart we're still both on the conference table, in the middle of a bunch of papers about cellular reproduction but I'm completely and absolutely sure that we're done talking about mitosis for the night.

"Take your glasses off," Wilder murmurs, and I realize his hand is still in my hair.

I do it, everything more than six inches away instantly going blurry, my heart thumping so hard against my ribcage I'm positive he can hear it as he brings his face to mine again and we kiss more, longer, a million hormones woken and raging at once.

He must have broken up with Melissa, I think.

I wonder if he did it for me. They must have broken up recently, I haven't heard anything, but it's not like I would.

We make out until I have to go home before curfew, hair wild and lips practically bruised, still not quite sure what just happened other than *oh shit Wilder Flint likes me.* Kissing is *all* we do, but the longer it goes on the more I think about other stuff. Other places his hands could go, other places our bodies could go.

It's not my first kiss, but it's the first time someone's kissed me like *that*.

Even as I'm standing, shoving my biology handouts back into my backpack, stumbling through some mono-logue about how I have to get home because of curfew, I'm hoping it won't be the last.

Wilder doesn't say much while I blather on, but when I'm finished he's got my glasses in one hand.

He hops off the table, opens them. I'm perfectly still as he slides them onto my face and suddenly he comes into crystal-clear view, the same cocky smile-grin-smirk expres-sion on his face that I developed a crush on in the first place.

"Thanks," I whisper.

"If I fail tomorrow, you'll help me study for the make up test, right?" he says, voice low and laconic as he leans back against the table. I'm too bowled over to notice the presumption there that of *course* I'll keep helping him, of *course* I'll do this again.

"Sure," I say, and he smiles.

My toes tingle, and I grab onto the straps of my back-pack for dear life, then walk for the door like a robot, no idea how I'm supposed to act now that I've *done French kissing*.

But just as I reach for the doorknob, Wilder grabs my arm.

"Wait," he says, pulling me back, spinning me so my backpack is crushed between the wall and my body.

He kisses me again, hard and urgent and this time our bodies are pressed together. Even though my coat I can feel his warmth, his urgency, and it's like he takes a flamethrower to a pile of dry kindling deep inside me. I have to fight the urge to wrap my legs around his thick frame, rub myself against him.

I don't even know what exactly I want from Wilder, but in this instant, I know it's something I've never felt before, something that just came *roaring* alive.

Then it's over. I fix my crooked glasses, breathing hard.

"Good luck on the test," Wilder says.

"You too," I whisper, and I'm already out three minutes past curfew so I run through the door and practically sprint home.

———

Present Day

WILDER SITS BOLT UPRIGHT, the rustle of his layers of coats and the parachute over top of us the only sounds in the dead-quiet night. I only realize that we were snuggled together when his absence leaves a cold space on my back.

"What is it?" I whisper, rolling onto my back, pine needles crunching under me, looking at Wilder's ramrod-straight spine.

He doesn't answer. I feel like I just barely went to sleep after lying awake for hours, and now Wilder's panicking over something, which instantly makes *me* worry that he's heard something dangerous, some new reason we're going to die here besides hypothermia, dehydration, starvation, or falling off a cliff.

I stare at the stars glimmering between tree branches, listening intently, holding my breath.

There's nothing. I strain my ears harder.

Avalanche? I wonder.

Something prowling? Airplane? Helicopter?
Are we getting rescued?

Then I hear it, off in the distance: a long, thin, solitary howl that wraps an icy hand around my heart and squeezes. Another answers it, then another.

"Wolves," Wilder whispers.

CHAPTER SEVENTEEN
WILDER

It howls again. This time it's more than one wolf, I'm pretty certain, two or three of them in tandem. That's a pack.

There's not a great chance of fighting off one wolf, but it's been done. I've heard stories.

Two? Three? No fucking way.

Another howl answers the first and I swallow, my mouth dry. This one sounds like it's from the other side of the valley, to our left and not our right, and my blood runs cold.

Colder. Every single part of me is already cold, but I've been cold for a couple of days now and I'm starting to get used to it.

Next to me, Imogen sits up, squinting and blinking, listening carefully.

The first wolf howls again, the sound clear and sharp in the cold night, and I just watch our breath puff in front of our face and disappear as the sound fades.

"We have to go," I say, shoving myself to my feet and offering my hand. "Come on."

She just looks at me, squinting because she hasn't got her glasses on.

"Why?"

"Because we're in wolf territory," I tell her, thinking it's fucking obvious. "Those aren't coyotes."

"I know they're not coyotes," she says, disdain in her voice.

"Then what the fuck are you waiting for?"

Imogen starts patting the ground around herself, like she's looking for something. She's wearing her big black parka, a hat, gloves, and snow pants, so the pale oval of her face is all I can really see in the half-moonlight.

"Wolves aren't interested in humans," she says, still feeling the ground around her.

"The fuck they're not."

She looks up at me, squinting vaguely because she can't see, but somehow, she still manages to look like she's about to talk down to me.

"The few wolf attacks against humans have largely been in liminal areas, where humans encroached on wolf territory and the wolves were therefore acclimated to a human presence, making them less afraid," she says, sounding like a sleepy academic paper. "I would hardly call this a liminal environment."

"Whether or not it's fucking *liminal* isn't really the point, the point is that I can hear them right now—"

"Liminal means transitional," Imogen points out.

"I know what *liminal* means," I snap, even though I didn't.

"Those wolves are very unlikely to take any interest in us, and frankly, I think the risk of us accidentally falling off a cliff in the dark is far greater than the risk of being attacked by wolves," she says.

Imogen raises her hand to her face like she's going to

push her glasses up, only to remember she's not wearing them.

"You know anyone who's survived a wolf attack?" I ask.

"I don't know anyone who's been attacked by wolves, though I do know several people who study them and have—"

"I do," I say. "He's got a huge chunk missing from his right side, no left eye, and his thigh is so fucked up he's gotta use a wheelchair most of this time."

"Was he fucking with the wolves?" Imogen asks, her voice flat.

There's another howl, crystal fucking clear and I swear to God it's getting louder.

"No," I say. "He was outside Yellowstone on a hunting preserve, tracking a deer or some shit when out of nowhere this wolf came and—"

"The wolf was *also* on a hunting preserve?" Imogen says, sounding bored.

I swallow, fists curled into balls in my pockets.

Sorry, am I boring you with my talk of vicious predators attacking? Am I just that uninteresting?

"If it was, it was likely already *quite* acclimated to humans and that's why it felt comfortable attacking one," she says.

Now I'm pacing back and forth in our little hollow, turning at every snap of a twig, imagining yellow eyes coming out of the forest at me, Mason's story of being knocked down and dragged around by a wolf in Wyoming haunting me.

I've seen the man's scars. He used to be a high-powered executive, the guy behind a wildly successful chain of pancake houses in the Midwest, and now he's in a wheelchair and terrified of dogs.

"Wolves don't want to deal with humans," she goes on,

turning her face away, like she's looking for something though I know for a fact that Imogen is blinder than a bat. "Same with mountain lions, grizzly bears, and whatever else you feel like being afraid of right now."

There's another howl, and I swear to God it sounds like it right on the other side of this boulder.

"Besides, those wolves are probably miles away," she says, sounding distracted. She's looking at the ground, raking her gloved hands over the pine needles, feeling along carefully. "Wolf howls can carry for miles, so could you stop pacing and help me find my—"

Something snaps beneath my boot, and it's definitely not a leaf or a twig or a branch. I freeze. Imogen freezes.

"Are you fucking kidding?" she whispers.

Imogen scrambles to her feet, throwing the yellow parachute off, hands held in front of her as my stomach drops to my feet.

She shoves me away and I stumble backward as she crouches down, face close to the ground as she picks up her glasses in the dark, cradling them like a dead bird.

"Shit," she whispers, sinking to her knees. "Fucking shit, Wilder."

She turns them over, held close to her face, my stomach churning with guilt and anger.

"You goddamn *moron*," she says, her voice clogged with tears. "What the hell am I going to do now?"

"Don't you have a backup pair?"

"Not here!" she says, her voice rising in pitch. "No, I didn't bring a backup pair of glasses to the middle of the wilderness because I didn't think I'd be walking through the middle of the Canadian Rockies while you ranted at me about wolves!"

"The fuck were they doing on the ground?" I ask. "That's where you put shit that you *want* stepped on—"

"Where else do I put them?" she says, her voice edging between high-pitched and whispered, obviously about to cry. "That's all there is here, Wilder, unless I'm supposed to somehow jury-rig my glasses into the trees with a pulley system so they don't get crushed by the only other idiot around for miles?"

"Try not putting black glasses down on the dark ground in the middle of the night!" I snarl, my voice also rising. "You've got a whole backpack, the hell is wrong with putting them in there?"

Her breath hitches in her throat, her lips trembling as she looks down at the glasses in her hands. I think she's crying, but it's dark and she's still kneeling so it's hard to see.

"Fuck it," she mutters, and drops them on the ground again. "Fuck this. Fuck you, Wilder, I hope you get eaten by wolves and I hope they eat your non-essential organs first and it takes you a long time to die."

She storms off, arms out in front of her, stumbling over the uneven ground, toward the nearest stand of trees.

"Imogen," I call, her glasses still at my feet, watching her disappear into the dark. "What the fuck are you doing?"

I don't get a response, but she disappears between some trees, her footsteps suddenly fading, the anger knotting in my stomach. I stand there, breathing hard, clenching and unclenching my fists until the snaps finally drift into nothingness and Imogen is either gone or very still, the night once more dead quiet.

The wolves howl again, and even though I'm *freezing* cold a trickle of sweat makes its way down my spine as I look up, through the trees. I can barely see anything past them beyond the vague shapes of mountains and my guess that we're heading down into a valley between two craggy peaks.

I hate this. They're all fur and teeth and claws, perfect killing machines, and I don't even have my gun because I don't take it when I fly into Canada. If one of those things were to jump from the shadows right now, I'd be defenseless against it.

I wait, wondering if that thought alone might trigger a wolf attack.

It doesn't, so I bend down to pick up Imogen's glasses from where she dropped them and hold up them up in the pale, watery moonlight.

They're in two pieces, the frame snapped right where it goes across the bridge of her nose, and it's the right piece that's had it worse. The left lens looks more or less fine — guess I didn't step on that part — but there's a single crack catching the moonlight diagonally across the right lens, and the right arm is bent back at a wrong, funny angle, but it all still seems attached.

Carefully, I bend the arm back and forth, and nothing snaps off. It's probably not *too* bad, but as I stare down at the pieces in my hands I think of Imogen, blindly batting her way through trees in the dark.

In a forest full of rocks and sticks and logs, a million things to trip over, a million holes to fall into and twist her ankle even worse than it already is, not to mention the wolves—

Fuck.

I unzip a compartment on my pack, slide the broken glasses in, grab the flashlight. We've only got one and I have no idea how old the batteries are, so I don't want to use it too much, but this seems like as good a reason as any, so I flick it on.

Instantly, I'm half-blind, looking away from the beam and blinking. Anything illuminated is blinding and anything not illuminated is pitch-black, giving me the creeping sense of being watched from all sides.

I shake my head and scramble up the side of the hollow we were in, showering down pine needles and entering the copse of trees, sweeping the beam of light side to side.

"Imogen," I call out softly.

The wolves howl again, like they're responding to me. I nearly turn off the flashlight, but then I remember what Imogen said, that they're probably miles away and not even interested in us.

"Imogen," I call again, pressing onward.

There's a light breeze, and it showers snow gently down around me, shaking it loose from the tree branches above. She can't have gone far, not blindly in the dark. Not in the few minutes since she stormed off.

I walk through the trees, slowly, calling her name. Every time I shine the light beam over a log or lump in the ground, my heart lurches for a moment as I think *it's Imogen's body*.

At last, there's a sniffle off to my left. I swing the light around and there she is, sitting on the ground slumped against a tree.

"Dammit, ow," she says softly, holding up one forearm to block the light, so I shine it at her feet in apology, but not before I can see that she's crying.

I've only seen her cry once before, and that was my fault too. I click the light off, and the two of us are just there, together, her breathing ragged while my eyes adjust to the dark.

She's so small right now. Tiny, even, huddled against the tree, her frame swathed and swamped in layers and layers of puffy black material, the only thing keeping her from a certain hypothermic death out here.

I step forward, hold out one hand. Her eyes narrow in the dark for just a moment, and then she turns her head away, like she can't see me.

"I'm fine," she whispers.

"Come on," I say.

"I can find my way back."

I've still got my hand out toward her, just waiting.

"Imogen," I say.

She exhales hard, her head tilted back against the tree, her face pale against the darkness.

"I know," she says, though I have no idea what it is that she knows.

"Don't make you call you Squ—"

"Wilder," she says, her voice a warning as she opens her eyes, looks at me.

My hand doesn't waver, still held out to her as she tries to focus her eyes on it.

"Don't call me that," he says, her voice softer now. "I didn't like it then and I fucking hate it now, so just let it die. Okay? Please?"

"You never liked it?" I asked, keeping my voice low and quiet. "Not even once?"

"Does it matter?" she asks, her voice still tear-soaked.

I don't answer her, but it does. Because I *know* she did. Because *Squeaks* was a secret between the two of us, the soft breathy sound she made the first time I got her panties off.

Squeaks was what I whispered to her in the hall sometimes at school, the single word that made her flush bright pink and shove her glasses up, and I know she liked it. I *know* she liked having a secret, liked knowing that behind the backs of everyone who was cooler and richer than her,

Wilder Flint had a nickname for her based on how she sounded when he made her come.

Until everything crashed and burned, her breathy voice playing over the loudspeakers. The door slamming behind her as I followed, only to watch her run away.

Imogen sighs, her eyes shut, and then reaches out and takes my hand. I haul her to her feet, her eyes glistening in the moonlight as she shoves her knuckles against them like I don't know she's been crying. She swallows hard, inhales deep, straightens her spine.

"I'm pretty blind without my glasses," she says softly, her voice a confession. As if I didn't know already.

"I'm pretty blind in the dark," I say. "Between the two of us we'll be all right."

I take her hand again, and she lets me. My night vision is coming back after the flashlight-blindness, and Imogen holds out her other hand in front of herself like she's warding off spirits as I guide her around stumps and past rabbit holes, pine needles softly crunching under our feet.

Then we're there again, at our hollow, and she climbs down backward holding onto my hand and we get under the parachute and the tarps again.

The stars blaze. The wolves howl.

"If they wanted to kill us we'd already be dead," Imogen says. "We can't see in the dark and we can't hear for shit, so we're pretty much the bottom of the food chain."

"Comforting," I say, and wiggle closer to her.

We should take off our coats, pile them on top of us, share body heat.

Imogen snorts.

"It wasn't supposed to be comforting, just true," she says. "Anything out here could kill us before we knew, so you can't worry about it, really."

"You're telling me not to worry?"

I *hear* her smile.

"Weird, right?"

"Right."

I wake up to full sun hitting my face and the sensation that for the first time in days, I might actually be *almost* warm, or at least not so thoroughly cold that I can barely think. I stay where I am for a moment, blinking, the pine needles pressing into my face and body, my eyes feeling sandpapered.

And I have the vaguest recollection of Wilder putting his arm around me, pulling me in as I fell asleep.

"We should get moving," he says.

He's already up, sitting on the ground not far away, chewing and swallowing something.

"The sooner we go, the more daylight we'll have," he says. "And the sooner we can find water, the sooner we'll be at a lower—"

"I know," I say, still blinking. Every single part of my body feels unpleasant, like my muscles are filled with something stickier and more viscous than blood and it's hard to move them.

He moves suddenly, and at the last second, I see something flying toward me and I flinch, deflecting with my arm as something small and light smacks into me and then falls to the ground.

"Sorry," Wilder says.

I pick it up, hold it close to my face. It's a granola bar. I'm starving, so I tear it open and sink my teeth into it before I can even start wondering how many we have left and whether I should be eating this one at all.

It's not very good. Cinnamon and banana and cardboard, tastes like, but I don't really care.

Wilder moves again, getting off the ground. His fuzzy shape comes toward me, and I squint at him, like it'll help.

"Hold still," he says, and crouches in front of me.

I freeze, mid-chew, unsure of what's about to happen.

Cold plastic hits my temples, and my glasses slide onto my face. Suddenly he's right there, crouching in front of me, his fingertips brushing my face.

"Oh," I say through a mouthful of granola bar.

"I couldn't fix the lens," he says, running one finger over the frames. "But I found a tent repair kit in my backpack, and that did well enough for the rest."

There's a crack running diagonally through everything over my right eye, splitting Wilder in half, and I take off the glasses and hold them close to my eyes, examining.

They're as good as they're going to get: held together with rugged, bright orange nylon, clearly glued on. But it'll work, *much* better than nothing.

I put them on, relief settling in the bottom of my stomach. Last night I laid awake for at least an hour after the *second* time I tried to go to sleep, just imagining how I was going to get down this mountain.

It would be slow. I'd fall constantly, talk to trees instead of Wilder, totally unable to see tree stumps or pits in the ground or logs beneath the snow, waiting to trip me. Everything would be a death trap and Wilder would have to lead me carefully, at a snail's pace.

I worried about whether he'd just leave me. I worried about whether he *should* just leave me so at least maybe one of us could make it out.

"Thanks," I say, sliding them back onto my face, a little uncomfortable and a little crooked.

Wilder pauses. He looks at me, from eye to eye, and I take another slow bite of my terrible granola bar, stomach making a rumbling nuisance of itself.

"I'm sorry I stepped on them," he says.

It's the first time Wilder's ever apologized to me, for *anything*.

I have no idea how to respond, so I just tear off another hunk and keep chewing.

———

ALL WE DO that day is walk, through a grindingly familiar landscape: cold, trees, snow, gray sky. We still don't find water, and even though I remember what I said about energy yesterday, I find myself shoving handfuls of snow into my mouth as I go, letting my body heat melt them as I trudge along behind Wilder.

We don't talk much. My mouth is too dry, and even though it's deadly cold, I'm sweating a little, afraid of getting dehydrated.

And I'm thinking about the past. *He's* making me think about it, my mind wandering all over the place as we walk downhill, trudging through the snow and making our own switchbacks as we go.

Even though he may as well be the marshmallow man right now, wearing ten puffy layers. Even though I can barely see him, just a backpack swaying in front of me and a coat.

Come on, Squeaks.

I hate him.

No. I just wish I hated him.

But instead I'm watching him walk, knowing that he has a nice butt under all that.

I'm thinking about why he called me *Squeaks*, the sounds I made in the passenger seat of his dad's Mustang, his tongue in my mouth and one hand in my panties.

What if you were going to die? I think.

If you were definitely for sure going to die, you'd fuck him again.

I'm probably right. But death still isn't assured, and my self-esteem is currently worth more than whatever Wilder's got to offer.

I don't realize he's stopped until I literally smack into him, though he barely moves when I do. The man is solid like a wall.

"You lose your glasses?" he asks without looking at me. "Not my fault this time."

"Sorry," I say, not bothering to answer the question.

I swallow, my mouth so dry it's sticking together strangely, and step up next to Wilder.

That's when I realize we're at the edge of a steep drop-off. Not a cliff, but not a hill, and in front of us is a long, steep, wide curve cutting into the side of the mountain, downed trees and rocks and dirt splashed through the snow, all parallel lines pointing downward.

An avalanche. Recent enough that the snow hasn't covered the debris again, an ugly scar slashed down the side of a mountain.

I wonder if anyone but us knows about it. Probably not, because why would they? If a hundred trees fall in the forest and there's no one around to hear them, et cetera.

"Well," I say, surveying the landscape, the broad expanse of destruction stretched below us. "Shit."

All day we've been walking along the edge of a mountain too steep to climb down comfortably, but it's starting to look like we'll have to risk it because we're closing in on sixteen hours with no water except melted snow.

I sigh, step back, ready to return the way we came but Wilder catches my arm.

He points.

It takes me a minute to figure out what he's pointing at, squinting hard because I probably need a new prescription on my glasses, but finally I see it: a dark slash down a granite cliff face, a couple hundred feet past the recent avalanche.

Water. A trickle, probably, but more than enough for the two of us.

"It's not far," Wilder says. "Five hundred feet? Six?"

"You're kidding me," I say.

He just looks over at me, eyes crinkled at the corner.

"I would never," he says, his voice low and teasing.

I swallow again, mouth and throat sticking together, cross my arms in front of myself.

"Look how recent this is," I tell him in the most reasonable voice I can muster. "It can't be more than what, a week old? There's no snow on it, and I know that you also know that an area that's recently seen an avalanche is *incredibly* unstable for a long time afterward, because all the debris could easily be set off again since all the organic matter that was keeping it in place to begin with is gone—"

"There's water over there," he says, pointing. "And past that, I think there's a way down that's easier than what we've been walking over."

"Sure, or we could end up at the bottom of the mountain the fast way, buried under a pile of trees and rubble," I point out.

The cold breeze ruffles our hair, sneaks in between the buttons on my coat.

"We could end up there any way," he points out.

"Trying to get across an area where there's recently been an avalanche is just stu—"

And he's gone, hopped down the three-foot embankment we were standing on, already setting off across the wide scar on the landscape.

My heart's in my mouth, and I honestly feel like I might throw up, though maybe that's just the hunger since we're not exactly eating well.

"Wilder!" I shout. "What the hell!?"

He turns, waves, gives me the thumbs up.

As he turns back he stumbles a little over a log, his foot hitting it awkwardly, and it starts to scoot downhill lengthwise, throwing Wilder off-balance in the other direction.

I gasp, both hands at my mouth as the log going downhill builds steam, catching other debris in its path, fluffy little snow flurries rising around it as it jogs and tumbles.

Wilder catches himself on his hand, the other thrown out for balance before hopping to another spot, turning to look at the log he dislodged, still tumbling downhill. Finally, it catches on a rock and stops with a jerk, the other stuff that was tumbling with it coming to a slow stop twenty or so feet below it.

I wait, holding my breath. Wilder adjusts his pack and keeps moving. I'm waiting for something worse to happen, for the whole mountainside to come unstuck and roll away, down into the valley below so I can be *really* screwed, alone out here.

Doesn't happen. Wilder gets smaller and smaller, lightly stepping through the snow and mud and logs and rocks like it doesn't bother him at all. Like it hasn't even occurred to him that *he could die* at pretty much any moment, with pretty much no warning.

The sun peeks through the clouds for a moment, bathing everything in sudden golden light. Wilder's almost across, close to the water and the easy way down, and I know that this means I either have to go or be completely alone in the wilderness.

He was fine, after all. I'll be fine, too.

And I should go before he gets to the other side and looks back, only to see me wussing out again. I jumped that chasm on the rocks, I can do this too, even if it's a hundred times worse and probably way more dangerous.

Come on, Squeaks.

I can't let him see me freak out like that again, so I hop down onto my good ankle and start across.

It's steeper than it looks. There's no cover, so I can see all the way down to the end of the scarred area, where it looks like an outcropping of rocks finally stopped the land-slide a thousand feet below. On it are freshly-splintered trees, branches askew, and I can almost hear the noise they must have made when they hit those rocks going forty, fifty miles an hour.

I don't even need an imagination to know what would happen to me down there.

I shake my head, wrench my eyes away from it. I force myself to only look at what's in front of me, to *only* work out the path I'm going to take and not think about all the things that could possibly happen.

Right foot on that dirt patch. Left foot on that rock, careful, it's rounded, right foot there, left foot there…

I make my way across slowly, carefully. I don't watch Wilder or the way he was practically leaping from spot to spot like a gazelle who didn't know he could die, and I hold my arms out for balance, my heavy pack making that even harder.

I get a third of the way across, halfway. The adrenaline shooting through my veins slows as long as I don't look down, and I don't.

Three-quarters and I'm almost there. I look up for a split second at Wilder, standing on the edge of an embankment that's only a couple of feet high, grinning while the breeze tosses his hair, looking for all the world like he's just won the lottery or something.

Asshole. I look down, keep going, until I'm ten feet from the end.

See? It wasn't so bad, I tell myself.

My left foot lands wrong on a rock and slides downhill, jerking me to the right. I catch myself only to gasp in pain as my right ankle, the bad one, gives way and twists, sending pains shooting all the way to my hip and I fall awkwardly backward, half on my pack and half on my ass.

And I slide. My legs and arms are akimbo, and I start sliding downhill, the dirt and snow around me so unstable I may as well be on a sand dune. I grab out helplessly, but everything I can grab is also moving, sliding along with me, the ground itself giving way.

I don't even scream. I can't.

The fuck are you supposed to do when you're in a landslide?

My mind goes blank except for one single thing: a scene from some James Bond movie where he skis down an avalanche, landing safely at the bottom with some witty quip. It's completely useless.

I stop. My right foot, the bad one, hits a rock or something that's sticking out of the ground and even though my vision goes fuzzy with pain and the rest of me jerks sideways, I stop. Snow and dirt and rocks clatter on downhill below me, bouncing and rolling, but I lean backwards against the earth, start breathing again.

I only fell about twenty feet. It's not even that far, and I turn myself over, crawl back up the steep slope on my hands and knees, get back to where I was.

Wilder's already there, his pack off, crouching in front of me.

"Can you get up?" he asks, breathless.

I don't answer, my chest heaving, my whole body shaking.

He doesn't ask anything else, but he reaches around me and unbuckles my pack from my back, lifts it away, heaves it onto his own back.

"Hey. Come on," he says, grabbing my shoulder.

I finally sit back on my heels, slightly unsteady, and look at my hands. My thick gloves are torn all over the palms, but they're still functional. My pants and coat seem like they've got some tears too, but I don't think anything's broken worse than it was before. My glasses are even still on my face, still patched together where Wilder fixed them.

"You okay?" he murmurs, pulling a glove off.

He puts his hand on my face, thumb stroking across my cheekbone.

I stare up at him in shock, at the way the rough pad against my face sends a shudder through my body, adrenaline ebbing and spiking.

I must have another concussion, I think, even though I didn't hit my head.

I don't move. I hardly breathe. All the focus in my entire body is concentrated in this one spot, his hand on my face, his eyes in front of mine and getting closer, the blue-green deepening, his breath puffing out in front of him.

I'm back on that conference table, biology handouts spread in front of me.

Your face is really close to mine.

Wilder kisses me.

Right there on the landslide, rocks and dirt and debris everywhere, both of us kneeling on the snowy ground. My eyelids stutter closed, and the same funny, warm feeling as always floods my stomach as his hand comes around the back of my head, holding me against him.

I open my mouth against his, my body betraying me as his tongue finds mine, his hand warm on my neck now, my whole body alive and tingling with adrenaline and endorphins and jubilation and fear and I don't even know what, I just know I kiss him desperately. Like we're teenagers again, like we might be found any second by the adults, so we have to make the most of this five minutes.

Finally, Wilder pulls back, running his hand over my cheekbone again, his eyes lit up, a smile curling around his mouth.

"C'mon, Squeaks, let's go," he murmurs, his face inches from mine.

I come to my senses and slap him.

CHAPTER NINETEEN
WILDER

For a moment, total silence.

Then I start laughing. Imogen's eyes are wide behind her half-broken glasses, like she can't believe she just did that, her pretty face smudged and dirty.

"That bad, huh?" I ask, still grinning.

It didn't hurt. She's got thick gloves on, plus it's pretty clear that Imogen's never slapped someone before, so honestly, I hardly even felt it.

"What the *hell?*" she whispers.

I stand, brushing my knees off, shifting her pack on my back. She does the same, unsteadily, glaring at the hand I offer her. Even though she just slapped me, not that it did any harm.

"What do you mean, *what the hell,*" I tease her, stepping closer.

My whole body is tingling with danger right now, that combination of adrenaline and endorphins, the constant rush of being alive and right here. We could both plummet to our death on the rocks below, sure, but the fire behind

Imogen's eyes right now is about ten times as potent as that possibility.

"I mean what the hell are you doing," she hisses.

I grin again, jam my hand back into my glove. I want to reach out again, touch her like I just did, but I'm afraid she'd jerk away and fall down a mountain.

"Only what you've been thinking of since you saw me again," I tell her. "You can play quiet and shy and angry all you like, Squeaks—"

She slaps me again. It hurts exactly as much as the first time she did it, but this time I grab her wrist on the follow-through, afraid she's going to go off-balance and tumble again.

"Hit me when we're on firmer ground," I tell her. "Don't worry, it's close."

I turn without saying anything else, carefully walk the last few feet to the embankment and climb up it, slinging her pack onto the ground next to mine before I turn to watch Imogen jump, trying to hoist herself up onto the other side.

I let her try a few times before I walk over, offer my hand. She doesn't look me in the eye as she takes it and I pull her up in one quick motion.

"Thanks," she says softly, not looking me in the eye. A muscle in her cheek twitches, and she look away at the gray smudge against the rocks, the trickle of water that's the whole reason we came over here.

We walk over, fill our water bottles, guzzle. The water's cold and clear and tastes wonderful, and even though I know that nasty stuff can still live in it, I know that dying of dehydration would be far worse.

As we put on our pack again, getting ready to keep up the long downward trek, Imogen pauses. She sighs, then comes right up to me, shoving her glasses up her nose, and stares me down like she's thinks I'm some sort of aggressive predator.

"I don't want you to kiss me," she says, her voice clear and firm.

Liar.

"No?"

"No."

"You kissed me back pretty well for someone who didn't want to be kissed," I say.

"I was surprised."

"Are you sure?" I ask, tilting my head to one side, studying her face. Her jaw's set, her eyes stubborn, her mouth a flat line across her face. "It didn't feel like surprise, Squeaks."

She flinches. Just barely, but I can see it: she blinks, a muscle in her neck twitches. In her pocket, one hand curls into a fist.

"It felt like you've been waiting for me to do that since I walked over to you at the airport," I go on, taking a step forward. "It felt like—"

"At the airport when you were standing next to your girlfriend?" she asks, her voice barely audible.

It stops me in my tracks, the way she says it, not even angry but just *sad*, like a kid who's just found out that Santa Claus isn't real.

"Amy's not my girlfriend," I say quickly. "She's just some girl, we see each other now and again, but it's nothing."

"Does Amy think that?" Imogen asks. "Or would Amy get her heart broken if she knew you kissed me?"

She turns, starts walking. It's mid-afternoon, the clouds coming and going, light slicing through the trees sometimes, the whole forest going dim sometimes. I've got the urge to catch up to Imogen, tell her that Amy's doesn't matter to me, but that's a losing argument and I know it.

———

TEN YEARS EARLIER

"THAT's because Coach Jackson's a fucking *dick*," Trevor says, shoving a chicken nugget into his mouth. "The hell does what you do off the field have to do with what you do on it? You can still fuckin' run, can't you?"

"Fuckin' pre-calculus, man," Jake sighs, poking at some sad, boiled vegetables on his plate with a plastic fork. "I'm never gonna need that shit ever, you know? And Coach is letting it fuck up my whole future and he doesn't even care. It's bullshit."

The fork clatters to his tray and he leans back in his chair, looking around us at the Solaris High School cafeteria. It's a Friday, the day after my biology test. Two days after I made out with Imogen.

It's game day, so we're all wearing our football jerseys and the cheerleaders are parading around the school in groups of two and three, hair in high, curly ponytails and tiny, tiny skirts on.

Trevor watches a group of them go by. Next to him, his girlfriend Nina glares holes through his head.

"Or, like, with English," Melissa says, sitting next to me. She takes a long drink from a can of diet coke, her half-eaten sandwich in front of her. "I already speak it, why do I have to be able to diagram sentences? Literally no one will ever ask me to that again in my entire life."

"*Literally* no one," Trevor says, his eyes still on cheerleader butts, mimicking Melissa.

She pulls a small, adorable frown, her eyes flicking to me because he's making fun of her again. Subtly.

Melissa probably doesn't know the word *subtly*.

"I'm just *saying*," she scoffs. "It's all just useless stuff. We're never going to use it, we have calculators and dictionaries and shit, why can't everyone just chill about this dumb stuff?"

"Why indeed," Trevor intones, very seriously, looking back at our group.

Melissa pouts. Even though I don't think she quite understands *why* Trevor's making fun of her, she knows he is and that's enough to piss her off.

"He should definitely let you play," I say to Jake, trying to change the subject. "If you failed the last test and got a D on this one, that's improvement, right? Improvement should be rewarded."

"You did get the D, right?" Trevor asks.

"Fuck you, man," Jake says, throwing a french fry as Trevor laughs.

"It's your favorite letter. Guys, Jake got the D!"

I can't stop myself from laughing, even though I know it's impossibly stupid.

But Melissa doesn't. Her face is still in her pouty frown, and when we finally stop, she pulls on the sleeve of my jersey.

"That weird girl is, like, staring at you," she says, nodding her head toward the cafeteria food line.

My stomach drops.

That weird girl.

Yeah, it's Imogen.

She's standing there with her cafeteria tray, back to the wall, shoulders a little hunched like she's a bird about to take off. When she sees me looking at her she glances at Melissa, then looks away, takes two steps, stops, backs up one step, looks around, shifts her weight on her hips, shoves her glasses up her face, turns to face the other direction.

Looks back at me, an impossible question in her eyes, looks away like she doesn't know where to look or who to look at. Her face is slowly going bright red, a deeper shade every time she glances over and sees Melissa and I looking at her.

I feel like there's a fist closed around my windpipe, just watching her flutter awkwardly like this. Melissa sort of shrugs, flips her red ponytail, and looks up at me through thick lashes as she sips her diet coke.

"Is *that* the girl who's tutoring you in biology?" she asks, sounding almost bored.

"Yeah," I say, glancing over one more time. "Imogen."

"What a weird name," Melissa says, looking back at her again.

Imogen's frozen there like she's trying to fold into herself. She's wearing a black shirt, black skirt that falls to her knees, fishnets and cargo boots.

I wonder what her skin feels like through the fishnets, little diamonds of soft flesh crisscrossed by black mesh, and then I instantly hate myself for wondering.

"It's from Shakespeare," I tell Melissa, only half paying attention to her. "Imogen's a character in one of the plays no one ever reads."

"How do you know that?" she asks, and I tear my gaze away from Imogen, look at Melissa again.

My girlfriend. In the cheerleader outfit, with the pouty lips and the skirt that barely covers the tops of her thighs. The one any red-blooded American male *should* be lusting after right now.

"She told me," I say.

Melissa raises her eyebrows, and I shrug.

"Dunno, we were studying, and it came up somehow," I say. "Why, babe, you jealous?"

I grin at her, knowing that it works. Knowing it *always* works, and it does, because Melissa rolls her eyes and scoffs.

"Of course not, silly," she says, putting her Diet Coke down on the table and playfully grabbing the front of my jersey. "Why, have I got something to be jealous of?"

She sounds like she's in a bad teen TV drama as she pulls me in, kisses me long and hard but chastely on the lips. Melissa tastes like marshmallows, like candy, and when she finally pulls back my lips are sticky with her gloss.

I slide an arm around her, glance over her head again. There's a flash of black disappearing around a corner, and then Imogen's gone.

Somehow, I feel even worse, even as I squeeze Melissa against my side, lower my face for another sticky candy kiss.

"How could I look elsewhere when I've got you?" I ask her, our lips touching.

There's nothing there, just flesh against flesh, pressed together for the correct length of time to make it a kiss. Not like the conference table, on the biology handouts, lips and tongues and hands and fingers, panting for breath, wanting and *needing* blindly.

Pressing Imogen against the wall before she left, getting just one final taste. Feeling completely helpless against the *weird girl*.

"Hey!" a teacher's voice shouts, and I disengage from Melissa to see Mr. Pike in full bulldog mode, charging over. "There is absolutely no PDA during school hours, you two!"

Melissa giggles, hiding her mouth with one hand.

"Sorry," I say, and Mr. Pike huffs.

"Next time, it's detention for both of you," he warns, shaking his finger at us.

CHAPTER TWENTY
IMOGEN

PRESENT DAY

Wilder strikes a match and I think we both hold our breath as it flickers, nearly dies.

Then catches, the pine needles going up in a quick whoosh. He shakes the match out, on his knees, carefully pokes the smaller branches into the pyramid he made. Gloves off, fingers delicate, the orange light flickering over his face and making him look somewhere between human and demonic.

Accurate, I think. *Given that Wilder Flint's probably somewhere between human and demonic.*

Human because right now we're sitting in a space between two huge boulders, their tops meeting over our heads, and I'm leaning against the rock with my bad ankle propped up on my pack. The moment we found this place Wilder basically ordered me to sit like this and not move, and for once I didn't fight and just sat here, exhausted and in pain, while he found firewood.

Demonic because of everything else, not least the kiss

on the landslide scar today. I spent a long, *long* time trying to forget everything Wilder Flint ever did to me, both human and demonic, and maybe more than anything I hate that he's right about when I started thinking about kissing him again.

It was at the airport. It was watching him with that girl, wondering if she had any idea who I was or what Wilder and I were to each other. I'd bet a thousand dollars that that answer is *no*, and I don't really have a thousand dollars to bet.

The twigs are catching fire, slowly. All the wood here is at least a little damp, and getting it to catch is an exercise in patience and frustration. This is Wilder's third try, after insisting that the only thing he wants right now is to not be freezing cold for ten minutes.

I've got my doubts. I think the cold is bothering me a whole lot more than it's bothering him, because even though we grew up in the same town, I've moved to Seattle. I've got a research position at the university there. My office has heat and air conditioning and so does my apartment. So does my car.

I've got a feeling that his years as a naval pilot mean he's a lot more accustomed to discomfort than I am.

"It's fine," I say for at least the third time since he started trying to do this. "It's not gonna help that much anyway."

Wilder ignores me, feeds it more sticks. I close my eyes and lean back against the rock behind me, the granite cold through my hat and hair against my head.

"There!" I suddenly hear him say, and I open my eyes to see that one of the bigger sticks has caught, flaring bright and high in our makeshift cave. Wilder sits back, legs akimbo, shoves his hair out of his face and grins at me.

"Third time's the charm," he says.

I just shrug, staring into the fire. I feel like I'm in high school again, like he's just kissed me in secret while he's got the pretty girl on his arm, out in public. Even though everything is different now and I *know* that, this all feels familiar.

Horribly, gut-wrenchingly familiar.

"Imogen," Wilder says slowly.

He's across the fire from me, staring into it and leaning against another part of the boulder, his elbows casually on his legs like he's hanging out in someone's basement, not lost in the wilderness.

I just wait. I know there's more coming.

"I'm sorry," he finally says.

His eyes flick up to mine, and I have no idea what to say. Seconds pass and all I can do is blink, stare back at him.

"What?" I finally say.

He looks back into the fire.

"I'm sorry," he says again.

"For what?" I ask, honestly curious. Not because there's nothing to apologize for, but because there are so many things.

"For everything."

I just wait.

"For cheating on you with Melissa for months," he says slowly. "For thinking that some popularity bullshit was important and for thinking that what anyone thought meant a damn thing."

I shift, staring into the fire, drawing my left leg under myself. For the first time in days — probably since I got on that plane in Solaris — I'm actually starting to feel the tiniest bit warm, and I lean in toward the fire, heat-seeking.

"I thought you cheated on Melissa with me," I point out. "She was your girlfriend. I was just the side piece."

He half-smiles, orange flickering over his face.

"You're the one I never lied to," he says.

"I wish you had."

"You're the one I took out in my dad's Mustang to the national forest," he says, still talking half to me, half to the fire. "You're the one who watched the northern lights with me that night. Melissa didn't give a shit about that stuff."

"But you weren't ashamed to be seen with her in public," I point out.

Silence from Wilder. We've never talked about this before, not even when everything ended in flames the way it did.

"I was awkward and nerdy, not a leper," I say.

"Those were basically the same thing back then."

My back stiffens. What, now it's my fault that he was a cheating asshole in high school? It's *my* fault that he didn't want anyone to know about us?

"I don't know if I forgive you," I finally say.

I look at the fire, not him. I keep my voice carefully neutral because I'm a little bit afraid that I'll break down into messy, ugly tears. For days now I've been tired, I've been cold, I've been hungry, I've been in pain, and now Wilder is apologizing for half his bullshit, but it just doesn't feel like I thought it would.

I thought it would feel good, or at least better. I didn't think it would feel like too little, too late, all that water already under the bridge and hundreds of miles downstream.

"I didn't think you would," he says. "For the record, I'm also sorry about prom."

We finally lock eyes over the fire, and suddenly it's not water under the bridge any more. Suddenly I'm *there*, in the ballroom of the Granite Pointe Resort, and everyone is slowly turning to stare at me while Wilder's up on a stage, his arm around Melissa, grinning.

I don't answer him. I'm not sure what to say, other than maybe *you can never be sorry enough*, but I think he gets it.

"I did it, not her," he goes on.

"I know," I say softly. "I always knew."

"I shouldn't have."

I swallow hard, anger bubbling inside me because this is too little, too late about something I was hoping to never remember again. Something that scarred my life for years, and he thinks that a couple of words are going to fix it.

"That's how you apologize?" I ask softly, trying to overcome the lump in my throat at the memory. "Like it's a side note? Like it's just something that casually happened, and you were there for it instead of something you *did* to me?"

"Maybe if the plane weren't busted I could skywrite you an apology," he says, a biting edge to his voice.

"I trusted you and you chewed me up and spit me out!" I say, my heartbeat picking up.

For years I've thought about everything I could say to Wilder now, the names I could call him, the ways I could make him feel like absolute scum of the earth, but of course it's not working. Of course I'm just some nearly-crying hysterical girl who's still upset about something that happened in high school.

"You *trusted* me?" Wilder asks. "What the fuck for, Imogen?"

"Don't you dare try and make this my fault," I say, fighting tears.

"You're the one who hooked up with me while I had a girlfriend."

"You're the one who had a girlfriend!"

"You *liked* it," he says, his cadence descending into a snarl. "You liked keeping our dirty secret, and you liked seeing Melissa every day and knowing that you were getting everything she wasn't. You *liked* hurting her without her even knowing about it."

"No, I didn't," I say, even though I know I'm lying. "I told her, didn't I?"

"And how'd that work out for you?"

I stare at Wilder for a long, long time, trying to pull together a coherent thought that isn't either sobbing or screaming. This all feels like a fresh wound, even worse than I thought it would, because I thought I could forget it, but it turns out I couldn't.

Not when he's here, poking a stick into the sore spot.

"It worked out to be a blessing in disguise," I finally say, shifting my body and my foot again because I don't want to look him in the eye. "I got out of that stupid hick town a year earlier than I thought I would. I got to college earlier than I thought. I got a jump start on my life away from that place and I haven't had to look back."

"Good. I'm happy for you," Wilder spits, and it's obvious he's not. He's still angry about some slight or perceived slight or I don't even know what, because I'm pretty sure I'm the one who had to leave, the one who never showed her face at Solaris High again.

"Thank you," I say, my voice hollow and stiff, ringing from the stone around us.

There's a long, long silence, and we both stare into the fire.

I'm thinking of ten years ago: a phone call that was nearly impossible to make, the panic attack I had when it was over.

The music cutting out suddenly at prom and the cruel smile on Wilder's face, the PROM KING sash over his shoulder.

And bolting through the doors, past the chaperones, out onto the melted slush of the late-spring ski slopes as my lungs screamed for air. Someone shouting my name behind me as I disappeared into the woods, feeling like I'd been stabbed through the heart.

———

Ten Years Earlier

I write paragraph after paragraph in my password-protected online diary about Wilder, the words spilling forth in some sort of horrible English diarrhea from my fingers. I've only got a handful of internet friends who read the thing, since it's private, and most of them just comment with useless bullshit like *he sucks* or *sweetie I'm sorry*.

Yeah, I'm sorry too. And yeah, Wilder sucks.

I spend the weekend inside, working on a history essay that isn't even due for two weeks, but I need something to do. Every time my mom looks at me she frowns a little deeper than usual, but I can barely see through the fog of my own hurt emotions to realize that she's worried about me.

Nope. Everything is pain, doom, and gloom. I write some poetry in my diary but delete it, because even I realize how awful it is.

Sunday afternoon, there's a knock on the front door of my house. My mom is humming to herself, clipping coupons at the kitchen table, my dad is watching golf on TV and my little brother is out somewhere, doing sports or something.

My mom sighs, and my dad glances up.

"I hope it's not those Mormon boys again," she says, her long skirt swishing as she walks. "I feel so bad telling them we're not interested, they're so nice."

I look back at the half-written paper on my computer

and scowl. In my head, Napoleon's started to look like Wilder Flint, and that's making me take a somewhat biased approach to the subject matter.

The door opens.

"Oh, Wilder!" my mom says.

Instantly, I feel like I'm going to throw up.

"Imogen must have forgotten to tell me you were studying together today," she says, all breezy and light. "Did you get your grades back yet on that test? I know she was worried about a few questions, and you know how she is, even though I'm always telling her not to stress."

We don't have a study session. If we did I'd have canceled it, for sure, because we are *never* studying together again, and I hope he fails everything forever.

"Not yet, Mrs. Gustavo," Wilder says.

My mom laughs.

"Please, call me Krista," she says lightly. "Mrs. Gustavo is my mother in law. Let me go grab Imogen, she must have her headphones on."

Quickly, I grab my headphones and jam them onto my ears so I can pretend like I've got an excuse for not greeting Wilder, then stare into my computer screen like I'm hypnotized.

My bedroom door's not even closed, and my mom knocks softly, standing in the doorway. I look up and she gestures at her ears for me to take the headphones off.

"Wilder is here?" she asks, crossing her arms over her chest.

I don't move or say anything. I think I might throw up if I do, so I just stare at my mom like a deer in the headlights.

"Look, sweetie, you know we're happy for you to have your friends over to study, but you've gotta tell us when they're coming. The poor boy is lucky I look decent today."

I have no idea why he's here and I wish he wasn't, I think, but I don't say it out loud because then I'd have to explain *way* more to my mom and I just… can't.

"Sorry," I say. I try to smile but my face refuses to cooperate, so I just stare at her.

She frowns slightly, glancing at my desk.

"It's okay," she says. "In the future just let us know, all right? Come on before your dad starts boring him with the time he almost made the Olympic Trials back in 1977."

I almost ask her to tell Wilder to leave, so I don't have to see him, but I also know that that will only open a whole other line of inquiry on her part, so I save my essay and stand, feeling like my whole body is filled with bees made of lead.

As I leave my room, I glance at the desk. My headphones aren't even plugged in. *Shit.*

My house is tiny, so in about five steps I'm down the hallway and Wilder is standing there, smiling like he hasn't got a care in the world, hands in his jacket pockets.

"Hey," he says.

My right foot kicks the back of my left and I stumble slightly, catching myself against the wall.

"Hey," I answer.

WE TELL my parents that we're going to the library to study. I take my textbook and everything, my stomach clenched and locked as I get into Wilder's shiny, brand-new Jeep and sit in the passenger seat staring straight ahead like I'm on my way to the electric chair.

He doesn't say anything as we drive past the library, past the hotel where we studied last time, past the driveway to his parents' enormous house, past the edge of town. We reach a rutted dirt road turnoff with a huge NO TRES-PASSING sign posted next to it, and Wilder just blows past it.

Of course he does. Rules aren't meant for *him*. Everyone here knows that. I'm just hoping that he's not taking me down here to axe-murder me and dispose of my body, though I don't think he's smart enough to not get caught.

I mean, my phone is on. Both my parents just watched me leave with him.

We still don't say anything. Both my hands are white-knuckled on my backpack, sitting stiffly on my lap as I watch the rocks and evergreens go past, the Jeep rattling from side to side. Finally, we get to a pool of water, granite-lined, a small waterfall running into it from one end.

Wilder pulls up next to an outcropping, kills the engine, and turns to me. I stare back, hugging my backpack to my chest.

"This is my secret spot," he says, leaning back against the driver's seat.

I swallow. My mouth's gone dry, and I glance around for a moment.

"You bring Melissa here?" I ask.

The words are out of my mouth before I even know it, and I feel my face go hot. I look away, at the waterfall, wondering how fast I could get back home if I just jumped out of the car right now.

"I haven't," Wilder says. I can feel his eyes boring into the side of my face, and I look ahead, stonily, because I'm a little afraid I'll freak out if I look at him. "Actually, I haven't taken anyone out here."

I can't help myself. I turn and look at him, but all I can see is him kissing her in the cafeteria, the smile on his face when he did. The way she curled her hand around the back of his neck and the way watching it felt like getting slapped in the face.

"But you're still going out with her," I ask, the words tumbling from my mouth because I *have* to check.

"Technically," he says, turning toward me, arm draped over the steering wheel.

Even through his jacket, I can see the bulge of his bicep. It's nice. A nice bicep.

"But I don't really *like* her," he says, his voice lowering, eyes boring into mine.

I swallow.

"She's all right," he goes on, gaze flicking out the windshield. "Melissa's pretty and she's popular and she looks good in a cheerleading uniform, I guess. But she's who I'm supposed to be seen with, you know?"

I nod, even though I don't really know.

"Once a week I promise myself I'm going to break up with her," he goes on, his eyes sparking. "And then, every single time, she bakes me cupcakes or some shit, and then I feel bad about dumping her, so I put it off."

He doesn't really like her, I tell myself. *It's like they're not even really dating at all.*

"She knows, though," he says. "She's gotta know. Maybe that's why I keep getting the cupcakes."

"Maybe," I agree, my voice quiet.

"I don't know what to do, Imogen," he goes on, his voice deep and low. "Here I am, dating some girl I don't even like, but I'm alone with the girl I can't get enough of…"

I blush bright red, glance through the windshield. There's a tiny voice in my head whispering *you're getting played*, but Wilder Flint just said he can't get enough of me and there's a symphony singing in my body, nerves alive and jangling.

"If I kissed you again, you'd forgive me, right?" he asks, a half-grin on his face as his eyes move to my lips.

He doesn't wait for an answer, but he takes my backpack from my hands and tosses it into the back seat.

"You shouldn't," I whisper.

His grin widens, and he reaches out, takes my cheek in his hand.

This is happening. THIS IS HAPPENING.

"I do plenty of things that I shouldn't," he says, and then he kisses me again.

It's hard and warm and soft and delicious and before I know it I'm straining against my seatbelt, trying to get closer to him, the same pit of longing opened up inside me as before but deeper, hungrier.

This is all I've thought about for four days. I've been standing in the shower as my dad pounds on the door, shouting about water conservation, while thinking about this. I've laid awake at night in bed, staring up at the ceiling, thinking about this.

He turns his head, grabs my hair, pushes his tongue into my mouth. A tiny noise, a squeak, makes its way out of me and Wilder pulls back, laughing.

"I like that," he murmurs.

"Me too," I whisper.

It's wrong. I know it's wrong.

But we don't stop.

CHAPTER TWENTY-ONE
WILDER

PRESENT DAY

I wake up before Imogen again. The fire's just coals, and in her sleep she's gotten so close that I'm almost afraid she'll catch on fire, nearly curled around it.

I let her sleep. We need to leave, need to get the rest of the way down this mountain and to the valley below because if we're going to find people or civilization, that's where it's going to be, but I let her sleep.

Just ten more minutes.

I go through my pack, do a quick inventory. We've got enough food for two more days, three if we stretch it though we're already stretching.

Supposedly it takes three weeks to die of hunger, but it takes way less time than that before you're too weak to fight the cold any longer, too weak to walk through the snow, too weak to do anything but sit under a tree and wish you were dead instead of cold, tired, and hungry.

At least we found water, and down below in the valley

there's a small river, the wide blue spot of a lake not too far away. But beyond that? I've got no idea.

Before I wake her up I head out from between the two boulders and climb up one of them, trying to get a better view of what we're dealing with. It's beautiful out here, the mountains all snow-covered sharp angles dotted with deep green trees and the forbidding gray of granite, wild and savage and terrible and glorious.

I take a deep breath of pine air, let it out. A breeze rustles through everything, and though it finds the tiny cracks in the zipper on my parka, the space between my hat and my hood, it's not so bad because at least today, the sun is shining.

It could be worse, I remind myself. *Remember how it rained the whole time you did wilderness training?*

Something flashes in the corner of my eye. Just once and it's gone, but I'm sitting bolt upright now, afraid to even breathe in case I see it again.

It was just water, I tell myself. *Ice or a waterfall or something, it caught the light the right way.*

I look for it, breathless, stone-still except my eyes.

"Come on," I whisper, scanning the valley below.

It seems like an eternity that I sit there, increasingly certain that I've made it up. Certain that I'm finally going snow-blind or just crazy, that I'm hypothermic and hallucinating. There are a million reasons I could have thought I saw something and only one of them is that I really did.

Finally, I give up, stand, turn so I can scramble back down the boulder and then there it is again, slower this time, like the sun's licking a flat, shining surface and wants to make sure I see it.

I do. I see it. I stare, holding perfectly still, at the spot where the flash happened. It's far away, miles away, but there's something *there*. Water or ice doesn't shine like this did.

This shines like glass.

There's a rustle below, and Imogen comes out of the makeshift cave, hair wild, looking like hell, but beautiful hell.

"I gotta pee," she says, glancing up at me. "Don't watch."

"Give me your glasses," I say.

She looks at me like I've grown a second head.

"Ew, no."

"Not so I can watch you pee. There's something over there."

"You don't even need glasses," she says.

"I know. I want to see better."

She blinks, holding up one hand against the light.

"That's not how glasses work," she says, sounding tired and annoyed.

I jump down from the boulder, brush my hands off, walk up to her. She takes a step backward but I'm faster, lifting the glasses from her face and holding them out of her reach.

"Don't!" she says, a note of panic in her voice.

"I'll be careful."

"You already fucked them up — *dammit* Wilder —"

"There's something down there," I tell her, and it sucks the fight right out of her.

"Where?" she asks, breathless.

I boost her up the boulder then climb up myself, point at the spot where I saw the flash. I look, then look through her glasses, then she looks through them.

"I can't tell," she says. "It might be something. It might be an empty vodka bottle left there by campers."

"That's something."

"It's not much."

"Something doesn't have to be much."

She sits there, perfectly still, cross-legged with her hands dangling on her knees, head bare, wisps of hair dancing in the breeze where they've come loose from her bun. For the millionth time in my life I wish I knew what she was thinking, whether it's about me or getting out of here or musk oxen or God only knows what.

"I don't know," she says, squinting and leaning forward as if an extra six inches will help. "It's the wrong direction, we'd have to either go across that part of the lake or around it, and I don't really like either option."

"What options *do* you like, Imogen?" I ask, staring at the spot. The glimmer's gone, but I'm fixated on where it *was*, an inlet from the lake, my eyes playing tricks on me because at this distance I can't tell trees from houses from cars from rocks and it could be anything.

But it could be something.

"Maybe we should just walk out the way we've been planning," she says. "Stay on this side of the lake, we don't have to go around or over anything, and we'll reach the mouth of the valley sooner and that's more likely to have people. Why would there be something there to begin with?"

We've come down from the mountains on one side the valley, near the spot where the valley dead-ends into a craggy wall. Down below is a frosted-over lake that turns into a river as the mountains narrow the valley toward a mouth that we can't see past.

The *thing* is across the lake from us, closer to the dead end than the valley's mouth. We'd be backtracking, but not much, and what if it's a house, or a cabin, or even just a broken down truck? Almost anything would help us.

"And if we're wrong and it's nothing?" she asks. "We don't have forever to keep going, Wilder."

She rubs her bad ankle with one hand, massaging it, though I don't think she realizes she's doing it.

"And if it's a house?" I say softly. "Even someone's summer cabin is gonna have food, a fireplace, somewhere we can hide out for a couple of days and recuperate before we get out of here for good."

Imogen looks down at it. There's purple spots under her eyes, and I know she's every bit as hungry and tired as I am, but in even more pain from two straight days of hiking on a sprained ankle. She never complains, not to me, but I have to wait for her to catch up a lot. Sometimes I look back at her and she's just standing there, face pale, like she's trying to summon the will to go on.

"Let's just go down," I say. "We can decide later."

I re-wrap her ankle before we leave, and she doesn't argue with me at all this time, just lets me do it.

Ten Years Earlier

Friday night, downtown Solaris. It's only about seven blocks long, seven blocks of tourist ski shops and cute little bookstores, coffee places and bars and restaurants that cater to the kind of people who can afford some of the best skiing in North America.

It's also the only place to hang out, and it's where everyone goes for date night. Whatever the single movie theater is playing we all go, then head to the diner nearby for burgers and milkshakes, like some dream left over from 1955, only it's real.

I take Melissa to see some rom-com about a girl who

bets her friends that she can make a guy dump her and a guy who bets his friends that he can date a girl for longer than two days, or something. It's kind of dumb but Melissa loves it, holding my hand the whole time, eating about three kernels of the popcorn I bought her.

On my other side, Trevor is *sucking face* with Allie, his newest girlfriend. I swear to God it sounds like someone trying to unclog a drain, it's so loud, but everyone ignores them and pretends to be watching this terrible movie as we really all watch each other.

I drape one arm around Melissa and she leans her head against my shoulder. I've never kissed her like I'm trying to unclog a drain. I've never even wanted to. I've never even touched a breast, though I tried once and she told me she wasn't *that* kind of girl.

It's been two months since the conference room, two months since I told Imogen that I wanted her and not Melissa. Two months of getting my cake and eating it too, of showing up places with a cheerleader on my arm for show and hooking up with the weird nerd girl behind her back.

Saturday, I tell my mom I'm going over to Jake's house to play video games. I think she hears me, but she's on the phone and her computer at the same time, sharp voice going on about branding or something as she waves me out the door.

I don't go to Jake's house. I go to the library, where Imogen's standing outside, and then we go to heavy equipment storage where Wayne waves me on.

"What's the surprise?" Imogen asks.

She's deeply wrapped up in a million layers, the hood of her coat lined with fake fur even though I've got the heat blasting in my car.

"If I told you, it wouldn't be a surprise, would it?"

She rolls her eyes as I pull up to the snowmobile aisle of the equipment shed and just leave my Jeep parked there. No one else will know. Our feet crunch across the frozen grass, and I head to the middle of the aisle, pull out the one that I've prepped, push it to the edge of the shed.

"Ready?" I ask, sitting on it and patting the seat behind me.

Imogen looks skeptical.

"Do you have helmets?" she asks.

I roll my eyes, but I toss her one. She makes me put on the other one, and then we're off.

It's so much better than the movies, than having Melissa's limp hand in mine. Imogen holds onto me tight, warm even through all my layers, her arms and legs tightening whenever we go around a steep curve, speed up, go downhill.

I swear to God I can feel her hips moving against mine from behind me, grinding, rolling, and I'm hard as hell just thinking about it. She does things to me that I don't understand, makes me want things I didn't know I'd ever want.

Up above, a single light flashes across the sky. It's the wrong shape and color for a light, curving and sinewy, winding through the sky like a snake and then it's gone.

Imogen squeezes me harder, and I know she saw it.

Good. I give the engine a little more gas.

By the time we get to the spot, a bare outcropping of rock surrounded by almost nothing but sky, the northern lights are in full force. Imogen leaps off the snowmobile, tears off her helmet, and stands there looking up, spellbound.

"This is incredible," she says, her voice hushed. "They're almost never visible this far south, the atmospheric conditions are almost never right and they're so hard to predict..."

She keeps staring. I grab the stuff I prepared, start spreading it on the ground.

"Did you know?" she asks.

Imogen sounds like she's looking at something holy, and maybe she is. A prickle of annoyance worms through my brain at the suggestion that I didn't know, that maybe I just took her here tonight of all nights by accident.

"Of course I knew," I say, walking up to her, my hand on her waist. "Why do you think I brought you here?"

She puts her hand over mine, both of us wearing thick gloves because it's January in northern Idaho and ten degrees below zero. It's not so bad as long as you dress for it, I swear.

"How'd you find out?" she breathes. "I was reading some weather blogs this week, and they said that it *might* be happening soon but none of them were sure. There's been a lot of debate because of the temperature inversions that've been happening, you know."

"Mhm," I say, pulling her closer, layers and layers and fleece and down still separating us. "I just asked Charlie. He says he's got a trick knee that hurts when it's gonna rain and an eye twitch that shows up just before the northern lights."

She's still looking up in awe, the writhing glow reflected in her glasses.

"There's a theory that they've got something to do with the earth's magnetic field," she muses. "Maybe Charlie is particularly attuned to that and so he can tell when it's going to happen."

"I think it might be a joke," I tease her, planting a kiss on the side of her head. "He was telling me he saw them a little last night, so I figured I had nothing to lose by bringing you here tonight. Worst case scenario, we're still in the middle of nowhere alone together."

I run my hand up her back until my thumb is on her neck, and I slide it over the knot of bone there as Imogen looks down at the spot I've laid out for us: two tarps, a couple of thick, old blankets, two sleeping bags zipped together, covered by another few blankets.

I did forget pillows.

"Oh," she says, a little breathless.

"It'll be a better view, Squeaks," I say, right into her ear, both my arms wrapped around her now. I'm already hard and she can probably tell despite the winter gear. "Wouldn't want you straining your neck."

"Is *that* why I should get into the sleeping bags with you?" she teases.

Even in the dark, I can tell she's blushing.

"Solely out of concern," I tell her. "If you don't, your neck could get stuck that way, you know, and imagine the difficulty."

She takes one of my hands in hers, pulls me over. Stands next to my setup, tilts her face up, and kisses me, rough and needy and fast, her hands already tugging at my coat. Every single time she kisses me like I've never been kissed before.

Every time feels new, wild, untamed, like I'm finding something I've never had before.

We take off coats, jackets, vests, get into the sleeping bags. By now we're ignoring the light show above as we keep shoving aside layers until we're making out skin to skin, our breath frosting into the air as our bodies are overheating.

"Did you get them?" Imogen murmurs.

I bite her neck, close my lips over it, suck so softly that I won't leave a mark.

"I thought you'd never ask," I growl, and reach for my pants.

Imogen's eyes follow the condom I pull from my pocket, her legs wrapped around my hips, and she takes it from me.

She unwraps it carefully, examines it for holes, bites her lip, clinical and careful as always, but she wouldn't be Imogen otherwise. I kiss her neck as she reaches down between us, rolls it on.

"Okay," she whispers, one hand on my hip.

In the years after that night I fuck *plenty* of other women, but no matter who or how many, I still think about the night I spent with Imogen under the northern lights.

CHAPTER TWENTY-TWO
IMOGEN

Reason #114 Wilder Flint is terrible: he's stubborn and impossible to talk out of something once he's got an idea in his head.

Reason #115: he walks too fast.

Reason #116: he's a bullheaded prick who won't listen to reason and who won't let the injured person in the party set the itinerary.

Reason #117: he just sucks, I just hate him, and the longer we're hiking *away* from the mouth of the valley and toward God-only-knows-what shiny thing, the angrier I'm going to get at him.

It's still there. We still can't tell what it is besides *something shiny not made by nature*, and for some reason, Wilder's completely convinced that it's our salvation. Even though it's in the wrong direction and across a finger of the frozen lake, and even though I'm pretty sure that at best it's just the windshield of a snowmobile or something that got left out here by some moron.

But at our last discussion, when we could have started walking for the shiny thing or for the mouth of the valley, he informed me that *he* was walking for the shiny thing, and I was welcome to do whatever the hell I wanted.

I've read enough survival guides and horror stories to know what happens to people who split up in the wilderness, so I go with him, lungs and ankle screaming in pain. We've got one more real meal for tonight, a couple more granola bars each, and honestly, I'm too cold and tired to even panic about the food situation.

Nice to know that there's a bottom to the anxiety pit, I think, stepping carefully over a fallen log, wobbling slightly as I balance on my bad ankle.

Who knew anxiety was a non-renewable resource?

I snort at my own stupid joke. Wilder glances back at me, eyebrows raised.

"I'm fine," I tell him.

He keeps walking, though I think he slows down. I still hate him for walking too fast, though. Just for the record.

On into the afternoon we're skirting the shore of the lake, the white-blue surface glaring through the evergreens as we hike lower and lower. We haven't been able to see *the thing* for a long time now, the tree cover totally obscuring our view, but now that we're closer to the frozen water Wilder's getting antsy, hiking way ahead of me, looking back impatiently.

Every time I lose sight of him my stomach knots, even though I don't say anything. I *need* him out here in a real, visceral way and I don't want him to know.

Finally, we find a way down to the lake shore and stand there, side by side, scanning across.

I don't see *shit*. I'm tired. I think I might be sunburned, because even though it's cold, ultraviolet rays are much more intense at high altitudes, not to mention the fact that when we're not under tree cover we're hiking through snow fields, light glaring at us from two directions.

My back hurts. My legs hurt. My quads and hamstrings are killing me, not to mention my ankle is throbbing and pulsing and pounding. I feel like it's a blood-filled water balloon that's about to burst inside my shoe and splatter everywhere, and all I want is to sit somewhere that's semi-comfortable for once and semi-warm for once and just... do *nothing*.

Instead I look out at the frozen lake, at the stark trees on the other side, at the craggy, rocky mountains above it, and I feel like crying.

"There," Wilder says, and points.

I squint. I think I need a new prescription, something I hadn't realized until we crash-landed in the wilderness and I couldn't see as well as I thought I could.

"Where?"

He steps behind me, takes one shoulder in his hand. I let it happen. He puts his face right next to mine, our hoods rubbing together, and points again, his finger bobbling and circling...

...something.

"I think it's a cabin," he says.

I push my glasses up, squint harder, but it doesn't really help. There's a dark shape in a blur of dark shapes, and this one *might* have straighter lines, might be squatter and a different color and look more man-made, but I can't tell.

I hold my breath, because my eyes are welling with tears.

You can't even see anything, what are you doing here? I think, suddenly drenched in self-pity. *You should have told him to leave you in the plane, he'd have been better off...*

"I don't see it," I say, forcing myself to swallow my tears.

"It's there," he says, his excitement barely contained. "Sort of on the other side, right across the one finger of the lake, it's not even that far. We can get there before dark, definitely. *Definitely.*"

I glance right, to where the mouth of the valley is, chew my lip.

But what if we're right outside a town or something and don't know it? I think, the same thing I've been thinking all day. *There could be a university or a superhighway or a ski resort just where we can't see it...*

Only I know he's right and I'm wrong. If there's something there, where are the lights at night? Where are the houses on the lake, where are the people going for day hikes?

"Okay," I say, swallowing my pride for once, trusting in Wilder again. "Let's go."

We edge along the lake. The ice is melted in spots, and way out in the center of it I think I can see water, or at least the flat, shiny spot where the ice is so thin that anything could break it.

I think of the rule my dad told me once about ice: one inch to hold people, two inches for horses, four inches for anything. I asked how they measured the thickness of the ice when he was a kid just going skating, and he didn't have a good answer.

The closer we get, the more it looks like a cabin: a square instead of a blob, brown instead of black, hard-lined manmade shapes instead of nature's curvature.

Wilder stops. I stop next to him, nothing but a thin finger of frozen water separating us from the shape that is almost definitely a cabin. We both stare at it without speaking, breath puffing in front of our faces.

I've never wanted to be somewhere more than I want to be in that cabin right now. My cold, tired brain is conjuring everything that it could have in it: a fireplace, blankets, canned food. A heater. A bed.

Running water, some sort of vehicle and a road to use it on. I worry at my lip with my teeth, head filled with cabin fantasies — *Scrabble, even* — as Wilder and I stare.

"It's still a long way if we go around the lake," he says. "That inlet cuts in pretty far, and from what I could see earlier, it looks like it gets pretty steep back in there…"

The inlet's what's separating us from the cabin. It's not that wide, maybe two hundred feet across, but it's tucked deeply into the mountain.

My ankle throbs. My spine protests. My fingers and toes are so cold I can barely feel them, and they've been that way for days now.

"The ice is plenty thick to walk across," Wilder says.

"One inch for people," I say. "Good thing we're not horses."

"I say that all the time," Wilder teases, looking over at me as I shut my eyes and shake my head.

"Something my dad used to tell me about skating on the pond," I tell him. "Though he never could answer how they could tell how thick the ice really was, all his answers sounded like guesses."

"I thought you'd insist on going the long way around," he muses, walking a little further along the shore.

"I guess you're in luck," I say, following behind him. The mud here is a little slushy, ice particles mixed in with the dirt. "I'm tired and sore and cold and just want to be inside a structure already."

We reach a spot where the land slopes into the water. Wilder goes first, stepping tentatively onto the ice with one foot, then the other. The shadow of the mountain is already stretching over the lake, and in a few more steps it'll consume him as he crosses.

My heart thumps as I pick a spot ten feet to Wilder's left, step on with one foot. The ice creaks but doesn't splinter, the sound sending a sickly feeling up my spine.

This is how ice sounds, I remind myself. *How many times have you done this? Hundreds.*

I take another step, then another. It's slippery but rough, and I hold my arms out for balance, knowing that if I go over on my bad ankle I'll make it even worse.

Every few steps, I look up at the cabin. From here I can finally tell that it's *definitely* a building, probably a hunting cabin. It looks like it's built from plywood and scraps, the roof tarpapered, the outside either unfinished or left for years and years to weather and decay.

But it's shelter. It's got a roof and a floor, and there's a chimney pipe coming out of the top.

I cross the lake slowly, fantasizing about a bed. About blankets, about canned soup that expired last year, about a flickering fire.

The ice creaks, but we make our way across without speaking. Halfway. Three quarters. The shoreline dips in toward me, so I've got ten feet less to go than Wilder does, and as soon as I'm close I find myself speeding up even though I'm still afraid of falling.

I reach the shore, one boot on the muddy ice and then the other, and I realize I'm shaking.

I could have fallen through.

I could be underwater right now, under the ice, breathing in cold water and beating at the ice with my bare hands as my clothes dragged me down...

"Quit it," I tell myself out loud because I'm probably losing my mind to cold and hunger.

I walk a few more feet inland, my eyes on the cabin. It looks uninhabited, an ugly curtain over the only window, and I doubt that anyone who had a cabin way out here would mind if a couple of lost souls broke in—

Behind me, there's a loud *crack.*

"Shit," Wilder says as I whirl around, fear squeezing my heart in an iron-clad hand.

He's perfectly still on the ice, one foot on a darker spot, bright white cracks radiating outward as my heart twists itself like a balloon animal.

"Watch out!" I shout uselessly.

Slowly, *so* slowly, he pulls his foot back, watching the ice. He unbuckles his pack, crouches, puts it on the ice.

I don't say anything. I stand stock-still, brain blinking like a neon light running out of juice, trying and failing to come up with a way I can help.

He starts walking, skirting the dark area on the ice, moving cautiously toward the shore, step by step.

I close my eyes, because I don't think I can watch. I can't do anything, I can't tell him anything that will help, I can only stand here and pray that the only other person in this godforsaken wilderness doesn't plunge into the water and die.

The water here can't be that deep, I remind myself. *He'll only get half hypothermia, the cabin's right there, he'll be able to climb out and*—

There's another *crack* and a splash, and my eyes fly open.

Wilder's on his back, cracks radiating outward. One foot's broken through the ice and he pulls it out instantly, wet to his knee, scrambling away from the hole on his hands and feet like a crab.

I cover my face with both hands, peeking through my fingers. I think I might throw up, the least helpful response of all, but I don't know what to *do* because anything I do will just make it worse.

He moves away from the water, his face pale, still backward on his hands and feet.

"Go here!" I shout from the shore, pointing at where the ice looks thickest.

He locks eyes with me, then pauses, looking around. Like he's trying to figure out the best course of action, his chest heaving under his thick coat.

Then he crashes through, the ice underneath his body just disappearing. He doesn't have time to move or react, he just disappears beneath the surface and then he's flailing, both arms coming up as the water drags his heavy clothing down.

"WILDER!" I shriek, bolting toward him.

I step onto the ice and slide instantly, my bad ankle going out from under me and sprawling me sideways, but I ignore the screaming pain and crawl toward him on hands and knees, fissures crackling around my gloved hands as I inch forward, the ugly groan of weak ice inaudible over the splashes and gasps.

I grab for his hand, miss. Wilder pulls himself up on the ice shelf, just his head and arms above water, and I grab for him again just as the ice crumbles, plunging him back down.

My hand goes in, but I scramble backward to safety, the water colder than cold, pure pain radiating up to my elbow.

Wilder thrashes. His face has gone bone-white, his hands and arms desperately flailing for purchase on the ice but not finding any.

I lay down on my stomach, face first, reach out again. This time I catch his hand and feel him kick, struggle to get up but the ice keeps crumbling away from the lip. My other hand dips in, the pain making me dizzy.

This isn't working.

You need something else, you're not strong enough, you're not at the right angle, you're just going to go through the ice yourself.

THINK.

I scramble backward, away from him, stumbling on the ice and wrenching my ankle again but I ignore the searing pain as I sit in the mud at the edge of the lake, tearing my pack off my back.

"Come on," I whisper. "Come on, please, *please*, fucking *come on.*"

There has to be something here, rope or another jacket or straps for something or a tent pole or—

I yank out a wide swatch of bright yellow nylon and instantly it billows over my head.

The parachute.

I stand, nearly falling over, tugging it from my pack with freezing, shaking hands. I don't dare look over at Wilder for fear that he's not there anymore, that he sank before I could help him and he's dead and it's my fault and I'm all alone out here now—

It's got straps. I tie some straps together with a square knot, the only kind I really know, hurl them at Wilder.

"Put it around you," I scream, and run the other direction, toward the trees along the shore. I'm praying that the parachute is big enough, that it won't tear, that this last-ditch thought I've had will work and isn't just stupid.

I trip over my own feet again, my bad ankle rolling and nearly pitching me forward into the dirt but I ignore the pain and look frantically up at the trees, trying to find the right one while Wilder shouts and splashes behind me, my own hands so cold after going in the water that I can't feel them and barely know what they're doing.

He's going to die, he's going to die…

There it is, a solid branch sticking out at ninety degrees, relatively smooth, maybe eight feet high. I hurl the other end of the parachute over it, miss, do it again, and it catches. I leap as high as I can and grab the yellow nylon in both hands, dragging it down until it's taut, the fabric scraping over the bark.

I land and my knees nearly buckle, tears in my eyes, but I ignore my ankle, look out at Wilder.

I *think* he's got it wrapped around him, still splashing and kicking though he's stopped yelling.

At least he's still alive enough to make a ruckus.

I jump again, grab the parachute, but my wet gloves slip and I fall back to the ground. My ankle gives out and I go down right on a pinecone, so I stand, brush it off my butt, tear my gloves off.

I leap, I grab, and this time I can hold it even though my hands are freezing, my body weight slowly pulling the parachute down, over the tree branch. There's the sound of fabric tearing above me, the sound of my own voice screaming, the sound of splashing and flailing and so I shut my eyes and just concentrate.

I keep going. I drag it hand over hand, hanging from it, clawing Wilder back toward me inch by inch using the worst pulley ever made until suddenly something gives and I fall again, my elbow smacking into a rock, pain shooting white through my vision but I'm back on my feet almost instantly, parachute still in both hands, wondering where it tore, what went wrong, whether I can fix it…

…and then I realize Wilder's out. He's lying on the ice, barely moving, but he's out of the water and I run toward him, grab the parachute, pull him to the edge of the lake and grab one arm.

"Are you okay?" I gasp, because it's stupid but it's the first thing that comes to mind. "Come on, you're okay, just stand up, *please* just stand up…"

I'm hauling him to his feet, or at least I'm trying. He's

pure white, lips and nose blue, eyelids fluttering, moving like he's still underwater. I have no idea if he can hear me, so I just keep shouting *get up, get up*, my own hands aching and icy as we struggle together.

Finally, he's upright, sort of. He's at least eight inches taller than me and is probably fifty pounds heavier, but I shove his arm around my shoulder and grit my teeth.

We start walking for the cabin. I can't get the parachute off from around him so we drag it behind us as we stagger toward shelter. It's only fifty feet away but it feels like it may as well be a thousand, because I drop him twice, fall over once myself, and by the time we get there I'm dragging him along the ground by the back of his jacket.

I throw myself against the warped plywood door and it flies open. The space inside is maybe twelve feet by twelve feet and austere as fuck but I don't care as I crouch one more time, right leg wobbling and shaking with effort and pain, and drag Wilder up the two steps and into the cabin, slamming the door behind me.

He's still awake, his mouth opening and closing, his eyes looking at me but I don't think he's really *there* as I tear his wet, freezing layers off, contorting his arms out of his jacket, yanking off his pants and his shoes and his long johns and his boxers until he's completely naked, his skin so pale it's got a bluish tinge.

There's a cot along the wall. I shove him onto it and he complies as much as he can, lifting one arm, blinking slowly.

What now? I think frantically, trying to remember all those wilderness training seminars I had to take to go to the Arctic. *Get them out of their wet clothes, and then….*

I look around again. There's a wood stove in the other corner but no wood and I have no idea how to start it.

Plastic crates stacked against one wall, and I pull down

the top one, start rifling through it. It's got camping supplies: flashlights, tarps, tentpoles, and then at the bottom a sleeping bag.

Two sleeping bags.

I'm crying as I pull them out, unzip them, throw them on top of Wilder. I've probably been crying this whole time, but it's only now that it registers what I'm doing.

"What else?" I cry-whisper, one shaking hand shoving the tears off my face. "What else, what else…"

He just looks at me. I think he's looking at me, but I have no idea if he's hearing me at all.

He has to get warm is what else.

I don't bother thinking about it, I just tear off my coat and my fleece and my down vest and my other fleece and my sweater, my fluffy snow pants and my boots. I shove everything underneath the sleeping bags and on top of Wilder, hoping my residual body heat will do something.

Then I crawl in next to him, wearing leggings and a tank top, and wrap my arms around him.

It's like hugging an iceberg.

"Come on," I whisper, and he doesn't say anything back.

CHAPTER TWENTY-THREE
WILDER

I wake up in an empty room, pinned under something heavy and soft, and I'm *freezing*. My whole body is trembling like a leaf, the shaking so hard that I can't do anything to stop it, my teeth chattering together. I'm shivering so badly it's hard to breathe, and I'm curled into a ball underneath this soft, heavy thing.

Wake up isn't the right word. I'm pretty sure I've been awake for a while, I just can't remember much because the past few hours have felt like I've been watching through a sheet of ice, dim shapes moving slowly on the other side.

I turn to my other side, careful not to disturb the blankets. That's what I've decided the soft, heavy things are, and I'm pretty sure I'm right.

It's a tiny room. Plywood walls, one window next to the door. Plastic crates stacked full of stuff against one wall, a single crate taken down, its contents strewn everywhere, my soaking wet outer gear still in a mound on the floor, surrounded by water.

I shiver harder, just looking at it and thinking of the crack of the ice underneath me, that one second before everything gave way and I plunged down, the water so cold it punched the air from my lungs.

Under the blankets I curl tighter, hug my knees to my chest, only my face sticking out of this pile. Vaguely, I wonder whether I'll get to keep all my fingers and toes after this.

The door slams open, but I don't move from where I am, curled and within reach of warmth even if I'm not there just yet. Imogen clomps in, her arms full of firewood, kicks the door shut behind her as she tracks snow across the floor of the little room and dumps her armful next to a blazing wood stove.

Her face is bright red and she's limping. She's limping *bad*, favoring her right side, and for a moment she stands in front of the stove, looking down into it, flexing and unflexing her ungloved hands like she's trying to warm them up.

Then she sighs, shoves her glasses up her face, turns around.

Sees me looking at her.

"Are you awake?" she asks.

I swallow, wiggle my toes. It all works.

"I think so," I say.

She reaches under the blankets, grabs my forearm, and even though I'm cold and nearly died today, I can't help but half-grin at her.

"You're still freezing," she says, frowning.

"You know what would warm me up," I say through chattering teeth, her hand still gripping my forearm, warm as anything to my cold skin.

Imogen just laughs, squeezes my arm. She pushes her glasses up again with her other hand, then leans in.

"Wilder, I have bad news," she says, pure mischief in her eyes.

If I weren't still shaking from the cold, I'd suck in a breath right now at that look.

"Your dick has gotten smaller in the past ten years," she says, cheeks flushing slightly pink.

I blink. I stare at her for a long moment, my brain still stupid and slow with the cold before I can think of anything to say back.

"That's not fair," I finally say, managing a smile. "You just saw the poor guy at his worst."

She just referenced your dick, you know. At least she's thinking about it.

"I'm a scientist," she says, taking her hand off me and standing. "I rely on empirical evidence, and the evidence in your case is…"

She shrugs, her eyes still sparking.

"The evidence in my case is tainted," I say as she heads for the door. "You know you can't always rely on that shit!"

She leaves, the door closing behind her, and I scowl around the cabin because whatever happens now, at the moment I've got one mission and one mission only: resuscitate my dick.

I take a deep, shuddering breath, fight my way out from under the blankets, get my feet on the wooden floor. It's cold, and there's nothing more I want than to get back onto the cot and pass out again, but this? This can't stand.

Even though deep down, I know she's just taunting me, I can't let this stand.

I get up, grab one of the blankets. I realize it's actually a sleeping bag, unzipped all the way, pull it around myself, and head for the wood stove.

When Imogen comes back in, carrying another armful of wood, I'm standing in front of the stove, sleeping bag held out to either side like a pair of wings.

Imogen stops mid-cabin.

"Are you…" she begins, the sentence trailing off.

"Warming up my dick," I confirm.

She limps over, drops the wood on the pile that she's already got, and stares into the stove, pointedly *not* at me.

"You nearly die of hypothermia and that's the thing that you're really worried about?" she asks.

I move the sleeping bag in my hand so it's shielding me from her view and grin back at her, giddy. The cold is like alcohol, something they teach you in elementary school when you grow up where I did: it impairs your judgement and makes you stupid.

"Not ready yet," I tease.

"I wasn't asking to look."

"You're the one who brought it up to begin with," I say. "I can't help what you've got on your mind, Squeaks."

The nickname comes out without me even meaning to say it, but Imogen doesn't freak out for once, just pushes her glasses against her face, a half-smile forming around her eyes.

"You nearly died, and your dick is tiny," she says. "You can have that one."

"We should have gone around the lake," I admit. "At least I was right about the cabin."

"You got lucky," she says.

"I know my shapes from far away."

"Luck," she insists.

Imogen walks to the cot across the cabin, grabs the other sleeping bag that was on top of me, comes back and sits with it wrapped around herself.

"If I was lucky it's about damn time I was," I say, and sit next to her.

I'm finally shivering less, still cold, but slowly returning to normal. I know enough about hypothermia to know that shivering is a good sign, a sign that means your body is fighting back. It's *not* shivering that's a sign of real danger.

I reach out, touch her knee. Imogen looks at me but doesn't flinch away.

"Let me see your ankle," I say softly.

She pushes at her glasses.

"It's fi—"

"You're limping like hell and I'm going to look at it one way or another," I tell her. "Voluntarily would be best."

She sighs, turns toward me, extends her right leg. Gingerly, I push her leggings up to mid-calf, unlace her boot, pull it off along with her sock.

Her ankle's swollen way worse than before, black and blue, the skin shiny.

"Shit, Squeaks," I mutter.

"I think I wrenched it or something," she says. "It kinda hurts now."

I'm fucking sure it more than *kinda* hurts. Just having it in her boot must be agony, not to mention walking around on it, hauling in wood from outside.

I have a vague memory of surfacing for air, her hand catching at me, Imogen stumbling and sliding and gasping in pain.

"You could've let me drown," I point out, running my thumb over the red welts on her foot where her boot cut into her flesh.

She just laughs, startled.

"What the hell?" she asks.

"It wouldn't have even been murder," I point out.

"Are you saying I should have just walked away?" she asks, half-teasing but half-serious.

"I'm saying I'm not sure I'd have blamed you."

"You know, even *I* think that something that happened

ten years ago when we were in high school is a bad reason to let someone die."

I start massaging her foot in my hands, a knot in my stomach, remembering.

Me, next to Melissa, up on stage. The music cutting out, Imogen standing in the back, against the wall, there with one of her other nerd friends. All I wanted then was to hurt her. Make her suffer for how she'd made me feel.

Even if maybe, *maybe* it was really my fault.

Her face when she realized what was happening, and the vicious surge of righteousness I felt when she ran through those doors. I thought then that it served her right, that it was what she got for trying to fuck up my life. Me, Wilder Flint.

And I remember looking down at Melissa, who faked a smile at me, her Prom Queen sash shining cheaply in the bright lights.

She dumped me not long after, and I realized way too late that I picked the wrong girl.

"So you've forgiven me?"

Imogen watches my fingers carefully, leaning back on her hands, the sleeping bag gathered around her shoulders as I press into the arch of her foot with one thumb.

"Not letting you drown and forgiving you are two different things, you know," she says.

"I really am sorry," I tell her.

She waits, not looking at me, her face closed off, but I can tell she's been crying recently, with her shiny eyes and blotchy cheeks. It feels like the cabin itself is holding its breath while I run my fingers gently over her foot, digging into the muscle and bone, her ankle delicately held on my lap.

"For prom," I say simply. "For not breaking it off with

Melissa. For giving a shit that you were a weird nerd and I wasn't."

She swallows hard, and I think her eyes behind her glasses might be filling with tears.

It's the smoke or something, I tell myself.

"For using you like that in the first place," I say softly.

Now she looks at me, pushes her glasses up with one hand, her eyebrows raised like she thinks something's funny.

"You weren't using me," she says, a note of laughter in her voice. "Don't go apologizing because you think I didn't have a good time."

I pinch her heel between my fingers and she winces slightly but doesn't move her foot from my lap. I shift, the sleeping bag sliding off my other hip, coming close to revealing everything. My skin's covered in goosebumps but I'm not shivering any more.

"Then I'm only sorry for everything else," I say.

She worries at the inside of her lip for a moment, looks at her foot, slides her eyes up to mine but lets them linger on me a heartbeat too long, a look I'd nearly forgotten but that I recognize in an instant.

It's a look that *always* made my mouth go dry and my dick spring to life. I tug the sleeping bag back over myself and pretend that nothing happened but secretly, I'm thinking of the kiss yesterday on the landslide.

The way that she kissed me as ferociously, as *needily* as she ever has, the way it told me she hadn't forgotten a damn thing.

"You weren't wrong the other day," she finally says, her eyes boring into mine.

"I'm not wrong very often."

She rolls her eyes.

"I was right about the cabin, wasn't I?"

"You were wrong about the ice."

"And I paid for it."

She wiggles her toes in my hand, and I pinch one between my fingers, massaging it back and forth.

"I'm trying to tell you that you were right about Melissa," she finally says. "I didn't hate knowing that I was fucking her boyfriend and she wasn't."

"Go on," I say, trying not to grin.

"She was such a *bitch* at first," Imogen says, turning slightly pink and laughing. "Did you know Sophomore year she started a rumor that she saw me make out with my little brother—"

"Ew."

"I know, right? So once I got over feeling bad, it was sort of… fun. Until I felt bad again."

I stroke my fingertips against her ankle and try not to look at her, because even though she's dirty and disheveled and wearing some really ugly clothes, it's also the easiest thing in the world to imagine pushing her down to the floor and pulling her legs around my hips as her hands claw at my back.

I tug the sleeping bag over my dick just a little more securely. The good news is that it *definitely* still works, and the bad news is that it's working great *right now*.

"You never told me she started that rumor."

"I didn't really like talking about her with you."

I grab her behind the knee, pull her closer, the sleeping bag underneath her scraping across the wood floor.

"Hey!" she says as I pull her leg across my lap. Now she's facing me, not *quite* straddling my lap but close, her leg thrown over mine.

"Ankle problems often lead to knee problems," I tell her, grinning, taking her knee in my hand. "I'm just being thorough."

"Is this what you learned since I saw you last?" she asks, pushing her glasses up her face again.

"How to treat sprained ankles?"

"How to perform the bare minimum of flirtation before just putting your mouth on whatever it is you want."

There's a bite in her voice when she says that, but she doesn't move away, doesn't take her knee out of my hands and I see her eyes dart to the crease between my torso and leg, the spot where the sleeping bag's come off again and it's pretty fucking obvious what I think about this situation.

"If I put my mouth on what I want, are you going to slap me again?" I ask, pulling her in closer. "You're not wearing gloves this time, so it might actually sting a little."

God, she's warm, and I swear I can feel her pulse beating in the back of her knee. Something else from today comes back to me in a flash: Imogen, sobbing, piling both the sleeping bags and her coats on top of me, crawling onto the cot behind me, holding me close.

She reaches out, fiddles with the edge of the sleeping bag where it's against my chest. I catch her wrist, my thumb against her palm.

"Don't go all demure on me, Squeaks," I say, my voice bottoming out at its lowest register, the sleeping bag getting practically thrown off my dick already.

"Don't tell anyone," she says suddenly, a hard note of urgency in her voice.

"There's nothing to tell yet," I say, and pull her onto my lap.

Now she's straddling me, the sleeping bag completely off, and I can see her determination not to look at my dick as I grab the front of her shirt with one hand, leaning back on the other.

"I mean about this, you idiot," she says, and I pull Imogen's face down to mine and put my mouth on hers.

CHAPTER TWENTY-FOUR

IMOGEN

Update: his dick didn't actually get smaller.

I haven't gotten a good look at it in its non-hypothermic state but Wilder pulls me in, his lips on mine, and I slide down his lap until we're crushed together, and it's trapped between us, hard and thick against me.

I shift my hips against him even though I try not to, because I can't help myself. Wilder brings one hand up, to the small of my back, fingers pressing into my sacrum and then grabbing my ass, making me do it again as his groan matches the slight gasp that escapes my throat.

He pulls back, my lip between his teeth, laughing.

"There it is," he murmurs, his voice so low I think animals hibernating underground could hear it.

"Shut up," I gasp.

"Nah," he says, and kisses me again.

It's rough and unpracticed, teeth and tongue, the angle awkward. I'm still wearing one hiking boot and trying not to use my busted ankle to balance but at the same time I can't stop pressing into Wilder, my body *screaming* for his.

I hate this. I hate how bad I want this. I hate how my body's reacting to his like this.

I hate that I'm not going to stop.

He slides his hand up under the layers I'm still wearing, hooks his fingers under the bottom band of my sports bra, pulls me in harder as I make another noise into his mouth, helpless against myself.

"Is this what I'm not supposed to tell anyone about, Squeaks?" he teases, still tugging. "That all it took to get you back in bed with me was a crash landing and a bout of hypothermia?"

"Shut up," I whisper, my fingers tracing down his chest.

"Yeah, you were a piece of cake," he laughs, tugging on my bra again.

This time he runs one thumb over my nipple, and even through the thick elastic it sends a jolt through my body that brings my hips forward, makes me squeeze his shoulder in my hand, make both nipples stiffen like diamonds.

He chuckles and tugs on the bra again, bringing my nipple to his teeth, biting me through the shirt and bra I'm still wearing. His teeth slide over me, the sharpness dulled by fabric, and then he shoves my bra over my breasts and does it again, only the thin fabric of my shirt in the way as he looks up at me, eyes twin glacial pools.

I gasp, and it comes out a squeak. Wilder grins, bites, lets his teeth slide off as I grind my hips against him one more time.

"You gonna tell me you don't like that?" he murmurs, then licks my shirt.

The fabric sticks to his tongue and he slides it around. I find purchase on his thigh with one hand, eyes closed as I pant for breath, afraid that if I don't hold myself up I'll fall over.

"It's dirty," I warn him, eyes still closed.

"Not yet."

His hand moves down, tongue working the other nipple through my shirt, and his fingers find the crease of my hip and in seconds, his thumb's brushing over my clit, nothing but the thin fabric of my leggings in the way.

"I meant my shirt."

Wilder just laughs, and I put more of my weight on his thigh, leaning back, pushing myself against his thumb and behind that, his hard cock.

No one ever has to know. Even if he tells, who's going to believe him?

He strokes me, thumb moving in little circles, teeth and lips around my clothed nipple, and I moan again. I can't help it and I can't stop myself, because this was always the problem: Wilder knows how to play my body like a goddamn Stradivarius, and somehow, he always has.

And right now? My strings are tight and it's been *ages* since someone came along who was any good at music.

"Get your shirt off," he growls.

"And if I—"

Wilder sits forward, bending his legs, grabs my shirt in both hands and tears it off over my head, followed moments later by my ugly bra before pulling me in and kissing me so hard our teeth nearly knock together.

"That's what happens if you don't," he growls, half-laughing, his lips moving to my neck. "Which is what you were gonna ask, right, Squeaks?"

"Maybe," I murmur, closing my legs around him.

"When has it *not* been in your best interest to take your clothes off around me?" he murmurs.

One hand shoves into my leggings, past my clit. He strokes my outer lips with two fingers, teasing me, and I push myself against his cock again, pure *want* pumping through my veins. He laughs into my neck and I curl my fingers into his hair, holding him there as his teeth and tongue are on me and it's all I can do to stay upright like this.

"Wilder," I whisper.

His fingers drag over my lips, start circling my clit, and my legs tighten around him.

"Don't make—"

"Who the fuck would see it if I did, Squeaks?" he asks, biting me again, fingers moving roughly over my clit as his teeth graze my neck. "It's us and the wolves out here."

He sucks the skin below his lips, a shower of sparks running down my spine as his fingers circle my clit harder, my body shuddering.

"Just come on," I say, my voice barely audible.

Suddenly he bites me, his teeth and fingers even rougher, and I moan, tangling my hands through his hair as hard as I can.

"Don't worry," he whispers savagely. "I'll make you come in secret if that's what you want, you know."

My whole body jolts, legs tightening, my teeth grinding together. I'd somehow forgotten this part, where I feel like a ball of yarn at the top of a skyscraper, looking down.

I moan into his ear, helpless against myself, against my own body's stupid wants and desires.

"Just our dirty secret," he murmurs.

I fall, and I unravel, unspool, spinning and tumbling down until I can't anymore and I open my eyes right into his, gasping for breath as he pulls his hand from my pants and grabs my ass with it, grinding me against him.

More. I need more, now, right now, and fuck everything else.

We crash together, tongues and lips and teeth. Wilder kisses me like he's trying to devour me. I have to pull my glasses off so they don't get crushed between us, my hair tumbling down around my shoulders as it comes loose and he shoves his hands through it.

Then I'm on my back, Wilder above me, between my legs and I finally reach down, grab his cock. He groans, bites my lip, kisses me. Grabs my other hand and holds it over my head.

Growls into my ear, "You like that, Imogen?"

I stroke him hard as an answer and he groans again. Lets my hand go, rocks back on his knees. Yanks my remaining hiking boot off, and I lift my hips as he tugs off my leggings too.

He takes my knees, pushes them wide, leans over me and kisses me again. This time his bare cock is right against me, resting against my wetness, making my nerves crackle again.

I slide my hand around his head, lock my fingers into his hair, his forehead against mine as we kiss fiercely, my legs wrapped around his hips. I can feel every muscle in his body as it moves and writhes, pure raw power behind them.

Wilder's like a caged animal ready to spring, both his hands clenching fistfuls of sleeping bag on either side of my body as I grab his cock again, stroking it, sliding the head against my clit until we both moan in unison.

I shut my eyes hard, forcing myself to slow it down for one second as I swallow hard, gasping for air.

"Are you—"

"I'm clean," he gasps, hips bucking, cock sliding against my clit again. "Are you—"

I just lift my hips and Wilder plunges into me with a shout, so hard and deep on the first thrust that I leave scratches up his back even as I *grunt* with the force of it.

Sparks explode in front of my eyes because *God* this feels good. I tighten my legs instantly, still holding his hair in my hand, our faces together as I try to pull him in and it feels like he's trying to push my hips through the floor below us.

"Jesus," he whispers into my mouth, just as I curl my tongue around his, fingers tightening on his back as he shifts and rocks, pulling one knee up, sliding half out and grabbing me and driving back in so hard I just whimper for more.

"Fuck yes," I manage to whisper.

I tighten my grip. I buck my hips up to meet him and he holds me down, his cock hitting every perfect place inside me and some I didn't know I had. In whispers I tell him to go harder, faster, deeper, *more* of everything as I twist and moan underneath him, my teeth on his lips and his neck and his shoulder.

I want him, and I want to hurt him, shred him to pieces, feel him explode like a grenade and get every ounce of pleasure I wring from his body. I want him unable to control himself, to shatter into a million pieces and not be able to stand properly tomorrow morning and I want it to be because of *me*. I want to do it to him, do everything, make him hurt and come and regret everything and forget the world exists.

Harder, faster, deeper, rougher because we're somehow not on the sleeping bag any more but my bare back is against the plywood and the floor is creaking and Wilder is shouting and I'm going to come again in seconds as he drives himself into me with no mercy, nothing but *need*.

There's one perfect, crystal clear, split second where I swear the whole blurry cabin comes into sharp focus and time stops.

I come like I'm being torn apart, gasping and shouting and fucking *begging* Wilder not to stop with teeth and lips and fingernails and he doesn't, not even as he comes inside me a second later, a string of curses growled into my ear as he pushes my legs up, getting as deep as he can while my body flutters and jolts.

We slow together, echoes washing over my body, unwilling to stop just yet. The floor's freezing beneath me but we're flushed, sweaty, my body trembling as Wilder finally sinks against me, his head in the hollow of my shoulder.

What did you just do? my brain whispers, even as I roll my head against the floor, rough plywood against my cheek.

That's the dumbest thing you could have done, everyone's going to laugh at you again, how could you give in again like this Imogen there was only one thing you weren't supposed to do again, and it was—

Shut the fuck up, I tell myself.

Miraculously, I shut up. I relax my grip on Wilder's dirty hair, running my fingers through it. I can feel him blinking against my neck, his breath warm on my shoulder, my head turned away from his.

It feels good to be like this, slow and drowsy and tangled together. It feels *right*.

And I kind of wish it didn't.

CHAPTER TWENTY-FIVE
WILDER

"All right," I ask. "Do you want meat lasagna with green beans and potatoes, or… chicken curry with steamed broccoli?"

I turn the second package over, holding it closer to the light of the stove. When the hell did MREs start coming in chicken curry flavor?

Imogen pulls the sleeping bag tighter around her, sitting on the floor, legs crossed. She's dressed again, and I'm wearing an enormous camouflage jacket and overall pants that I found in the plastic bins stacked against the wall.

Hope Bubba doesn't mind that I've borrowed some of his stuff. Maybe if he ever finds out what happened I'll give him a gift card to a hunting store or a free heliskiing trip or something.

Not that whoever owns this cardboard-and-plywood place has any business heliskiiing. The ramshackle cabin has more of a *drinking beers and racing souped-up snowmobiles* vibe to it.

"I'll take the chicken curry one," she says.

"Great," I say, and shove them both into the MRE heater.

I wonder again if this is the last two, because Imogen says she couldn't find my pack after she dragged me in here. She also said she didn't look that hard, and Christ knows I'm not venturing out to look for it tonight in bare feet and a sleeping bag.

It might be sitting there, somewhere she didn't see it.

It might be at the bottom of the lake. I've got no clue what happened to it, and I can only cross my fingers and hope that it's the first, and not the second, particularly since Bubba didn't seem too hot on stocking his little getaway with, you know, *food*.

The MREs finish heating. I give Imogen hers, open mine, and for a couple of bites we eat in silence together.

"You know, something occurred to me," Imogen finally says.

"Mmm?" I ask, spoon in my mouth.

"There's a woodstove here," she says slowly. "There's a bed frame, there's a twin mattress, there's all these sheets of plywood and everything. This stuff didn't get here on someone's back."

"No," I agree.

I don't think we're going to talk about what just happened, how it feels a little right now like my world's flipped again and somehow I'm right back where I was ten years ago.

The last time it took me forever to get over her. Even though I never saw her again after prom night — not until Amy called me over to the counter at the Solaris airport — I was nearly twenty years old before I stopped seeing Imogen's face on every girl I looked at.

And there were *plenty*. I rebounded like hell, plowing through the cheerleading squad at Solaris High, even though most of them were Melissa's friends who'd *sworn* to her that they'd never touch me.

I taught ski lessons sometimes the next winter, after Imogen was already in California, and I met rich men's daughters, took them to the *secret* hot tub in the resort, the one where I first saw Imogen naked. I sat them in the same spot and whispered the same things and got what I wanted but it was never what I *needed*.

Sometimes it was the rich men's wives, purring cougars who knew what they wanted and weren't afraid to have a barely-legal kid give it to them.

It took forever to get over her, is my point. The only thing that finally worked was joining the Navy and going to flight school, the thrill of the air the thing that made her face disappear, only for her to come back.

"So there must be a road," she says, opening her MRE and peering inside. "And that road must go somewhere that has plywood and wood stoves and big plastic tubs."

I open my own MRE, stab into it. It isn't really *good* — it tastes like an MRE — but I'm so hungry right now that it could taste like vomit-flavored dirt and I wouldn't care.

"Did you see a vehicle?" I ask.

Imogen shakes her head slowly, stirring her MRE together. The only light is the low fire in the wood stove, so she's lit from the side, her face orange and shadowed, her glasses darkening crazy lines across both eyes.

"I didn't look," she says. "I figured we weren't leaving until tomorrow, anyway."

I look at her ankle, pointedly.

"Maybe if we find a snowmobile," I tell her. "But I don't think we will, and you're not walking anywhere on that."

She pulls the edge of the sleeping bag over her ankle, even though she's got her thick wool socks back on, like not being able to see it will make me forget that it's black and blue and swollen.

"We can tape it again," she says, not looking at me.

"We taped it before you did whatever the fuck you did to it."

"Whatever the fuck I did to it was pull you out of the lake," she fires back. "I can do that, I can walk out of this stupid valley on a road."

"So you can turn it again on a rock or something, halfway out, and then I can carry you the rest of the way?" I ask, a knot in my stomach slowly unfurling. "If you go I'm not going with you, and if you go I might also haul you back here so you can sit the fuck down and heal for a minute, Imogen."

"I'll be *fine*," she says, not looking at me, her voice quiet and sharp.

I swallow hard, look through the tiny window and into the fire inside the wood stove. She's always been like this, fucking stubborn, and something about her being this way always makes me even more pigheaded than I already am. Something inside me hates giving way to Imogen even though I know she'll never bend or break.

Like when she said she wanted me to tell Melissa.

Barricade the door, carry her back here if she leaves, tie her down and make her stay until her ankle's better—

"You're not fine," I say, trying to keep my voice even, reasonable.

I try not to react like we're both seventeen, because we're not.

"You're injured, and by going out there, you run the risk of injuring yourself further and putting us both in danger," I continue.

I sound calm. I sound reasonable.

"We've got shelter, we've got warmth, we've got some food, let's stay here another day or two," I say.

"We're low on food," she says quietly. "These were the last two, we lost your pack into the lake—"

"You said you weren't sure."

"It's not looking good," she says, her eyes boring into mine. "There are a few more bins but I don't think those have anything in them either."

"A day," I tell her.

"I don't want to starve in the warmth," she says quietly.

I finish my MRE, and my stomach growls. Imogen's already finished hers, drawn her knees to her chest. I want to pull her to me, stroke her hair, tell her that we'll be fine, but the girl's like an iron gate that slammed shut.

"I bet we could catch a bunny," I say.

She leans her chin on her arms around her knees, looking at me skeptically.

"At least call them rabbits."

I grin at her.

"Why, you don't want to eat a bunny?" I ask. "You know they're the same thing either way."

She shoves her glasses up her face, the ghost of a smile around her mouth.

"Semantics matter," she says. "Though I'll believe you can catch a bunny when I see it."

"I went on a hunting trip once with my dad," I point out.

Imogen snorts, but now at least she's smiling.

"I'm *so* sure the two of you hung out in a camouflage shelter all day where you ate jerky, peed into bottles, and stayed cold and miserable in the hopes of seeing a deer," she says.

"Not exactly," I admit.

I can't even begin to imagine my dad *actually* hunting. I

can barely imagine the man wearing anything but a suit and tie. Camouflage? *Pissing in a bottle?* Hell no.

"It was on a preserve," I tell her. "And we were shooting… what's the bird that flies up out of the bushes and then you shoot a shotgun and some of them fall down?"

"Quail? Partridge? One of those," she says. "So you did that and now you think you can catch, kill, skin, and eat a bunny?"

"I thought we were calling them rabbits."

"Apparently, we are, now that I've made you think about killing one."

"I think the hard part would be catching it," I admit. "I'm not a bad shot, but there's no gun and I've got no clue how to build a rabbit trap."

I let it go unsaid that I've got no problem with the thought of killing a rabbit, even if it's fluffy and cute.

"And here you had me thinking you were Mister Survivalist," she teases.

"Did I?" I ask. "I guess I was doing all right until I fell into a lake and you had to drag me here."

"That wasn't super impressive, no," she agrees, sitting back on her hands. Imogen straightens her leg, making a face as her right ankle moves. Even through her thick socks I can tell that her ankles are different sizes, and it worries me all over again.

"And you did scare the hell out of me," she says, suddenly, her voice brittle but soft.

She's staring into the wood stove, suddenly rigid, like she's holding an invisible shield against whatever I'm about to say. There's that haughty look I know, that holier-than-thou manner that she has that fucking *infuriates* me, makes me want to drag her down to earth.

Her guard is up. She just told me something real, something true, something that makes her vulnerable and that's all. I don't know why I never saw it for what it was before, but right here, right now I feel like plate glass just shattered over my head, shards raining down around me.

"I'm fine now," I say, just so my mouth is making noise because it needs to do something. "I think it was worse for you than it was for me. I was barely conscious for most of that."

It's not true. I still remember crashing through the ice in sharp relief, the sudden plunge into the cold that burned like I'd been launched into the sun. Imogen grabbing at me, slipping away, the certainty at that moment that I was going to die there.

Wrapping something around myself. Imogen screaming, leaving, being pulled toward the edge and kicking and pulling like hell to get myself out, getting half-dragged to the cabin because I could barely think, let alone walk.

Imogen, piling up blankets and coats, wrapping herself around me. She must have been freezing.

"It was pretty bad," she says, her voice still flat, that tone that makes my hackles go up instantly.

Defense mechanism, I remind myself.

"We should get some sleep," she finally says. "I can grab a couple of blankets and sleep on the floor, you're still recovering—"

"Bullshit," I say.

She raises an eyebrow.

"Bullshit that you're still recovering?"

"Bullshit that you're taking the floor."

Imogen rolls her eyes, shoves her glasses up her face.

"Look, the floor is colder, and it takes a couple of days to recover fully from a bout of hypothermia, especially if you're—"

"I don't mind sharing."

Something flickers across her face, this moment of

uncertainty that I don't see, so much as I *feel* punch me in the gut. I want to shout *I was inside you an hour ago, where the fuck was this then,* but I swallow it and don't. Imogen's a deep lake, bottomless depths.

I stand up, brushing myself off. I open the grate on the wood stove and fill it up with the wood that Imogen brought in while I was still sleeping earlier, make a mental note that if I can, it might be nice to chop some more wood for whoever owns this cabin.

Then I remember the food situation. My stomach growls. I'll have to fulfill my karmic duties some other way if we're gonna walk out of here.

Imogen stands, unsteady. She grabs the sleeping bag she was using, tosses it on the floor, straightens it out.

I grab it and throw it on the single bed, followed by my own, and she crosses her arms, *glares.*

I take her by the shoulders in the dim orange light, and for long seconds, I just look down at her.

Imogen looks like hell. There's no getting around that. We crash-landed a plane in the wilderness and then walked out for a couple of days. She's listing slightly to one side, favoring her good ankle. She's got deep purple circles under her brown eyes, the shadows of her glasses making them look worse. There's dirt and leaves and twigs stuck in her hair, which is back in some kind of messy bun.

She's got dirt on her face, scratches on her neck. Her jaw clenches as she looks back up at me, waiting for whatever I'm about to do but I don't know what I'm about to do.

Yes, I do.

I kiss her.

I kiss Imogen with no excuse, no ulterior motive, no impulsive adrenaline rush. I kiss her because I want my lips on hers and that's all I want, to kiss her and have her kiss me back.

She does. Soft and gentle this time, like we're being careful. Like we're doing this for the first time even though it's anything but, like we suddenly have everything to lose.

I turn my head, put my hand against her face like she's a bird that could fly away. Her skin's warm under my fingertips and I swear she leans into me slightly as I stroke my thumb along her cheekbone.

Our lips separate but we don't move apart, our faces still touching. Hesitantly, she puts her hand to my face, her eyes closed like she's blind and trying to find out who I am.

"Imogen," I whisper. "What are you afraid of?"

"That I haven't learned a thing from my mistakes," she murmurs. "That I'm doomed to repeat the same pattern forever and never break out of this stupid cycle that led me back to you."

"This is different," I whisper. "I swear this is different."

Imogen doesn't say anything, just presses her lips to mine again. I don't know if it means that she believes me, or she just wants me to shut up, but it works and I go quiet.

"C'mon," I murmur when we separate again. "It makes more sense to share body heat."

She doesn't answer right away, just leans her head against my shoulder, turning her face in toward my neck as I slide my arms around her and she lets herself relax into me.

"All right," she finally says. "Try not to kick me too much."

The bed's not very big — maybe smaller than a twin bed, I've got nothing for comparison — but for the first time ever Imogen falls asleep in my arms, and I let myself be rocked gently on the waves of her breathing.

CHAPTER TWENTY-SIX
IMOGEN

"Oh my *God*, did you see him trip over the curb the other day and just sprawl on the sidewalk? Peyton said that when all his textbooks fell out of his bag there were also a bunch of drawings of naked elf women, like with pointy ears and everything."

Jessica, the blonde siting at the desk right in front of Melissa, giggle-gasps.

"Of *course* he gets off on pointy ears," she whispers back. "He's such a weirdo, remember the time he wore a suit to school to ask that girl Diane to Homecoming?"

"Peyton said the drawings all had Diane's face," Melissa confides, leaning forward over her desk. "Like, all these naked elf girls, all with her face, kind of."

"Ew."

"I know, right?"

I'm sitting one row over, pouring all my concentration into the shapeless doodle I'm making, lines in circles in triangles in lines. My face is slowly going bright red, because they're talking about my friend Pete.

Pete's a nice guy. He's not weird, just awkward, but he's friendly and smart and kind of funny when he relaxes, and he volunteers with Habitat for Humanity every summer.

And he does *not* have weird elf-girl naked drawings of Diane. At least I don't think he does, but who cares? He's not hurting anyone.

"We should steal one and put it up on Facebook," Melissa says.

Jessica giggles, and I just turn brighter red, even though I don't dare say a single thing.

I just think about how I spent last weekend. Midterms are coming up, so Wilder told Melissa that he *really* needed to study or he'd get kicked off the football team, and then he drove me in his dad's Mustang to this amazing view, out in the national forest.

Not that I saw a ton of the view. I mostly saw the back seat of the Mustang, because I recently discovered reverse cowgirl and wanted to see if it could be done in a car.

You know, for science.

For the record, doggie style can *also* be done in the back seat of a Mustang.

And this, right here — Melissa spreading rumors and lies about people who aren't cool enough for her, no matter that they're *good people* — is why I don't really feel bad about sneaking around behind her back with her boyfriend.

If I'm being really, *really* honest with myself, I kind of like it. She's famously *saving herself for marriage*, something that she brings up constantly and obnoxiously, like that simple fact makes her Princess of the World and everyone else is her sinning, dirty peon.

She's the one people look at, the one they get judgy

about. People spread rumors about the stuff she does with guys — for example, the one that she lets Wilder put it in her butt *only* — and leave me out of it.

I get jealous. Every single time I walk past them holding hands or kissing in the cafeteria or when I got the voting ballot for Prom King and Queen, I get jealous. When I see the pictures of them on Facebook looking cute out on a date somewhere, when she posted the flowers and candy he gave her on Valentine's Day, I got jealous.

Even though I got something way better than shitty chocolates and roses that'll just die.

But it's hard to *stay* jealous when he calls me midweek, begs me to meet him at the resort and bring my swimsuit. Hard to stay jealous when he sneaks me off to the spot where the butterflies are migrating, and *really* hard to stay jealous when he asks me, straight-faced, if I've ever come twice in a row.

For the record, the answer is now *yes*.

I know it's immoral or whatever, but I have a hard time caring. Maybe that makes me a bad person, but I'm pretty sure that all that is relative and there's no heaven or hell anyway.

———

"Hey," a voice says behind me.

I jump about a mile, dropping my Calculus textbook into my locker with a loud thud and whirling around.

Melissa's *right* behind me, one hip cocked, both her hands holding her backpack straps.

Oh shit she knows oh fuck—

"It's Imogen, right?" she says, her forehead crinkling ever so slightly.

I swallow, my mouth dry.

"Yeah," I say.

"Listen, Wilder's my boyfriend—"

Oh God oh God oh God—

"—And he was telling me that you've been helping him study for biology lately?"

I nod mutely.

—Oh God oh God—

"And so, like, he was telling me that you're really helpful and his grades in bio have gone way up so he can stay on the football team? And you're really good at explaining stuff?"

My heart's still thumping, beating nearly out of my chest.

"Uh huh?" is all I can muster, still certain that in the next second she's going to accuse me of exactly what I've been doing.

"I'm like, failing English?" she says, her blue eyes going wide and worried. "And I can't be head cheerleader any more if I don't keep my GPA up, and that's like *really* important because otherwise I can't go to the University of Arizona and that's like really *really* important to me, so I was wondering if you could help me?"

I wait, but she doesn't say anything else.

For a long moment I'm wide-eyed and open mouthed, and then it finally hits me.

This has nothing to do with Wilder.

This has nothing to do with last weekend in the back of his dad's Mustang or the weekend before that in the hot tub or the weekend before that—

I swallow, blink, make myself smile.

"Sure," I say. "When are you free?"

———

MELISSA TAPS A PEN against her English notebook, then against her pink lips, her mouth forming a perfect little O as she frowns, looking down at what she's written.

"Wait," she says, slowly. "The *priest* is the little girl's father?"

"Right," I confirm, even though he's technically not a priest, just a preacher.

Her eyes go wide.

"Oh," she says softly. "But she could have totally said something, right? And then he'd be banished from society too because that's also adultery, when you sleep with a married woman even if you think her husband is dead?"

"Well, that's sort of the point," I tell Melissa, grabbing a handful of popcorn from the bowl her mom brought us earlier. "She's kinda letting him hang himself here, that's the whole reason he dies at the end, because of the guilt or something."

"But he could have told someone."

"Mhm," I confirm, crunching the popcorn.

"Huh," she says reflectively. "So… okay, I think I get it. I think I'm gonna write the paper about *that*, about how like, sometimes guilt is the worst punishment there is because it can really eat you alive."

I look at the popcorn, not Melissa, my stomach shuddering in nervous little waves, because even though I'm 99% sure she's just struggling with the themes of *The Scarlet Letter*, maybe she's secretly telling me that she knows about me and Wilder, that she knows that every time I see her I feel a little guiltier about the situation, a little more like sooner or later she's going to get her heart really really broken and it'll be my fault.

"I think that's a great essay topic," I say, talking more to the popcorn than to her.

Melissa sighs dramatically.

"Thank you *so* much for helping me with all this," she says. "I had such a hard time with this book, it's written so old-fashioned and stuff, and I know this is gonna sound dumb, but I honestly wasn't even quite sure who the little girl's father was."

I chew on the popcorn, kind of unsure what to say because I'm starting to feel really bad for Melissa. It's true that she's not the smartest person I've ever met, but it's also true that there's not a single person in her life who seems to expect her to be anything other than a pretty idiot.

Her dad barely notices that she exists. Her mom's an obvious trophy wife, a good fifteen years younger than her husband who plays the clueless, helpless housewife role to a T. I'm pretty sure that when my parents were giving me lab sets and taking me on a road trip to Wyoming so I could see the dinosaur skeletons, hers were entering her in beauty pageants.

Also, I think she might be dyslexic or something. God knows I'm not an expert, but she picks things up pretty quick when she hears them. It's her reading comprehension that's total shit, but it seems like everyone's just assumed she's dumb this whole time.

"No problem," I say, pulling one foot in and sitting cross-legged on the couch in her parents' den, my own notebook still in my lap. "It's a weird old book, and a lot of the stuff doesn't actually make sense, like the one guy dies of guilt."

She smiles at me and laughs a little, a nice, pleasant laugh, and I laugh too. Melissa's still the girl who spread the rumor that I made out with my younger brother and that my friend draws elf-girl porn, but I get the impression that she just… thinks that's what she's *supposed* to do. There's not much real malice behind it.

Her phone buzzes, and she grabs it, biting her lip.

Then she puts her thumb between her teeth, smiling secretly to herself.

"Sorry," she says, batting her eyelashes at me. "It's Wilder, he wants to know if I can come to dinner at his parents' house Friday night."

I swallow my jealousy and look at the blank TV across the room. I've never even met his parents, let alone had dinner with them. I'm not *that* girl to him, the sweet, charming, dumb one who can say the right things and bat her eyelashes the right way and be pretty on his arm.

No, I'm just the girl he fucks in the back seat of a car. Since I got to know Melissa better it's been harder and harder to take pleasure in being her boyfriend's secret lover, and the whole thing just feels... *bad.*

"Cool," I tell her, even though I think it's anything but.

"Did I tell you about the present he got me for our six-month anniversary?" she gushes, texting away, giggling to herself. "It's a Build-A-Bear! He had to go all the way to *Spokane.*"

"Wow," I say, my voice plastic and brittle in my ears. Spokane's a two-hour drive, one way, and even though I couldn't care less about an ugly stuffed bear I'm jealous of the drive, of the effort, of the fact that now she gets to parade this stupid thing around in front of everyone and all I get is to be his secret side piece.

My grandmother once told me that men would never buy the cow if they got the milk for free. I was eleven, so I didn't *really* get what she meant, not to mention that my mom overheard and instantly admonished her for putting sexist notions like that into my head, but maybe this is what she meant.

I'm the milk, and Melissa's the cow. And only cows get stuffed bears.

"Okay, sorry," she says, enthusiasm practically bubbling over. "I *love* Mrs. Flint's spaghetti! Do you want some Diet Coke? I think I'm gonna go get myself one."

CHAPTER TWENTY-SEVEN
WILDER

PRESENT DAY

I wake up on my back, one arm around Imogen, her leg draped over mine and her hair everywhere, taking over the whole pillow. We're buried under both sleeping bags, and the wood stove has pretty much gone out, the morning freezing cold.

I don't move. I'm barely awake myself, and even though I feel like I just slept for the first time in a week, I want to stay here a few more minutes while she's asleep.

Like this, she's warm and soft and trusting. Like this, she doesn't remember all the shit that I did to her, shit that she didn't deserve just because I wanted to feed my ego. Shit I did purely because I was the high school big shot, the golden boy, and I could get away with it.

Slowly, I turn my neck. I put my lips to Imogen's forehead slowly, softly, so carefully that she doesn't even stir.

My CLOTHES still aren't completely dry and her ankle's not much better, so I talk her into staying at the cabin for another day. She's all for me taping her up and hobbling out into the woods, but I tell her that if I wear my clothes the way they are, I'll die of hypothermia.

That's what gets her.

We go through the plastic bins, quietly apologizing to whoever's stuff we're messing up. I find some galoshes — camouflage print, of course, apparently the cabin's owner doesn't own anything else — and I go outside, grab more wood from the giant pile outside.

Somewhere toward the bottom of the bin pile, Imogen finds a case of canned chili, and when I get back she waves one at me.

"I saved us from eating bunny," she says, holding one out.

I examine the thing. It expired a couple of months ago, but does canned food *really* expire?

"We can still have bunny dinner if it's what you really want," I tease, tossing the can in my hand. "Just give me the word and I'll be back with the cutest, fluffiest critter I can find."

Imogen just scrunches her nose.

"I've got a surprisingly fond recollection of you showing no mercy in biology lab," I say.

"Those animals were already dead," she says, a smile playing around her lips. "Killing something is harder, trust me."

I raise one eyebrow.

"I've killed some experimental mice in my time," she says. "It wasn't much fun."

"If I catch a bunny I'll let you kill it, then," I agree.

She shoves her glasses up her face, takes the can back from me.

"My point is, now we don't have to," she says. "Did you find cooking stuff anywhere in here? I think we can just put a pot on top of the wood stove and we'll be good to cook this… stuff."

———

THERE'S STRANGELY little to do when you're lost in the wilderness, in some hunter's cabin while you wait for your stuff to dry and your ankle to heal, and we mostly end up talking. Imogen tells me about Stanford and Seattle, about her life since the last time we saw each other. She doesn't say it out loud but it's obvious that leaving Solaris was the best thing she ever did for herself, that a small town in the middle of nowhere, Idaho, wasn't for her.

She tells me about the drama in the department while she was getting her Master's degree, and how all the politics are the reason she's not sure if she wants a PhD or not.

She tells me about last summer at the research station, spent observing musk oxen in their natural habitat. That sounds like it was pretty dramatic too.

We repack her pack. We find another backpack in the bins — not as big or as good as what we've got, but all right — and we pack that with stuff we've taken from the cabin as Imogen tries to memorize everything we're taking so that, in theory, someday we can find the owners and repay them.

I'm less concerned about that. I'm more concerned with making it out alive first, repaying them second.

———

THE SECOND NIGHT we're there, I wake up to pitch blackness and Imogen's gone, the wood stove no longer burning. There's a moment where I can't remember where I am and for some reason I think I've been shot down over enemy territory, that they've put me in a tiny hole in the ground with no light and left me here to die.

It's a dream I used to have a lot, but that's not this. Seconds later it comes rushing to me where I am, on a tiny bed under a pile of blankets, and then the door opens, a rhombus of moonlight falling across the floor, her shadow dim inside it.

"I thought you left," I say, my thoughts raw and unfiltered.

She closes the door, steps lightly toward me. I hear her coat drop to the floor beside the bed, the *thunk* of her boots and then her weight is next to me on the bed again, still warm and sleepy like she must have been when she left.

Imogen snuggles up. Imogen's never *snuggled*, not even in high school, and definitely not since we've been out here. It's always been me holding, her acquiescing. She's still wearing her thin long-sleeved shirt and leggings, but I can feel every inch of her skin and curve of her body through them as she undulates lightly against me.

I run my hand down her back, lightly, even though my heart's pumping hard. Whatever's happening, I'm not about to ruin it.

Her hand moves down my side, stroking me from shoulder to hip, her fingers finding the notches in every muscle, her head on my other shoulder, her lips tilting toward my neck and suddenly I'm *awake* to the nip of her teeth on my collarbone, her fingers pulling at me, her hand on my back as I roll toward her until I'm on my side and her lips are in the hollow of my throat.

Her hips push against mine, her hand still on my hip as she licks me, bites me, lips and teeth and tongue moving over my jawline until finally her mouth is on mine, hard and needy and ravenous.

I wonder again if I'm dreaming, if maybe I'm actually going to wake up sleep-humping Imogen. I pray I'm not going to have my first wet dream in fourteen years, but this feels too real, too sharp to be a dream.

It's still black in here, so dark I can't see more than the faint outline of the door, a few spots where there are cracks in the space between the plywood walls and the plywood ceiling. Imogen's not making a sound besides her breathing, and all I've got to go on is touch. So I touch her.

I slide my hands up her soft warm body, pull her shirt off, no bra beneath. I cup her shoulders in my hands, run my fingers over her collarbone, flatten my palms over her nipples and listen for the change in her breathing, a shudder, a quick hitch that tells me she got what she wanted.

There it is, the soft sigh I was looking for, so I let my hands drift lower as she nips my neck again, lips on my chin, then finally on mine as she digs her fingers into my side, practically using me to pull herself up.

She makes another noise, a soft squeak from the back of her throat, and I grin in the dark, catch her bottom lip between my teeth until she makes it again.

Imogen grinds herself into my erection, her body moving with a ferocity I haven't felt in a long, *long* time. The kind of ferocity that makes me glad Imogen's always kept her nails short, otherwise I'd be shredded to ribbons in five minutes.

She bites my lip. I grab her ass, squeeze hard, let my fingers dig into the muscle, through her leggings and she just makes a *noise* into my mouth, swipes her tongue along my lower lip.

I slide my hand down, between her legs from behind, feel the jolt move through her body as my fingers find her lips, just barely reach her clit through the fabric, brushing over her as her nails rake down my spine.

I tease her through her clothes, the fabric of her leggings slightly rough against my bare, hard cock, the friction delicious, the thought of what's coming next intoxicating. I nearly ask her *is this all it's gonna take to make you come again, Squeaks*, but I shut up for once, savor the silence and the darkness.

Imogen moves, wriggles, turns over and moves away and when she's next to me again the leggings are off, her bare skin soft right next to mine as she hooks one leg over my hips, my cock trapped against her lower belly, the pressure making me growl.

So I grab her thigh and roll onto my back so Imogen's straddling me, invisible in the dark, but I can imagine what she looks like: pink lips in an O of slight surprise, brown hair tousled and down around her shoulders, eyes wide and then half-closed. Nipples hard as rocks, *begging* to be touched, so I reach out blindly and roll them both between my fingers and thumbs at the same time, probably a little too hard but Imogen gasp-moans again anyway.

She's over my lower belly, my cock against her ass, and before I know it she's reached behind her and grabbed it in one hand, stroking me from root to tip slowly, surely, and *God* I wish I could see right now.

Her hips flex against me. I take one hip in my hand, my thumb at the soft juncture where it meets her thigh, slide it in until I've found her clit and she's made *that* noise again, grinding into me, her pussy leaving a wet spot on my treasure trail.

Imogen gasps, moans, whimpers. I can tell from the sound she makes that she's biting her lip against the sound, her hand stroking me the entire time, the constant pressure and friction of her hand on me driving me completely insane.

She whimpers again, and I exhale hard, force myself not to open my mouth and *beg* her to climb on already, my cock aching to be inside her again after last night.

Finally, she lifts her hips, arches her back, one hand lightly on my chest, and I hold my breath. *Growl* like an animal as she finds her entrance with the tip of my cock, then groan as she slides down me slowly, like she wants to make sure I can feel every fucking millimeter of this.

I do. I feel every single one as she takes me, panting for breath, both her hands on my chest and her hips flexing, her muscles tight around me as I sink deep.

There's that sigh of satisfaction, her hand opening and flattening on my chest as she puts her weight on me, her fingers dragging over my chest like an afterthought. Another squeak of pleasure as she moves her hips and I push back, slightly, in that way I know presses me against every nerve and pleasure center she's got, my hands curled around her thighs like it'll help me control myself.

She starts riding me, going so slow that at first, I'm not even sure she's moving until I can feel her flex and clench around me, the sensation followed by a soft sigh, by the gathering heat in my lower belly.

Fuck, I wish I could see her. I want to see the way her eyes are closed and her mouth is open, the roll of her hips. I want to see myself slide into her, her juices on my shaft. *This* is new, this slow and sensuous Imogen, this girl who seems like she knows what she needs from me and is willing to take it.

And hell yes, I'll give it to her. I meet every soft thrust of her hips with my own, angling myself into her, feeling her muscles tremble and shudder, the soft grip of her bare skin against mine.

She shifts one leg, leans back, her foot suddenly next to my side and her hand anchored on my thigh, right above my knee. The angle changes and we both moan together, her full-throated and me between my teeth because I didn't think this could feel better, but it *does* and I know she's right there, her fucking glorious body stretched out where I can't see it, her ribcage rising and falling beneath her skin.

I'm clenching my fists on her thighs, grinding my teeth, fighting myself as Imogen takes me exactly the way that she wants to, and it drives me absolutely fucking crazy, but I don't stop her even though I'm afraid I'm going to come first.

I find her clit again with my thumb. She makes a noise, pushes herself down my shaft, taking me deep and hard as I circle her button lightly, trying to focus on anything but *this*.

It doesn't work. Of course it doesn't work because Imogen moans, she flexes, she pulls back and does it again but a little harder this time. She's *demanding* this of me, using me for her own pleasure and in this moment there's nothing I've ever wanted more than for her to do exactly this, use me and ride me and do whatever she wants.

She gasps, whimpers, squeaks, moans. Her hips move faster, and through the dark I can see the barest outline of her form like a wraith in the dark and I have to clench my teeth again, force myself not to come before she does even as her muscles flutter and clench around me, getting close.

I squeeze my eyes shut, focus all my willpower on holding off when suddenly she slows again, gasping. Her nails dig into my thigh as she pushes me deep and then suddenly she shudders, moans.

Imogen tightens around me like a fist as she comes, a moan escaping her throat as she rocks back and forth, getting every last ounce of pleasure that she can from me and I give it up, willingly, angling myself so I hit *that* spot over and over again as she comes wordlessly but loudly.

I follow her. There's nothing else I can do when I feel the slow, hard pressure of her release, no way I can fight it. I pull her down hard, sliding against her skin-to-skin as I come inside her, the thrill of something we've never done before spiking white-hot pleasure through my brain.

I let it wash over me, over us. I feel like we're in a slow-motion film because I'm sure I've never come this hard or this *long* before, until we're both trembling, shaking, beads of perspiration on my chest despite the cold.

She moves her leg, hinges at the hip, leans over and kisses me. Her tongue is in my mouth and I'm still inside her, feeling the aftershocks rock through her as we kiss like we didn't just fuck but like we're about to.

Slowly, she moves off me, back to my side. She curls against me, and I put my arm around her shoulders, pull her head into my shoulder, her arm going around my belly, and suddenly I understand something.

This is what I want. This is what I wanted all along, these quiet moments in the dark, this feeling like you share a body and a soul with another person. This feeling that, even though you're deep in the wilderness and might be doomed, everything is fine because she's here.

This is what I wanted. This is what I missed, what I fucked up back when I was too stupid to see it.

Imogen's breathing slows, evens out, but I keep holding her tightly, staring into the pitch-black dark of this tiny, ugly hunting cabin.

I have to keep this, I think to myself, over and over again.

CHAPTER TWENTY-EIGHT
WILDER

TEN YEARS AGO

Imogen crosses her arms in front of herself, feet planted shoulder-width, chin jutting forward.

She's serious. I can't believe that here, after all this time — *months* — she's serious. For fuck's sake, I'm not even wearing a shirt, and she comes in here with this?

"No," I say, crossing my own arms, leaning against the hotel room's dresser, mimicking her stance.

"If you don't, I will," she says.

I just laugh.

"I *will*," she insists, her chin jutting out a little more. "I swear to God, Wilder."

The fire behind me crackles. Jesus fucking Christ, there's a fire and everything, even though it's a warm May night. Relatively warm, anyway, warm for northern Idaho. The room's free because the skiing season is over, so I can have my run of the place again.

Fuck, I can't believe I finagled this room just for Imogen to come in here and act like she's the morality police, for her to give me this bullshit ultimatum out of nowhere.

She thinks just because we're fucking she can tell me what to do?

I just laugh at her, putting every ounce of scorn and derision I can manage into the sound.

"And you think she's gonna believe you?" I ask. "You think that, if *you*, Imogen Gustavo, tell literally anyone in the whole school that you've been screwing *me*, they'll believe you?"

She swallows hard, and I can practically hear the gears in her brain grinding, trying to think of some proof she has.

But I don't think there *is* any. It's more an accident than on purpose, but we only ever texted or emailed about class stuff, and we spent plenty of time together in public, *studying*.

"I can't do this anymore," she finally says, looking at the floor. "I can't—"

Her voice cracks and she turns around, paces to the door, into the bathroom, paces back out, still won't look at me. Instead she stares at the wall.

Here she is, tearing my heart into pieces and she won't even fucking *look* at me.

"I can't watch you *be* with her and know that she doesn't know about us," she finally tells the wall. I think she's crying, but I look away instead of at her. If she won't look at me I won't fucking look at her, that's fine.

"She doesn't care," I insist, even though I'm pretty sure I'm lying.

"She doesn't care because she doesn't know!" Imogen says, and starts pacing again.

Still no eye contact.

"Melissa *likes* you," she says. "Like, she really *likes* you,

Wilder, the other day she was telling me that she hoped you guys went to the same college and stuff—"

I snort, and finally Imogen shoots me a look. It's tear-stained and acidic, but at least she looks at me.

"—And that she really sees you together in ten years, and how sweet you are for never pressuring her about having sex, and how that's why she's thinking of maybe letting you *do stuff* with her, because you're *such* a fucking gentleman."

"You're jealous," I tell her, letting a smirk settle onto my face.

I'm determined to stay cool, stay calm in the face of Hurricane Imogen. She doesn't get to decide what happens here, I do, and fuck her for thinking she can make me do what she wants.

"Of course I'm jealous!" Imogen yelps. "Everyone thinks you're with her! You hold hands in public! You kiss her in the cafeteria, you tell people she's your girlfriend, she's met your parents…"

"No," I say slowly. "You're jealous that you might not have *this* to yourself anymore."

I gesture at my dick.

Imogen makes a very unladylike snort.

"You're not going to fuck her," she says, and she's *so* certain and *so* cocky about it that it makes me want to prove her wrong.

"Why not? She's my girlfriend. That's who most people fuck."

Imogen opens her mouth, closes it, opens it again and looks away like she's hoping for backup from somewhere, but obviously no one's coming to her rescue.

"No," she says, like she's astonished. "If you fuck her we're over. Are you kidding me? No."

I just shrug.

"I didn't know it was an option until now," I say.

I'm being deliberately cruel and I know it, but it feels *good* to watch Imogen cry after she came in here, all high and mighty, demanding that I tell Melissa the truth about us.

Imogen thinks that this is how she gets me. She thinks I'm going to break up with Melissa — my picture-perfect cheerleader girlfriend — for *her*, the weird nerd.

And it's not even that. She thinks she can fucking *tell me* what to do and how to do it.

She swallows, shakes her head, crosses her arms in front of herself again.

"If you don't tell her about us I will," she says again, stubbornly. "She doesn't deserve you doing this to her."

"She won't believe you," I warn, still smirking at her. "I'm telling you, Squeaks, no one's going to fucking *believe* you."

Her mouth settles into a hard line as another tear drips down her face. The sight of her in tears pleases me in a terrible, hard, bright way. At least I know I have *this* power over her, even if she's got the power to rip my heart out of my body by basically telling me we're over.

I'm not stupid. We're not going to survive this fight. Imogen and I are fucking done for as of tonight, even though she clearly thinks that I'm going to roll over and break up with Melissa to date her.

Hell no. Imogen can barely string two sentences together when she's in a group of people. I can't tell my friends that she's my girlfriend, I can't take her on dates and shit. No one would ever talk to me again.

"Yes, she will," Imogen whispers, and then she turns on her heel, grabs her backpack, and she's gone through the door.

I just stand there, staring at it, long after it closes. I'm still shirtless because my plan for tonight was to light this fire, wait for Imogen on the plush faux-fur rug, and then have her sit on my face for as long as she wanted.

It didn't fucking happen, clearly. It's never going to fucking happen again, and that fact twists my stomach into a pretzel of regret and sadness and ten thousand other bad feelings I can't even begin to identify.

But it won't work. She can tell Melissa all she wants, but I know about Imogen's reputation in ways that she doesn't, and she's a quiet, strange, off-kilter girl who's super smart, a little delusional, and has an enormous crush on me, the guy she tutors in biology.

I haven't done much to dissipate that reputation, for the record.

So she can tell Melissa anything she wants. It doesn't matter. At worst, Melissa will come to me, crying prettily, and ask me if it's true and I'll say of course not. I'll wipe away her tears and it'll be everyone's word against Imogen's, and in a couple of months maybe I'll get up her short little cheerleading skirt.

Done and done.

CHAPTER TWENTY-NINE
IMOGEN

PRESENT DAY

"You're the one who was so hot to trot yesterday," Wilder says, towering over me as we both stand in the doorway of the hunting cabin, looking out at the dawn.

"Hot to trot?" I murmur, not moving, just staring out at the mostly-frozen lake that nearly killed him. "Who are you, my dad?"

"Gross," he laughs.

Wilder puts one hand on my shoulder, slides his thumb onto my bare neck, massages one of the tight muscles there.

I let him. Part of me still feels like this is dangerous, like we shouldn't be touching each other at all, like I shouldn't be falling for this anymore, but that part might be stupid.

It's nice. It's been ten years. I'm different now, why can't Wilder be different too?

He can act like this now because there's no one to see, that part of me whispers.

Out here he doesn't have to explain that he actually likes the weird girl. The wolves and squirrels don't give a shit if the awkward nerd is his girlfriend.

He's being nice because it's a secret.

I swallow hard, trying to shove all those feelings down along with the shock of nerves and apprehension I feel about leaving the cabin, but it's pretty obvious that no one is coming, at least not in the next couple of days, and there's no method of communication in there.

My ankle's taped again and doesn't hurt nearly as much when we first got here. Wilder's clothes are all dry. We ate plenty of disgusting store-brand canned chili, we took the sleeping bags.

And we found the road. It's a fire road, hardly more than a couple of ruts through the forest, but it's ten times better than trying to find our own way through the trees and bushes only to end up on a cliff we have to go around or at a body of water we can't cross or something.

If we just *go*, it looks like a two-day hike. A long and miserable two days, yeah, but only two days and then maybe, *probably*, civilization at the end.

We hope there's civilization at the end. If not, I don't know.

"I'm gonna miss the wood stove," I admit.

"C'mon, Squeaks," he says, and pushes me gently forward, down the three rudimentary steps and to the mostly-frozen, half-muddy ground. "On and into the wild. We're almost there."

"We're not," I point out. "We're technically not that much closer than we were when we first—"

"Just walk," he says, his voice steady and calm.

I think about arguing, but instead I adjust the pack on my back — I've got the smaller one that we found in the cabin, Wilder's got the big one that I had before, since his is at the bottom of the lake — and I start walking.

WE WALK. And walk. And walk, until my ankle screams and I think my feet might fall off, and then I walk some more.

The road is easier, at least, rudimentary as it is. It's still just dirt, and it's full of things to trip over in the just-melting snow, full of mud and holes and all that stuff, but it's nice to know that we've got the way out in our grasp.

As we walk, we talk. Wilder tells me about realizing that he wasn't going to get into college, and if he *did* get into college he was just going to fail out, so he infuriated his father and joined the military. He tells me how now Flint Holdings will probably go to his younger brother Grayson, because his dad doesn't think he can handle it.

Later that night, we zip together the sleeping bags and huddle together, still in most of our layers and our coats. The wolves are howling again, but they're further away now. I think.

We walk another day. I tell him about how my life was hell after prom, how I became a hermit in my parents' house just so I wouldn't have to see anyone while I took enough summer school classes to get my diploma and then a semester's worth of courses at Solaris Community College before somehow miraculously getting into Stanford mid-year.

I tell him how that wasn't a piece of cake either, but it was better than Idaho. *Anything* was better than Idaho, back then.

We talk about basic training and flight school, how the Navy actually has more planes and pilots than the Air Force. We talk about going to therapy and actually getting diagnosed with an anxiety disorder and how it felt like *finally* someone gave me a user's manual to my brain.

We sleep in the sleeping bags again, too cold and too exhausted to do more than sleep.

Day three dawns darker than the first two, and even as we're packing up the sleeping bags, re-taping my ankle, and eating cold store-brand chili, it feels like something is wrong, like the light is different, like there's something bad coming.

It feels like I'm being watched by eyes I can't see, like behind every tree is some vague menace that I can't name or understand, but that's definitely *there*.

I don't mention it to Wilder, because I don't want to sound crazy. Even if I'm not a wilderness survival expert like he seems to think he is, I know that constant cold and hunger and exhaustion can mess with your brain. I wonder if I'm having a low-level hallucination — not enough to have a chat with someone who's not there, but enough to feel like reality is different.

Wilder seems uncomfortable too, but he doesn't say anything. Maybe he doesn't want to make me worry, either, so we walk for most of that morning in silence. Comfortable silence, but still silence, filling our water bottles every time the fire road crosses a stream.

It's a couple hours after we leave that there's a break in the trees overhanging the road and I look back at where we came from. I've been doing that every so often, trying to spot the ridge where we crashed so I can see how far we've come already.

Only this time the skyline looks different, like there's another set of mountains behind the ones we came from and it takes me a moment to realize what it is: storm clouds.

Massive, ugly, heart-twisting storm clouds. They're tall, taller than the mountains beneath them, sharp shadows delineating each and every fluffy, dangerous billow. Their undersides are so dark they're nearly black, making the midday sun look strange and pale.

I just stop, fear prickling through my limbs.

They're so far away, I tell myself. *You don't even know that they're heading in your direction, they'll probably blow right on past or go somewhere else.*

"They're twenty miles off," Wilder says, standing next to me, staring in the same direction, like he's echoing my thoughts.

I hope he's right. I hope we're both right, but I don't know that I believe it.

"How far are we from the valley mouth?" I ask.

He sighs, adjusts his hat on his head. The maps we were looking at are at the bottom of the lake, so I know it's a guess at best.

"Not that far," he guesses. "A few miles, maybe?"

I just nod and don't ask the other question that's on the tip of my tongue, because I know he doesn't know the answer: what then? Is there anything out there *then*?

We just keep moving. I make a rule that I can only look over my shoulder at the clouds every five hundred steps, so I count to distract myself.

The valley mouth looked obvious from higher up in the mountains when we first saw it, but now that we're close there's no real way to tell. The mountains just keep looking like mountains, high and forbidding, and it seems like they go on forever. We could be through already and maybe we wouldn't know.

Maybe the whole thing was a false hope. The clouds behind us keep getting closer, the sunlight getting paler, like it's being sucked away.

Then we hear the noise.

It's late afternoon, the sun on the decline. The wind is picking up just enough that we've both noticed but haven't said anything to each other, because what is there to say? What is there to *do* except keep walking, counting my steps, looking over my shoulder every five hundred so I don't jinx it?

But we both stop, stand there, still as stone, and just *listen*.

It doesn't happen again. There's nothing but perfect, crystalline silence, the slight crackle of birds hopping from branch to branch, the faint drip of the snow *just* starting to melt from the trees.

"It was the wind," I tell Wilder, still holding my breath.

He tilts his head, turns in a slow half-circle, listening.

"Are you sure?" he murmurs.

I go silent again.

"No," I finally say. "But I don't want to get my hopes up."

He nods, and we keep walking. I'm pretty sure we're at the mouth of the valley that we could see from the cabin, only it doesn't look like that close-up. Close-up it just looks like it opens onto more mountains and then mountains behind that, all white peaks shot through with gray, wispy clouds around them, nothing more to see anywhere.

We walk until we hear the noise again, maybe thirty minutes later, and *this* time it's not the wind. This time it's louder, more of a grunt than a whisper, and my heart leaps in my chest when I hear it.

"That was a truck!" I shout, grabbing Wilder's arm.

He goes still, listening, his eyes searching through the trees over my head like he'll be able to see something there.

"It was," I whisper, grabbing him harder. "That was the sound of a semi engine-braking, it used to wake me up all the time at night when I was a kid because we lived near this highway—"

It sounds again, the unmistakable deep stutter that's so

obviously mechanical, and I start laughing, one gloved hand over my face.

"I think you're right," Wilder says, a smile ghosting across his face.

"I *know* I'm right!" I yelp, letting him go and practically hopping up and down with excitement. "It sounds like it's *right* through those trees, I bet we could cut through and——"

"Stay on the road," he says.

I eye the trees to my right just as I hear the truck's groan again, further away now, fading into the distance.

"Imagine breaking an ankle when we're this close," he points out. "Come on. We'll hit the main road, I'm positive."

I'm tempted to argue with him, but I'm too giddy, too happy that maybe my days of being cold and hungry and in pain are almost over, that maybe I'll spend tonight in a real bed wearing something besides the same outfit I've worn for longer than I want to think about.

Just as I let Wilder's arm go, a single drop of something lands right on my nose, like it's mocking me. I blink in surprise, then wipe it away with one finger as Wilder frowns, his eyes on the sky over my head.

"Shit," he says quietly, and I turn.

The black sky is closer, though up this close it's more of a hard steel gray, the color of shark skin. It's moving, undulating, and as we stand there more drops fall, dotting the sleeves of my coat. I can't tell if they're freezing rain or just regular rain, but I know they're not snowflakes. It's just a little too warm for that at this lower elevation, this time of year.

"We gotta move," Wilder says, adjusting the pack on his back. "Come on."

CHAPTER THIRTY
WILDER

This is bad. There's a heavy feeling in my gut, and there has been all day, watching the storm get closer and closer. It's got that ugly, dangerous color, and worst of all it's not even dropping snow.

Snow would be one thing, but now we're at a low enough elevation that, at this time of year, it's *just* above freezing during the day. That means the snow is dropping rain that'll freeze at night, or it's dropping freezing rain. Snow would be almost okay, nice and fluffy and easy to brush off your jacket.

But that doesn't work when the precipitation is liquid. This stuff sinks in, no matter how waterproof your gear is. At night it'll probably go below freezing, but the ground will be wet and we'll be wet and that's dangerous as hell.

We have to get to that road, and we need to do it while it's still light. I'm tempted to take Imogen's suggestion and go through the woods, but we've come so far that I don't want to find ourselves on a cliff again or have her step in a hole, finally snap her weak ankle.

"Slow down," she gasps behind me.

Imogen's limping pretty bad, even though I've been re-taping her ankle every morning. She hasn't said a peep, but I *know* it has to hurt.

"Sorry," I say, slowing my pace to wait for her. "I got excited."

She just nods, droplets of water adorning her hat.

"I know," she says. "Me too."

We keep moving. The fire road we're on slopes gently downhill, staying close to the base of the mountain. I *think* we walked out of the valley today, or at least what we thought was the valley — with no map it's hard to tell, and God knows I've been focusing mostly on putting one foot in front of the other.

We're silent. The precipitation starts coming down a little harder. The light gets lower, and I can't tell if it's because the sun's dipped behind the mountains or if it's the storm cloud overhead, but either way it's not good. Time passes, maybe an hour, maybe more.

Suddenly, the road we're on forks. One branch goes straight, still hugging the mountain, but another branch curves right, through the trees and more sharply downhill. It's the first time in days we've had a choice, and we both stop, look at each other.

"That one," Imogen says, pointing to the sharp downhill.

We haven't heard another truck sound, but I follow her lead anyway even though I know that the road we heard might have curved earlier, might be miles away by now, but we slog. It gets muddy. Our trail crosses a couple of streams and we have to hop carefully from rock to rock so we don't dunk our feet in the cold water.

I carry Imogen over one because I don't think she'll make it with her ankle.

And then, just when I think we should have stuck to the other trail, it's there in front of us.

Salvation. Rescue.

Heaven is a two-lane blacktop with a thick yellow dotted line down the middle, the trees on either side of it lashing back and forth as the wind picks up, cold half-frozen rain pelting down even harder.

We stop and stare. Imogen shoves her glasses up her face, dotted with water droplets, and we both look left, then look right, then look left again.

"It's a road," Imogen says, even though we obviously both know it's a road. "Did your map say which way we should walk?"

"The map wasn't even sure there was a road here," I say.

"Pick one."

The wind picks up again, shaking slush out of the tree branches, snow sodden with freezing rain. The light is getting dimmer by the minute, and we haven't heard anything since we heard a truck engine braking an hour or two ago.

We might be sleeping outside again, this time in the cold wet. We're both hungry, we've been walking for three days now, and even though she won't admit it I can tell that Imogen is flagging.

"Left," I say.

We walk down the middle of the road, and it's mercifully faster than the trail we've been on for the past few days. Imogen's limp is better on the asphalt than it was on the uneven dirt, but she's still limping. I'm shivering, she's shivering worse.

Come on, I think. *We didn't get all this way just to freeze to death on a highway.*

The sun goes down, I think, though it's hard to tell with

the storm slowly picking up, the wind driving the rain into the creases of my coat, slowly creeping through the layers I'm wearing until it's chilling me, right next to my skin.

Imogen's trudging along next to me, and I have the urge to reach out and take her hand, but I know we're both warmer with our hands shoved in our pockets.

"We should think about stopping soon," I finally say. "The sun's nearly down and it'll take us a while to figure out shelter."

She doesn't respond.

"Hey, Squeaks," I say, trying to fire up some kind of reaction from her, but instead of listening to me, she takes a step forward, staring down the highway. Then another step, and I squint into the near-dark, trying to figure out what she's so intent on.

Then I see it: white lights playing on the trees to one side of the road, moving and flickering.

It's a truck, two blazing headlights barreling through the darkness, and it comes around a bend and then it's headed straight for us, the rain nothing but sharp lines through the light.

"Hey!" Imogen yells, waving both her arms over her head.

She limps forward, hops, tries to jog, limps faster.

"HEY!"

The truck doesn't slow down, just keeps barreling toward her, but I can see the set of Imogen's shoulders as she stands dead in front of it, letting it bear down. Now she's waving her arms, screaming at it, and it's getting closer and closer in a horrible game of chicken that I *know* she can't win.

"STOP!" she screams, still waving. "Goddammit you fucking asshole just stop, *please* just fucking stop, just stop, please—"

The truck's horn blares, practically sending a shock-wave through the night, but it doesn't look like it's slowing down at all. A million possibilities run rampant through my head — drugs, guns, military stuff, illegal shit — as I sprint forward to Imogen.

She screams. I shout. The truck honks again, and then I grab her and pull her to the side of the road, just barely out of the way of the truck.

We stumble through the mud and gravel as the huge vehicle whooshes past, misting us with even more water, so close we can feel the breeze of its wheels.

Fuck, that was close. The first thing we do when we find civilization and we nearly get hit by a truck.

"He saw me!" Imogen shouts, my hand still around her arm. "That motherfucker saw me, he *had* to see me—"

I pull her in, close my arms around her, press my face against her hair because she's right. I know she's right, and we're both *so* cold and *so* tired and *so* hungry that in the moment, standing in front of a truck seemed anything but insane.

"I know," I murmur.

Imogen bursts into tears. She wraps her arms around me and just *sobs*.

She's never done this before. Not with me, at least; the few times I've seen her cry she's been angry and fighting tears the whole way, but now she just leans against me in the rain, on the side of this road, and she cries.

I hold her. There's nothing else I can do, no way to make this any better. All I can do is stand here, let her cry, and hope that someone else will come along who's not a dick.

"We're gonna be okay," I whisper, even though I'm not at all sure. "It's a road, there will be more…"

I glance over her head and my words trail off, because

there are two pulsing red dots way up ahead in the road, blurry with rain.

Flashing brake lights.

"He stopped," I tell Imogen.

She jerks her head up, looks behind her. Sniffles hard and wipes a glove across her face, leaving a smear of dirt as she squints through her wet glasses.

I grab her hand.

"Come on," I say, and practically pull her back onto the road.

I walk as fast as she can handle, and even though I want to sprint as fast as I can before this guy has a chance to drive away, I don't leave her behind.

"Hey!" I shout, waving my other arm.

We reach the back of the truck and Imogen reaches out, touches it like she wants to make sure it's real.

"There you are," a man's voice calls back. "Shit, I thought I was seeing things."

The sound of feet hitting the pavement, and then a man's shape is outlined in the yellow light from the truck cab: middle-aged, slight paunch, flannel shirt.

"Sorry," he goes on. "These things take a while to stop, 'specially when it's weathering like this."

We close the last few steps between us, stop in front of him. Imogen's gasping for air, balancing on her left leg, and I'm trying to take as much of her weight as I can as the cold water drips from my hair and into my clothes, soaking me to the skin as the rain lashes us.

The trucker frowns, steps closer, peers at us.

"Shit," he says quietly. "What the hell are the two of you doing out here?"

CHAPTER THIRTY-ONE
IMOGEN

TEN YEARS AGO

Melissa just *stares* at me, her pencil suspended over the rough draft of her English paper. We're in her parents' den again, sitting on the couch. This time her mom made rice krispy treats, and they're neatly arranged in a small pyramid on the coffee table in front of us.

"You're lying," she says, slowly sitting up straight.

I just shake my head. My heart is beating so fast it's practically fluttering in my chest, and I feel like I've got a vise around my lungs. I know my face is beet red, and I think I might cry with sheer nerves any second now.

It took me three days to work up the courage to tell her. I threw up four times, and I've already been at her house for an hour before finally blurting out *I'm sleeping with Wilder!* while trying to answer her questions about passive sentence constructions.

"I'm not," I say quietly, my voice shaking.

"He would *never* sleep with you," she says, her voice sharper with every word, filled with disdain.

"Yes he would," I say. "He did."

"Why are you doing this?"

I swallow hard, forcing myself not to cry in front of her.

"I felt too guilty lying about it any longer, and I told him that he had to tell you or I would—"

"I mean, why are you lying?" she says, crossing her arms in front of herself. "There's no *way* he'd sleep with you. He told me he loves me last week, and everyone knows that you have some weird *thing* for him which is why you're always asking if he wants to study and stuff, and he only says yes because he feels so bad for you."

I'm stunned, open-mouthed. My mind goes totally blank and I can't think of anything to say while Melissa sits there with her perfect pink lips and her pretty blue eyes and looks at me like I'm some sort of circus sideshow.

"Is that what he said?" I whisper.

She rolls her eyes.

"Did you think everyone didn't know?"

I can't speak.

"Look, you have some weird thing for my boyfriend and I let it slide because you've been helping me with this English paper but you seriously have to *stop*, Imogen, it's really weird and I think maybe one of these days you're gonna make a flamethrower or something and come to school with it…"

I tune her out, because I suddenly remember something.

It was an accident. Most of the kids at Solaris High have smart phones by now, but I just got my first cell phone a couple of months ago, an older-model flip phone that my parents have reiterated a thousand times is *only* to be used for emergencies.

But it turns out that if you press some combination of the buttons on the side, it starts recording audio. I found that out a few weeks back when I accidentally recorded Wilder going down on me.

Meaning it's mostly me, gasping and moaning and squeaking, trying and failing *miserably* not to make too much noise, but he's on there too.

I pull my phone out. My hand is shaking, and Melissa stops talking when she realizes I'm doing something.

I hit play.

From my phone, Wilder laughs.

"No, it's because I like the way you turn bright pink when I say stuff like *I'm gonna lick your pussy until you come*," he says, his voice tinny and hushed, but obviously his.

My recorded voice joins his in a nervous giggle, and I have to put one hand over my mouth because I'm afraid I'll throw up.

Melissa's gone white, her mouth open.

"You made this up somehow," she whispers, tears wobbling in her eyes.

I just shake my head, terrified of speaking.

"That's not—" she stutters, tears falling prettily onto her cheeks. "He would never— You can't—"

"I'm sorry," I say, stumbling over even those simple words.

In a flash her eyes harden, and her jaw tightens. Before I know what's happening she's grabbed my phone, leapt off the couch, and run to the bathroom, the lock clicking seconds before I reach the door behind her.

"Melissa!" I hiss, rattling the knob.

"Go away," she says, her voice dripping with tears.

"Give me my phone."

"Go *away*."

"Melissa, seriously," I beg, trying to keep my voice down because the absolute last thing I want is for her parents to come see what's going on.

No answer. It goes on like that for a couple of minutes, long enough for her to listen to the whole thing a few times.

Through the door I can just barely hear myself, and even though it was hot at the time — hot enough that I didn't delete the recording, because honestly, I kind of liked it — right now it's the worst thing I've ever heard. I crumple against the bathroom door, tears sliding down my face.

How could you be so stupid? I think, over and over again.

Who cares if she believed you? It's true, what does it matter if Melissa knew or not?

I've got a bad, bad feeling that I might have just really fucked up.

Finally, the bathroom door opens. I look up at Melissa, ugly for once with puffy eyes and blotchy skin.

She drops my phone on the floor next to me.

"Get out," she says, and ten seconds later I'm gone.

Present Day

THE NEXT TWENTY-FOUR hours are a blur, as for once I give up my own will and just let people do things to me.

I let the trucker put us in his cab, turn the heat on full blast, and drive us through the rain to Black Mountain Junction.

I let the Black Mountain Junction volunteer fire department load us into their ambulance and drive us to McBride Mills, the nearest town with a hospital.

I let the hospital staff take off my clothes, layer me with heating pads, put an IV in my arm. I let them do whatever the hell they want as I answer their questions, lie still while they X-ray my ankle.

All I know is that I'm warm, I'm dry, and they're giving me soup. Wilder's somewhere too, and I make a half-hearted effort at telling the people whirling around us that he fell into a lake, that he was hypothermic for a while and they should check him out for that, but they don't pay much attention to me.

Finally, I accept that they know what they're doing and relax into the sweet, sweet arms of comfort.

———

I WAKE up the next morning groggy, almost like I'm hungover. I feel like I've slept for twelve hours and like it wasn't enough, but the phone next to my bed is ringing and ringing, and I finally wake up enough to realize that I should answer it.

"Hello?" I ask

"Oh my God," my mom's voice says.

She bursts into tears.

"Hey Mom," I say, still groggy. I sit up in the hospital bed, blinking, trying all at once to get a handle on where I am and what I'm doing here and how I even got here, not to mention how to comfort my mom who's now out-and-out sobbing on the other end of the line.

"Uh, I'm fine, I'm in the hospital in…"

I try to think of the town name and fail.

"…I'm in the hospital somewhere, but I'm okay, don't worry. Sorry."

"I know," my mom says between sobs. "No, sweetie, it's not your fault, don't apologize, I just—" She breaks into a fresh round of sobbing, and in the background, I hear my dad say something.

"I don't know how to do that, Barry, I told you it never works for me and it always hangs up the pho—"

Suddenly all the background noise gets louder, cutting into my mom's sentence. I raise my eyebrows at the opposite wall of my hospital room, not that listening to my parents try to figure out how to use their cell phone is anything new.

"Immers, honey, it's your dad," he says, his phone voice a little too loud.

"Hey, Dad," I say. "Can you tell Mom that I'm gonna be fine, I promise?"

The revelation that the person with me was Wilder Flint can wait, because the only two people on this planet who hated him more than me were my parents.

"We're in the Edmonton airport," he booms.

I can practically see the two of them, standing somewhere and probably blocking foot traffic, my dad holding the phone about a foot in front of them, speaking very loudly and clearly.

They're hippie types, kind of old school, and they never really took to technology.

"We're trying to get a flight closer to where you are, so we can rent a car and come see you," he says. "We originally booked a flight with AirCanada, but it was one of those flights that's actually operated by their regional jet service and it got canceled because there weren't enough people on the flight, only you know how these airlines are and if they tell you why it was really canceled they've gotta refund your ticket and pay for your meals so they're claiming it's a weather issue but you know I can watch the weather channel too and there's nothing but blue sky between here and McBride Mills, those greedy corporate bastards…"

I close my eyes, lean back against the pillows, and let my dad rail on about corporate greed for a while, occasionally punctuated by my mom telling me how glad she is that

I'm okay. My dad's got a habit of ranting on about whatever's in front of him at the time when he gets stressed or upset — something my therapist pointed out — so when he moves on to checked baggage fees and having to pay more for the same seats he'd have gotten for a better deal thirty years ago, I just smile and nod at the phone.

I'm pretty sure I know what he's *actually* stressed and upset about.

"Okay, Barry, that's enough," my mom finally says once my dad's gone on for a while. "We've gotta go talk to the airline and see what they can do—"

"Got half a mind to rent a car right here and just drive to the hospital."

"We can't drive, there are mountains, Barry," my mom says, suddenly the reasonable one.

"Might have to if we want to see our daughter before the dawn of the next millennium."

"Sweetie, we're so glad you're safe and sound and all right," my mom says, her voice tearing up again. "We'll be there as soon as we can get there, okay?"

I swallow the lump in my throat, because I feel absolutely awful. It didn't even occur to me, the whole time I was out there, that my parents were probably looking for me like crazy.

"Okay, Mom," I say. "Thanks."

CHAPTER THIRTY-TWO
WILDER

Man, hospitals suck. There's nothing on TV except talk shows, and even though I'm watching two rednecks throw chairs and threaten each other right now, it's *boring*. Something about a dog coming into the wrong yard or some shit.

I don't have my phone. I've got no idea where it is, since it was pretty much useless in the wilderness, except now I wish I could at least play Angry Birds or something while they keep me another day or two for observation and fluids.

I'm very much under the impression that that McBride Mills hospital doesn't get a whole lot of exciting action. It's pretty small, as hospitals go, and nearly everyone else I've seen here has gray hair and a walker.

They won't tell me how Imogen is, other than *fine*. They won't tell me where she is, either, and since I already got sternly admonished once for getting out of bed and trying to walk around with my IV stand, I'm gonna hold off on trying it again for a few hours.

I mean, the hospital's not very big. I'll just keep trying to find her until I actually do.

I flip TV channels. Some weird cartoon, a close-up of a crying woman, a telenovela. Jesus, I'm bored.

There's a knock on my door and before I can say anything it's pushed open, the curtain in front of it swishing back.

"There you are," my mom says, her upper body practically sagging with relief. "The front desk told me the wrong room—" she tosses her purse on a cart "—but the person in there was some old guy, and then I started worrying that I'd gotten the wrong hospital or something or that someone had told me *wrong* and you were still out there—"

She leans over me and kisses my forehead, one hand on my shoulder.

"Hey, Mom," I manage to slip in between sentences.

She sits, and I realize her eyes are watering, brimming with tears.

"Hey, baby," she says, taking my hand. "You look terrible, are you okay?"

I squeeze her hand, and she squeezes back.

"I'm gonna be fine."

"I got here as soon as I could," she says. "I almost got in a screaming match with the guy behind the desk at the private air terminal in Solaris when he tried to tell me that our jet was already being used by some big shots in the oil industry who were headed back to North Dakota, but luckily one of them was standing right there and he was *so* nice and made me take the plane instead," she says, sighing.

I wonder, very briefly, where my dad is or if he's coming. I don't ask, though, because I'm pretty sure I know the answer and I'd rather be pleasantly surprised if he *does* show up.

"*Then* I get to the airport only to have the rental car people tell me that they've got the car I've booked, but they didn't realize I was driving to McBride Mills and if I do *that* then they're gonna have to put chains on the tires, and that'll be an extra hour of waiting unless I want to upgrade to all-wheel drive but then of course when they go to check, they haven't got any of those available and — God, baby, I'm sorry, I'm just going on and on, aren't I?" she says.

I squeeze my mom's hand again, reach over, pat hers with my other hand.

"It's okay, Mom," I say. "Don't worry about it."

"How are you feeling?" she asks, brushing hair off my forehead. "Are you warm enough? When they called, the nurse told me you were being treated for hypothermia, and…" she trails off, concern in her eyes.

I swallow hard. My mom is usually impeccably put together, the perfect CEO's wife, but right now she's messy, frazzled. There are dark circles under her eyes and her hair's pulled back from her face, strands poking out here and there.

I feel *awful*. Even if my dad and I have some differences — even if we've barely spoken for almost a year at this point, despite the fact that I technically work for him — my mom's always been there for me. She was at every football game, sent me emails and letters constantly when I was in the Navy.

"I'm doing great, Mom," I say again. "The bad part's over."

"I hope so, baby," she says.

———

BY AROUND SIX THAT NIGHT, the nurses have finally convinced my mom that she should go get a hotel room in town and some rest. Even they can tell how stressed and frazzled she is, and the longer she spends with me, the more obvious it is that my disappearance took a toll.

She won't go into details, but I know two things: they were looking for us in the wrong place, and she is *pissed* at my dad for reasons she won't say. I don't pry, at least not right now.

As soon as she leaves, I push aside the food tray that she insisted on keeping filled, going to the bakery across the street a couple of times and berating the nurses for giving me *lukewarm* soup. I make sure my IV isn't tangled on anything, and I kick my feet over the side of the bed, then stand.

And head out in search of Imogen. By now the nurses who see me up and around don't do anything to stop me, probably because they're afraid that my mom might come back and threaten their jobs, pensions, dogs' lives, and the existence of this very hospital if they dare lift a finger against me.

For the record, my mom is lovely about ninety-nine percent of the time.

I shuffle along the hall in my socks and gown until I finally reach someone behind a desk. I ask her which room Imogen Gustavo is in, and *finally* I get an answer: room 214, just down that way.

When I open the door, three heads turn. Conversation ceases.

Imogen's sitting up in the bed, and she's pale with deep circles under her eyes, but she smiles.

"Hey, Wilder," she says.

CHAPTER THIRTY-THREE
IMOGEN

I was kind of hoping this wouldn't happen.

I've been thinking about Wilder all day, obviously. I've been wondering if I haven't seen him yet because maybe he was in worse shape than I thought, or maybe he's fine and checked out without seeing me, or God forbid maybe something happened and he had some sort of heart attack brought on by the cold and he was dead.

My tired, frenzied brain got a little carried away with the possibilities, running through them all ceaselessly even as I kind of hoped that I wouldn't have to explain just yet to my parents *who* I got stuck in the wilderness with for over a week.

"Hi," he says back, coolly, one eyebrow raised. "Nice to see you, Mr. and Mrs. Gustavo."

They're silent and still for a beat, my dad standing by the window with his hands on his hips, my mom staring up at him like the language centers of her brain just evaporated, hands wringing together in her lap.

At least I know where I get my penchant for awkwardness from.

"It's Mrs. Catton," my mom says without moving. "I kept my maiden name."

"Right," Wilder says, because he already knows that. Or at least he did, back when he'd pick me up from my parents' house for study sessions.

My dad squints at him, a frown deepening on his slightly lined face.

"Are you Marcus Flint's boy?" he asks.

I swallow, because somehow this is already going off the rails.

"Wilder, these are my parents," I tell him. "Mom, Dad, you remember Wilder. He was flying me to Yellowknife."

I don't know why I made the formal introduction. They all know each other, and the way that they're staring each other down proves that they all remember *everything*.

More dead silence.

Great.

At last, my mom clears her throat.

"It's nice to see you again, Wilder," she says, her tone so stiff and formal I think it might shatter on impact. "You were flying the plane?"

I can see his grip on the IV pole he's dragging behind him tighten.

"Yes, I was the pilot," he says.

"Wilder's the reason we made it out," I say quickly, hoping to fend off whatever's about to go down. "He's the one who said we needed to leave the plane behind, if it weren't for him we'd still be there, and you'd have never found us since you were looking in the wrong place, haha!"

"What exactly happened?" my dad asks, moving his arms from his hips only to cross them over the ugly sweater on his chest.

Even though Wilder's wearing socks, a hospital gown,

and has an IV in his hand, he still someone manages to give my dad this cocky, collected look that irritates me instantly.

"Instrument failure," he finally says, jerking his head so his hair's off his forehead. "One minute they said everything was fine, the next we were at fifteen thousand feet and dropping like a stone."

"You lost altitude that fast and you couldn't tell?" my dad asks, incredulously. "My ears pop in an elevator, for crying out loud. How did you not—"

"Dad, could we do this later?" I interrupt.

"He's right, you know," my mom pipes up.

"This boy crashed you into the side of a mountain and nearly killed you!" my dad says, starting to get excited. "How do you not want to know—"

"He *also* crashed himself into the side of a mountain," I point out.

"He didn't break a leg, did he?" my dad asks.

I shove my glasses up my face, frustrated. My parents have perfectly valid reasons to hate Wilder, but this isn't one of them.

"Dad, I don't think he managed to crash-land a small plane so precisely that I broke an ankle and he didn't," I say, forcing my voice calm. "It was an accident. Neither of us wanted it to happen, I promise."

"I'll come back later," Wilder says, his eyes on me. There's a hint of something in their blue-green depths, though whether it annoyance or amusement I can't entirely tell. Maybe some of each.

"—Linda, you *know* that his father, that son of a bitch —" my dad says on the other side of my bed as I try to smile at Wilder.

"Now you're just being ludicrous," my mom answers him. "Honestly, who would crash their *own* plane…"

"That's probably a good idea," I tell Wilder, trying to smile.

———

I FINALLY GET my parents out two hours later, still arguing, though now it's over something that happened thirty years ago with some sweater.

It's kind of how they communicate, especially since they just had a long, sleepless, stressful week, so I don't pay much attention to it. Maybe after we all get some rest they'll be back and better.

When they're finally gone, Wilder comes back, peeking around the curtain, grinning at me.

"Safe?" he asks, raising one eyebrow.

"The coast is clear," I tell him.

He walks in, around the bed. I sneak a peek through the back of his hospital gown, and even though the gown itself us ugly as hell, he somehow makes it look good. Even with socks and an IV pole.

Unfair, I tell you.

He comes up next to my bed, leans in, kisses me on the temple, sits. He acts like it's the most natural thing in the world that he'd kiss me like this, keeping one hand on my shoulder even after he's seated.

My heart's drumming an unfamiliar pattern in my chest. Even though my brain's been going nonstop since I woke up, I haven't *really* thought about the ramifications of our time together in the cabin.

I've got no idea what it all means out here, where there are other people around. Where we'd have to figure shit out because it's suddenly much harder than *I'm here and you're also here and I've been thinking dirty thoughts about you for days and hating myself for it.*

"Is it really broken?" he asks, nodding at my right foot.

I wiggle my toes through my cast.

"Spiral hairline fracture," I confirm. "I got X-rayed this morning."

Wilder sighs, leans back in the chair.

"Shit, Squeaks," he says, his voice suddenly quieter, rougher. "I'm sorry."

I reach up to my shoulder, take the hand that's perched there and hold it, feeling suddenly brave.

Maybe this is something after all.

"Why?"

"For telling you it wasn't."

I start laughing. Wilder smiles after a minute, leaning back in the ugly vinyl armchair, still holding my hand.

"The hell are you laughing about?"

"What if you'd known it was broken? What were you gonna do differently?"

He shakes his hair out of his face, a cocky little head-jerk that I'm realizing I remember from years ago.

"Be nicer," he says.

"Liar."

"I might not have made you cross that landslide."

I just look at him, trying not to laugh.

"Okay, I probably would have," he admits. "It wasn't that bad, you know."

"You didn't fall."

"You could have watched where you were going, that rock was *obviously* going to—"

"Wilder?"

"Hm?"

"Shut the fuck up," I say, and he just laughs.

"Can I at least sign your cast?"

"If you can find a marker."

He grins, stands, winks.

"Be right back," he says, and leaves the room, IV tower in tow. I crane my neck one more time to catch a glimpse of his butt as he walks through the door.

Thirty seconds later he's back with a Sharpie, crouching at the foot of my bed. I can't see what he's writing, but the devilish look in his eyes has me worried.

"What'd you write?" I demand when he stands again, capping the marker.

"You can't read?"

I make a face, craning my neck and just barely lifting my leg so I can see what my cast now says.

Wilder Flint
You're welcome for everything.

I blush. I blush *hard*, and at a loss I push my glasses up my face again even though they haven't moved since the last time I did that.

He just keeps grinning at me, tosses the Sharpie into the air and catches it.

"Jerk," I say, but I'm somewhere between trying not to blush and trying not to laugh.

"No one will know what it means," he says. "Not unless you tell them, and why on earth would you do that?"

"Anyone who reads it is gonna guess exactly what you mean," I counter.

"They'll all know that I'm saying you're welcome for carrying the heavy pack through the wilderness?" he asks, teasing me. "They'll all know that you're welcome that I fell into the lake and not you?"

He's at the foot of my bed, leaning over it, one hand on my other shin. It shouldn't be sexy — the hospital gown, the IV — but between the look in his eyes and the way he's walking his fingers up my leg, that rakish smile… it kind of *is*.

"Well, if that's what you meant," I tease right back. "Though maybe you could write a footnote on there that says something like, 'By that I mean you're welcome for normal, wholesome stuff and definitely not anything dirty.'"

His hand reaches my knee, my thigh. Carefully, slowly, Wilder climbs onto the bed between my legs, certain not to bump my broken ankle.

"But that'd be lying," he says, planting his hands on either side of my hips, his face right in front of mine.

"Are you suddenly opposed to that?" I murmur back.

There's nothing between us and the open door except a curtain. Outside, I can hear two nurses chatting about which movies are coming out this weekend.

"I'm opposed to lying where you're concerned," he says.

I swallow hard, bite back a sarcastic *oh, that's new* response.

"So you just want to brag?" I whisper. "Is that it?"

He grins, moves forward another few inches until the tip of his nose is right at the tip of mine. Somehow, I've moved my good leg up to his side, hugging it against his torso though the other leg is a lost cause at the moment.

"I just want everyone to know, Squeaks," he says. "Everyone on this whole damn planet."

He kisses me, and it's fucking *sensuous*. Even in this hospital bed under the fluorescent lights it's slow and sexy, his mouth exploring mine, his hand on my face, our tongues moving together.

We pause. We turn. We try a new angle, touch lips again experimentally, like it's the very first time we've ever kissed. It *feels* like the first time we've ever kissed, everything somehow new and strange, a wild discovery.

He pulls away, still kneeling between my legs. He runs his hand down my side, beneath the sheets, finds the bottom of my hospital gown, pushes it up, and grins.

"No one gave you underwear either?" he asks.

"Guess they're not standard hospital issue," I say.

He runs a thumb along the crease between my hip and thigh, my whole body going rigid.

I glance toward the door. I can tell it's still wide open. It's still *visiting hours*, and even though I don't know who else might visit it doesn't mean no one will. Hell, a nurse could waltz in here any time she wanted.

"Leave it," he murmurs in my ear.

"But it's *open*," I point out.

"So be quiet for once, Squeaks."

He bites the lobe of my ear, making a thrill run the length of my spine.

"Even if it's not your strong suit."

I bite my lip, letting my eyes drift closed. I hate admitting it but there's something hot about the idea, about knowing that twenty feet away there are people just going about their jobs.

Even if it's also kind of horrifying. It's not like I have a good record with people knowing my sex noises.

"Or tell everyone what we're doing in here," he says, his lips on my neck, hand up my hospital gown. "I'm done with keeping you my dirty secret, Squeaks."

He brushes his fingers over one nipple, bites the other through the gown and I clench my teeth, determined not to make a sound.

"Well," he says, his head moving lower. "I'm done keeping you secret, anyway."

Without warning, the hospital bed buzzes slightly and

tilts backward. I gasp, grabbing the rails, but Wilder just laughs.

"The dirty part can stay," he says.

Then he hikes my thigh over his shoulder, done talking, and within seconds I'm white knuckling the bed rails. I come with my head turned to one side and the pillow pressed to my face, clenched between my teeth, wave after wave rocking my whole body.

Holy shit, I think when it's finally over and I'm practically in a daze, the pillow still in my mouth.

I can't believe he got even better at that.

"And you're completely sure about that?" my dad asks, his voice crackling through the phone. Surprise surprise, McBride Mills, Middle of Nowhere, Canada, has bad cell reception.

"Yeah, Dad, I'm sure," I say, staring out the hospital window, onto the parking lot. It's not even a big parking lot. It's not a big hospital.

In the distance is the angular, faded metal of mining equipment, then more mountains. God, I'm sick of mountains right now, but at least I'm looking at them through a window.

"You know that Flint Holdings does a very thorough monthly inspection of our entire fleet," he says. "For one of our aircraft to suddenly malfunction like that would be very unusu—"

"Do you not believe me?" I ask, my voice blunt and hard.

There's a long pause on the other end of the line, and I clench my jaw.

"Of course I believe you," he finally says.

"I didn't crash-land a plane in the Canadian Rockies for fun."

"Son, I'm not suggesting—"

"Walking through the snow for five days and barely making it out before winding up in the hospital for hypothermia wasn't *fun*," I point out.

I'm staring at the parking lot but I'm seeing my father's face. In a suit, impeccable, as always. Watch on one wrist, and I'm probably on speakerphone while he's driving his BMW to some lunch meeting because God forbid the man take thirty minutes to do nothing but have a conversation with his older son.

"Of course not," he says.

"Then start looking at your planes," I say. "Start looking at who you're hiring and what their problems are, because the plane got fucked up."

He clears his throat. Unperturbed, as always. I wonder what it would take to perturb the man.

"Most plane crashes are caused by pilot error," he says. "And the insurance company is going to grill you five times harder than I am right now, son, so you had better be prepared to explain what exactly happened before they decide you fell asleep while flying."

Suddenly, I remember something else.

"The beacon was missing," I say.

Another long pause. The man is all long pauses, I swear.

"The emergency beacon?"

No, all the other types of beacons that you'd find on a small plane, I think savagely. I don't say it out loud.

"Yeah. It wasn't there."

"You checked the—"

"I *promise* you I checked every single goddamn place on that plane for it," I say through clenched teeth.

Another long pause. I know my father doesn't appreciate being cursed at, but that's not exactly my biggest concern right now.

"I see," he finally says.

Now it's my turn to say nothing. I can practically hear the wheels turning in his head, because *plane crash* is one thing, *emergency beacon missing* is another entirely. The crash could be my fault, but not the beacon.

"I'll have it looked into," he says carefully. "I'm glad you're all right, son."

That, at least, sounds true. He may not believe me about anything else — he may think I was drunk and high and too irresponsible to be flying — but at least he really *is* glad that I'm all right.

"Thanks, Dad," I say, and hang up the phone.

My mom is in and out all day, driving the nursing staff absolutely bonkers by doing stuff like complaining about the croissants in the cafeteria or the way that one of the fluorescent lights in the women's bathroom down the hall blinks too many times when she turns it on.

When she's not there — when she goes back to her hotel room for a bit to have a nap, or when she goes for coffee or something, just to get out of the hospital — I head out of my room to go look in on Imogen.

Once she's asleep, her dad sitting by her bed. He just glares, and since she's not even awake, I just leave.

Another time I peek in and she's got a doctor and a nurse in there, both buzzing around her foot, carefully bending her knee, talking to her and her parents with very serious expressions on their faces. Bending her knees again, turning her leg very lightly side-to-side, and I figure

I may as well let them do their job and show up again later.

———

LATER TAKES A WHILE, because my mom comes back, and she's got croissants. Still not up to her standards — surprise — but apparently there's one "decent-ish" bakery in McBride Mills.

I don't tell her about the conversation I had earlier that day with my dad. I don't see the point, because sooner or later it'll either come out between them or it won't, and neither way is really my problem.

I think I might be done working for Flint Holdings, Inc. I think I might be done with my father's company completely. Something went wrong with the plane, I know it, and he won't admit that *maybe* Wilder the Disappointment actually knows what he's talking about sometimes.

"I don't know why they want to keep you any longer," my mom is saying. She's standing at the sink in my room, wiping down the mirror. There's no reason for her to be doing it, other than the fact that my mom is constantly moving, brimming over right now with nervous energy while I sit in the vinyl chair next to the hospital bed.

The nurses make me get back in the bed every time they want to check me for something. I'm really starting to hate the bed, which isn't even comfortable for five minutes.

"Well, besides the obvious, which is that you've got great insurance because you're American, and they want to bleed that honeypot dry before sending you back to the states," she says. "You know, the same thing happened to Nancy years ago when she went skiing up in Banff and ran into a tree. Just a little concussion, but they absolutely *insisted* on keeping her for two nights for *observation* or some nonsense instead of just letting the poor woman go home…"

I don't respond. My mom's been going on like this for a while now, annoyed at everyone and everything, and the best I can do is just ignore it while wondering when I can get away to visit Imogen again.

She's probably not supposed to be moving her leg a whole lot yet, but we can work around that. Maybe tonight I'll even close the door for my visit, so she doesn't nearly pull my hair out by the roots as she tries not to make too much noise.

"…I mean, honestly, don't you think you'll be recuperating better back at home? You can come stay with us for a few days, sleep in your old bedroom…"

Having a cast on shouldn't keep her from putting her legs over my shoulders, and with the adjustable hospital bed I can still—

There's a knock on my open door, and my mom and I both turn.

"Wilder!" Amy says brightly.

I forgot about her. I completely forgot that Amy even *existed*, let alone might be worried about me, but now here she is, wearing her flight attendant uniform and standing in the door of my hospital room with a very large stuffed bear holding a heart.

The heart says GET WELL.

My mom looks at her suspiciously, both eyebrows raised.

"I knew you weren't dead," Amy says, ignoring my mom. "A touch of the sixth sense has always run in my family, and I knew you were still alive somewhere out there. I *knew* it, and I'm right! I told them not to give up on you and that poor girl."

"No one was considering giving up," my mom says,

speaking up for the first time, and Amy looks over at her like she didn't realize she was there.

She blinks, like she's confused. Not that it's hard to confuse Amy. I wasn't seeing her for her brains, after all. I wasn't really seeing her, to be honest, at least not outside her bedroom.

Shit.

"Mom," I say, standing. "This is Amy."

"Oh gosh of *course* you're Wilder's mom! I'm *so* pleased to meet you, Mrs. Flint, though I wish it were in better circumstances if you know what I mean!"

She beams, her white teeth practically fluorescing. My mom takes her hand and shakes it, though she gives me an obvious *who is this girl* look.

"Wilder and I are—" Amy's voice drops to a whisper "—*dating*, even though I wasn't supposed to tell anyone since we sort of work together and didn't want anyone to know, but after all this, you know how it is…"

"Isn't that lovely," my mom says, her tone perfectly flat and neutral. "And what brings you here?"

Finally, Amy seems to realize that something is slightly off, that maybe she got off on the wrong foot with my mom by suggesting that she was the only one who wanted to find me.

"Well, we're dating," she says again, as if my mom didn't hear her the first time. "And, I, you know, had this feeling about him, and one of the girls switched flights and took my Vancouver to Edmonton route so I could take her Calgary to Prince George route and then one of the air traffic controllers from that airport lives down here, so…"

Amy keeps explaining *how* she got here to my mom, which isn't the *why* that my mom wants to know. I've got a feeling that I'm going to get grilled about Amy the minute she leaves, and since Amy's obviously not someone I was ever going to bring home to Mom and Dad, I'm not looking forward to that conversation.

I wish she weren't here. I want her gone. I'm human enough to feel kind of bad that she somehow got all the way here, just to see me and give me this fucking ugly bear, but I wish she'd leave so I can tell my mom that she's just some girl.

And I don't want Imogen to see her, because the last time the three of us were in the same room I was so desperate to show Imogen that she didn't mean shit to me that I practically stuck my tongue down Amy's throat, and... yeah.

Shit's changed.

"Hey, Mom, could you give Amy and me a minute?" I ask.

"Sure," she says, the hint of a smirk around her lips, and she leaves the room, closing the door behind her.

"Listen," I tell Amy.

She's still holding the bear with the heart on it, her lips in a pretty red pout. I don't know what the hell she was thinking coming here, but now I have to make our relationship status crystal fucking clear in a hospital in the butthole of nowhere, Canada, and I really *really* wish she hadn't bothered to make this journey.

"We're not dating," I say bluntly. "We're fucking, and we're not even doing that any more as of whenever the last time we fucked was."

She looks puzzled. Then she frowns, her pretty face slowly scrunching together.

"You *used* me," she says.

"You had a pretty good time too," I counter.

"You used me for sex and now you're throwing me away. Here. After I came *all this way* to visit you in the hospital, after I *told* everyone that you were still alive and they kept looking—"

"I'm sure that was your doing and your doing alone," I say.

She picks up on the sarcasm just enough for her mouth to flatten into a line.

"I should have known you just wanted an easy lay," she says, eyes flashing.

I just shrug, because I can't argue with her. That was *precisely* the point — she's hot and I only had to buy her two drinks before getting into her panties.

"You men are all the same," she accuses. "You only want what's between our legs, you never care about anything else, about our brains or personalities. I should have never let you sleep with me without at least going on a date first—"

"That wasn't gonna happen," I tell her.

She looks unsteady.

"What wasn't?"

I snort.

"A date, Amy," I say. "If you weren't interested I was gonna move on, not try harder."

Both her hands are white-knuckled on the bear. She's practically murdering the poor thing.

"And you tell me this here?" she hisses. "Now?"

I just hold my hands out, palms-up, as if to say: *yes, I'm obviously telling you here and now.*

"You're an asshole, Wilder Flint," Amy says, her jaw set hard.

She takes a step backward, toward the door, and relief prickles through me.

"You're an asshole because the *least* you could do is wait until we're back in Solaris because now I'm here and I've got nowhere to go, everyone will know I'm humiliated…"

She trails off, like she's waiting for me to offer some solution.

I don't.

"I hope you crash your stupid plane again and the next time it's way worse," she spits at me.

Amy stomps to the door, her heels clicking against the tile, flings it open, and marches through with her head held high.

I roll my eyes.

Of all the fucking things, I think.

CHAPTER THIRTY-FIVE
IMOGEN

I take a step, frowning. The weight distribution on my walking cast is weird, and so is the way it rolls a little bit back-to-front in a way that normal feet don't.

I've still got crutches until I get used to it, but I'm trying to practice so I can shed them. The summer research season is pretty short in the Arctic, and if I'm going to do any useful observation, I *really* need to get up there, stat.

I take another step, then another. I hobble in a small circle around my hospital room, glad that my parents have finally taken a break to go do whatever there is to do in McBride Mills. I love them and I'm glad they came, but they were starting to drive me a little crazy.

The window in here overlooks the parking lot. I've already spent a couple hours staring down there, waiting for something interesting to happen — it's better than TV, which isn't saying much — but it hasn't yet.

Until now.

Because now, crossing the parking lot, is a woman in a red flight attendant uniform, complete with long shiny hair and high heels.

I limp closer to the window, the hairs on the back of my neck starting to prickle.

You're being insane, I tell myself. *There are tons of flight attendants in the world.*

Wilder said they weren't dating. He wouldn't have called her, there's no way for her to have gotten here, right?

But I can't shake the bad feeling in my gut, the gnawing suspicion that this has happened to me before. The feeling that history just repeats itself if you let it.

The flight attendant down below turns, glances up at the hospital, and for one moment I see her face perfectly.

It's Amy.

I turn away from the window because I can feel myself starting to sweat.

What are the chances? I think. *Don't bother being rational, it clearly doesn't work.*

I take a deep breath. I can feel the prickle of perspiration starting in the valley between my breasts, on the back of my neck, the skin all over my body hot with nerves and anxiety and the horrible feeling that I've been humiliated, again.

Go talk to him. It doesn't mean anything that she's here, maybe the airline sent her because...

I blink, unable to come up with a reason. My palm is sweaty against the handhold of the crutch, and I wipe it on my hospital gown, grab the crutch again, hobble out of my room and into the hall before I can think of a reason not to.

It takes forever. I'm slow, and I'm gimpy, and I'm forcing myself not to turn around with every step because I *don't* want to talk to him about this, I want to go hide in my room and avoid the topic forever, maybe move to a cabin in the middle of nowhere and become a total hermit rather than face humiliation again.

It's tempting. I don't know where I'd get a cabin, but I'm tempted nonetheless.

I hobble past other hospital rooms, past the nurse's station, past medical professionals bustling to and fro until I'm outside Wilder's room, and I take a deep breath.

The door's open. I go in.

Two heads turn, and the room hushes instantly, the kind of sudden quiet that makes it obvious I interrupted something.

"Hey," Wilder says after a moment. "Imogen, this is my mom—"

Mrs. Flint has her arms crossed over her chest, and they were clearly mid-argument about something. She gives me a long, hard look up and down, then shoots a glare at Wilder.

"What, are you a collector now? I'm going to go get a coffee across the street," she says, grabbing a jacket from a hook on the wall and huffing out of the room.

I have no idea what to say, so I don't say anything. Neither does Wilder, his mouth an annoyed, flat line until his mom leaves.

"Sorry," he says. "She came all the way here just to get on my fucking case—"

"I saw Amy," I blurt out.

"Shit," Wilder mutters, and that one simple word feels like it closes a hand around my airway.

"You said she wasn't your girlfriend," I say, the words coming out a whisper. "But, I mean, she's *here* and why else would she have come all the way here if…"

"She's a flight attendant, it's easy for her to get places," he says. "I didn't know she was coming, Imogen, I didn't ask her to come. I broke up with her, just now, I swear."

There's a stuffed bear on his bed, lying askew like it was tossed there. I blink back tears, trying to shove away a memory: Valentine's, ten years ago, Melissa prancing around the halls of Solaris High School with that stupid build-a-bear from Spokane.

"You broke up with her?"

"Yeah," Wilder says, stepping forward, reaching a hand toward my shoulder.

I step back.

"I was serious when I said it was different this time," he says, his eyes flicking over my face. "I fucked up before when I was young and stupid and I'm not doing that now. I promise."

"You broke up with her," I repeat. "Meaning you were dating."

"I told you, we weren't *dating*, we were just sleeping together. It was different."

I glance at the window. A tear falls out of my right eye, and I brush it away angrily.

"Squeaks," he says. "This isn't the same."

I want to believe him. I do. I want to look into his eyes and say *yes, of course*, but when I do all I can think of is his arm around her shoulders as she looked up flights to Yellowknife. The way he kissed her while I was standing *right there*, across the desk from them, feeling ugly and invisible and unimportant.

I'm afraid that we'll have this conversation a dozen times about a dozen women. That his mom will never recognize me, just forever think that I'm one of his collection.

Worst of all, I'm afraid that I'll never believe him, even when I should. Maybe I should right now, but I *can't*.

I can't look at the past and ignore what it's telling me.

I shake my head.

"It's okay," I say, even though I know it's nonsensical, and I hobble for the door.

"What?"

"It's fine," I say, still hobbling. "Just—"

My hand's on the doorknob. Wilder's behind me, and he reaches out, his hand brushing my shoulder. I straighten my back, stare into the oak-color wood grain and try to collect myself.

"I don't think I can trust you," I say, willing my voice not to shake. It doesn't work. "This already happened. It's going to happen again. So maybe we should let it be over, yeah?"

I jerk down on the door handle, yank it open, stumbling. Wilder catches me, holding my arm.

"No," he says, his voice stronger. "No, I'm not going to just let this go because you matter to me, Imogen, everything that happened *matters*—"

"Stop it," I say.

"This isn't the same. I've changed, I'm different—"

"Let me *go*," I say, just a little too loudly as I jerk my arm out of his grasp.

The nurses standing in the hallway, discussing someone's chart, look up, alarmed.

Wilder lets me go. I hobble out of there as quickly as I can, tears now streaming down my face. The two nurses look at each other, and I don't need to be psychic to know what that looked like.

As a small mercy, Wilder doesn't follow me.

———

Ten Years Earlier

I DON'T KNOW why I came to prom. Who in their right mind thinks this is a good idea or even wants to *be* here?

Because God, it sucks. The music is awful. The DJ

makes *me* cringe and he's played the same song three times already. The dance floor is full of girls wearing ugly, sparkly, full-length dresses grinding up against their boyfriends like putting their butts somewhere near a dick is exciting and transgressive.

I roll my eyes for the thousandth time, lean against the back wall, arms crossed over my chest.

"I *told* you I shoulda brought my flask," my friend Art says.

"They patted you down at the door," I say, just as annoyed with him as with everyone else. "Also, you don't actually drink, you're just saying that because you're within earshot of Grant Newport and you want to look cool."

Art goes scarlet. Grant is the tall, blue-eyed, blond-haired center of our soccer team, and is completely unaware of Art's crush on him.

Though, by the way he's trying to get a look down Trisha Murray's dress right now, it wouldn't matter. I don't think Art's got much of a chance.

"Well, at least I'm not here to moon over someone so unavailable that there may as well be a sign hung from—"

"Shut up," I say.

I didn't tell him about Wilder and me. I didn't tell *anyone*, except Melissa at the very end. Even after the huge fight Wilder and I got into the next day, and even after he made it very clear that he was picking her over me for reasons I'll never understand, I didn't tell anyone.

It just seemed… pointless.

"I'm just saying," Art says, and goes back to staring at Grant.

Yeah, going to prom is about the worst idea I've ever had, and of-fucking-*course* Solaris High has one of those 'no leaving' policies regarding school dances, because it's supposed to keep students from doing drugs or having sex or some shit.

Clearly it never keeps anyone from having sex, and given the glazed-over look plenty of people seem to have tonight, it's not going great on the drugs front either.

"You're not even dancing," Art says. "I thought you'd at least want to dance, but nooooo."

The thought alone sends a chill down my spine. Back here, with the lights pulsing and the loud music and everyone all wrapped up in what they're doing, no one is paying me much attention.

Keyword: *much.* I've gotten couple of weird looks, and I'm totally certain I've seen a couple of people lean into their dates and say *what's that weird girl doing here, I didn't think she'd come.*

I don't need them watching me dance. The thought alone makes me feel kinda nauseous. I just came because, you know, it's my junior prom and it's one of those memories you're supposed to treasure forever, something that will mark a milestone in my life going forward, a day that maybe I'll look back on fondly…

Fine. I came because I knew that Wilder would be here, with Melissa, probably getting crowned Prom King, and as much as I hate myself for it I also love to make myself miserable. Dumb, right?

This terrible song ends, but instead of another one starting, the DJ interjects over the speakers, sending circles of spotlights spinning through the crowd. Everyone cheers for no damn reason at all.

"How's everyone liking their Night! To! Remember?" he booms.

That's our prom theme. Apparently proms have themes. Everyone cheers again. Even Art claps.

"Well, now I'm pleased and honored to announce that

it! Is! Time! To crown the Solaris High School Prom King and Queeeeeeeen!"

Jesus, you're not announcing an NBA game, I think. *It's just a dumb high school prom.*

"Could all the nominated couples please come to the stage?" the DJ asks.

My eyes land on Wilder and Melissa, holding hands. She's flushed with excitement, and somehow her hair still looks great. Her makeup hasn't melted, not even a little, and I think about how deeply unfair the world is.

"I shouldn't have come," I mutter to Art.

"No shit," he mutters back.

They all get arranged on the stage. Five spotlights, five couples, but everyone knows who the winners are. It's a popularity contest, nothing more.

"If I could have a drumroll please," the DJ announces.

He plays himself a canned drumroll. God, I hate it here.

"Solaris High School's Prom Prince and Princess are... Justin Brennon and Lila O'Connor!"

Cheers. Applause. A tightening, sick feeling settles into in my chest as some girl who I'm pretty sure is in my gym class drapes them both in sashes, then gives Lila an ugly tiara.

For at least the thousandth time, I wish I hadn't come. I don't know what I was *thinking.*

"And now!" says the DJ. "For Tonight's! Solaris High School! Prom King! And! Queen!"

Lights flash over the crowd, strobing and blinking, washing a few hundred high school students in a sea of color. I back further against the door, suddenly afraid I might either puke or cry because I hate seeing him with *her.*

Even if she never did anything wrong. Even if that burden's entirely on my shoulders and even in the blackest depths of my heartbreak I *know* it. I just hate that he picked Melissa, the empty-headed popular girl, over me.

I'm interesting, dammit.

"With a full *fifty-four percent* of the vote, coming in first place…"

I look up at the stage, my heart so far in my throat I think I might choke on it.

Wilder's standing there, wearing a tuxedo that he actually looks *good* in, unlike all the other high school boys around me. He's got Melissa's hand on his arm, her dress a sparkling green cascade, just a *hint* of freckled cleavage visible.

He's so fucking sure he won. I can read it in his face, in the way that he's holding himself. In the slight cock of his hips.

I'll never know why she didn't dump him. She *knows* he cheated on her. She knows that he wasn't saving himself the way she was, and she's still up there, looking at Wilder like he's the cherry on top of an ice cream sundae.

"May I present Prom King Wilder Flint and Prom Queen Melissa Hedder!"

More lights. I shade my eyes, turning away, but from the corner I can still see the girl put a sash on Wilder and a crown on Melissa as the crowd of other teenagers goes completely wild.

I'm fighting tears. Art gives me a weird look, because he has no idea why. I just shrug at him.

"I'm really sensitive to strong light," I say, praying that my voice doesn't sound as miserable as I feel right now.

He shrugs, leans over to me.

"Wilder sure does clean up nice," he says.

"Yeah," I agree, my tone as flat and neutral as I can make it.

"Think he might be… curious?" he asks, cocking an eyebrow.

My fists are clenched so hard that I think my fingernails are cutting into my palms.

"I wouldn't know," I say.

"Now I'd like to take it down a notch," the DJ cuts in. "And congratulate Wilder and Melissa on being Prom King and Queen! You're all invited to join them as they dance to their song, *Hey There Delilah!*"

Wilder doesn't even like that band. He told me once that he just doesn't get the hype, that that song is terrible and stupid.

She puts her arms around his neck. He puts his hands on her waist, cranes his neck down.

I look away just as he's about to kiss her and wish for the thousandth and first time that I hadn't come tonight.

"I mean, I don't think he's even that into her," Art opines. "Look at how he kinda scrunched his face up when he went in, like he doesn't even want—"

"He's not interested in you, either," I tell Art.

The opening chords of this song I hate are playing, some stupid acoustic guitar part that's all fluff and sweetness and did I mention that I hate this song?

"You don't know that," Art says. "Maybe he just needs—"

Just after the lyrics start, the sound cuts out. A murmur passes through the crowd, and Melissa looks over her shoulder at the DJ, her pretty face frowning slightly as she and Wilder keep swaying.

Art sighs and rolls his eyes, but I'm secretly glad because watching them dance to *their* song was a form of torture I'd just as soon not subject myself to.

Until a loud moan echoes through the room. A moan

that goes up at the end, finishes in a high-pitched squeak, the obvious moan of a woman having a *really* good time.

The crowd murmurs, giggles.

I can feel the blood drain from my face. My vision goes gray at the edges, my fingers and toes starting to prickle.

My mind is filled with pure white blank panic as I moan again through the speakers, gasping, squeaking as Wilder eats me out and I try desperately not to scream.

"Imogen," Art frowns. "Is that…"

People are turning toward me, whispering to each other. I lurch for the doors, one hand over my mouth.

"Don't stop," my recorded voices whimpers, *begging* Wilder for more.

I shove through the doors, stumbling, nearly blind with panic. There are two teachers out here in the lobby, talking to each other, but I barely see them.

Right in the middle of the fancy carpet, I puke. I think I puke up everything I've eaten in the past week, I puke so hard, until I'm crying and dry-heaving, the bottom of my skirt splashed with my own vomit.

"Are you okay?" someone asks. "Did you drink—"

I can hear another, louder moan from the other side of the doors and I take off again, my stride building to a run when I get outside.

People are shouting after me. I don't stop. I don't think I *can* stop, my legs just go and go, beyond my control. I run through the parking lot of the resort where we're having prom, through the street, into the woods beyond.

I stumble. I trip. I fall. I keep going, blind and deaf to everything, face slashed by branches and knees scraped from falling.

All I can see is Wilder's face. The way he looked at me when the music cut off, that ugly, cruel smirk he had on his face.

He did this. I *know* he did this. I don't know why, but that doesn't really matter.

They find me an hour later, balled up against the roots of a tree, crying my eyes out.

I never step foot in Solaris High School again.

CHAPTER THIRTY-SIX
WILDER

PRESENT DAY

At ten-thirty, Imogen's door is still closed. It's the third time this morning I've checked to see if she's awake yet, and that's after checking twice last night.

I should have just chased her when she left. I should have made her believe me, shouldn't have let her go thinking that maybe she wanted some time alone...

I don't know. I don't think that would have worked, I think we'd have had a shouting match in the hospital corridor and *that* would never have fixed anything.

But now she's *still* asleep. It's been eleven hours, which I guess isn't all that much if you're trying to heal a fractured ankle and you've been walking through the cold for days, but I'm kind of worried that something happened.

Could a blood clot or something...?

Did she fall...?

I turn around, head to the nurses' station again, and there's finally someone there who barely looks up at me as she types something into the computer.

"Yes?" she asks, still not looking at me.

I put on my most charming smile.

"Sorry to bother you, but do you know if Imogen in room two fourteen is still asleep?"

"The girl who was in the plane crash and walked forty miles?"

"Right."

"She checked out first thing this morning," the nurse says, tapping on a keyboard. "We wanted to keep her for another night, but she—"

"She's gone?"

I feel like a trap door opened underneath me, and I put my hands palm-down on the counter in front of the nurses' station.

The nurse just nods, and I'm suddenly unmoored, unanchored.

You lost your chance, I think. *You fucked up and now your chance is gone, you idiot.*

"Did she say where?" I ask, swallowing hard.

"Most people go home when they leave a hospital," the nurse deadpans.

My jaw tightens for just a second, and I have to fight the urge to grab her, shake her, *demand* to know where Imogen went.

But instead I walk away. The nurse doesn't know, either. When I get back to my room my mom is there, unpacking bagels from a brown bag and placing them on the tray that swings over my hospital bed along with little plastic tubs of cream cheese.

"Not that Solaris is exactly New York City, but at least they have all right bagels," she murmurs to me. "I'm afraid that up here they've confused them with donuts or something. Look at this."

She pokes one, her finger leaving a deep impression.

Imogen's gone.

Most people go home when they leave the hospital.

Imogen lives in Seattle now, but did she go there? Or did she go home to Solaris, with her parents, maybe to recuperate for a bit before going back to her research job?

"*Wilder*," my mom says.

"Sorry."

"Do you want the everything bagel or the sesame one? If you can even call these bagels."

I swallow, my mouth dry, my mind still completely elsewhere.

"Sesame," I say.

"What's wrong?"

I sit in the vinyl-covered armchair next to the bed, lace my fingers together. I feel more at loose ends than I can remember ever feeling before, more like something important has slipped through my fingers.

She left. Without saying goodbye, and the knowledge is like a rock in my gut. The last time I saw her before this was ten years ago, and she was running away from me then.

She's running away from me now.

I clear my throat. My mom arches one eyebrow, still waiting for an answer.

"Sorry," I tell her. "Imogen already checked out and… I've still got something of hers."

"That's the second girl from yesterday?"

"Yeah. The girl I was stranded with."

My mom spreads cream cheese on her subpar bagel, radiating disapproval, because as much as I don't involve my parents in my sex life, they're not blind, deaf, or stupid. They know that I've got a habit of going through women and never bringing one home.

Hence my mom's *collection* comment yesterday. Even if

she's never said anything, it's not a secret that she thinks it's more than time for me to, if not exactly settle down, at least *date* someone.

"And you're so upset that she's already out of your hair?"

I pause, a bagel halfway to my mouth. I close my mouth. I put it down.

She might not take you back, I think. *Maybe you shouldn't tell your mom about this, because what if she doesn't and it gets around Solaris that the dork from high school turned you down?*

"Wilder?"

Don't be fucking stupid.

"Imogen and I went to high school together," I say slowly, looking at the bagel and not my mom. "And I fucked up pretty bad then."

"I don't remember her," my mom says.

"You wouldn't," I say.

And then, before I can stop myself, I tell my mom everything.

She's the first person I've ever told, the whole story spilling out of me in fits and starts, from studying for biology to getting rescued on the side of the road to being afraid that the love of my life slipped through my fingers twice.

It feels good to get it off my chest.

When I finish, she wipes her fingers neatly with a napkin, poised and ready.

"All right, let's get to work," she says.

I clear my throat, not really sure what she means.

"There's only so many places she can be," my mom says, perfectly reasonable. "Let's find her so you can grovel and *finally* have a girlfriend you'll let us meet."

———

FIRST THING the next morning I'm sweating, shaking, my heart rate skyrocketing. I haven't been able to eat for ten hours because the only thought I've had this entire time has been a loop on continuous replay: dropping out of the clouds, instruments going haywire. The mountain, up close, rushing in.

It plays again. And again.

"Thank you for flying CanadaAir to Edmonton!" says a perky female voice over the loudspeaker. "Please be aware that since the first half of this route is pretty bumpy over the mountains, we'll be delaying beverage service…"

I turn my head to look out the porthole, but my mom's closed it. There are only two seats on this side of the aisle and one on the other, so the outdoors is never far away enough.

"I wish you'd take some Xanax," my mom says, her voice worried.

I just shake my head, sweat rolling beneath my collar.

"My head's gotta be clear so I can fly," I say.

She looks away, because as gung-ho as she was about Imogen at first, she hates my plan.

"At least spend the night in Edmonton," she says.

I don't answer her, just tilt my head back against the seat rest and close my eyes. If I spend the night somewhere I'm afraid I'll lose my nerve and wind up back in Solaris, no closer to Imogen than before.

And I can't do that. I have to get to her, even if I have to spend hours and hours sweating and shaking in tiny planes, even if the mere thought of flying makes me vomit up everything I've eaten for the past day.

I wish I could take the Xanax, or get drunk, or do *anything* to make me forget where I am and what I'm doing, but I can't. Not if this is going to work.

And I want it to work more than I've ever wanted anything.

CHAPTER THIRTY-SEVEN
IMOGEN

When I finally make it to Tekkeit, I sleep for seventeen hours straight and only wake up to go to the bathroom a couple of times. Other people come in and out of the tiny bunk room, which has four beds in two sets of bunks, but I barely notice them.

It's the Xanax. Generalized Anxiety Disorder aside, I rarely take the stuff, because I mostly don't like the way it just… flattens everything out. It's harder to feel anxious or nervous or insecure, sure, but it's harder to feel *anything*.

Plus, it knocks me out cold for seventeen hours. Anything with that kind of power kind of freaks me out.

But I needed to get here. The Foundation was willing to extend my grant, in light of circumstances, and let me do this next summer, but I couldn't handle the thought of going back to Seattle and having to see lots of people, deal with other academics, explain what happened and how I got my ankle broken again and again.

Easier to be here, with a few other scientists who'd rather talk about bacteria than relationships, and who think that *hey, Imogen, I saw rutting marks on some trees yesterday, so I think the bulls are getting pretty frisky* is a perfectly good conversation starter.

That's why I took the Xanax and then slept, because getting here, to Frisky Musk Oxen Paradise, necessitated several flights and the exact same kind of tiny plane that *someone* crashed less than two weeks ago. They weren't thrilled when I showed up in a walking cast, but they didn't send me back, either.

The first morning I'm awake, after the pro tip about the rutting marks on trees, I pack my bag for the day, grab a walking stick, and head in the direction of the horny oxen.

It's beautiful up here. It's chilly, unsurprisingly, but as I walk *very* slowly toward where my colleague marked the trees on the map, I unzip my outer parka and then also my inner fleece, warming up.

Late May here is the beginning of spring, so there's bright green new grass poking through the marshy soil, spotted with gray rocks. Water is *everywhere*, with much of the snow and ice melting after the winter, revealing the tundra underneath.

A little further away are the pine forests, less dense than the ones further south, the trees smaller, stunted. The sky above is the perfect, clear blue that you only see in commercials for antidepressants or somewhere hundreds and hundreds of miles from the nearest city.

I find the rutting trees without much of a problem. I spend my day recording everything I find there: the marks, the poop, the tracks. I follow them for a bit, watching for evidence of changed behavior, and though I don't find the oxen before I need to leave, it's a nearly-perfect day.

I don't see anyone else. I don't talk to anyone else while I'm out there, and no one talks to me. I could be stark naked or wearing a glittery evening gown and no one would care, because *I'm all alone.*

It's great. It's the best.

And I can't wait for a whole summer just like it.

————

THE NEXT DAY is promising again. I find a clear watering spot for the oxen, not to mention plenty of fresh dung. I take samples of it along with the fresh, new grasses that look like they've recently been feasted on.

A few plants around have strands of their long, shaggy fur stuck to them, so I collect those too. Global warming means that, among other things, the northern skin mite has been making inroads with the oxen population, and no one is quite sure what that means for the animals themselves.

I set up my camera trap — it's not really a trap, just a motion-activated video recording device — by around three, and start heading back. I've got plenty of sunlight left, but I'm hyper-conscious of not wanting to overdo it. I'm not so far from the research station itself that I'd die out here if I couldn't walk, but I'd hate to inconvenience anyone else.

Besides, they'd be really, really annoyed.

I'm about halfway back to the station when I hear a noise that does *not* belong, a loud buzzing that has nothing to do with the wind whispering through the pine trees or the distant, constant drip of water seeping from earth's every pore.

I glance behind me, make sure I'm not being attacked by a vicious male ox. Nothing. But the noise doesn't stop, and I scan the horizon, my brain lazily flicking through the possibilities.

Bees? Birds? Motorboat?

Really far-away mining equipment, even though I thought we were on protected lands?

Finally, I look up, to the pure blue sky punctuated by puffs of white cloud, so big it feels like it could engulf me if I look too long.

There's a plane. Heading in from the southwest and toward the research station. I think it's either the same kind of plane that Wilder and I took—

Nope, I tell myself. *Everything about that is officially off-limits right now. You visualized locking it into a bank vault, remember? So you can deal with it later but not right now?*

Right. I'm not thinking about being cold for all that time, about being trapped, about Wilder fixing up my ankle or luring me down those rocks or across that landslide.

I'm not thinking about how he apologized, and I didn't even ask him to. I'm not thinking about how that made me think that *maybe* he'd changed, about how maybe now the boy who'd been both the best and worst thing in my life at one point could finally just be good for me.

And I'm not thinking about the lake, the cabin, the terror of thinking that he might die, the relief when he didn't. How I let my guard down then and now I regret it again.

Nope. Not thinking about that stuff.

Just heading back to the station, where I'll help load in the supplies from the plane so the pilot can get on their way back to Inuvik and make it before nightfall.

Is it Friday? I think.

Don't supply planes come on Fridays?

I shrug to myself, stab my walking stick into the ground, take yet another unsteady step.

"Must be Friday, then," I say out loud to absolutely no one.

CHAPTER THIRTY-EIGHT
WILDER

My hands are still shaking as I cut off the tiny plane's engine. My shirt's soaked through with sweat, and I feel like I just got run over by a bulldozer after running two back-to-back marathons.

A small knot of people, all wearing hiking pants, sweaters, fleeces, and hats are collecting at the edge of the airstrip. They look somewhere between upset and confused, but I don't even care right now. I don't care about *anything*.

My nerves are fucking shot. I'm pretty sure that an enemy squadron could come screaming down out of the sky at me right now and I wouldn't budge, because there's nothing left in my mental reserve.

Getting on the plane to Edmonton was hell. Getting on the smaller plane to Yellowknife was a worse hell, and even though both times I was tempted to drink myself into oblivion before the flight, I knew I couldn't.

Because come hell or high water, I was getting to Tekkeit Research Station. Even if I threw up twice before I got on this plane. Even if I couldn't stop the camera in my brain from replaying the crash, over and over and over, even if every tiny bit of turbulence made me obsessively check my instruments again and again, certain that they were failing.

On the runway in Yellowknife, I almost bailed. There was a moment where I didn't think I could take off and decided to just taxi around, figure out some other way to get here. A boat, on horseback, by Jeep, I didn't care.

But then I thought of Imogen asleep next to me in that tiny bed in that ugly cabin, the wood stove fire nearly dead. I thought of the way she looked at me when I woke up after nearly freezing to death.

And I got that plane in the air. I nearly had a panic attack, but I did it, and now I'm here on the ground again, sweaty and shaking and in desperate need of collecting myself, but I'm here.

I just hope this is the right one, because Imogen's not there. She's not one of the people standing next to the air strip, looking faintly puzzled and faintly like they might start observing me through a microscope.

I take a deep breath. I open the door, I wipe my sweaty palms on my pants, I jump down and swing the door shut.

The gathered people just keep looking, obviously confused. That's okay. I can only imagine that I'm confusing.

Finally, a woman steps forward. She's slightly round, slightly short, and has gray hair and a gaze I'd describe as *piercing*.

"It's not Friday and you're not the usual delivery pilot," she says.

"I'm not a delivery pilot at all," I say. "I'm here for Imogen Gustavo."

The others — two men, two women, all between twenty and sixty — move in. They remind me of a flock of birds, moving as one curious-but-shy knot.

"Here for?" she says, blinking.

I didn't think this part through. In my imagination, as soon as I landed the plane she'd be there, standing at the end of the air strip, and she'd run — well, hobble — into my arms and I'd twirl her around and birds would sing and the sun would shine and all that shit.

"I need to talk to her," I say, the only explanation I can really come up with.

"Imogen?"

"Yes," I confirm.

The woman looks to her left and to her right, into the eyes of two other equally puzzled scientists. At least I assume they're scientists. They're sure not welcome ambassadors.

"Is that the girl who was in plane crash?" one of them asks.

"Yeah, musk oxen and busted ankle," the other says.

"So I'm in the right place."

The woman just snorts.

"No, *you* are not in the right place," she says, adjusting her round glasses by the frames. "She's in the right place. *You* are most certainly not supposed to be here. How did you even get here?"

I swallow, shove my hands into the pockets of my jeans, and even though I'm still coming down from the most nerve-wracking hours of my life, I manage to smile at her.

After all, why be charming if you never use it?

"I flew," I say.

One side of her mouth twitches, and one of the other scientists snort-laughs.

—————

THE SHORT, round, gray-haired woman is Wanda, and she lectures me even as she leads me into the big, ugly, squat, semi-industrial building that houses Tekkeit Arctic Research Center.

"Should make you just leave back the way you came," she says, turning her head so her voice drifts over her shoulder and to me. "Unauthorized visitors are completely unheard of, I don't even know how you got through border security and all that, I hope you've got enough fuel to get you back somewhere because there's none here, you know…"

I'm barely listening to her. She let me in and didn't shoot me with a giant grizzly bear gun or something, and that's all I really care about. The woman goes on and on about how I'm lucky they've got a bunk free, but food is rationed, so unless I'm going to be catching some fish and sharing it with the group, they haven't got too much for me to eat.

My sweat-soaked shirt is cooled against my body, and I start to shiver a little. It's cold up here, but given how close we are to the Arctic Circle, that's not a huge surprise.

Wanda leads me into a room that's got tables and chairs, a projector up front, and a couple of couches in the back. The entire research station is much nicer and less clinical than I thought it would be — from how Imogen described it, I thought it would be nothing but sterile white, microscopes everywhere, with cold concrete-and-metal hallways.

But it's kind of nice, though it has a very space-efficient, semi-Ikea vibe to it.

"Sit," she says. "I guess I'll go see if I can find Gustavo? It's not like there's a protocol for unannounced visitors, you know."

I sit down, trying to behave myself. My shirt sticks to

me. This seat has a lime green cushion with light wood all around it, and I lean back, stare at the empty projector.

I've changed, I think, still searching for what to tell her.

There has to be something, right?

There's gotta be something I can do, something I can say, someone I can be that will make all the hurts and the scars and the betrayals fade.

I'd take it back, I think, desperation crawling its way into my heart. *I'd take it all back if I could.*

There are no windows in this room, no natural light, so I lean my head back against the back of the chair and close my eyes, miserably trying to figure out what to do.

CHAPTER THIRTY-NINE
IMOGEN

When I checked out of the hospital, I got a pretty long instructional lecture about how to care for my ankle. Things I *should* be doing including taking it easy, keeping my leg elevated when possible, *taking it easy*, drinking plenty of fluids and getting lots of calcium, *taking it easy, seriously*, and make sure I'm gentle with the cast.

I've at least been getting lots of fluids and calcium. The other stuff is more… guidelines, right?

"They'll really fuck up a watershed, you know," Grace says, walking into the kitchenette.

I turn and look at her, blinking. She's even more direct than most of the other scientists here — not a group known for tact, if I'm being honest — and I have absolutely no idea who's been fucking up watersheds. I didn't know anyone was fucking up watersheds.

"Pollutants?" I guess as the electric kettle clicks off.

Grace gives me a blank look, blinking once.

"Musk oxen," she says, as if it were completely obvious what she was talking about. "That herd you're chasing down really fucked up the stream I'm trying to study and now all my samples are filled with silt."

She shakes her head like it's my fault, her shiny black top knot bouncing slightly.

I'm at a loss for words. That's not exactly unusual for me, but Grace is proving to be kind of a mystery, even for a fellow scientist. She's got a weird habit of being unnecessarily accusatory.

Like right now. With the musk oxen.

"Walking through streams is what they do," I point out, pouring hot water over my teabag. "They're animals. They walk over stuff. It's their thing."

Go on, sound less professional, I tell myself.

Grace exhales loudly, pouring the last dregs of a mostly-empty mug into the sink.

"Well, their *thing* is fucking up my *thing*," she says, even though she says it without malice or annoyance. It's just a fact to her, I guess.

I say nothing. She says nothing. There's a long, awkward silence in the kitchenette while I stare into my tea as it steeps, feeling baffled about human behavior.

Does she want me to do something about the oxen? Should I build a bridge over that stream? There are other streams.

"Can't you use a different stream?" I finally ask.

She looks at me like I just farted.

"Of course not," she says. "I've been measuring the phosphate levels in that one since last summer, and I need to know how the bacteria that naturally live at these climates are adversely affected by..."

The door to the kitchenette opens, and she trails off. We both watch as Wanda, the most senior person here and thus our de facto leader, pokes her head in and looks at us both for a long moment, blinking behind her round glasses.

"Imogen, there's someone here to see you," she says.

I'm stirring my tea, and I stop. I tilt my head in confusion, like I'm a baby bird.

"Someone here to see me?"

She just nods.

"Here."

"Yes."

"To see me?"

"Yes. He said he had to talk to you?"

I'm just dunking my teabag again and again, trying to wrap my brain around this even as my stomach tightens.

Suddenly I remember that plane a little while ago, as I was walking back to the station. I didn't *think* it was Friday. Maybe I was right all along.

"You mean on the phone or something—"

"I mean *here*, Imogen, I didn't misspeak."

I toss the teabag into the trashcan, because at the moment my lungs feel a little like they're being compacted, and I can't breathe, because there's exactly one person who has the means, ability, and reason to show up at my arctic research station.

And there's only one who'd just show up without consulting anyone first, someone who thinks that he's God's own gift to the world. Someone who takes what he wants and doesn't care if he has to lie about it as long as *he's* happy, as long as he gets what he wants.

Flying in unannounced sure does look good, I'll give him that. I'm sure the other scientists here are all *very* impressed, and I'm sure that was the entire point of his dumb, stupid, immature stunt—

"It's too late in the day to send him back, so just come talk to him before everyone starts gossiping, will you?" Wanda says. "It's bad enough that Jim and Tandy are practically doing elaborate mating dances at each other—"

"Jim and Tandy?" Grace asks. "They are?"

Wanda sighs.

"I'll come talk to him," I say, walking quickly for the door before we start speculating about which bird Jim and Tandy's dance most closely resembles.

"In the lounge-slash-viewing room-slash-cafe," she says, pointing. "And he's not supposed to be here, you know!" she calls after me.

"I know," I mutter to myself, my mug of tea still held in one hand, sloshing dangerously side to side as I limp quickly down the hallway.

He wasn't supposed to come, I think, heart pounding. *He did something stupid and showy, and now he's here, and now all summer I'm going to be that girl who had some guy fly in just to beg her forgiveness, and they're all going to wonder why and either I'll have to explain it all or make up some lie...*

It's not a long hallway. I'm already there, standing outside the lounge/viewing room/cafe, staring at the metal doorknob, desperately wishing I didn't have to go inside.

More than anything, I feel like an idiot. The first time I let Wilder chew me up and spit me out, I was in high school. I was seventeen. I'd never really had a boyfriend before, I'd never done more than kiss a guy.

I wanted it. He wanted it. None of the other stuff really mattered over the roar of our hormones, and look where *that* got me.

But now I'm older and I'm *supposed* to be wiser, but I fell for it again. He lied to me and I believed him only to realize that I shouldn't, that I *can't*, not if I don't want the past to repeat itself.

I can't do it again. I won't. Wilder already tore my heart out and played baseball with it once, and that was more than enough.

I tighten my grip around my mug of tea. I grasp the

metal doorknob in my other hand, firmly, square my shoulders, and open it.

Wilder looks up. He's got the bomber jacket on again, leaning his elbows on his knees, his hair flopping in front of those jewel-tone eyes.

I almost close the door and run away, a wave of anxiety crashing over me the moment I see him. I didn't come here after all that with a broken ankle because I want to confront my problems, I came here — to the Arctic, for crying out loud, it's pretty far from everything — because I want to ignore my problems and spend my day researching oxen.

"Squeaks," he says, and he smiles.

Over in the corner are two of my colleagues. They're pretending to play chess but it's incredibly obvious that now they're just eavesdropping.

"Wilder," I say, and it comes out sounding stiff and formal. I glance at the chess players again, nerves crawling up my back because I do *not* need to be the butt of gossip here for the next two and a half months, I don't want to look across the cafe area at someone and wonder if they're talking about me and the guy who flew a plane in unannounced…

I jerk my head backward, telling him to come out into the hallway, and when he rises from the chair I realize that underneath his jacket, his shirt's weirdly wet, sticking to his chest.

That must be cold, I think, but before he fixes it I can see his chest muscles flex and move as he walks. I realize I'm staring. I step into the hallway to make myself stop, but I do it a moment too soon, the door closing into Wilder who catches it gracefully with his shoulder.

Of course he does. I'd be on my ass if that happened to me, but of *course* not him.

We face each other, surrounded by concrete and drywall and bright lights.

"Why are you here?" I hiss. "You're not—"

He leans in and kisses me.

I jump and step back, stumbling a little. The hot tea in my mug sloshes out, burns my hand, and without thinking I drop it with a yelp.

It shatters on the floor, splashing our feet and legs.

"What the *fuck*?" I hiss at Wilder, shaking my hand.

He's holding his shirt away from himself, brushing liquid from his jacket sleeves.

"You okay?" he asks.

"I'm fine, but what the *fuck*, Wilder?" I say again. I'm trying to keep my voice down but it's not really working, because I've pretty much just announced to the whole station that I'm having some sort of lovers' spat out here and that is *not* what I need.

"I can't let you go again," he says.

Suddenly, the smirk is gone, the funny little smile, the *God's gift to the world swagger* is gone and Wilder just stands there. Staring at me like he's piercing my soul with those eyes, hands wet with now-cold tea, a brown spot on the front of his shirt.

A whirlpool opens up in my stomach.

"Yes, you can," I say, shoving my glasses up my nose. They're not even properly fixed yet, though I glued them together last night since Wilder's tape job was starting to come apart.

"In fact, it's pretty easy, all you have to do is *leave me alone* and not get in a plane to an Arctic research station just because you think you can do whatever you want and have whoever you want with no consequences," I go on. "Maybe I came here without telling you because I didn't want you around and didn't want you showing up and trying to kiss me again. You think of *that*?"

"Yes," he says.

"Then what the hell?"

"I couldn't forgive myself if I let you go again," he says quietly.

"You say that to all the girls you bang?" I snap.

I've got that unsteady feeling in my throat that means I'm about to cry, and I clench both of my wet fists, trying to get myself under control.

"Or do you only say this shit to the girls you bang on the side while you've got some *other* girlfriend who's prettier and funner and has bouncy hair and laughs the right way at your jokes? The girls who you can string along so you can laugh about it later with your buddies when you crawl back into whatever hole you crawled out of and tell them *oh hey, I really had that girl Imogen going again, she thought I was into her for real can you even believe it—*"

"You think I flew to the end of the earth in that tiny fucking plane so I could laugh about it later?" he says, incredulous. "I know you know how getting in one of those things felt."

I sigh, shutting my eyes because he's right and I hate it.

"I got into that thing because I had to come see you," he goes on, his voice quiet and serious. "I got into that thing and flew it for almost ten hours even though I was shaking the entire time because I wanted to see you again. I want to listen to you talk about musk oxen family sagas and I want to hear you laugh when you make an awkward joke and I want you to wake me up in the middle of the night to—"

The door opens, one of the chess players comes out. He's middle-aged, gray-haired and wearing a puffy vest.

"Everything okay?" he asks, brow slightly furrowed as

he glances at the broken mug at our feet, the tears streaming down my face.

"Fine," I say, and point at my foot. "Just clumsy."

He nods and starts walking away. I try to wipe some tears off my face, but I just smear tea on myself, which makes me cry harder.

I'm sure the flight attendant never breaks mugs and sobs like a little kid and then smears tea all over herself, I think self-pityingly. *I bet she's even pretty when she cries.*

"Imogen—"

"I can't do this again," I tell him.

I finally manage to look into his eyes, holding my breath for strength. Tears are still leaking down my face, and I'm barely holding it together without sobbing, snot going everywhere.

"I already did this once," I go on, my voice a miserable stage whisper because I don't trust myself. "And, you know, I can forgive myself for believing you when we were out there because it was a weird situation, and there was a lot of stress, and I thought I was going to die and people make bad decisions when they think they're going to die."

I swallow hard and force myself to take a deep breath.

"I'd do it again," he says.

"Don't be stupid."

"Don't tell me what to do," he murmurs, teasing.

I laugh despite myself, wipe my hand on my pants, finally wipe off some of my tears.

"Once was enough," I tell him. "That's all I've got in me."

"Squeaks—"

"Don't. Please."

Wilder reaches out, smooths a strand of hair back against my head. His thumb brushes tears off of one cheek and I breathe deep, force myself not to lean into his touch like a cat.

"Let me say something," he murmurs, his hand still on my face. "You don't have to believe me. You don't have to say anything back, you don't even have to acknowledge me, you can just walk away. Just let me tell you."

I don't want to hear it. I don't. I know that whatever he's about to say is going to make this a billion times worse and harder and then I'm going to spend ages second-guessing any decision I make, but despite myself I nod.

"I loved you ten years ago and couldn't admit it," he says. "That's why I came. Because even if it took a plane crash and a broken ankle and a bunch of nearly dying, I finally figured out that I love you, I did then, I do now, and I'd crash the plane again in a second if it led me back to you."

I push my glasses onto my head, rub my eyes with my hands.

"Please don't crash another plane," I whisper.

"There's no one else," he says. "Amy was just… a distraction. She's nice, but she was a way to pass the time."

I want to believe him. I do. My whole body wants it, from my busted ankle to the top of my head, all my nerves harmonizing in a symphony of *this feels right.*

Just say yes.

"It's different this time, I swear, Squeaks," he murmurs. "Please believe me."

I bite my lip, trembling, my voice untrustworthy as I look up at Wilder again, pure desperation in his eyes.

He's telling the truth this time, I think.

He came all the way here. He has to be.

Once burned, though.

"I can't do this again," I whisper.

Twice shy.

CHAPTER FORTY
WILDER

She turns and walks away, leaving faint wet footprints down the hall until she finally picks a door and heads through it, not looking back even once.

I feel like I'm tearing down the middle. I feel like I've got a part of myself that I didn't even know could get hurt that's being slashed to pieces with a dull knife, hacked through until the edges are ragged and ugly and bleeding.

I could call after her. I don't. I could chase her, but I don't, because what good is going to come of that? I already followed her all the way to the tundra, a thousand miles from real human civilization. Following her another twenty feet down a hallway isn't how I fix this.

Slowly, I bend down and grab the big pieces of the shattered ceramic mug that's at my feet, careful of the sharp edges. I'm suddenly aware that the tea's cold, that it soaked through my shoes, that my shirt is still damp from how much I sweated while I was flying here.

And it didn't work. Maybe the craziest thing I've ever done. Probably the hardest, and it didn't work. I don't know what I was expecting, but not this.

I guess I thought she'd at least kiss me back. That she'd at least agree to think about it, give us a trial or something.

I stare at the pieces of broken mug in my hand, and I want to throw it back on the floor, maybe against the wall. Break it even harder than it's already broken, storm out of the station, jump into the tiny plane I rented and take off.

I want to find another woman here — literally any woman would do — seduce her in five minutes, tell her my name just so she'd scream it loud enough for Imogen to hear when I fucked her. I want to pull someone's hair and imagine Imogen, on the other side of the wall, crying.

And for a moment I nearly do something. I nearly throw the broken mug and storm down the hallway, anger seething through my veins that I didn't get what I want.

That I came all the way here and she still doesn't believe me. That I flew here, in the exact same kind of plane we crashed in, that for hours and hours in the air I had visions of crashing again, alone this time. That I did it just to see *her* again, and she turned me down.

At the far end of the hall, a door opens. My head snaps up but it's not Imogen, just another girl with thick black hair in a topknot. She gives me a weird look, then turns and walks the other direction, but in that moment the spell of my anger is broken, cold tea dripping through my fingers as I crouch on the floor.

You can't do the same thing you did before and expect different results, I suddenly think.

I pick up another shard of ceramic, this this one slips and when I grab it tighter it cuts the pad of my finger.

"Shit," I mutter, dropping it as a drop of blood blossoms out of me, but the sharp pain breaks the spell, red liquid dripping into the spilled tea.

This was a disaster. It didn't work and now I'm out several thousand dollars in plane rental and jet fuel, not to mention I'm fucking lucky that the Canadian Air Force didn't get called on me for pulling this stunt.

I stand, ceramic pieces in my hands. I head back to the lounge where I was waiting, and I pull the door open, nod at the two other people in there still bent over a chess board. I throw the ceramic pieces into the trash and grab about twenty paper towels from a dispenser, head back into the hallway.

I clean up the mess I made. I wipe down the floor and the wall where it splashed until there's no trace whatsoever, going back for more paper towels twice.

When I'm done I stand there, in the hallway, and I look at the shiny sealed concrete floor and I think: *there, I made one piece of this better.*

———

I LEAVE THE NEXT MORNING, early, after one of the most awkward nights of my life. Imogen avoids me like the plague, and even though we're two people in the same fairly small building, I don't force the issue.

It's not that I'm giving up. But I did, finally, realize something: doing the same things will produce the same results. She doesn't want to talk any more, I won't make her.

Instead, I try to come up with a cover story for the other scientists, who all seem to regard me as a particularly interesting specimen, like I'm an insect who can walk and talk.

Grace, the girl with the black hair in the top knot, frowns at me over the lasagna someone makes for dinner.

"You flew here alone because you thought it sounded fun?" she asks.

It's dead clear that she thinks I'm an idiot, so I grin at her, idiotically.

"Sure!" I say, false enthusiasm in my voice. "Imogen kept talking about how much she likes doing research here, so I figured I'd stop by and see her! All day outside, watching some funny animals have sex, what's the downside?"

"It's cold, it's uncomfortable, and it's for serious scientific inquiry. It's not a resort. There are no drinks with umbrellas," she says, still dead serious.

I'm still grinning as I fork lasagna into my mouth. If they want to think I'm a total moron, it's fine with me, mostly because I know that if I want to completely and utterly tank any chance of ever speaking to Imogen again, I'd tell them the real story.

So, *rich kid mistakes research station for Club Tundra* it is.

"Guess I got it wrong!" I say. "Neat place you got here, though."

She gives me another baffled look, so everything's going according to plan.

———

THEY GIVE me a pair of sweatpants that someone left here last research season along with a hoodie, and let me sleep in one of the mens' bunk rooms, but not before the woman in charge — Wanda, the short round one who was also my welcoming party — lectures me at length about what a risk I took flying in unannounced and how lucky I am that they didn't shoot me and how it's a good thing they didn't refuse to let me land, how they're able to feed me for a day, etc.

I smile and nod through all of it, even though I'm not sorry in the least.

Even though I feel like I carved Imogen's name onto

my still-beating heart and she just walked away, I'm not sorry.

I leave the next morning, still in the borrowed sweatpants, and before I get on the plane again I puke my guts out in the bathroom. I can't stop remembering the way it felt to plummet out of the sky, the sense of complete and total helplessness I felt when I realized that nothing I did had any effect.

The ground rushing up and up. The certainty that I was going to die, that my last thought was going to be *what the hell just happened?*

And then I get up, I flush the toilet, and I get on the plane. I force myself to taxi and take off even though my whole body is trembling, even though my mind is nearly blank from panic.

Hours later I land in Yellowknife, and thirty minutes after that I'm drunk on cheap whiskey in the tiny airport's only bar, trying desperately to knock the endlessly looping plane crash from my head.

CHAPTER FORTY-ONE
IMOGEN

Pierre opens the freezer in the lounge as I open the trash can, tossing my tea bag in. Luckily, no one's said anything about the mug I broke, even though I was afraid I'd be relegated to only sipping water from my cupped hands or something.

"Travis!" Pierre shouts, his wiry frame perfectly upright, his eyes closed.

"Yo," Travis responds from across the room, where he's sitting on a couch, using his laptop.

"You *cannot* put samples in the lounge freezer," Pierre says, his eyes still closed, his back rigid. "I'm well aware that the proper storage facility is in another building, and you don't like going outside because it's cold, but this freezer is for food and you absolutely, positively—"

"It's just dirt," Travis says, looking bewildered. "It's not like, meat or shit or anything."

"If it's dirt, *why* is it in the freezer?" Pierre asks, exasperated.

"So it doesn't thaw."

"What does it matter if dirt thaws?"

"Well, there's organisms in the permafrost," Travis says, twirling his pen around in his fingers. "And so I need to put them under the microscope when I get a chance, but I dunno if thawing them—"

"If there are organisms then it is not *just dirt*, is it?!" Pierre exclaims. "That, Travis, is precisely why we have *separate* storage for…"

I take my leave of the lounge, because while it's true that Travis shouldn't be storing dirt samples in the same freezer where people get ice for drinking, Pierre can really get going sometimes, and I just can't take it right now.

I hobble down the hallway. Past the spot where I last saw Wilder, where he kissed me and I broke the mug and then ran away, and just like I have for the past two days, I wonder if I fucked up.

I wonder if I'm too cautious, if I should be more trusting, more open, more willing to believe that people can change. I wonder if I should follow my heart more instead of my brain, because while my brain seems great for most things, I'm not sure this is one of them.

I just know that there's still a few tiny splotches on the wall where whoever cleaned it up missed a spot, and looking at them hurts. It feels like there's a fish hook connected to my ribcage and someone's trying to reel me in, pulling me backwards with a sharp pain somewhere in my heart-region.

It feels a little like I can't breathe when I think of him saying *I loved you and couldn't admit it.*

Then I shake my head slightly and continue on. I've got movement data that needs transcribing, some scat samples waiting in the proper storage area that I should really deal with, and I've been thinking of starting a blog about the many and varied romantic tribulations of the musk oxen I've been watching.

It's much more dramatic than you'd think.

"Hey, Imogen!" a voice calls out behind me.

I turn, careful not to spill my tea.

"Phone call," calls Kelly.

My heart clenches and my skin goes cold because I *immediately* wonder what awful thing has happened that would make my parents call out of the blue like this, instead of emailing or Skyping or something.

My brother was in a car crash, I think.

One of my parents had a heart attack.

My dad fell while skiing and broke his hip, and since he's starting to get up there in years that's pretty bad, though replacement hip technology has come a really long way lately…

The research station has a landline, sort of, though it's through a satellite so I don't know if you can exactly call it that. I head into the office-type-room, where the receiver is just hanging out on a desk and Kelly sits down again, looks at her computer.

Wilder crashed his plane again. He really did it, just to prove something, that moron…

"Hello?" I say, panic clutching my chest.

Mentally, I run through all the bad things that could have happened, my mind a cacophony of crashes and spills and hospital beds. Why else call here, like this?

"Hey there, Squeaks," Wilder says, his voice perfectly relaxed and casual.

I freeze, blinking in surprise. I wasn't expecting him, not at all.

I swallow hard, my mouth dry.

"What's wrong?" I ask. At the desk, Kelly ignores me studiously, trying to act like she's not listening but of course she is. She's five feet away.

Wilder chuckles.

"What's wrong is I hadn't talked to you in a few days," he says. "I like the sound of your voice."

I turn toward the wall, where there's a safety poster about how to treat hypothermia. Every room's got one.

"You called the station," I say.

"Your parents wouldn't give me your phone number so I had to get creative if I wanted to talk to you," he says, his voice low and slow, almost a drawl. "I might have made up some story about needing to double-check a serial number on a microscope so that my company could send up a replacement. You do have microscopes up there, right?"

"Of course we have microscopes," I say, off-handedly. "You just called to… call?"

"Is it *that* strange?"

"Kind of," I say, still feeling hesitant. "You're sure that nothing terrible has happened and you're not just soft-pedaling it because you think I'm going to freak out if you tell me my brother was in a car crash?"

"Squeaks, I promise that if your brother was in a car crash I'm the absolute last person on this green earth that your parents would tell," he says, a smile in his voice. "If he has, I don't know shit about it. I just know I wanted to talk to you."

I'm relaxing, slowly, though I'm still suspicious of this new *called just to talk* thing. Doesn't Wilder know that people don't do that, at least not anymore? I mean, my mom will call her friends just to talk, but she's in her fifties.

"Okay," I say slowly, excruciatingly aware that I'm in a semi-public place where Kelly is half-listening and anyone else at the station could waltz in at any second.

"Do I have permission to proceed?" he teases. "If you've got musk oxen *telenovela* drama to go observe, I can call you back."

I could tell him no. I could tell him never to call me

again, tell him that I'm not interested in hearing about rich peoples' skiing foibles or telling him about how hard Pierre freaks out every time someone leaves something in the fridge for more than three days.

And I shouldn't be. I should have moved on ages ago, should have forgotten all about the boy with the bottomless eyes and the smile that makes me feel like the rest of the world's evaporated.

But I didn't, and now here I am.

"Don't call me on this line," I say, my heart squeezing in my chest. "It's really for official station business, and there's no cell reception up here, but we've got Wi-Fi and Skype."

Beep boop beep, beep boooop beep.
No answer on the other end of the call.
She wouldn't give me the wrong info, would she?
Just to get me to stop calling her?
I brush my hair out of my eyes. I need to get it cut, but after getting out of the military I've been pretty lazy about that. I never thought about my hair much before I went in, but ever since getting out, doing whatever I want with it is pure freedom.

Beep boop beep, beep boooop beep.
Come on.
She wouldn't give me the wrong number to get me off her back. Hell, after some of the shit she said to me out in the woods, I can't imagine her being anything less than perfectly candid and totally straight with me if she never wanted to hear my voice again.

Imogen would just tell me off if that were the case. God knows she's done it enough times.

Beep boop beep, beep booo—

"Hey?" says a staticky voice on the other end of the line, though the picture doesn't change.

"Civilization calling," I say, grinning and leaning back into my leather couch.

"You don't have to sound so smug about it," she says, a smile in her voice.

Springs creak, and the Skype image breaks into static for a moment, then freezes again.

"I happen to really like canned green beans, dried ramen, and reconstituted meat products," she says.

"The lasagna the other night wasn't half bad," I admit. "Better than half the food in the service, honestly."

Imogen goes quiet for a split second too long, like I shouldn't have brought up the other night.

"Ben — he's one of the geologists up here — keeps joking that he's gonna make jerky from some of the invasive species," she says. "And then someone has to tell him that the problematic animals are mostly tiny crabs and microscopic bacteria."

The image on the screen jerks, pixelates, flattens, but it doesn't reveal anything beyond a moving, blocky shape that might be Imogen and might be a polar bear. It's impossible to tell.

"Are the crabs any good?"

"I'm not sure it's worth it to find out," she says. "They're a couple inches big, by the time you got through the shell to the meat there'd be almost nothing there, plus we're situated on more of an estuary than on the seashore proper, so it's kind of a hike to go even find the crabs…"

Imogen tells me about invasive species for a while. The picture never does come through, and after a bit, we switch to just voice. I'm disappointed — I like looking at her — but I'm aware that it's a miracle we can talk at all.

She talks about the work she's doing, about the other

scientists. About how there's already been a fight about someone leaving too much hair in the shower, and about how some uptight climatologist named Pierre has already been dubbed *The Refrigerator Nazi* after a mere four days at the research station.

"So one day you're going to open the fridge looking for creamer and it's just going to be him in there, all curled up and shouting about expiration dates?" I ask, enjoying the mental image.

Imogen laughs. It's somewhere between a laugh and a giggle, a light, carefree sound that comes bubbling up out of her like she hasn't got a care in the world.

It makes something deep in my chest pleasantly warm and fizzy-feeling, even as it twists, and I remember the last thing she said to me in person: *I can't do this again.*

"Well, if I do find Pierre in the fridge, I'll be more than well enough equipped to cure his hypothermia," she says dryly. "It's too bad we crashed on the way here and not the way back, because *now* I'd do a bang-up job of fixing you."

"I thought you did an okay job," I tell her. "I made it, didn't I?"

I close my eyes despite myself, because I barely remember anything about falling into the lake — hypothermia does that, nearly shuts your brain down — but I remember her hands tearing my clothes off, her warm body behind mine as she held me tight.

"It took a whole day," she says. "I think you almost didn't come back. The right answer would have been to light the wood stove much earlier."

I frown at the far wall of my apartment, where there's a huge TV, speakers, and not too much else.

"I was asleep for a day?"

"Just about."

"I never realized that. I thought it was a couple of

hours. One minute I was freezing and you were in bed with me, the next I was awake and the fire was going," I say.

Imogen sort of laughs, like she's trying to play it off. I'm astonished that I lost a whole day without realizing it, but from this distance, I'm thinking of her — all alone in that cabin, in the middle of nowhere, not sure whether her only companion was going to live or die.

"Yeah, it was a while," she says.

"Shit, Imogen," I say. "I'm sorry."

"For falling into the lake?"

"For leaving you alone for a whole day."

"If it helps, I mostly slept too," she says, her voice suddenly sounding far away. "I got up to pee a couple of times, but I was afraid that if I left for any longer I'd come back to — you know."

"Thank you, Squeaks," I say softly.

We both pause, and I know we're thinking of the exact same thing: my lips on hers, in front of the wood stove, warmth like I've never felt before in my life.

"Imogen, I mean," I say, swallowing.

That was something I decided while drunk as hell on the way back from Yellowknife, miserable in a window seat on an airplane but glad to be drunk instead of sober since it kept me from thinking much about how far off the ground I was.

From now on, I call her Imogen. I stop reminding her of the asshole I was to her ten years ago, even if I still remember why I called her that. Even if after all this time, I still think about her sometimes when I rub one out.

She laughs again, softly.

"Call me Squeaks if you want," she says. "I don't mind anymore."

"No?"

Her voice is like steam, curling through the phone, warm and soft.

"I got over it," she says. "I think it was somewhere around the time you carried my pack a million miles for me and kept me from freezing to death that I decided you could call me whatever you wanted and I didn't care."

"Anything I want?"

"Well, not poopface or something."

I burst out laughing, and after a moment, so does she.

"You really think poopface is my go-to?" I ask. "You think that, of all the ten thousand nicknames I could come up with for you, *poopface* would be one of them?"

"Shut up," she says, but I can hear her grin through the phone, and I grin back at my empty apartment.

———

I CALL her again two days later, via Skype first this time, and we talk for an hour about absolutely nothing. Pierre still hasn't cracked — which is probably good, since as Imogen points out, a crazy person in a remote location is how three-quarters of horror movies start — and since it's nearly June, it's not like I'm doing any heli-skiing runs.

Which is fine. I'm not terribly enthusiastic about getting back in the air right now, anyway.

I end up telling Imogen that I got shitfaced in Yellowknife, on the way back, once I wasn't going to have to fly anywhere any more. I don't tell her how hard it was to get on that plane to the Tekkeit Research Station in the first place, and I don't tell her that I threw up three times before I even took off, but I think she knows.

I tell her that I nearly got kicked off the plane before it left Yellowknife, but I don't tell her about the revelation I had after my sixth whiskey in the airport bar, my head in my hands, blissful numbness finally coursing through my veins.

The revelation that, if she couldn't do this again, the only option left was to do something else.

It sounds fucking simple and obvious, but it felt like the sun coming up after a cold night. Imogen and I were always fire and ice, love and hate and spikes and thorns. High and lows, hot and cold, and maybe she was right. Maybe *that* was fine when we were teenagers.

Maybe flying to her, showing up out of nowhere, and making a hell of an impression would have worked ten years ago, but any idiot can make a big romantic gesture once.

So I start calling her every other day. Sometimes every day. Sometimes every third day, if one of us is busy.

And we *talk*, the one thing we never did much of before.

And somehow, in the place of all that emotional wreckage, all the fire and ice, all the spikes and thorns, Imogen and I become friends.

———

"You can go on in," Ginger says, smiling at me.

She's new. She's cute. This time last year I'd probably have chatted her up, gotten her number, taken her out behind my father's back. I'd probably have kept it up until I got bored of her in a week or two.

Now I just smile at her, knock my fist against her wide mahogany desk, and walk on past.

"Thanks," I say, and push the door to my father's office open.

He's behind his desk, wearing his usual blue suit. A man I faintly recognize but can't quite place is sitting in one of the expensive-but-austere leather chairs, and both of them stand, all formal business.

I've got on a pair of jeans that aren't my worst but that aren't my best and a flannel plaid shirt rolled up to the elbows.

"Thank you for coming in," my father says, and his tone is too stiff and formal by half.

"No problem," I say, crossing my arms in front of myself as my spine straightens.

I've got a feeling that I know what this is about: a formal announcement that my younger brother Grayson will be the one taking over the reins at Flint Holdings, Inc., not me.

He went to the University of Chicago and majored in business; I joined the Navy, flew planes, and then came back here and didn't make too much of myself. It's not exactly a surprise that he should be taking over, not me.

Hell, I'd pick him, too.

"You remember Elijah Lininger," my father says.

Suddenly the man's face snaps into place: my dad's lawyer, someone who's been to dinner at our house more than once, though I clearly wasn't paying too much attention.

"Good to see you again, Wilder," he says as we shake hands.

"Likewise," I lie.

Does he think I'm going to have a shitfit? Sue him?

Demand that I be given control of a massive company I'm barely interested in?

The two men glance at each other, then sit. My father gestures at the other chair in the room, but I shake my head, preferring to stand. Sitting too much makes me antsy.

"I'll just get down to it," my father says, lacing his fingers together on top of his dark wood desk. "It was recently discovered that one of the aircraft technicians in our private fleet had something of a cocaine problem."

Wait. What?

I frown.

"It was *also* recently discovered that he had been... removing things from our aircraft here and there," my father goes on. "Largely, he stole smaller electronic equipment that he thought might go unnoticed — handheld navigational units, radios, that sort of thing."

I lick my lips, because they've gone dry. *Now* I know what he's getting at.

"Like emergency transponders?" I ask, an edge to my voice.

I look over at the lawyer, but he's intently reading the papers in his lap, refusing to return my gaze.

"We don't have an exact list of the things that this individual has taken from aircraft," my father says carefully.

He doesn't have to admit to it, because I can read between the fucking lines.

"What else?" I ask, taking a step forward, my voice dipping dangerously. "Emergency beacons, what else, *Dad?*"

"I'm afraid it's impossible to tell," my father says, his eyes icy, his voice betraying nothing. "But I can tell you that he was caught when he tried to remove some copper wiring from a Cessna 172."

My skin shivers cold, then hot. I can feel fire creeping up my cheeks, my hands clenching as I lean onto my father's desk, sweat suddenly trickling down my back.

That's the plane I was flying. Removing the right wires could *sure* fuck it up.

"Where's he now?"

"Fired," my father says. "Promptly, once his actions were discovered."

"And?"

"And what?"

I pause, feeling the lawyer's eyes on the back of my head. My father doesn't flinch, doesn't budge, because the man is half steel and half ice and always has been.

"Has he been charged with a crime?" I ask, keeping my voice soft. "Think he'll be doing jail time for deliberately sabotaging a plane or for attempted manslaughter?"

Elijah, the lawyer, clears his throat. I look over my shoulder at him.

"Unfortunately, there's no evidence for anything beyond the crimes he was caught during," he says, his voice cool and calm. "Frankly, it's more than enough to fire him and sue for the amount of the replacement items, but even that is a losing cause. Any money the man had has gone up his nose long ago, so it's really pointless to sue."

"You can't press charges?" I ask, my voice a quiet snarl.

"I'm afraid it wouldn't be worth our time," the lawyer says.

For a moment, I'm not there. I'm on top of a mountain, just coming to, still strapped into the pilot's seat of the tiny Cessna. The windshield is nearly covered with the snow I've just plowed into, and even as I'm trying to undo my restraints, I can't quite get my hands to move the way I want them to.

I shake my head, and I'm back in my father's office.

My father, who's caught the man responsible for me nearly dying, and who isn't interested in pressing charges. My father, who brought his lawyer with him to this meeting, presumably to make sure he didn't say something that might make him liable to me, his son.

I stand up straight, taking my hands off his desk. I look from him to the lawyer and back: my father cool and calm, stony as always; the lawyer slightly shifty, nervous.

"All right," I say.

I turn and walk out of his office, past Ginger, into the hall, out of the building and to my car and I drive back home, to my apartment that I don't pay for because it's in a complex owned by Flint Holdings.

But I don't go in. I walk to the nearby ski slope, turn around, look down at Solaris nestled in the mountains.

And I start saying goodbye.

CHAPTER FORTY-THREE
IMOGEN

I pause for a moment, not sure I heard Wilder right. The line has been particularly patchy tonight — Travis keeps swearing that it has something to do with the twenty-two hours of daylight — so I take a moment, let my heart beat a little faster.

"Where?" I ask, hoping my voice doesn't sound this nervous on the other end of the line.

"Boeing," Wilder says, less staticky this time. "Third round of job interviews, baby. They want me in person this time."

"Where is that?" I ask, even though I know perfectly well where Boeing's headquarters are: the suburbs of Seattle, about thirty minutes away.

About thirty minutes away from me and the life I'm going back to in a month. My heart feels like it seizes and stutters in my chest, a thousand questions racing through my mind: *why's he doing this? Is it his dad or me?*

How do I feel about it? Do I want him closer? He hasn't said anything else about us.

There could be someone else. We could really be just friends now, he could have some girl and I'd never know because I'm here and he's there…

Suddenly it's all real. For the last eight weeks Wilder's been a voice on my laptop, disconnected from the real world. *I'm* disconnected from the real world up here, but this brings it crashing back.

"Tukwila, Washington," he says. "Though I've got the feeling you knew that, Squeaks."

I laugh, awkwardly.

"There are other Boeing locations."

"You knew which one I wanted, though."

I swallow hard, even as a tight warm whirlwind thrums through my chest at his words.

"I had a feeling," I murmur.

"A good feeling?"

I bite my lip, trying to keep myself from smiling even though he can't see me. We gave up on the video part of Skype a long time ago, so for weeks now he's just been a teasing, gravelly voice from my laptop.

"It was a feeling," I demure, because *I'm* not even sure what the feeling was.

Part excitement, part disbelief, part mistrust at both of those things.

Wilder just laughs.

"Well, don't go too crazy with the feelings until I get news one way or the other," he says. "One step at a time, Squeaks."

I swallow hard, because he's right.

"If you get it?"

"I'm moving to Seattle and you'll have to put up with me in person."

"And if you don't?"

"Squeaks, I have a confession."

I lean on one elbow on my desk, moving my face in

toward my laptop speakers. I want to bathe in Wilder's voice, low and just a little husky, let it wash over me.

"Confess."

"I wasn't looking for jobs at Boeing, I was looking for jobs in Seattle."

"That's your confession?"

"What, it wasn't good enough?"

I grin at my laptop.

"I guess I was expecting more," I tease, and Wilder laughs through the speakers.

"All right, Squeaks," he says. "Do you really want a confession? You think you can handle one?"

Suddenly my stomach twists and my toes scrunch in my shoes, because *what if I can't?*

What if his confession is *I bang a new woman every night after we hang up and I'm never going to change my ways?*

"I don't know," I whisper.

"I spend every day looking forward to the next time we talk," he says, his voice gone quiet and growly. "The only thing on the walls in my apartment is a calendar that I use to count down the days until you're back in the states, even though I have no idea if you'll want anything to do with me. I've applied for seventy-three jobs in the greater Seattle area, and I'm going to keep at it until I find something that gets me closer to you. And if you turn me down again, I'll still be there, waiting for you somewhere in the background, just hoping you look my way sooner or later."

I feel like someone's knocked the air out of me. There are tears in my eyes, and I cradle my face in my hands, try to swallow the lump in my throat.

"It's fucking pathetic, Squeaks," he says, half-laughing. "You're what I want, you're all I want, and it took me so long to realize it. Want another confession? Something less romantic?"

I don't answer. I don't think I can, the lump blocking my throat.

"I never stopped thinking about you in the back seat of my dad's Mustang," he goes on. "I still jerk off to that at least once a week. I have for *years*."

And *now* my face is on fire, cheeks burning.

"That was almost really sweet," I manage to say.

Wilder just laughs again, and it makes me grin down at my laptop even though I'm still tearing up with *no* idea what to think.

"I'm probably too honest sometimes," he admits. "But I can't have you thinking I'm all sonnets and roses."

"I promise I wasn't about to," I laugh, my face still hot. "I know you just as well as you know me, Wilder."

"I know," he says, voice bottoming out. "Trust me, Squeaks, I remember."

"WHERE ARE YOU *TAKING* ME?" Wilder teases. "I demand answers. Right now."

I roll my eyes at him on my laptop, walking down the main concrete corridor in the research station, headphones in.

"I feel like I'm being kidnapped. Are you gonna be holding me for ransom?"

"Are you always gonna be this obnoxious about surprises?" I ask.

Wilder laughs.

"Probably, Squeaks," he says. "I'm like a cat on the wrong side of a door."

I've been saying stuff like that more and more lately, stuff that assumes we've got some kind of future, even though I've confirmed or denied nothing.

But Wilder's got an apartment outside Seattle now. He's working at Boeing, forty-five minutes from where I live.

None of that means I ever have to see him again. Avoiding him in a city the size of Seattle wouldn't be too hard.

But we both know I'm not going to. For the past ten weeks we've done nothing but talk, sometimes about absolutely nothing and sometimes about the deepest, darkest parts of ourselves. Mostly, it's about all the in-between stuff.

And somehow, even though we've talked for probably a hundred hours now, every time my laptop makes that *beep boop beep* sounds that means I've got an incoming call, my heart skips a beat.

"Okay, okay," I say, just to shut him up. "I'm taking you outside and hoping that the Wi-Fi is good enough that you get signal out there, too."

Some of the other scientists here finally got fed up with the slow Wi-Fi at the station and they did... something. I know way more about animal poop than about technology, so I'm not precisely sure what they did, I just know that suddenly it's fast enough that I can actually use the video portion of my video chat.

"And what's out there?" Wilder asks. On my laptop screen he tilts a beer back into his mouth, sitting on his couch.

"You'll see," I tell him.

I hope.

I'm weirdly nervous, because as much as we've talked about everything under the sun we haven't talked about us. Not exactly. We've talked about high school and we've laughed about stuff once or twice, but we've shied away from *really* talking.

But this... might bring some stuff up.

I open the inner door, put on my coat, and heave open

the research station's outer door. There's a black gravel path leading toward the airstrip and another path leading toward some outbuildings, but I take the middle way between the two of them, boots tromping over tufts of the green grass that shows up on the tundra mid-summer.

"Do I owe you an adventure next?" Wilder asks. "I'm not sure I know anywhere in Seattle that you don't yet."

Then he leans forward, his elbows on his knees, peering at his own screen.

"Can you see?" I ask, and turn my laptop so the camera can take in the sky.

Wilder laughs.

"I thought they were only visible in the winter," he says.

I sit down, computer in my lap, and we look up at the sky together.

"Usually, they are," I tell him. "But they're especially strong right now, so you can see them even though it's barely sunset. One of the climatologists told me why but I forget."

The green and pink lights dance across the sky, sinuous and winding. It's barely sunset even though it's eleven-thirty at night, so they're faint, but it's incredible that we can see them at all.

"I haven't seen those in years," Wilder's voice says in my ears.

"Me either," I say.

"Was Solaris the last time?"

He doesn't have to tell me what he means by *that*. We both know without having to say anything.

"No," I say slowly. "I did a two-week research stint in Alaska a year or so ago and I saw them there."

But Solaris was the best time, I think.

"I went on a family trip to Norway," Wilder says. "Three years ago, I guess? It was supposed to be a vacation but really, my father ended up networking and doing resort research the entire time so he could write it off as a business expense. Anyway, we saw them there."

"Were you riding reindeer?"

"Just snowmobiles."

"I'd have demanded a reindeer ride," I say, eyes still on the sky.

We're both quiet for a long time. I think a million thoughts, all cascading and crashing through my head at once, like a stampede of people trying to shove through a single exit: *I wish he was here* and *I wish I were there* and *I should say something, I should tell him why I'm showing him this.*

I miss him. I do. I'm up here living my dream life and wondering what he's up to all day.

"Do you want to know another secret?" he finally asks.

I shift positions, stretch my legs out, turn over onto my belly and point the laptop so it's showing my face with the Northern Lights behind me.

"What kind of secret?"

"That was my first time."

I blink. I straighten my glasses, looking into my laptop screen suddenly unsure what to say.

"When I took you up the mountain in the snowmobile," he says. "With the sleeping bags out on that meadow way up there..." he goes on.

"I remember."

How could I forget?

A flush creeps up my cheeks, but I don't think he can tell over Skype.

"I didn't want you to know," he admits, a smile creasing the corners of his eyes. "I don't even know why. I think I was afraid that you'd think I didn't know what I was doing."

I snort quietly, pushing up glasses as they slide down my nose.

"How on earth was I gonna know?" I tease. "I'd never tongue-kissed a boy until you came along, so why lie about the older woman the summer before?"

He shrugs, leaning forward, and even over twenty-five hundred miles, our talk feels close and intimate.

"Why'd I do anything back then, Squeaks?" he asks. "I was afraid of what you'd think. I was afraid of what other people would think. I was mister football guy, son of the richest man in town, and I thought I was some big hotshot that everyone looked up to."

I'm holding my breath, because he's not just explaining why he lied about his first time.

He's explaining, as well as he can, about our relationship and Melissa and prom and why he threw me under the bus the way he did.

"Turns out I was just some asshole in high school," he says. "No one gave a fuck. When Melissa and I broke up the next summer, no one batted an eye. I had it in my head that what I did back then mattered to the world in some big, dramatic way, and… it didn't."

"It mattered," I say softly.

"I wish I'd told you then," he says. "I should have at least given you that."

"Why, so I could secretly lord it over your girlfriend like I did everything else?" I ask, shaking my head and laughing. "When I was tutoring her in English Lit she told me she was thinking about giving up her virginity to you."

"She didn't," Wilder laughs. "We broke up instead without ever getting past—"

He cuts off suddenly, and I raise one eyebrow.

"Don't tell me you're suddenly too shy to say," I tease.

"Second base," Wilder admits, and I laugh. "It seems rude to bring it up to you, now."

"After everything, admitting that you got to second base with someone else seems rude?" I ask, still laughing.

He grins and shrugs.

"Let me tell you a secret," I say, leaning my chin on one hand. "I have *also* been to second base with other people in the past ten years."

"I can't believe you weren't sitting in your laboratory, pining away and waiting for me to come back into your life," he deadpans, making a face.

"If anything, I was hoping you wouldn't."

"I can't imagine why."

Strangely, talking about this doesn't hurt any more. It finally feels like the past is the past, like it's not haunting me anymore. Like now it can stay there, and I can move on with my life, whatever that's going to mean.

Though I've got some strong ideas about that, too. In the past ten weeks I've realized that I hate imagining a life where I don't talk to Wilder all the time, where I don't see something wonderful or strange or funny and immediately tuck it away to tell him about it.

"Wilder," I say, taking a deep breath, fighting down the nerves that are always there, right below the surface, even when they don't need to be. "When I get back to Seattle—"

"—You need someone to pick you up at the airport?" he asks.

I can't help but smile at his suggestion that this is step one of a million.

"Exactly," I say.

CHAPTER FORTY-FOUR
WILDER

I'm standing next to a guy who's practically a walking Valentine's day boutique, even though it's late August. He's got a giant sign, written entirely in pink glitter, that reads WELCOME BACK HONEYBOO, festooned with hearts and cut-out Cupids and fake flowers.

He's *also* got a giant basket filled with red and pink tissue paper, a huge teddy bear, and an enormous heart-shaped box of chocolates.

I think Imogen would murder me if I greeted her at the airport like that. I'm pretty sure that the last thing she wants right now is to have her existence pointed out to the entire baggage claim, so it's just me, standing here, next to a guy who's practically glowing neon with romance shit.

Hopefully he's not making me look bad, but I'm not too worried.

According to my flight tracker, she landed thirty minutes ago, and with every passing second I get more keyed up waiting for her to come down the escalators.

There are business travelers. A family with three kids, all of whom sprint across the baggage claim toward two people who must be grandparents while their parents, lagging behind, tiredly shout at them not to run.

A bunch of girls all wearing matching *Everett Cheer!* shirts, more families, more men in suits already talking on their cell phones.

I start to hope that she didn't get hung up in customs or something. I hope that she didn't absentmindedly put a sample of musk ox fur in her carry-on only to get endlessly questioned about why she's illegally smuggling animal parts. It does seem like something she might do.

But then, finally, there she is.

She's got on leggings and an oversized sweater, because she's always cold, even in August. Her hair's up in a messy bun and she's blinking behind her glasses, looking like she just woke up.

When she finally sees me, she smiles. I take a couple more steps toward the escalator, and a woman in a suit with a briefcase gives me an annoyed look as she gets off and swerves around me.

I'm grinning like an idiot. Imogen's half-smiling, still looking mostly asleep, one hand on the railing of the escalator.

"HONEYBOO!" a woman's voice shouts.

We're all surprised, even the sign-holder, as a girl wearing a pink sweat suit runs at top speed across the baggage claim and makes a beeline toward the guy holding the sign, then launches herself at him, landing with her legs around his waist.

They kiss. Sloppily. The poster flies out of his hands and settles on the floor next to them. I stare for a second too long.

"Hey," Imogen's voice says, and I whirl around.

She's here. Now. In person. I've waited months for this moment and suddenly, I don't know what to say.

"Hey," I say back.

Behind her glasses, her pupils are big, almost the size of her irises, and she's got this dreamy, lost look in her eyes.

She's on the *good* anti-anxiety drugs, much better than mine, which were 'all the whiskey.'

"Welcome back to the—"

Imogen grabs my jacket by the lapels, pulls me toward her, and kisses me.

I wrap her in my arms and kiss her back.

It's a long, slow kiss. It's hard and gentle all at once. It takes its time, and when it's over, I'm out of breath, feeling spun sideways here in this airport.

Imogen lowers her eyes, a secret smile in them, her fingers still on the zipper of my jacket. It looks like she's trying to say something but can't think of what it is, and finally she turns, glances at the Honeyboo couple next to us.

She's still straddling him, held in the air. They're spinning and insisting that they each missed the other more.

Imogen moves in another inch, tucks her head below my chin and I rub her back. I think she's still high as fuck, but I don't mind.

"Should I have gotten you a sign?" I ask quietly into her hair.

Her body shakes slightly as she laughs.

"I took the right amount of Klonopin, but it wasn't working, so I took more," she says, her voice faraway and dreamy. "I almost didn't make either of my connecting flights. I think customs thought I might be a drug mule who had something burst in her stomach. I'm not sure I can even read right now."

"How about I take you home, then?"

She nuzzles her nose against my neck, her arms around my waist underneath my jacket.

"I have luggage."

"I *was* going to get that first."

"Yeah," she says softly. "*Yeah.*"

———

IT'S ALMOST nine by the time we get to Imogen's apartment on University Hill, a small-but-nice one bedroom on the second story of an unassuming building. She doesn't talk too much during the half-hour car ride, but I don't mind.

If anyone understands needing to be drugged out of your mind to get on a plane, it's me.

When we're in her living room, she looks around. Turns on a light. Shakes her head slightly, takes a deep breath, pushes her glasses onto her head and rubs her eyes.

I laugh.

"Get some rest, Squeaks," I tell her. "I'll call you tomorrow when you're back with the living."

"Stay," she says.

She puts her glasses back down and just looks at me. I feel like I'm looking into her soul, raw and vulnerable.

"Please?" she asks. "Just for a while. You can go home later, just… just stay, Wilder? For a little while?"

There's no possible way I can say no, and we both know it.

"Only if you promise to go to bed," I tell her. "You're gonna fall asleep standing up."

She smiles, softly, her face radiant as she walks past me, toward the bedroom.

"Thanks," she says, and closes the door behind her.

———

Half an hour later, we're both in her bed and Imogen's curled against me, her breath warm against the hollow of my throat.

"Thank you," she says. "Every time I close my eyes I swear I feel the plane crash again. Over and over and over, even through the drugs…"

Her voice trails off, and I rub a circle on her back through the worn t-shirt she's got on.

"You're not on a plane, you're in your apartment," I rumble, trying to sound as soothing as possible. "In bed. Solid land. There's nothing to crash."

She nods against me, and I keep rubbing her back. Slowly, I can feel all of Imogen's muscles relax, the anxiety and tension melting away.

"Wilder," she says suddenly, her voice nearly a whisper.

"I'm here."

"You haven't been fucking anyone else, right? This summer?"

I wonder how long she's been waiting to ask this. Knowing Imogen, the question's been on the tip of her tongue since I first met her in the airport, and she's been trying to figure out how to ask until she finally blurts it out, seconds away from sleep.

"Nope," I tell her, and I can feel her muscles loosen again. "Why, did you have a fling with the Fridge Nazi?"

Imogen sighs, snuggling into me even harder.

"Jesus, no," she murmurs.

I don't say anything else, just keep still, rub a circle on her back. In another few minutes she's asleep and snoring so softly it's cute.

I stay there all night, in Imogen's bed, letting her toss and turn. I don't know what time I finally fall asleep, but when I do, I dream of her face in the northern lights.

CHAPTER FORTY-FIVE
IMOGEN

I sleep for a *very* long time. Luckily my flight got in on a Friday, so I've got the weekend to collect myself, get my shit together again, recalibrate my brain from 'arctic research' mode to 'regular workday' mode.

And also figure out what's going on with Wilder. Forty-eight hours should be about enough to talk through years and years of misunderstandings, trauma, hurt feelings, and longing, right? Right.

I lie in my bed and stare at the ceiling. It's an ugly, popcorn ceiling, and it's somehow gotten dusty. How does a ceiling even get dusty?

On the other side of the wall, the shower cuts off. In the sudden silence I realize it was on in the first place, and that's *clearly* where Wilder was.

I sit up in bed, cross-legged, push the comforter off myself. I run a hand through my hair, shaking loose some tangles, yawning and trying to feel like an alive person even if my brain is all clouds and marshmallows right now, the effect of the Klonopin yesterday and then twelve-plus hours of sleep.

The clock on my bedside is glowing red, and I reach for my glasses. The time comes into focus: 11:12.

"Damn," I say out loud, because it's the latest I think I've slept in years. Well, aside from flying into the research station, when I *also* took Klonopin first.

I kick the comforter down. In the next room over I can hear the floor breaking slightly as Wilder walks back and forth, drying off and moisturizing and giving himself finger-guns in the mirror or whatever boys do after they shower.

He was in the shower, I think.

Finally, the ramifications of that make their way into my brain.

Wet and warm and naked.

Water just dripping down his chest, over that V that's between his side-abs and his hips. God, I have two degrees in biology and I don't even know what that thing is called.

Also biceps. Also, those forearms, with the veins sticking out just a little, strong hands soaping himself up and then rinsing himself off…

I clear my throat and wonder if I should stop thinking dirty thoughts about Wilder, who was sweet enough to call me almost every day, who stayed here last night and rubbed my back until I went to sleep and told me again and again that I wasn't in a plane and it wasn't going to crash.

I nearly laugh at myself. It's Wilder. The man was practically *designed* for dirty thoughts, and if I can be certain of one thing in this uncertain world, it's that he doesn't mind it when I think them about him.

On cue, the bathroom door opens and a split second later he's standing in the doorway to my bedroom, a towel slung low around his waist, skin still damp.

There's the V I don't know the word for. The abs, the chest, the biceps, the faint treasure trail of fur leading into the towel from his bellybutton.

The slight bulge beneath the towel.

"I used your shower," he says, rubbing one hand through his hair. "You were asleep."

Finally, I look at his face.

He's smirking. He knows what I was looking at, and he takes a step forward. The towel moves lower by a centimeter.

"I figured as much," I say.

"Sleep well?"

"Mhm."

I'm looking at the V again, and this time Wilder grins. He walks around the bed until he's standing in front of me, wet hair tousled. It's taking most of my willpower not to pull the towel off, so I'm not spending the rest of it making sure I look at his face.

What a waste of willpower.

"You're not still high, are you, Squeaks?" Wilder asks.

He leans down, one hand on either side of my hips, and now his face is right in front of mine, steam rolling off him. There are a couple of water droplets on his shoulders and I fight the urge to suck them off his skin, because I'm enjoying this new side of Wilder.

The teasing side. The you-want-me-and-I-know-it-and-I'll-make-you-want-me-worse side. Before, he just told me what he was going to do to me and did it, and while I never had any complaints, this also has its merits.

"Sober as a monk," I say.

He leans in, nips at my bottom lip with his teeth, pulls back and I gasp at the sharp pleasure that races through my mostly-awake brain as lightning bolts through my body.

I squeak, and he laughs, a dark, husky sound.

"There it is," he says as I lean forward, one hand in his damp hair, pulling his head down to mine.

I've thought about this a *lot* for the past three months

and it's better than I remember, the feeling of Wilder's mouth on mine. The way that now, this time, it feels like it's something more than purely physical.

The way my brain whispers *it's right this time* as he licks my lower lip, my mouth opening, the tips of our tongues sliding against each other.

When we pull back, we're both breathing hard. Wilder's eyes have gone unfocused, his forehead against mine. I realize I've unfurled my legs and I've got one loosely wrapped around him, the damn towel *somehow* still in place even though the bulge below it is now considerably larger.

I swallow. I can tell my nipples are poking through the thin fabric of my *STEM Women Rock!* t-shirt, the pajama shorts I'm wearing pushed all the way up my thighs.

"So," he murmurs. "Should we talk about this first?"

"Fuck no," I whisper into his mouth, then bite his lower lip.

He growls. He kisses me so hard I think he nearly draws blood, my teeth against my own lip as I fall backward onto the bed with him on top of me.

The towel's gone, utterly forgotten, one of my legs still wrapped around him. He's got one hand on the inside of my other knee, pushing me open, his hard length sliding against the shorts I'm still wearing, the friction stuttering through my body.

"Good," he says, that same grin in his voice. "Action first, Squeaks. I like it."

He bites my ear, my neck, teeth and tongue making me gasp on the sensitive skin.

"Don't, I've got work Mond—"

Then there's fingers across my mouth, slurring my words.

"I'm housebroken," he teases.

"Are you?" I whisper, and lick the pads of his fingers.

I don't wait for an answer, just suck one into my mouth, lips wrapped around it as a low noise rumbles from the bottom of Wilder's chest, his hips grinding into me even harder.

I bite down, gently, the head of his cock slipping against my clit, and even through my shorts I swear to God he knows what he's doing.

Strong fingers pinch one nipple, through my shirt, just hard enough to make my back arch off the bed.

"Not always," he says. "Say the word, Squeaks, and everyone from here to Tijuana will know you've been with me."

He pinches again, lips on my neck. I dig my fingernails into his back despite myself as his head moves lower, rough hands shoving my shirt up. Now my fingers are raking through his hair, my legs just under his shoulder blades.

"Will you still get flustered if I tell you what I'm going to do to you?" he asks.

I feel myself turn bright red, and Wilder takes one nipple between his teeth, pulling his head back slightly as I gasp.

"No," I say.

"So if I tell you that I'm going to lick your pussy until your legs shake and then fuck you as slow and hard as I can possibly stand it…"

He grins, his face feral, his blue eyes sparking.

I blush harder, despite everything, and he just laughs.

"I'm not flustered," I say as his mouth moves back to my other nipple, tongue swirling around it.

I grab his shoulders, back arching. He grabs my shorts in his hands, slides them off along with my underwear.

"Then what are you?" he asks.

His lips are on my sternum, my belly, his tongue quickly dipping into my bellybutton as I squirm.

"Excited?" I whisper, even that one word hard to get out.

Talking dirty has never exactly been my strong suit. I'm always a little afraid of saying something weird, something wrong, and then the activities come to a screeching halt.

Wilder slides his knuckles softly along my lips, his mouth on the curve of one hip. My thighs are already pushed apart, both my hands in his hair, and I moan as he touches me.

"Excited is one word for it," he says.

He slides his knuckles again, brushing my lips along his hand. I'm aching, pulsing, half a second away from clenching my fists and shoving his face into me, because he's making me crazy right now.

"But what you are right now is wet as hell, Squeaks."

"I know," I whimper.

"Then why didn't you just say that?"

He's teasing me. As he talks his lips are brushing my clit and my lips, goddamn *teasing* me like he never has before.

It sends another rush through me, a surge, a pulse of arousal as I throw my head back against the mattress.

Finally, he licks me. He licks me slow at first, tongue flicking back and forth as I hold my breath. All my muscles go rigid and then limp and I turn my head to one side, moaning.

He goes faster. His tongue gets rougher, twisting around me, slow and then fast and then slow, dragging over my clit in a steady rhythm that has me clutching the blankets in one hand, nearly screaming.

"Come on," I beg.

Wilder just groans, his low voice vibrating through me.

I moan again, helpless, as he drags his tongue over me again.

I'm right on the edge, right where he's keeping me. Fucking teasing me because in this moment he could do absolutely anything he wanted and I'd say yes, just for the sweet release of Wilder's tongue.

He flicks me. He slides down, between my lips, the tip teasing at my entrance as it takes every last ounce of willpower not to grab him again, push him inside, but I don't.

And I'm rewarded because he laps at me again, fast and slow and rough and gentle and in moments I'm shouting, moaning, shuddering out his name while he's got one hand on my breast and the other pushing one knee wide, his face still between my legs.

I can't move.

I can't think.

He's gotten better at that.

His tongue is still teasing at my lips, as if he likes tasting me, lapping and circling as his hands keep moving and I pant for breath, swallowing hard, trying to come back down.

Finally, I open my eyes and look down. He looks up at me, grinning, the look in his eyes wickeder than I've ever seen it before.

In a second, he's on his knees, legs between mine, and he pulls me roughly to sitting and kisses me. I taste like myself and he wants me to know it, grabs the back of my head and pulls me in.

It's sexy. It's kind of dirty, kind of wild and untamed. Utterly impolite, and I kiss him back hard, plundering his mouth for evidence of me.

After a long kiss Wilder pulls back. He strokes my cheek once, with his thumb, staring straight into my eyes. He's still got that feral, untamed look, a look that I can feel in the bottom of my soul and the base of my spine.

My glasses came off at some point and the rest of the room is blurry, nothing but the soft line of his mouth, his eyes that could cut glass. My voice sticks in my throat and I'm left speechless, totally certain that I don't have words for this moment.

"I still love you," he whispers, his voice harsh.

"I know," I say.

The words slip out before I can think about them, and for a moment they hang in the air between us, utterly true and never meant to be spoken aloud.

"I mean—"

"You mean exactly what you said," Wilder grins.

He pulls my face to his, one hand on the base of my spine, tugging me in.

"Good," he growls. "I want you to know it."

He kisses me again, harder, teeth and tongue, his hand on my face.

Then in one fluid motion he pulls back, grabs my knee, flips me somehow and the next thing I know I'm on my elbows and knees on the bed and he's on top of me.

He pushes my hair off the back of my neck, kisses me there so it sends shivers down my spine, somewhere between tender and rough or maybe both.

I reach behind my head, slide my fingers through his thick dark hair, as if I can coax him into more, faster, *now*.

"What else do you know, Squeaks?" he muses.

His knees push mine apart, my hip collapsing onto the bed and I bite my lip, arch myself into him like I'm a wild animal.

"I know lots of things," I whisper.

"Do you know how many times I've thought about those nights in the cabin?"

His hand is on my hip, pulling at me, and I writhe against him, toes curling at the frisson of flesh on flesh.

"Do you know that every time you mentioned another man at the research station, it lit a spark of jealousy deep inside me just because they got to see you and I didn't?"

He kisses my neck again, angles himself between my legs and his cock bumps against my inner thigh. I clench the sheets in my hands, arch my body, try to wrap my leg around his because even now I'm desperate for this contact, for every inch of me to be touching every inch of him.

"You know I never could help myself around you, Squeaks," he whispers into my ear.

Just like that he's at my entrance, his girth easing in, and I gasp because every single time I forget what it's like but the instant my body remembers I lose control.

I arch back, one knee halfway under me again, pushing back and demanding more because *this* is what I need, *this* is all there is. Someone's making a guttural growl and it might be me or it might be him.

Wilder pulls me back, down, and we're half on our sides, my hand a fist in the sheets, his bigger hand over mine as he pushes himself deeper, hits the spot that makes me see stars.

I gasp.

"I know," he growls in my ear.

He keeps his promise.

He *does* know.

He knows, somehow, that hard and slow was exactly what my whole body craved. It was what I needed, all along, the chain reaction of spark to spark to spark to fire.

Wilder shoves a pillow under my hip, pushes me into it. I arch into him, the new angle making my eyes roll back as I grab at him over my shoulder, trying to latch on in some other way, feeling so possessive that I want his skin to sink into mine.

He squeezes my hand harder, his fingers lacing into mine as he fucks me deeper, harder, pleasure blossoming through my body like it's springtime.

I think I'm blind. I think Wilder's got his teeth in my shoulder, growling. I think I'm moaning into the mattress as we rock together, our bodies moving in slow sync like we're one creature. The world could fall down around us and I wouldn't even care.

I come slow and hard, so slow that I barely realize what's happening until I realize I'm shouting Wilder's name over and over again, shuddering and sweaty, feeling like the first day of sunshine after the winter.

He doesn't speed up, slow down, or relent, just fucks me hard with his whole body until suddenly there's a catch in the rhythm, a sigh. Wilder moans my name and still shivering I push back against him, taking him in as deep as I can with the desperate desire to give him every part of myself that I can.

Wilder pulls me in, my name on his lips as they brush my shoulder. I'm his and he's mine and I think it's always been that, since long before I knew, and we keep rocking together even as the aftershocks of pleasure drift through us, diminishing with every bolt.

Then we lie on the bed, spent. His hand is still around mine and I flex my fingers, squeeze his between mine, secure our hands together a little more tightly. I let go of his hair in my other fist, suddenly hoping I didn't rip out a chunk.

He presses his body against me, pulls me closer. Buries his face against the back of my neck, in my sweaty hair. I wonder if I'm supposed to say anything. I wonder *what* I'm supposed to say, but all I can think of is *that was fun* or *how long until we can do that again?*

"Mmm," I finally say, wriggling back against him.

Wilder laughs softly against me, moves up, tucks my body against his.

"Yeah," he agrees.

CHAPTER FORTY-SIX
WILDER

Half an hour later, we're still in bed. The strong August sunlight is filtering through the blinds, the blurry light covering both of us in stripes, Imogen's back and my front as we lie there, one of her arms thrown over me.

I wonder, vaguely, if we should talk *now* but I also feel like everything that needs to be said has been said in one way or another.

"Do you need to be anywhere?" Imogen asks.

She hasn't put her glasses on again yet, her soft brown eyes blinking at me behind a fine curtain of hair.

"Not until Monday," I tell her. "How far can you see?"

"You mean how far can I see well?"

"And even *now* you're a smartass."

She grins, moves her hand off my chest and up to her face. Pulls it away slowly, until her fingers are eight or nine inches from her eyes.

"About here," she says. "It's a little bit blurry before that and really blurry after."

I wriggle toward her on the bed, kiss her hand, put my face where it was.

"There," I say.

She laughs.

"Thank you for the gift of your face, I guess," she says.

"I wouldn't want to deprive you in this important moment," I say, putting her arm back over me. "I wanted to make sure you imprinted properly or whatever."

Imogen makes a face and scrunches her nose.

"Humans don't imprint and they especially don't imprint after sex," she points out.

I raise my eyebrows, wait.

"What?"

"You're about to tell me all about what imprinting really is and why I'm *so* wrong right now."

"Well, not any*more*," she says, her eyes crinkling. "Now you're going to have to suffer in ignorance for being a dick about it."

"Oh, come on, Squeaks. You love correcting me."

She laughs, silently.

"Maybe it's because you imprinted already, and now every time you think sexy thoughts you, I don't know, impose my face onto whatever else is happening at the moment. Like when you hear a song that makes you want to dance dirty—"

"Okay, that's *really* not what it is," she says, finally breaking.

Now it's my turn to laugh.

"Baby animals do it to their mothers, sometimes. Right after birth, so they follow the right one around."

"Are you saying you're gonna be following me around now?"

"Mammals don't even imprint. It's just birds. And *ew*, Wilder."

"You do have to go to work sometimes," I tease her. "I wouldn't want your career hurt just because I sex-imprinted you so well that you're following me around all day every day."

"Oh, my God," she mutters, but she's laughing.

I grin, because it can be so easy and fun to get a rise out of her. Even though I'm the one who's followed her everywhere, the one who flew to the Arctic just to see her face.

"Do you know about anglerfish?" she asks, her eyes still dancing.

"Know what about anglerfish?"

"They're these crazy, super-deep-sea fish," she says.

I shrug.

"Anyway, they're called anglerfish because they have a single glowing antenna that sticks out, because it's always pitch black when you get that deep in the ocean, and they have these enormous mouths and horrible teeth and jaws that can unhinge so they just eat anything that wanders close enough to their forehead light. Super ugly," she says, helpfully.

I just wait to see where this is going.

"And it's really hard to find other fish in the dark down there, even though they're got the glowing forehead thing," she says. "So when a male anglerfish *does* find a female, he uses his big horrible mouth to latch onto her, after which he fuses to her body and basically becomes a parasite that shares the same circulatory system. That's how they mate."

I blink.

"They fuse into one body?"

"Gross, right?"

"Shit, Squeaks, is this a warning?"

She laughs.

"I was only gonna ask if you wanted to have dinner tonight," I tease. "But if that's too much…"

"Sorry," she grins. "I get carried away with cool biology stuff sometimes."

"As long as the anglerfish isn't a metaphor for something else," I say. "See, I know big words too."

"I'm *so* impressed."

"If you're gonna be like that I can start going through flight preparation checklists for *several* different models of fighter jet," I tease.

"Are you going to tell me about lubing up the coxen?" she asks, batting her eyes.

"No, because that sentence was total nonsense."

"But you've gotta lube *something*, right?"

"Did I interrupt you while you were telling me how fish fuck?" I ask, laughing.

"That was fascinating and sexy," she protests.

"Sexy?" I say. "*Sexy*, Imogen?"

She just laughs, turning her face into the pillow.

"Okay, point taken," she finally says, her voice blurred.

She turns her head back to me.

"I'd love to have dinner tonight," Imogen says.

I take her hand, kiss her folded knuckles.

"How about next weekend, too," I say.

"Sure."

"And the weekend after that?"

She raises one eyebrow.

"Okay."

"Just get dinner with me all the time," I say. "And sometimes I'll spend the night and we can post cutesy pictures of ourselves being ridiculously happy on the internet and sometimes we'll argue about whose turn it is to drive or do the dishes or what shows we're going to binge-watch next. How about that?"

She wriggles in until her body is halfway across mine,

warm and supple and inviting as hell. My cock twitches once, but it's still too soon.

"I can't imagine us ever arguing," she says.

"Now you're just lying."

"Do you at least have good taste in television shows?"

I grin over at her.

"You know I don't."

Imogen sighs, blows a strand of hair out of her face, wriggles against me with the bars of light playing across her naked body.

This isn't what I'd imagined. Not even in high school, the few times that I wondered what my life could be like if I chose the *other* girl.

Back then I thought it would be… normal, the way it is for anyone who ends up with their high school sweetheart. We'd date, we'd be long distance, we'd both go back to Solaris where we'd get married and I'd work for my father and she'd get a marketing job or something.

But now, I can't imagine anything else but this. Fuck, I'd cross the Rockies on my hands and knees for this.

"Well, maybe I'll learn to love dumb superhero shows," Imogen sighs. "I accept your offer anyway."

I reach out, trace her bottom lip with my thumb.

"It worked," I say.

"What worked?"

"Bothering you until you said yes."

She laughs, ducks her head slightly, kisses the pad of my thumb.

"You mean the part where we did nothing but talk for a couple of months and you didn't break my heart again? The part where you put your money where your mouth was?"

"I still can't believe you didn't fall for my big romantic gesture."

"I'm a scientist, Wilder. I believe things when there's evidence for them."

"So, charts and graphs for Valentine's Day, not flowers and chocolates?" I tease.

"I'm still human," she laughs. "I'd take chocolates."

I close the distance between us, kiss her again. It's lazy and slow, both our faces half in the pillow.

"I do love you," I murmur. "You need proof of that?"

She kisses me, bites my lower lip, her body curling toward mine. My cock twitches again, only this time it comes halfway to life because *now* it's been long enough.

"What kind of proof are you offering?" she says, her mouth still against mine. "Theoretical, physical, what?"

With one move I push her shoulder, flip her onto her back, climb on top of her. Imogen gasps, the noise half-squeak, and I press myself into her belly, her legs already winding around me.

"You're so smart," I growl. "*Guess.*"

EPILOGUE
IMOGEN

Two and a half years later

Wilder's words hit me right in the chest, momentarily pushing the air from my lungs.

"What do you *mean* he doesn't know?" I ask.

Wilder's face is tense in the dark, headlights and taillights and street lamps washing over his features.

"I mean I haven't told him," he says evenly.

"But your mom must have told him," I counter. "She must have. I mean, for fuck's sake, she's practically already started ordering monogrammed china—"

"She said she hasn't told him," Wilder says, his Adam's apple bobbing as he swallows. "And I don't think you monogram china."

"Not my point."

He sighs.

"They barely talk," he admits. "Honestly, I think she mostly stays at the condo and he's got the big house all to himself. I don't know what he does there, I don't know if he has affairs or what. He probably sleeps on the couch in his office most nights. God knows he did when we were growing up."

Something in Wilder's voice softens my heart a little, the muscles in my ribcage thawing.

"Gray knows," Wilder says. "I told him the very next day. Promise. It's not a secret, Squeaks, literally all he'd have to do is ask my mom how I'm doing—"

"That wasn't my point at all," I say. "You just don't think it's weird that your dad doesn't know you're getting married in six months?"

He sighs, shoves his hair out of his face with one hand.

"Yeah, it's weird," he admits. "But there's a lot that's weird about our particular relationship, and he's not exactly the guy I go to when I'm bubbling over with good news."

I look down at my hands. I'm holding an enormous arrangement of pale-blue-and-white flowers that we just picked up from the florist in Solaris, who was kind enough to stay open fifteen minutes late a couple days before Christmas.

I've been more nervous than a basket of squirrels on crack cocaine about this visit for a couple of weeks now. It's not like I'm particularly good with people, and it'll be the first time I'm really spending *time* with Wilder's family.

Actually, the only time I met his dad I was in seventh grade, and he was giving out a civic award at the middle school. I think he sponsored it or something.

I doubt he remembers me, or at least, I *hope* he doesn't. Seventh grade wasn't my best year.

The rock on my ring finger glimmers gently in the low light, sparkling even now. I told him a thousand times that I didn't want a big engagement ring, that I wanted something small and understated, maybe not even a diamond.

He didn't listen. It's the only time he's touched his trust fund since moving to Seattle.

And, even though I kind of hate to admit it, I like it. I wasn't sure I would, honestly, but it's *gorgeous*. Plus, there's something about going out with Wilder and the moment that other people see him, see me, then look at the ring.

Something that says *yeah, bitches, he's all mine*.

But it's weird as hell that his own father doesn't know we're getting married. I'm really only mostly sure that Marcus Flint — owner of Flint Holdings, Inc., as well as about half of Solaris, hated by my own parents — knows we're dating.

"He knows we're coming, right?" I ask, stomach twisting again as Wilder drives us down the dark road.

"That he does," Wilder says dryly. "I talked to his secretary about what time we'd be having Christmas Eve dinner."

"And he knows *I'm* coming?"

Wilder reaches over, puts his hand on my knee, squeezes through my jeans.

"I'm sorry I didn't tell my father we got engaged," he says, glancing over at me every few seconds, eyes mostly still on the road. "I kind of avoid talking to the man."

"I get it," I say, softly.

One more time, I wish we were spending the first night with my parents — my lovely, normal, not-crazy-rich parents — who know all about our engagement. My mom texts me several times a week with suggestions of absolutely hideous wedding dresses, and every single time I have to talk her down.

But a while back, I decided a 'get it over with' approach was best, this got scheduled, and now… here we are.

Wilder slows the SUV, puts on his blinker, turns left into a snowy driveway, angled up. There's a moment where the wheels don't grip properly, but Wilder just shoves the car into all-wheel drive and gives it more gas.

My knuckles are white on the huge flower arrangement.

It's fine, I tell myself, over and over again.

You've met Brenda a million times, and Grayson was just out in Seattle last month, they're both very nice...

I breathe deep. I force myself to relax, because new people and new social situations will *never* be something I'm good at. It's better now than it used to be, at least when Wilder's by my side, but I don't think it'll ever be easy.

He pulls into a driveway, yanks up the parking brake, puts the car in park.

"They'll love you," he says, his hand on my knee again. "I mean, my mom and Gray already do, and if Dad doesn't, fuck him."

I put one hand over his, squeeze.

"I know," I say. "Thanks."

He leans over, kisses me quickly. Up ahead the huge chalet house is glowing from within, the roof outlined with Christmas lights, the snow making it look like something out of a storybook.

"Okay," I say. "Let's do this."

We get out of the car. It's freezing out here, and immediately my breath puffs into the cold air, my snow boots biting into the thin layer still on the driveway. It's the first time I've been back to Solaris in the winter since Wilder and I got together, and I'd somehow forgotten what the biting cold is like.

"I'll come back for the suitcases in a little while," he says, coming around the front of the car. He takes the heavy flowers from my hands, leans over them, kisses me one more time, and I follow him up the stairs, to the front deck where there's a fire pit and benches all around.

As he rings the bell, I glance over my shoulder, then gasp.

The view from here is *amazing.* All of Solaris is spread

out below us, and even though it's nighttime, it looks like a cheesy painting or a photograph or something. It doesn't even look real, just a beautiful valley of light.

Of course this is their view, I think. *This way they can survey all they own every time they leave their house.*

Before I can get any further, the front door opens, and I plaster a smile onto my face as my heart hammers in my chest.

"Oh, thank *God,*" Grayson says, the moment he opens the door. "I was about to start sending up flares. Get in here. Ooh, lilies, my favorite."

Wilder laughs, and already, I feel better. The first time I met Grayson he was absolutely nothing like I expected — I knew that he was the *good* son, the one who was being groomed to take over the business, the one who was straight-laced and went to a good college, serious and studious.

Except he's got the same wicked sense of humor the Wilder does, only more deadpan. He and Wilder could almost be twins, except Grayson's eyes are an unearthly amber brown, his hair a few shades lighter.

He's also my second-favorite member of Wilder's family, and I'm already relieved that he's here. Even if he's the only one who's got some idea of what happened between us in high school, since he was a freshman at the time.

"Mom's made mulled wine and Dad's had three glasses already, so he's telling us his opinions on the latest Range Rover and Mom is looking at her phone instead of paying attention. Welcome to the circus," he says, and gives us a grin over his shoulder before leading us into the living room.

"They're here," he announces.

"Wilder!" Brenda exclaims. "Oh, my gosh, I *love* them! Lilies, my favorite!"

Standing next to her, Grayson smirks.

"This is just *gorgeous*," she gushes. "Here, put it down on the new sideboard, I've got just the spot…"

She leads Wilder a few feet away, directing flower placement, and Wilder's dad steps in to take her spot.

Instantly, my heart ties itself into a knot. Grayson's wandered off to the mulled wine, so I don't even have *his* backup.

"You must be Imogen," Wilder's dad says. "Marcus."

He holds out his hand as if we're about to make a business deal, and the first thing I notice is that he's wearing a white button-down shirt and gray slacks, even now, relaxing at home.

The second thing I notice is that he's got Wilder's eyes, only where Wilder's seem like they change from one moment to the next, soft to warm to laughing to cool, Marcus's eyes are brittle as diamonds in his face.

"Yes, of course," I say.

Of course what? Of course I'm Imogen? Jesus.

"I've heard so much about you," I say, smiling as much as I can and making sure I'm not slacking on my end of the handshake.

"Likewise," he says, though I'm pretty sure he's lying. "Good, firm grip. Be good in the boardroom someday."

I just keep smiling, because I've got *no* idea what to say to that. I'd be terrible in a boardroom, not to mention I've got zero desire to go anywhere near one.

After a moment, the handshake ends, but he keeps looking at me with those eyes like lasers, like he's adding and dividing and running the numbers about me in his head, calculating something I don't even know.

Still at a loss for words, I push my glasses up my nose with my left hand.

His eyes alight on the ring, and a split second too late, I realize what just happened.

Shit.

I meant for Wilder to at least tell him, with words, not just find out sort of by accident...

But Marcus just nods once.

"Congratulations," he says, his tone neither pleased nor dismayed, just perfectly businesslike. "Excuse me, I ought to go help my wife with those flowers."

And with that, Marcus Flint steps away. I glance over at Grayson, at a loss for words, and he holds up an empty white mug, a question on his face.

I nod. I'm *definitely* gonna need that wine tonight.

———

LATER THAT NIGHT, after Wilder's parents have gone to bed, the two of us and Grayson are sitting in their chalet's upstairs lounge, which is a couple of leather couches, a huge fireplace, and an *amazing* view. We've got the lights out, wrapped in blankets, looking out at Solaris, drinking hot cocoa.

"He really just said *congratulations*?" Grayson asks.

He's on the couch opposite us, his feet on a marble-topped coffee table that probably cost more than my monthly rent.

"Yep," I confirm, leaning back against Wilder's shoulder. "That's weird, right?"

"It's weird for most people," Wilder says, taking another sip of his cocoa.

"Is he pissed? Upset? Angry? Hurt?"

Wilder and Grayson just look at each other and then shrug in unison.

"It's a fucking mystery," Wilder mutters. "Is he man, or machine?"

"It's not that bad," Grayson says, but I can already tell the defense is halfhearted.

"No?" Wilder says, looking into the fire. "Not as bad as the time he told me why I nearly died in a plane crash and he had to have his attorney present to make sure he didn't accidentally admit fault?"

Grayson ignores that and looks at me, his gaze steady. I take another sip.

"Look, Imogen, it's not you," he says. "I don't think he noticed when I got into college or when I graduated. I know for a *fact* his secretary got those cards and he just signed them, but you should see the man read a positive quarterly report."

Wilder just snorts.

"He lights up like a goddamn Christmas tree," Grayson muses, looking into the fire again.

"It doesn't matter," Wilder says, kissing my hair. "Everyone else loves you."

———

A WHILE LATER, Grayson goes to bed, and it's just Wilder and me, on the couch, with the fireplace and the view of Solaris, spread out in the valley below, lights blanketing the soft white of winter.

"You know, I never really thought I'd leave," Wilder says.

We're both a little drunk and pretty tired. We *should* go to bed, but it's so nice and warm right here, so lovely to sit in the dark with a fire and a view that neither of us wants to move.

"Leave Solaris?"

"Yeah. I mean, I knew I was leaving once I joined the Navy, but I didn't think it was permanent."

I snuggle into him, the mulled wine still faintly winding its way through my veins.

"Do you want to come back?"

He laughs softly, his chest like a tiny earthquake.

"No," he says, his voice steady and sure. "I liked it here because it was easy to be a big fish in a small pond, but that's all. Turns out there's way more out there in the world."

He kisses the side of my head.

"Stuff like weird nerd girls who get very excited about newly-discovered mating behaviors of large shaggy mammals."

"I was here," I say, pointing out the obvious.

"You never belonged here," he says, tilting his head back against the couch. "You needed a bigger pond."

I laugh.

"That's one way of putting it," I say. "If it helps, I never thought I'd find much good in this place."

"Can't blame you for that," he says. "This is pretty good, though."

"It is," I agree, snuggling down. "Against all odds, it really is."

A memory drifts to the surface of my mind suddenly, like garbage floating to the surface of a lake: Melissa, on her couch in her den, casually mentioning that she was having dinner with Wilder's family.

God, back then I was so jealous I must have turned bright green. But right now, remembering it and sitting next to Wilder myself, the memory suddenly doesn't hold any power over me.

I don't attach anything to it. I don't wonder, even for a split second, whether his parents would rather see him marry her than me. I don't think how unfair it is that I had to wait almost thirteen years just to hear a totally unexcited *congratulations* from Marcus Flint.

I'm over it. I really am. Nothing that happened back then has any power over me anymore.

"We should head to bed too," Wilder says, his voice sleepy.

"I love you," I say.

"I know."

I laugh, burying my face into him, wrapping one arm around his waist underneath this blanket.

"Are you *ever* going to let me forget that?"

"Do you mean I should take it out of my wedding vows?"

"You're impossible," I tease.

"That's why you like me so much," he says. "If I weren't, just think of how fast you'd get bored."

"I would never."

"Liar. You like a challenge, Squeaks, and you know it."

He kisses my forehead.

"It's one of the things I love about you, you know."

The fire crackles. My eyelids are drooping, warm and comfy under this blanket, and for a few moments I'm back in that hunter's cabin in the middle of nowhere, the two of us buried under sleeping bags on that cot, Wilder's body still colder than it should be even after a few hours.

I don't think I've ever cried harder in my life than I did that night. I was terrified of having to go on alone, sure, but I think I'd already fallen back in love with him.

Deep down in my heart, I knew that there was one

person for me, and even though he was the last person I was hoping it would be, I couldn't bear losing him already.

"Bed?" Wilder asks, slowly rubbing my shoulder. "Gray said something about a Christmas Eve snowshoeing expedition tomorrow, and we should get rested up for that."

"Is that his idea of fun?"

"Yes," Wilder laughs. "You know all the survival advice he gave me for *next* time I get stranded after a plane crash."

I sigh. We get off the couch, toss the blanket back onto it, grab our mugs from the coffee table.

Before I can step away, Wilder takes my face in his hand, brushing his thumb across my cheekbone. He's highlighted by the fire, orange light flickering across the chiseled lines of his face, casting deep shadows.

"Thank you, Squeaks," he murmurs, and kisses me.

I don't even ask for what. It doesn't matter.

I just kiss him back.

THE END

ABOUT ROXIE

Roxie is a romance author by day, and also a romance author by night. She lives in Los Angeles with one husband, two cats, far too many books, and a truly alarming pile of used notebooks that she refuses to throw away.

www.roxienoir.com
roxie@roxienoir.com